Praise for Mari Hannah

'Brutal and engaging. Mari Hannah writes with a sharp eye and a dark heart'   Peter James

'A satisfyingly meaty read'   *Guardian*

'Hannah is especially good at portraying the emotional interactions and office politics of a fraught police force'
The Times

'If proof were needed that Hannah's DCI Kate Daniels is a great addition to the crime scene, then here it is, a third corking case to keep you up at night'
Peterborough Telegraph

'Brutal, shockingly realistic and satisfyingly unpredict-able, this is a thrilling, chilling tale with a formidable star player and charismatic location, ideally suited to the small screen. Move over DCI Jane Tennison, there's a new kid on the block'   *Lancashire Evening Post*

'Joining Val McDermid and Ann Cleeves is a new and distinct voice in crime fiction . . . page-turning'
Journal

MONUMENT TO MURDER

Mari Hannah was born in London and moved north as a child. Sponsored by the Home Office, she graduated from Teesside University before becoming a Probation Officer – a career cut short when she was injured while on duty. Thereafter, she spent several years working as a film/television scriptwriter. During that time she created and developed a number of projects, most notably a feature-length film and a pilot episode for a TV crime series based on the characters in her book, the latter as part of a BBC drama development scheme. She lives in Northumberland with her partner, an ex-murder detective. In 2010, she won the Northern Writers' Award. *Monument to Murder* is her fourth novel.

www.marihannah.com
@mariwriter

By Mari Hannah

The Murder Wall
Settled Blood
Deadly Deceit
Monument to Murder

MARI HANNAH

MONUMENT TO MURDER

PAN BOOKS

First published 2013 by Macmillan

This edition published 2014 by Pan Books
an imprint of Pan Macmillan, a division of Macmillan Publishers Limited
Pan Macmillan, 20 New Wharf Road, London N1 9RR
Basingstoke and Oxford
Associated companies throughout the world
www.panmacmillan.com

ISBN 978-1-4472-4607-7

1 3 5 7 9 8 6 4 2

A CIP catalogue record for this book is available from the British Library.

Typeset by Ellipsis Digital Ltd, Glasgow
Printed and bound by CPI Group (UK) Ltd, Croydon, CR0 4YY

Visit **www.panmacmillan.com** to read more about all our books
and to buy them. You will also find features, author interviews and
news of any author events, and you can sign up for e-newsletters
so that you're always first to hear about our new releases.

For my very special sons
Paul and Chris

1

The unrelenting din beyond his cell door dropped out. It was as if someone had pressed a pause button inside his head. With the signal lost there was silence from within – no yelling, foot traffic, steel doors slamming, keys turning or locks driven home. Those noises were drowned out by the sound of a motorcycle throttling down, changing gear. There was no mistake. He'd heard it many times before. He'd been waiting, praying, to hear it again. If he was any judge, it was around a mile away, heading towards him like a bullet.

She was coming back to him.

Walter Fearon closed his eyes as the flashback began. In his mind's eye he imagined her as he'd last seen her, sobbing as she left the wing. No furtive glance in his direction. No lover's kiss goodbye.

Shame that.

He'd been on his knees scrubbing the floor as she approached the exit gate, close enough to reach out and touch her bare legs as she hurried off escorted by one of the screws. The scrawny git had his arm around her too.

That wasn't on.

No, sir.

Bad news had taken her away, according to his source. The prison grapevine was all well and good but the gen it provided was sketchy. Unreliable. He sucked in a breath, smiling. Good thing he had alternatives.

He had to admit her sudden departure had shaken him up. As the weeks dragged into months, panic had set in. He'd feared she might never return. His heart hammered inside his chest and his hands shook now he knew that not to be the case. He craved her smell. Ached to be close to her. To engage her in a conversation – of his choosing, of course – he was good at the stuff she called manipulation.

Relaxing back on his bunk, he calculated the length of time it would take her to pass through security. He had it down to a fine art. He'd be at the window when she appeared on his side of the perimeter fence. He'd drink her in as she walked across the prison grounds, every step and movement – a couple of hundred metres of poetry in motion. It was time to execute his plan, something spectacular to regain the chick's attention.

The razor should do it.

What the hell were they staring at?

Hadn't they ever seen a widow before?

Through her dark visor, Emily McCann could feel the weight of a dozen pairs of eyes following her as she skirted the packed car park looking for a vacant space. Keeping her revs steady, applying gentle pressure to her right handlebar, she completed a perfect U-turn manoeuvre, recalling little of the five-mile journey along narrow lanes from home, an isolated cottage in the Northumbrian countryside.

Her mind was on Robert and, to a lesser extent, on her

only child. Rachel had begged her to stay home for one more week. But Emily knew that one would've stretched to two – two to three – and so on. A further postponement was in no one's best interests. Let alone hers. She wanted, needed to immerse herself in work.

Stopping short of the gatehouse, she cut the engine and removed her gloves. Pocketing the key, she sat for a moment before pulling her bike on to its stand. Dismounting the machine on shaky legs, she took a deep breath, trying to calm the butterflies in her stomach. A sign on the wall welcomed her back to HMP Northumberland, a Category B prison, the most northerly in England, home to almost a thousand men.

More eyes at the windows . . .

More sympathy . . .

She couldn't cope with sympathy.

Hesitating then, she was in two minds whether to enter the establishment or climb back on her bike and ride away. That wasn't really an option. Now more than any time in her life she needed to work – if not for herself, then for Rachel. That thought urged her on, lingered in her head as she approached the gatehouse with a sense of dread, the thick metal chain firmly fastened around her waist feeling heavier than it ever had with each step forward.

Once through the reinforced security gate, Emily removed a numbered tally from the end of the chain, placed it in a chute in the wall and heard it slide into the well beneath. On the other side of a thick glass screen, an officer traded it for a bunch of keys. He smiled politely and went back to his newspaper without a word being exchanged between them.

3

Attaching her keys to the empty chain, Emily walked away feeling much like she had on her first day at the prison four long years ago: apprehensive, the subject of others' curiosity, a stranger in an unknown world.

Was the officer in the gatehouse new?

Emily assumed so. She didn't think she'd seen him before. Or, if she had, she couldn't recall the encounter. Just as well. She didn't feel like small talk. Maybe he was too embarrassed to welcome her back for fear she'd lose it in front of everyone. Even people she knew well had dodged her in the street in recent months, darting into shop doorways to avoid a face-to-face encounter, making her feel like a leper when she needed them most.

The majority of prisons are grim. Emily hadn't noticed how grim until today. Today, the cold steel keys felt strange in her hand as she unlocked the gate to B-wing and took her first tentative steps towards some form of normality. Today she was seeing things in sharp focus, as if doing so for the very first time. Today, as she made her way past officers and inmates going about their business, things were different.

She was different.

When the commiserations were finally over and prison staff had returned to their duties, she shut her office door hoping they'd leave her be. Her desk was exactly as she'd left it on that fateful day: her blue cardigan slung over the back of her chair; the file she'd been reading still open at the same page; the fountain pen Robert had bought her abandoned without its top; a half-empty bottle of water.

Nothing had changed.
Why would it?
Life goes on . . .
For some.

2

The call had reached the control room at 9.43 a.m. from a mobile phone. A child playing 'hunt the dinosaur' with his father had stumbled upon an exposed skeleton where a section of dunes had broken away and slid on to Bamburgh beach below – a horrific end to what should have been a perfect morning.

'*Definitely* human?' Detective Chief Inspector Kate Daniels asked.

'According to first responders,' DS Hank Gormley replied. 'Then again, would your average copper know a human from a Stegosaurus?'

Kate laughed.

At a signpost for the village of Bamburgh she left the A1 taking the B road towards the coast. It was a better road in her opinion than one she could've taken a few miles back – which meant she was approaching the coastal village from the north side.

Her new Audi Q5 handled well as they passed through the small hamlet of Waren Mill along a winding country road bathed in winter sunshine, a nature reserve and the sweeping sands of Budle Bay on their left.

The car picked up speed, climbing gently now.

Hank had gone quiet. Kate didn't need to turn her head to

know that he was fast asleep. He could nap at a moment's notice, on a clothes line if he had a mind to. She smiled, keeping her eyes on the brow of the hill, anticipating the glorious view on the other side. She'd seen it many times before and yet it still took her breath away. And there it was – Bamburgh Castle – rising majestically out of the ground on which it stood, a sight of power and beauty, its distinctive red sandstone walls impenetrable to the enemy without, the royal seat of the Kings of Northumbria in days gone by.

Flinching as a bird flew across her windscreen, Kate slowed on the outskirts of the village to observe a thirty-mile-an-hour limit. There were buildings on her right. Some fairly flash houses. The Grace Darling Museum with an RNLI flag on top. Dropping a gear, she turned left into The Wynding and drove downhill past some large seaside villas, one particular art deco example catching her eye.

An overhead sign came into view, a warning: MAX HEIGHT 6' 11" – 2.1 MTRS. And another sign: NO OVERNIGHT PARKING.

There would be tonight.

The car park beyond was a piece of pot-holed rough ground with a mound of grass in the centre but no vehicular access on to the beach. It was full of police vehicles, CSI vans, a couple of Area Command pandas and search teams waiting for instructions.

As Senior Investigating Officer it was Kate's job to direct operations, tell them exactly how she wanted them to proceed.

She sighed, steeling herself for a long shift.

She'd planned a rare half-day – a swim and a sauna – then

dinner with her old man on his birthday at the Black Bull in Corbridge, the Tyne Valley village where she grew up. Secretly she was pleased she had a good *public* excuse to cry off. Ed Daniels couldn't argue with that, though she was sure he'd try. She'd fled their last birthday celebration – hers – for much the same reason. Only that wasn't strictly true. In order to avoid a confrontation she'd used the excuse of being needed at the office, leaving him to finish his dinner alone.

A blustery wind whipped around the car as it came to a halt, shaking it like a toy. A man and a small boy Kate assumed were her witnesses were sitting together in a four-by-four with police insignia on its side. The child had a mop of blond hair and striking blue eyes. His face was pushed up against the window, staring out at her.

A podgy little hand appeared, waving.

Waving back, Kate turned away. She'd interview the boy and his father later.

The detectives got out of the car, put on their coats and walked the short distance down on to the beach where clumps of rotting seaweed rolled like tumbleweed in a desert landscape. This part of the Northumberland coast was stunning but unforgiving too, completely open to the elements. They had to shade their eyes from a sheet of sand being whipped along the shoreline, making wave-shaped ridges on the surface beneath their feet.

A large section of the beach had been taped off to keep the public out, an outer and inner cordon already in place. The crime scene itself was dwarfed by Bamburgh's fortified ancient castle, inhabited to this day. Built on a plateau of volcanic rock, the magical castle had inspired many a film director to shoot there. But Kate Daniels was less enthused by the isolated location. This exposed stretch of coastline was more often than not deserted. If it *was* a human skeleton, whoever had buried the body there had chosen the spot carefully. She knew she'd have her work cut out to crack this case.

'DCI Daniels?' an officer in uniform had fixed his eyes on Hank Gormley.

Wincing, Hank pointed at Kate.

Realizing his mistake, the PC blushed. 'Oh, I'm sorry, ma'am—'

'So you should be . . .' She was pulling his leg. 'Don't let it happen again.'

Relieved at having been let off the hook so easily, the constable lifted the police tape allowing the detectives to duck underneath. Kate scrambled up the dunes to where a tent had been erected, giving her DS a hand up.

Turning when they reached the top, they stood for a moment looking out to sea – a tranquil shoreline with stunning views over the Holy Island of Lindisfarne. A place of pilgrimage and spirituality, a tidal island, accessible only over a causeway, forever at the mercy of strong tides. A draw for visitors from around the world, Christians flocked there in their droves, using the island as a focal point. At school, Kate had studied the island's long history, learning of Christian martyrs and pagan attacks, developing a fascination with Celtic Christianity.

'You thinking what I'm thinking?' she said without shifting her gaze.

Gormley scanned the horizon. 'Religious significance?'

'First impressions are often the best ones, Hank. Hold that thought.'

Tread plates marked a single route to the crime scene tent. On this occasion they were probably superfluous but the detectives used them anyway. Showing ID to a uniformed officer guarding the tent, Kate entered first, Hank close behind.

The skeleton inside was without question human. Surrounded by golden sand and tufts of rough grass, it looked as though it had been carefully placed there, not just dumped in a hole and covered up. It was partially exposed: lying face up, arms bent at the elbows and crossed over the chest, one bony hand resting on top of the other. Some clothing was intact, a flash of red polka dots, a sandy necklace, a high-heeled shoe.

'Not prehistoric then,' Gormley said.

'No . . .' Kate looked at her watch, then back at her DS. 'There's nothing we can do here until Stanton turns up. Summon the squad and give the Super a ring. Tell him I'm setting up an incident room at Alnwick station. If the clothing remnants are anything to go by, the remains are relatively recent.'

As Hank pulled out his phone to make the call, Kate glanced at the skeletal remains. With no detailed physical description of the deceased to go on, she had the uneasy feeling that this case would run and run.

3

Emily McCann spent the morning going through a pile of case notes that had been left on top of her filing cabinet. She was almost up to speed, having paid careful attention to the new and, by definition, vulnerable inmates who'd arrived at the establishment in her absence. Their sentences ranged from just a few years to life imprisonment, covering a variety of offences: robbery, arson, rape and murder among them.

As resident psychologist, Emily was responsible for the whole of the prison population – staff as well as prisoners. Just over a year ago, her office had been moved from the admin block to B-wing, a sensible decision given that it housed some of the most dangerous offenders, the troublemakers and downright disturbed. There was a downside. Although directly responsible to the prison governor, Emily now had to contend with another man, Principal Officer Harrison.

Pushing that unpalatable thought aside – she hadn't seen Harrison since Robert's death – Emily set about prioritizing the most urgent cases. Making a list of those she wanted to call up for interview, she filed the rest away and made herself a cup of tea. Then sat back down to concentrate her efforts on one particular inmate, a young man serving seven years for the rape of a woman old enough to be his grandmother.

Emily felt sick.

It had nothing to do with Walter Fearon's heinous crime or the prison governor's insistence that she treat him as top priority on account of his impending release. Letting a dangerous offender back on the streets was deeply troubling and required careful handling but that was not the cause of her nausea. No, the wave of grief came out of the blue – a panic attack – the first that morning. She knew there would be others. Despite her best efforts to suppress them, there was no escape, no rhyme or reason, rarely any warning. That was the way it was. The way it had been since Robert had been snatched from her so unexpectedly.

She wept, quietly at first, then in huge sobs as the flood-gates opened. She wasn't the only one struggling to cope. Poor Rachel had fallen spectacularly apart since her father's death. She'd clung on to Emily before she left for work, terri-fied to let her out of her sight. Her moods were getting worse, her anger more potent. Her stubborn refusal to accept Emily's suggestion that it was time to move on with their lives had led to hurtful accusations and emotional blackmail designed to stop her mother doing just that.

Emily wanted to *feel* again. She wanted to function in the real world, not merely exist as a punchbag, a target for her daughter's fury. If the truth were known, returning to work had been her escape, her route to salvation from the night-mare of bereavement. But she was, first and foremost, a mother. Leaving Rachel alone was the hardest thing she'd ever had to do.

But was her daughter right?

Was it too soon to return to work?

Emily didn't feel ready to face the harsh reality of such a

taxing job within the suffocating walls of a prison. Maybe she never would be again. But what alternative did she have?

She was the breadwinner now.

She had to start sometime.

Wiping a tear from her cheek with the palm of her hand, she forced her grief away and focused on the file in front of her. An hour later, as satisfied as she could be that a probation hostel afforded at least half a chance of keeping tabs on Fearon, she picked up her pen and signed her name to his discharge report.

He'd had his chance.

She'd tried, without success, to unpick his history and modify his behaviour. To demonstrate how different choices might have altered his path in life. She'd been wasting her breath. Despite all the work she'd put in, he'd steadfastly refused to take responsibility for his actions or show a willingness to cooperate in his sentence planning. If anything he'd got worse in prison. He was stronger and more dangerous than he'd been on reception. One thing was certain: *he'd be back.*

4

Taking his phone from his pocket, Hank Gormley swore under his breath when he saw there was no network signal. It didn't surprise his DCI. Kate Daniels had worked in Northumberland long enough to know that mobile coverage this far north could never be guaranteed.

'I'm going to have to find a phone.' His face brightened. 'We could try the Lord Crewe.'

'Or wait 'til we get to Alnwick?' Kate wasn't buying a visit to the nearest pub.

'Boss, I'm busting for a pee!'

They turned their faces from the next gust of sand-blasting wind.

Hank blinked, closing one eye. 'How long would I need to lie down before this lot covered me up, d'you think?' He pointed at his shoes, specifically at the thick layer of sand that had formed on the uppers. 'Maybe Ms or Mrs Bones in there was doing a bit of bronzing and stayed too long. Could be natural causes, couldn't it? Wind blows, covers her up. No one comes along for weeks and hey presto! She could've lain undiscovered for years, never to be seen again.'

'That's the most rubbish theory I ever heard!'

'Why so?'

'She's not wearing any sunnies,' Kate said.

'Clever! Why didn't I think of that?'

'Because you're rubbish?' she teased.

They walked back to the car park. Kate was surprised to see the police four-by-four still parked up. A chubby hand reappeared at the window. The little boy attached to it looked frozen now. His shoulders were hunched. His lips, blue. At a rough estimate, he'd been sitting there for a couple of hours at least.

Cursing under her breath, Kate turned to the sound of chattering radios. There was a muddle of bodies to her left, all wearing uniforms. The nearest one binned her cigarette when she saw the DCI heading towards her pointing at the police vehicle.

Kate wanted to punch the dozy cow. 'Who's supposed to be looking after my witnesses?' she asked.

The PC's expression was blank. 'Er, not sure, ma'am.'

'Well find out! And when you have, tell them to shift their lazy arses and get their act into gear. I want that child and his father transported to Alnwick police station and given something to eat and drink immediately. They just found a body, for Christ's sake!'

The policewoman hurried off.

Rolling her eyes at Hank, Kate got in the car, started the engine and turned left out of the car park heading back towards the village.

There were no parking spaces outside the Lord Crewe on Church Street so she carried on driving with the village green on one side, a short row of pretty cottages, galleries and gift shops on the other – the Copper Kettle Tea Room among them. Not far away, a Japanese tourist was taking a photograph of a traditional red phone box with his mobile. The group he was with were looking through the window of the Old Pantry, a deli Kate knew sold delicious goods like onion marmalade and Francesca's Figgy Pear Relish, her late mother's favourite.

'Fancy stopping at Carter's for a pork growler?' Gormley asked.

'Thought you were dying for the loo?'

'Doesn't mean I'm not hungry.'

Hank could always eat, no matter what time of day or night it was. It made no difference if they were, or had recently been, viewing fresh blood and guts or a corpse crawling with maggots. Nothing came between him and his food.

Giving in to his plea for sustenance, Kate stopped further along the road at the Mizen Head Hotel, a place to warm up, grab a quick coffee and make some urgent calls. As Hank went off to find the Gents, her ears pricked up as a woman at the bar recounted a developing weather situation to the big guy serving her. There was no sign of it through the window but snow was apparently moving in from the north, forecast to last several days. A Met Office severe weather warning had been issued.

That was not good news.

Northumbria force covered a wide area. Bamburgh was about as far from its centre as it was possible to get. The high-tech murder investigation suite in Newcastle was fifty-odd miles away, an hour and a quarter by road. Unbelievable though it seemed in the twenty-first century, numpty politicians hadn't yet recognized the need to dual the A1 through the border regions to Scotland. From Kate's point of view, that made it too far away to function effectively as an operations base from which to run a case, particularly in winter. The weather here could change in minutes. She couldn't expect detectives working extended shifts to spend an additional three hours on treacherous roads between home and office.

Returning to the table with a latte for her and a pint of John Smith's for him, Hank sat down, taking in her disapproving look. 'What?' he said. 'I'm only having the one!'

'Did I say anything?'

'You didn't have to. What's up?'

Kate nodded towards the bar where the prophet of doom was telling her growing audience that the blizzards currently engulfing Berwick were heading their way.

Hank listened in for a moment, then turned to face Kate. 'You think we should get digs?'

She nodded. 'Seems sensible. Local boys will be on house-to-house *eventually*. There'll be nowt doing until we hear from Stanton. We'll be kicking our heels a bit, but we can get an incident room up and running while we wait. Drink up, we'd better get moving.'

5

Concerned about the threat Fearon posed to the general public, Emily called the manager of the hostel who had reluctantly agreed to take him on release, gave a précis of her report and then hung up.

Through her barred window, dark clouds gathered on the horizon, matching her mood. Shutting her eyes for a moment transported her back in time to the last occasion she'd sat there looking out. It was a memory so vivid she could almost feel a warm summer breeze on naked arms through the narrow opening, smell the scent of flowers being blown across the prison grounds.

The gardeners had worked well that year. The raised beds were awash with colour, softening the austere buildings. It never ceased to amaze her how such able young men could waste their lives in places like these.

A gentle knock on the door pulled her from her reverie.

She looked round as the handle turned.

Psychiatrist Martin Stamp reversed into her office with coffee in both hands, a smile creeping over his handsome face as he caught sight of her. On a year's secondment from the Home Office, he was conducting research into the dangerousness and treatment of life-sentence prisoners with another of Emily's closest friends, criminal profiler, Jo Soulsby, who had followed him into the room. Because their work was strictly confidential, they were using her old office in the admin block, well away from prying eyes. She'd called them to B-wing because she wanted their help.

Jo walked round the desk to Emily's chair, bent down and kissed her lightly on the cheek, patting her back gently, acknowledging the tough day she must be having. Taking a chair by the window, she sat down, crossing her very long legs. 'There's hell on in Walker's office,' she said.

Emily looked past her to the open door as Stamp kicked it shut.

He grinned at her. 'She's right. He's giving Kent a right dressing-down. You should see his face!' Handing Jo a coffee, he held the other up to Emily. 'Want this? I can nip out and get another.'

Emily shook her head as he took off his jacket and made himself at home. She'd been so engrossed in her work she hadn't noticed the row building in the office beyond. But now her colleagues had mentioned it, she realized she *had* heard something. It just hadn't registered on her radar. Muffled angry tones or even full-blown raised voices were not un-usual in prison. What might have worried her once had become commonplace over time. She'd learned not to react to every yell, every fight, and there had been a fair few of those in recent years.

Leaving her desk, she walked to the door and peered out. The area directly outside her office doubled as a recreation room. A wing cleaner dressed in prison blues was mopping the floor. Another was placing a triangular sign by the gated entrance warning those entering that the surface was wet.

They were giggling like a couple of five-year-olds over the heated exchange taking place in the wing office further down.

Emily's eyes followed their interest . . .

In a room no bigger than ten by twelve, a prison officer was standing to attention, feet slightly apart, hands linked behind his back. Facing him, Senior Officer Ash Walker, an attractive man in a pristine uniform, stared him down, an angry expression on his face.

Wondering why he was in such a state, Emily returned to her desk, focusing her attention on Stamp. If anyone knew what the story was, *he* would.

'Any idea what's going on?' she asked.

'I haven't a clue,' he said.

Emily pulled a face.

'I don't!' he declared. 'I'm a psychiatrist, not a mind-reader.'

It was an old joke. Nevertheless, Emily grinned. She'd known Stamp for years. He'd been a brick since Robert died, holding her hand, both literally and figuratively, trying his best to fill the void – resented by her daughter for his trouble.

Rachel could sulk for England sometimes.

'You OK, Em?' As well as a good friend, Jo was an astute psychologist attuned to the sudden change in Emily's mood. 'Not worried about anything, are you?'

Emily blushed, realizing she'd left the room temporarily and arrived someplace she'd rather not be. A regular occurrence she could ill afford now she was back at work.

Concentrate.

'I'm fine,' she said.

The other two weren't buying her bullshit.

'I am! It's just strange being here, that's all.'

Taking a Daim bar from his pocket, Stamp ripped off the wrapper and bit into it. 'Had to bribe a prisoner for this,' he said. 'Canteen was closed. Paid double for it, too. Friggin' daylight robbery. Who says crime doesn't pay?'

'You should know better,' Emily scolded. 'If Harrison gets wind of it he'll have you out of here quicker than you can say P45.'

B-wing's Principal Officer was a formidable figure who ruled his kingdom like a dictator. Harrison was not a man to mess with. Main-grade officers referred to him as 'God' behind his back, though never to his face. Ex-military, he'd swapped one institution for another – *big fish, little sea* – a moron with no respect for inmates or civilian staff. If you weren't wearing a uniform, your views didn't count. The next time he smiled would be a first. Martin Stamp was the exact opposite, the consummate professional with a wicked sense of humour and a complete disregard for rules and regulations.

'Come on then, spill.' He screwed up the sweet wrapper and lobbed it towards the bin. It missed by a metre. He didn't bother picking it up. 'What's so urgent it couldn't wait 'til lunchtime?'

'Walter Fearon . . .' Emily pushed a prison record across her desk. 'I'm calling a pre-release case conference. I'd appreciate your input. He's due out in two weeks and the receiving hostel need to know who they're dealing with.'

Jo reached for the file.

Stamp shot a hand out and got there first.

Opening the front cover, he studied the contents carefully,

his eyes sliding over a long list of sexual offences, each one more serious than the one before. He turned a few pages, his brow creasing as he took in her final handwritten note. Closing the file, he handed it to Jo, keeping his eyes on Emily. 'He's not a prisoner who falls within our remit now, but give him time. He's a lifer in the making, Em. No doubt about it.'

'How is he presenting?' Jo looked up from the file. 'Is he still in denial?'

Emily shook her head. 'Anything but.'

'He's not your average sex offender then?' Stamp butted in.

'Believe me, there is nothing average about Walter Fearon,' Emily replied. 'He relishes the opportunity to talk, to shock. Oh no, Walter isn't at all shy. The more detailed he can be about what he's done, the better he likes it. This guy makes Hannibal Lecter look like a charity worker. He may look and even act like a wimp on occasions, but he's no such thing – especially where women are concerned. In my view he still needs intensive therapy. I agree with Martin. He'll kill his next victim.'

6

Alnwick Police Station was situated in the market town of the same name. The office offered as a temporary incident room was far from perfect. When the DCI complained she was given two choices: take it or sling your hook.

Most of the Murder Investigation Team had arrived and set to work, fixing up the communications, getting the room ready for a new enquiry. Kate didn't require an archaeologist in the historical sense, but she did need the expertise of a forensic anthropologist to oversee the excavation and determine how long her victim had been in the ground. Before she'd left the crime scene, she'd made it known that she wanted to be present when the body was moved. In the meantime, she'd asked Detective Constable Lisa Carmichael to ring round and see what accommodation was available for her team.

At the height of summer, finding somewhere to stay would have posed a problem. But at this time of the year there would almost certainly be plenty of spare beds. The rest of the squad were already on the phone advising loved ones they wouldn't be home. There had been no dissent. Even DS Robson – the only detective with a young child at home – agreed to stay local until the enquiry got underway, joking that he'd get a better sleep sharing with a snoring colleague than being prodded by his two-year-old son in the middle of the night.

Various suggestions were thrown in the hat: Hog's Head, White Swan, Queens Head, hotels conveniently located, not far from the town's police station. The incident team voted on it, deciding that a B & B might be more practical. As well as offering peace and quiet, it would be less likely to attract the weirdos and groupies who inevitably hung around murder detectives, stifling their ability to do their jobs.

Sitting down at a computer, Lisa Carmichael slipped her warrant card into a slot. She looked different with her hair cut short. It suited her features perfectly, framing her stunning green eyes. Picking up the landline, she dialled out and identified herself. After a very brief conversation, she rang off abruptly, a worried expression on her face.

'Problem?' Daniels asked.

Lisa looked up, frowning. 'Maybe.'

'No rooms?'

'Yeah, plenty.'

'But?'

'Word's out already . . .' Carmichael glanced at the phone. 'That hotelier was rather curious about the bones we found. As well as owning a hotel, he's a volunteer archaeologist involved in a local research project. He claims there was a dig going on inside and outside of Bamburgh Castle last year. There's more planned for this summer too. Channel 4's Time Team filmed there, he said.'

'Our victim was dressed in modern material, Lisa. Not that there's much left of it. The bones aren't old, not in the archaeological sense. But I *will* need to talk to whoever's running the project to establish where and when they were digging. Maybe they can throw some light on how and why a section of dunes suddenly broke off like that. Action it, will you?'

Carmichael nodded.

'Your hotelier too,' Daniels added.

Lisa's fingers were already tapping away on the keyboard. In addition to being a lightning-fast typist, she had considerable know-how when it came to the Internet. Not long ago, she'd received a commendation for her work after proving conclusively that a serial killer the team were investigating had used the World Wide Web to track and target his victims. Her tenacity had been instrumental in apprehending Jonathan Forster, though not before he'd confronted Kate in a chilling encounter that could so easily have proved fatal. The events of that night still haunted her in the small hours when she couldn't sleep. Though the case was considered by many to represent Northumbria MIT's finest hour, in Kate's opinion it was the biggest failure of her career to date. Forster had killed seven times before being stopped.

'Boss?' Lisa Carmichael pointed at her computer.

The screen was now open at the website of the Bamburgh Research Project. On the left-hand side of the home page was a menu bar. She clicked on *Get in Touch*. The names and email addresses of the project's directors and administrators appeared instantly, along with relevant phone numbers.

She looked at her boss. 'I'll copy these and send them to your BlackBerry.'

Just then, said BlackBerry rang.

It was Home Office pathologist, Tim Stanton.

'Hi, Tim . . .' The DCI tried to sound more upbeat than she felt after a heavy workload the previous week, half-spent preparing a murder file, the other giving evidence in a trial that had lasted a couple of months. Covering the speaker, she thanked Carmichael and moved away, talking into the phone. 'You done already?'

'There wasn't much *to* do . . .' Stanton broke off as someone spoke to him. Clearly he was still at the scene. Wind distortion on the line prevented Kate from hearing what was being said. Then he was back: 'Sorry to keep you . . . permission to move is granted. There's nothing more to be done here until we get her to the morgue. Not an easy task for you guys, due to the physical geography of the area.'

Daniels couldn't agree more.

If the skeleton had been found in concrete it would have been possible to remove it in one solid slab, but with shifting sands, a worsening weather picture, and the risk of further slippage, time was of the essence. She rang off, telling her team that she was heading back to the crime scene to witness the excavation.

7

No more than twenty metres from Emily McCann's office, the door to the shower block slammed shut. A single drop of blood hit the floor. Then another . . . and another . . . followed by a loud thump. A pair of steel-rimmed spectacles with one smashed lens skidded across the floor through pubic hairs and lost bars of soap. They came to rest in a pool of watery blood trickling into a nearby drain.

A few feet away, a young man lay on cracked wet tiles, his childlike face drained of all colour, blood pulsing from gashes to both wrists. Fearon's steel-grey eyes were open and trained on the door. The last thing he saw and heard before his eyes fluttered closed was a pair of squeaky uniform boots rounding the corner as the door opened inwards.

'Oh fuck!'

The prison officer wearing those boots slammed his fist against a red button on the wall, sounding the alarm. He took out his radio to report what he'd found, his action resulting in immediate lockdown. And suddenly all hell broke loose as officers ran towards the wing from every direction, yelling and herding the cons back to their cells, summoning medics to the shower block.

Hearing the commotion, Martin Stamp, Jo Soulsby and Emily McCann abandoned their meeting and came out to investigate. In the recreation area, inmates were arguing with jailers. Emily understood why. Following any emergency situation or security threat there was always an enquiry: questions asked, fingers pointed, blame apportioned. Prisoners could find themselves banged up in their cells for hours on end.

A giant of a young man Emily didn't recognize was reluctant to leave. In no mood to be pushed around, he squared up to a rookie officer, shoving him hard against the wall. Within seconds, the prisoner was pinned to the deck, his arm twisted behind his back as half a dozen uniforms rushed to their colleague's aid.

Seeing one of their peers so easily overpowered and restrained, other inmates who'd been on the verge of making a fuss thought better of it. They shuffled away to their cells, craning their necks to see what was going on, moaning about rough treatment and the untimely interruption to their daily routine.

Following the direction of their gaze, Emily rushed towards the shower block, heart kicking hard inside her chest. She pulled up short when she reached the open door.

Walter Fearon was lying on the wet tiled floor, stark naked, so still she was sure he was dead. Emily tried to speak but no words came out. She looked away, trying to focus on something other than the pool of deep red blood surrounding him. Fearon's prison blues were folded in a neat little pile in one corner of the steamy room. A pair of worn black plimsolls placed neatly on top reminded her of the ones she had worn at school.

She looked back at the lad.

He had multiple injuries on his muscular body, the majority of them self-inflicted. In his right hand he was holding an improvised scalpel: a toothbrush with a razorblade melted into the end.

The sight of it made her shiver.

Movement . . .

Fearon's eyes fluttered open and shut as he slipped in and out of consciousness. Instinctively, she moved towards him, kneeling down at his side as others arrived at the door . . .

'It's OK, Walter,' she whispered.

'Emily, no!'

Senior Officer Ash Walker's tone was fierce enough to stop her dead in her tracks. Emily's hand froze in mid-air as she reached out to touch the bleeding prisoner. Walker rushed to her side, kicking the weapon from Fearon's fingers, at the same time pulling on a pair of rubber gloves, the significance of which she understood.

Was the risk of HIV the reason why the officer who'd found him hadn't stayed around to offer assistance? At least tried to stem the blood? Do *something*.

God Almighty! Where was his compassion?

Emily backed away leaving Walker checking for a pulse. Of all the scenarios she'd imagined, this had never crossed her mind. She felt guilty now for having discussed the prisoner with Jo Soulsby and Martin Stamp, even though everything she'd said about him had been true. Fearon *was* a dangerous young man. But was it any wonder? From an early age he'd been systematically and brutally abused, both physically and emotionally. The transition from child victim to high profile offender was almost inevitable, sadly.

He wasn't born that way: he'd been *made* like it.

He'd endured an upbringing of horror beyond imagination.

But why had he cut himself now when release was imminent?

In her darkest hour, Emily had contemplated suicide. Only Rachel had stopped her from taking such drastic action. Fearon had no one. It occurred to her that he didn't want to get out. That the prison afforded him order: food, warmth, a roof over his head – basic requirements the rest of us took for granted. But then so would the hostel she'd arranged for him. Still, when you'd been inside for a lengthy period, change was unsettling.

She looked up as a medic was bundled into the room to revive him.

His escort, Officer Bill Kent, arrived by her side, taking in the bloody scene. For a moment, Emily mistook his silence as distress. Glancing to her left, she was taken aback by his indifference. Kent's eyes were ice cold and unsympathetic, full of loathing, not pity. Not an ounce of concern for a young man's life. When he spoke, his words rendered her speechless.

'Let the nonce croak,' he said. 'The bastard won't be missed.'

8

DCI Kate Daniels gave the go ahead for the victim's body to be removed from the dunes, plus two metres of earth around it in order to preserve any forensic material that may have been accidentally dropped at the scene. Forensic anthropologist Abbey Hunt had arrived with a couple of assistants in tow. They were fresh from another 'dig' that had turned out to be no more sinister than a set of ancient bones unearthed by a JCB on a building site.

Listening to her describe her day brought to mind a call Kate had received the previous February following the discovery of human remains beside a medieval tower in a different part of the county. It had caused quite a stir at the time. But foul play was quickly ruled out, and the Murder Investigation Team stood down soon after. She later learned that the bones had been radiocarbon dated. According to the council's archaeological team, they had given a fascinating insight into the area's history.

Hoping for some 'fascinating insights' of her own, Kate studied the ground beneath her feet. It was now marked out in a complicated grid system she and Abbey had agreed upon before work commenced. There were all manner of archaeological tools to hand: a tarpaulin for holding sand already sifted, trowels, brushes and Ziploc bags for any foreign bodies that may or may not turn out to be evidential material she would later use in a court of law.

Abbey had loads of experience of working with the police. She was fifty-three years old, a formidable figure who didn't suffer fools lightly. She preferred to work with the minimum of people breathing down her neck and was directing operations in her inimitable way, her tone reserved and businesslike, her attention to detail second to none.

The crime scene was in the very best of hands.

So why did she look so worried?

'Abbey?' A camera flash lit up the tent, blinding Kate momentarily. 'Abbey, is everything all right?'

'No, it bloody isn't!' The woman stopped combing a mound of rough grass from around the skull area. A black beetle made a run for it as she stood up, arched her back and crossed her arms. 'You want the bad news or the really, *really* bad news?'

Kate, who hated games, waited for her to continue.

'In their present state these dunes are highly unstable.' Abbey swept her hand out. 'This whole area could collapse at any moment. As a result, I need to extricate these bones much quicker than I'm comfortable with, which is like asking a tortoise to move like a cheetah. I'm hardly built for that, am I?'

It was a rhetorical question.

Not expecting an answer, Abbey ploughed on. 'I prefer daylight, to be perfectly honest. Things get missed in artificial light . . .' Glancing at the CSI photographer, the archaeologist pushed her glasses up on to the bridge of her nose. 'Leave that, please! Can you step outside a moment? I need a quick word with your SIO.'

When Abbey said 'jump', people usually asked: How high? The photographer made himself scarce.

As soon as he'd cleared the tent, the scientist turned to Kate, an inscrutable expression on her face. Whatever she had on her mind was obviously better said in private.

Kate suspected it wasn't going to be good.

She wasn't wrong.

'There's a discrepancy between what you thought you saw and what's actually here, Kate.' Abbey swept a gloved hand out towards the corpse. 'This body is not what it seems.'

'It's male?' Kate asked.

'No, you got the gender right. Let me show you something . . .' Beckoning the DCI nearer to the corpse, Abbey used the tool in her hand to move a fragment of red-and-white material away from the lower abdominal area. 'The width of the pelvic bones are a dead giveaway. They're much wider in females to facilitate childbirth. Not that this poor unfortunate will ever have children of her own. I'm sorry to have to rain on your parade, but what's left of the clothing and pearls around her neck aren't age appropriate . . .' Abbey pointed at the sandy high-heeled shoe on the ground near the body. 'And that *definitely* isn't.'

'It's a kid?' Kate knew the answer even before she'd asked the question.

'No more than ten years old, I'd say.'

'Are you absolutely sure? I thought it was tricky determining age.'

'Not so much in children. I can tell from the skull mainly. I'll do some further tests at the lab. Without getting too technical, it's all to do with calcium and mineral deposits that form the bones. That'll determine her age for sure. With the aid of X-rays I'll be able to give a very accurate prediction. Look here . . .' Using a soft brush Abbey dusted loose sand away from a perfect set of teeth. 'See, little evidence of wear or dental decay.'

Kate hoped that in due course an odontologist would be able to give her an identity for the child. But that wasn't something she could confidently rely on. In any event, it might take weeks or even months before a match was found. In the meantime, it was gratifying to have Abbey's expertise on board.

'I'd better get on.' Abbey pointed at the entrance to the tent. 'Your colleague can come in again now.'

Kate nodded and stepped outside.

Her crime scene photographer was frozen. He was standing with his back to the biting wind, collar pulled up around his ears, fag in one hand, hot drink in the other. The light was fading as they re-entered the tent. But before he'd even got started, the ground beneath him gave way and he toppled over, almost landing on the corpse.

Hunt went ballistic. 'Get him out of my bloody crime scene!'

Apologizing – although technically it wasn't his fault – the photographer scrambled to his feet, sand dropping off his clothing and landing all over the place, giving the scientist even more cause to rebuke him. Simultaneously, they turned toward the DCI complaining about each other. But Daniels was otherwise engaged, staring at the area of ground her CSI colleague had just vacated – her worst nightmare staring back at her.

'Hold it! Hold it!' she yelled.

Abbey and the police photographer froze, their focus switching to ground level. To the right of the skeleton being excavated there was a size-ten footprint where the photographer had fallen and two projectiles sticking out of the ground.

With or without skin, Kate knew fingers when she saw them.

9

Once Principal Officer Ted Harrison got going there was little anyone could do to shut him up. The man was holding court with representatives of no fewer than four departments sitting in a semi-circle round his desk. The meeting, scheduled to last just forty-five minutes, had already been going on for the best part of an hour.

The room itself was stuffy, littered with used coffee cups, the remains of a packet of digestive biscuits, empty water bottles. Prisoner profiles lay in untidy heaps on the floor, along with psychological assessments, parole dossiers and sentence-planning reports. Casting her eye over the mess, Emily McCann felt guilty. Her colleagues were exhausted, itching to draw the meeting to a close. She wanted to go home too but as soon as the day's business was concluded, casting caution aside, she'd dared to criticize one of Harrison's men, tackling the thorny subject of Officer Kent – specifically his attitude towards inmate Walter Fearon following his suicide attempt.

As she waited for a response, her attention strayed to the PO's desk where a hefty document had been pushed to one side. Her eyes scanned the title page: Amanda Drake: *Punishment v Rehabilitation – Both Sides of the Argument*.

Yeah right, Emily scoffed.

Harrison was incapable of seeing both sides of anything.

As flexible as a steel girder, he was a patronizing, self-opinionated bully. Someone who liked the sound of his own, very loud, voice. Sensing that a sermon was imminent, Emily fixed him with a glare and got in first.

'This is not Abu Ghraib, Ted. Fearon is entitled to as much protection as any other prisoner. Deal with Kent or I *will* take it further.'

'I hear what you're saying, Emily, I do . . .' Harrison paused. His mouth was smiling but his eyes were not. Placing his elbows on the desk, he linked his hands in front of him and rested his chin on top of them. 'You're making a serious alleg—'

'No!' Emily hit back. 'I'm stating a fact. Ask Ash Walker if you don't believe me.'

'Are you *trying* to make yourself unpopular?' Harrison asked. 'Why don't you go away and think about whose side you're on. Come and see me again when you've given it more thought.'

'Don't patronize me, Ted. I—'

'I wouldn't dream of it,' Harrison said. 'I've worked with Bill Kent for a very long time. He's not perfect, but then who is? As a matter of fact, he's a fine officer.'

'Is he now?' Emily could feel the colour rising in her cheeks. 'May I remind you we have standards on this wing.' She thumbed over her left shoulder. 'Last time I looked at the nameplate on that door, your name was on it. That means it's *your* job to ensure they're upheld!' She glanced at other staff in the room. 'Well? It isn't the first time Kent has stepped out of line, is it?'

Two of those present avoided her gaze – too bottleless to

acknowledge a problem existed – not wanting to get involved. The prison chaplain adjusted his dog collar and looked at the floor. Fortunately for Emily, the woman sitting to his left had more nerve. A probation officer of long-standing, she nodded her head and spoke up.

'She's right, Ted. For what it's worth, I also think Bill Kent has a problem.'

Harrison bristled at the overt challenge to his authority. His views on women were common knowledge: the prison would be much better off without them. He was in charge of this wing; he'd made that clear often enough. Leaning back in his chair, he looked down his nose at them like a headmaster rebuking a pair of insolent pupils.

It was a childish game.

His expression said: toe the line or you'll be out on your ear.

The probation officer looked away.

Harrison turned on Emily. 'You don't want to rock the boat on your first day back now, do you?'

Resolute, Emily made no comment.

'Suit yourself.' He was almost smirking. 'You want to make a complaint, be my guest.'

'You think I won't?' Emily countered.

'You know where to find the guv'nor,' Harrison said. 'It's your call. This meeting is over.'

10

Each violent death scenario is different: location, motive, modus operandi. Kate Daniels had never worked on two that were the same. Some were straightforward: detected almost immediately. In others, the Murder Investigation Team had a pretty good idea of who might be responsible. All they had to do was put in the legwork to prove it. The rest – thankfully, the minority – were a complete mystery right from the off.

Kate had the distinct impression that her current case would fall into the latter category. Not only because of the time lapse between burial and discovery, but because the perpetrator had gone to great lengths to mask the victims' ages. The question she was asking herself was: why?

Was this a case of human trafficking gone wrong?

This stretch of coast was remote. A boat could easily sail in unnoticed. Perhaps the girls were foreign. If they were dead on arrival in the UK, maybe someone had buried them in the first accessible spot . . . Except that made no sense. Why would anyone bother when it was so much easier to chuck a body overboard while you were out in deep water?

Calling the room to order, she was about to start the briefing when Detective Superintendent Ron Naylor suddenly appeared in the doorway. He was wearing a pair of green wellington boots and a three-quarter-length parka jacket covered in fresh snow.

'Decided to have myself a little trip to the seaside,' he said.

Bearing in mind his appearance, his comment sounded ridiculous.

Everyone laughed, Naylor included.

He extracted something from his pocket and held it out to Kate with a curious look on his face. Her personal mail: three postcards from three different locations, the same message on each, just four words – *Are You Hungry Yet?* Each card signed with a flamboyant: *F*.

Fiona Fielding.

Kate could feel herself blushing. These cryptic messages had been dropping into her in-tray with alarming regularity in recent months, sent by an artist who was never far away from her consciousness of late.

Gormley was grinning.

He knew she and Fielding had more than a love of fine art in common.

Popping the cards into her bag, Kate made a mental note to text the artist her home address. She couldn't keep receiving these curious messages at work. It was funny but rather embarrassing too. It had to stop.

Taking off his coat, Naylor shook it violently and hung it over an open cupboard door. DC Andy Brown passed him a mug of something hot. The Super sat down, cradling the cup in his huge hands, confirming what the team already knew. There was little to be done until the results of the post-mortem were in.

'And then there were two,' the DCI said sadly. 'Abbey filled you in, I take it?'

Naylor nodded. 'She's gone with the bodies to the morgue. Her team will continue digging in the morning. For now the scene is secure with an officer posted on overnight watch. Shit duty for some poor sod, but we have to assume there could be more until we're told otherwise. For all we know that's a mass grave out there.'

'What a cheery thought.' Kate drew in a big breath, wishing they were back at the purpose-built major incident suite in Newcastle. Something was telling her she would need its state-of-the-art technology at her fingertips. 'I'm already regretting my decision to run the incident from here.' She sighed, looking around her. 'What a dog's bollocks!'

'What's up with you?' Naylor said. 'It's not that bad!'

Either Abbey hadn't told him or Naylor was being very understanding.

Kate cleared her throat. 'I hadn't realized the first one was a kid, guv.'

'Don't beat yourself up over it. You weren't to know. You called it as you saw it. I'd have done the same in your shoes.'

She thanked him for being so understanding, adding, 'The second victim is a little older. Mid-teens is Abbey's best guess. Knowing her, it'll be spot on.'

'Is she ever wrong?' Naylor made a face. 'Bloody woman gets right up my nose.'

'What is it with you and her, guv?' Gormley asked. 'You got history we don't know about?'

'You *are* joking?' Naylor's mouth turned down at the edges. 'She'd eat me for breakfast!'

Ignoring their banter, Kate moved on.

'Lisa ran the unsolved cases through the system, guv. There are none where two young kids went missing together. The press are going to be all over this if we don't keep a lid on it.' Kate wondered why he'd come, what on earth possessed him to venture out in such atrocious weather. He normally ran from encounters with Abbey Hunt and there were easier ways of being briefed on a new case. Unlike her former boss, Detective Chief Superintendent Bright, Naylor had never been one to interfere. 'You sticking around for the briefing or heading back to town?'

'I might sit in for a bit. Actually, I'm meeting Jo at the Railway later for a bite to eat. Two birds, one stone, seeing as I'm up here. Forty pence a mile doesn't go far these days. By the looks of the weather, I might have to find a room too.'

'Win win . . .' Kate tried for a smile but it didn't come off.

Naylor didn't notice. 'Filled my car up the other day,' he griped. 'Cost me nearly ninety quid!'

As he continued his rant about the price of diesel, Kate's mind strayed. Jo Soulsby was a psychologist who'd worked for Northumbria Police as a criminal profiler for the past few years. She'd resigned recently in order to take up a post at HMP Northumberland. Right now she was probably hard at work only ten short miles away from where they were standing. She wasn't just an ex-colleague either. She was Kate's ex: her lover, confidante and the best friend she'd ever had. Their relationship, or former one to be precise, was a closely guarded secret only Hank knew about.

Yeah right, Kate thought.

A run-in with former Assistant Chief Constable Martin –

who'd since retired in disgrace – had outed her in spectacular fashion when an offender she was chasing sent him an
anonymous letter. Though the ACC had no proof of her relationship with Jo, he'd sure as hell be making his mouth go
about her private life now, dishing the dirt to anyone who'd
listen. Whatever he was saying would eventually filter down
to the whole damn force.

Kate sighed.

She found it hard to accept that she and Jo were finished,
harder still to define her feelings for someone who steadfastly
refused to return her texts. Recent attempts to contact her
on landline or mobile had failed. Fair enough. If she didn't
want to talk, Kate wouldn't push it. No point in chasing a lost
cause.

'Kate?'

A combination of her boss's voice and Hank's interest
dragged the SIO back into the room. Apologizing for the
lapse in concentration, she said, 'Give her my love when you
see her, won't you, guv?'

'Are you even listening to me?' The Super put down his
empty mug, a curious expression on his face. 'I said why don't
you join us?'

'Maybe next time. I want to get stuff up and running here
first.'

Puzzled, Naylor looked around him. The temporary
murder wall was almost blank. There wasn't a thing going
on. The squad were bored out of their brains, itching for the
enquiry to get under way. A couple of detectives were playing
cards. Others were texting or tweeting on mobile phones.

Naylor didn't question her in front of the troops. Not in

words. But when he turned to face her, he held her gaze long enough to let her know that he wasn't fooled by her avoidance tactics. He knew something was up. He also knew that, whatever it was, it had nothing to do with the investigation.

11

Incensed with Harrison for giving her such a hard time, Emily didn't hang around after the sentence-planning meeting. As soon as it broke up she was out of there, returning briefly to her office to dump her case-notes before heading straight for the medical wing with her bag slung over her shoulder.

As she shut the gate behind her, she glanced back through the thick steel bars. Like a smiling assassin, Principal Officer Harrison was standing in his doorway shaking hands with the chaplain but looking right past him in her direction. Wishing she could wipe that supercilious smirk off his face, she turned away, determined to deny him the satisfaction of knowing that he'd got to her.

She'd felt vulnerable since losing Robert. It was as if her confidence had died and been buried along with his body. It had taken all her resolve to crawl out of the black hole she'd fallen into when the news of his death reached her. Now this ignorant arsehole was trying to push her back in it again.

Well, she'd see about that.

Turning the key in the heavy metal gate, she rattled the bars to make sure it was properly locked, a habit she'd developed years ago. Her shoes squeaked on the highly polished floor as she turned and hurried down the corridor feeling the weight of Harrison's beady eyes between her shoulder blades.

Emily couldn't afford to dwell on Harrison.

She had more important things to do.

Once out of sight of the wing she slowed her gait, took a long, deep breath and tried to focus on the task ahead. It was then she realized she should've called first. Medical staff liked to be informed when staff wanted to visit the sick. She hoped it wouldn't lead to yet another row. *Assuming Fearon was even there*. Last she'd heard, he'd been shipped out by civilian ambulance to Alnwick Infirmary for treatment, attached to a burly prison officer, despite his poorly condition.

It wouldn't be the first time an escape plan had masqueraded as a suicide attempt.

Preoccupied with that thought, she failed to notice Martin Stamp emerging from the prison library. But he saw *her,* more especially the look on her face, a confusion of worry and anger.

Doing an about turn, he fell into step, asking what was up.

Emily kept on walking, giving chapter and verse on her spat with Harrison, ranting about his superior attitude, how embarrassed she'd been when he slapped her down in front of fellow professionals.

'Welcome back to the mad house,' Stamp grinned.

Unable to see the funny side, Emily didn't respond.

'C'mon, lighten up! Don't make a crap day even worse—'

'The man's a bloody moron! If he talks to me like that again, I swear I'll . . .' Emily didn't finish her sentence. Inmates were fast approaching from the opposite direction, escorted by two prison officers who were members of

Harrison's inner circle. They said hello as they passed by. She could tell by looking at them that they already knew what had taken place. Word spread quickly in institutions like this.

She waited until they were out of earshot.

'See that?' She glanced at Stamp. 'They'll all close ranks if I go running to the guv'nor.'

'Then use that psychology degree of yours and tackle Kent yourself.'

'That's easier said than done, Martin. The PO has marked my card. He'll be watching every move I make. It's all right for you. For a start, you're a bloke. In twelve months you'll be gone. I, on the other hand, will be here banging my head against a brick wall ad infinitum with that fucking idiot making my life hell at every opportunity.'

'Ever thought Kent might be in need of counselling?'

Emily stopped walking. 'You know something I don't?'

'Maybe . . .'

She caught his arm. 'Well? Are you going to tell me or what?'

'I'm not at liberty to say.' He seemed profoundly troubled all of a sudden.

Emily bristled. He knew her well enough to know that whatever was said wouldn't go any further. Besides, she'd helped him out in the past. They had always been close. Back when they were at university, they'd dated for a while, going their separate ways after graduating. Even in those days Martin would cheerfully break every rule in the book but he would never betray a confidence. Where secrets were concerned, his sense of morality was delightfully old-fashioned.

Endearing almost. She knew she'd be wasting her time trying to pry information out of him.

More was the pity.

He opened his mouth to speak and then closed it again.

For a moment, she wondered if he was going to reconsider and compromise his precious principles. But if the thought had crossed his mind, he dismissed it in a flash.

'Have a word with Ash Walker,' he said. 'Maybe *he* can throw light on Kent's behaviour.'

That wasn't a bad idea.

SO Walker had always been her go-to man for help and support. He wasn't the only decent prison officer at HMP Northumberland by any means. There were plenty of those. But he had been her first ally on the wing when she'd taken up her current post. He knew Kent as well as anyone.

'I'll do that,' Emily said. 'I'll catch you later, Martin. I really need to see Fearon now.'

'Be careful . . .' Stamp looked deep into her eyes, ramming home the warning. 'I mean it, Em. He may be weak, but he's extremely dangerous.'

Emily gave a curt nod and raced off before he could stop her.

12

Detective Superintendent Naylor paced the incident room. He grew more like former Newcastle United and England striker, Alan Shearer, as each day passed. Except, and this was unusual in this part of the world, what he knew about football you could write on a postage stamp. His hair was so thin on top he'd stopped trying to comb it over, opting instead for a virile baldness. He had nice eyes and a ready smile, more accurately described as a cheeky grin.

A fiercely ambitious man, Naylor had climbed the ladder to his present rank without difficulty. He'd recently confided that the higher position was not all it was cracked up to be. He longed to get his hands dirty instead of sitting at a desk delegating the interesting stuff to others.

Probably the reason he'd visited the crime scene.

His obvious discontent made Kate question her future too. Could she really give up the job she loved to attain the next rank, knowing full well she'd be forced back in uniform before she made detective super? The very thought made her angry. She'd already given up so much in pursuit of her career, including a close and loving relationship with Jo Soulsby.

As her boss moved away in search of a decent place to park himself, Kate scanned the room. Hank Gormley was sitting close by, facing the murder wall, Detective Sergeant Paul Robson to his left. Both had their legs stretched out in front of them, crossed at the ankle in relaxation pose. Next to them DCs Andy Brown and Neil Maxwell shared a desk but were otherwise ignoring each other in favour of their mobile phones. Maxwell was getting to grips with a new 3G device, the signal of which kept dropping out, displeasing him no end. At the back of the room, three civilian indexers were crammed together in a confined space waiting for something to do: phones to answer, intelligence to input into the HOLMES system, *any bloody thing*.

The identity of the victims would be a start.

Waiting for news from Alnwick mortuary was frustrating, not to mention a complete waste of everyone's time. But the hiatus provided Kate with the opportunity to ring her father and cancel her arrangement to take him out to dinner, a task she'd managed to avoid thus far.

With a sense of unease – expecting an earbashing – she picked up the nearest internal telephone, dialled nine for an outside line, followed by his home number.

He answered on the fourth ring. 'Three-o-three.'

A wry smile crept over Kate's face when she heard his voice. Rigid was the word that best described her father. He was stuck in a time warp, viewing change as a threat rather than an opportunity, insisting on answering with his old phone number, ignoring the additional three-digit prefix that had been introduced years ago.

'Happy birthday!' she said, heart in mouth.

She shook her head as Hank hauled himself off his chair and made a 'drink?' gesture by waggling a hand in front of his face. In her right ear, her father was expressing surprise at the number of cards he'd received.

'That's nice.' She hoped she didn't sound patronizing. 'Have you seen the news?'

'No, should I have? I've been out for a haircut.'

Kate winced.

Ed Daniels always visited the barbers for a short back and sides when he wanted to look his best. Torn by conflicting emotions, she felt guilty for having to disappoint him on his big day. Dinner was out of the question now, *unless* . . . did she have time to nip out and see him before Stanton's report came in? She looked out at the snow falling in big fluffy flakes. Corbridge was almost fifty miles away. She'd never make it.

'There's been an incident, Dad.'

'You don't say.' He sounded more angry than disappointed.

'I'm sorry,' she said. 'It's not like I arranged it just to piss you off.'

She could feel his irritation down the line. Her swearing and backchat angered him. It wasn't how he'd brought her up. He held the view that children should know their place and show respect to their parents at all times. Earning that respect didn't come into it. His crackpot philosophy got right up her nose. As did his silence, calculated to provoke her.

And it was working . . .

Had he forgotten how old she was?

What she did for a living?

Kate was annoyed too now – with herself, for allowing him to get under her skin. She'd tried her very best to meet him halfway. At every opportunity the stubborn old git made it so bloody difficult. He'd never forgiven her for joining the police when she had won a place to study veterinary medicine at Edinburgh. *His* choice, now she came to think of it. Since then, each time she cried off on a prearranged social event due to the demands of her job – a frequent occurrence, unfortunately – he took great pleasure in reminding her that there was more to life than work.

Well, actually there wasn't.

She'd made her choice fifteen years ago . . .

It was time he got over it.

Kate sighed. She ought to be used to her father's disapproval by now. He'd behaved the same way when she told him about her relationship with Jo. Now *that* was a hanging offence. A complete abomination in his eyes and no doubt those of his precious church.

Taking a deep breath, she counted to ten, wishing her mother was still around to let her off the hook and share his special day. But mentioning her now would only upset him further. So the dutiful daughter apologized again.

He put down the phone without another word.

Kate needed some air. Putting her coat on, she left the building, telling the others she wouldn't be long. It was only a short trudge to Alnwick morgue. Tim Stanton, the on-call Home Office pathologist, was about done by the time she arrived. Unfortunately, he had no news on how her victims had met their deaths. But he did have information that might help, he told her.

'That's quick.' Kate glanced at the skeletons lying on adjacent slabs. 'I was steeling myself for a longer wait, given the condition of the bodies.'

'We aim to please . . .' Stanton scratched his head. 'Abbey's observations are correct. They *are* both children, one much younger than the other.' He pointed at the nearest set of bones which were shorter than the others but not by much. 'This unfortunate young girl is about nine or ten years old, the other around fifteen or sixteen. Their clothing was a definite ploy to mislead—'

'Or a prop in someone's bizarre fantasy,' she reminded him.

'Indeed,' he said.

'Don't suppose you can tell if there was a sexual element from the remains?'

'Sorry, I can't help you, Kate.'

That's what she'd thought. Maybe it was better not to know.

13

The small medical ward had barred windows and four beds, all of which were occupied. That wasn't unusual. By their very nature prisons were unhealthy pressure-cooker environments locked down tight. People got sick. Was it any wonder, with hundreds of repressed men forced to live cheek by jowl – all vying for a place in the pecking order – resentful of being under the microscope 24/7?

Hell-bent on corrective measures, successive governments had spent substantial sums building and improving institutions like HMP Northumberland in an effort to curb criminal behaviour and punish wrongdoing. But within the walls of prisons, a subculture of aggression reigned. Racism was rife. Violence and hostility between individuals and groups was commonplace, resulting in physical as well as psychological damage to inmates, some of whom required hospital treatment from time to time.

Emily scanned the room.

Three patients were sitting up in bed: two reading, one staring into space – almost catatonic. In the bed furthest from the door, Fearon lay pale and childlike, both wrists bandaged, a male medic keeping observation from a nearby desk. A short, stocky, Asian man of indeterminate age, he smiled at Emily as she crossed the room. He didn't question her turning up on spec, just advised that Fearon's prognosis was favourable. His wounds had been sewn up and he was otherwise fit and healthy. He'd live to fight another day and would be back on the wing before she knew it.

'Tonight, in all probability,' he added.

'That soon?' Emily was appalled. 'Surely not!'

The medic levelled steely eyes at her. 'You didn't buy that crap, did you? It was a con.'

'I saw it with my own eyes.'

'You saw blood, Emily. It always looks worse than it is. His wounds were superficial. He'd have run the blade the length of his arm if he really wanted to end it all, but these cuts were lateral. Disfiguring, yes, but carefully choreographed. No question. Designed to shock, to draw attention. Who knows what's going on in that depraved mind of his.'

'He was unconscious!'

'Was he?' The medic smirked. 'He cut over old scars, Emily. He knew exactly where to do it and he knew that it wouldn't kill him. Pathetic. Anyway, we need the bed.'

We need the bed?

She took that as a euphemism for the medical team not wanting Fearon on the hospital wing for any longer than was absolutely necessary. And who could blame them? This particular patient was an unknown quantity – unpredictable in the extreme – an individual who could flip at a moment's notice. It was a question of ward security; the needs of one patient balanced against the safety of the other three.

The medic was warning her off, just as Stamp had done.

Emily felt a shiver run through her.

Watch out.

Fearon is trouble.

She took a deep breath. 'Despite what you say, I insist you place him on suicide watch tonight. I want assurances. If he's sent back to B-wing before I come in tomorrow, please make sure the night shift get the message.' She was leaving nothing to chance. 'I'd be grateful if you would write my request down too.'

'As you wish.'

Emily waited for a note to be made. 'OK if I sit with him?'

The medic nodded. 'Be my guest.'

She turned away and walked over to Fearon's bedside. Lying there, he seemed so ordinary: asleep, peaceful, innocent, a young man without a care in the world. Looking at him now, it was hard to imagine that beneath those closed eyelids lurked the hardest, certainly the coldest, pair of steel-grey eyes she'd ever seen. Eyes that looked through you like you weren't even there: the manifestation of a psychopath. And yet he was not much older than her only child.

Emily looked at her watch. Four p.m.

Despite the fact that it was her first day back at work, she was in no rush to get home. After their terrible row that morning, Rachel had gone off in a huff and sent a text informing her mother she would be staying overnight at a friend's place. She hadn't said which friend. *That would be far too easy.* When Emily called to find out, Rachel got stroppy all over again, reminding her she was nearly twenty years old.

Whatever.

It wasn't like her to be so secretive. She'd spent a few nights out lately and Emily had a feeling she might be seeing someone new, although Rachel had refused to confirm or deny it. As far as she was concerned, there could only be one explanation for that. Whoever it was, you could bet your bottom dollar *she* wouldn't approve of him. Emily had spent many a sleepless night recently going over the possibilities in her mind: an undesirable rogue, an older man, a manipulative freak who might be taking advantage of her daughter's vulnerability.

Or was she the weak one, unable to face the prospect of going home to an empty house? It was bad enough with Rachel in it, but it was totally insufferable being alone there. So, in the vain hope that a gesture of kindness might do some good, Emily sat down to keep vigil at Fearon's bedside, taking a book from her bag in order to pass the time.

Within a matter of minutes she became so engrossed in the exploits of a fictional hero that she was oblivious to her surroundings. Which was a little unfortunate because the patient in the bed was awake and watching her.

14

The work of the forensic pathologist had always fascinated Kate. Tim Stanton was one of the best she'd ever come across. A Bachelor of Medicine, Fellow of the Royal College of Pathology and honorary lecturer at Edinburgh University, he'd made significant contributions to major investigations over the years, examining scores of murder victims, young and old.

As devoted to his work as she was to hers, Kate regarded the married father of two as a personal friend as well as a professional colleague. Watching him now, she mourned the fact that they rarely, if ever, saw each other socially. There was a simple explanation for that: their meetings only took place across the stainless-steel slab of his examination room or at her grim crime scenes. Either way, there was always a third party present – one who'd drawn their last breath.

Hardly dinner-table conversation, was it?

Tim had barely mentioned Abbey Hunt when the door burst open and the woman herself marched in fresh from the shower. At least a foot shorter than the DCI, her hair was still damp and tied in a bun at the nape of her neck. She wore no make-up, a pair of navy cargo pants and a pale blue V-neck T-shirt revealing a flabby spare tyre.

Her barefoot technology footwear obviously wasn't up to much.

Grabbing a newly laundered white coat from a shelf near the door, she slipped her arms into it and walked towards them buttoning it up. A smile played on her lips as she came closer, an I-know-something-you-don't expression forming on her round face.

'Have you told her yet?' she said.

'Told me what?' Kate said.

Stanton shook his head.

Abbey turned to face Kate. 'That's what I love about Tim, he's so self-sacrificing, *so* gallant. He knows how much I ache to be the one to drop a bombshell.'

'Bombshell' sounded ominous.

Kate waited, her eyes darting left and right between the two medics, the hairs rising on the back of her neck at thoughts of a breakthrough in her case. Abbey was savouring the moment but itching to divulge her findings. Despite her casual appearance and jocular attitude, which for some reason was never on display when Naylor was around, she was a meticulous and committed professional of international standing. If she had something to say, it was probably worth hearing. No matter how small her insight, Kate was sure it would kick-start her enquiry.

At least, she hoped it would.

Walking between two stainless-steel tables, Abbey glanced at the skeletal remains lying on each and then refocused her attention on Daniels. 'Tim probably told you that the manner of death is undetermined. Accidental is out of the question. If that *were* the case, the girls would've been found before now. A suicide pact only works if they had the ability to bury themselves after the event—'

'Unless a third party was involved,' the DCI cut in.

'Quite so. Thank you for reminding me.' Abbey dropped her head a touch, peering over the top of square-framed specs. 'So . . . given the fact that they were buried together, are we all agreed that these two unfortunate young women were in all probability murdered?'

Trying to work out where this was leading, Kate cocked her head on one side, her eyes sliding over what was left of her two young victims. Apart from a well-healed fracture in the older girl's right tibia that might prove useful in identifying her, preliminary examination of the bones had proved inconclusive. Stanton had already told her he'd found no obvious signs of trauma that would indicate fatal violence on either victim: no caved-in skulls or bullet holes; no nicks on hands or arms to suggest defence injuries; no ligatures round their necks. Furthermore, no instruments of death had been found by crime scene investigators in the vicinity of the bodies. In short, there was nothing at all on which a reconstruction might be based.

Replaying Abbey's monologue in her head, Kate suddenly realized what she was getting at. The anthropologist's words had been chosen carefully, designed to mislead in the short term so she could emerge victorious and put the SIO in her place. *Again.* No malice intended, simply a bit of humorous banter between fellow professionals to lighten the seriousness of the proceedings.

Kate wasn't fooled.

The words '*buried together*' could be taken two ways.

Abbey grinned. 'I see our clever DCI is awake and paying attention, Tim.'

'Her default setting,' Stanton replied. 'But then I guess you already knew that.'

'So, they were buried in the same place . . .' Kate interrupted, 'but not at the same time. Is that what you're telling me?'

'And we're not talking weeks.' Abbey pointed at the shorter of the two skeletons. 'As a ballpark figure, I'd say this one's been buried for around ten years, the other about five. I need to complete more tests to be absolutely sure, but I'm confident enough for you to work on that assumption, yes.'

Thanking them, Kate left the morgue immediately. No point hanging around any longer; better to let the medical examiners get on with it. She didn't need telling that cause of death might never be established. To be certain how her victims died she might even require an offender to cough.

No pressure there then.

15

It was almost five-fifteen when their squash game ended. Having a court within the confines of the prison was a wonderful facility, Jo thought. What better way for staff to end a shitty day than by smashing a little green ball around to the point of exhaustion? Especially when it represented Principal Officer Do-As-I-Say Harrison from B-wing who'd upset Emily McCann on her first day back.

'Good game!' Stamp said. 'I see you haven't lost your touch.'

He was being kind; he was much the better player, the more athletic of the two. Always had been, even at uni. Jo's cheeks were burning, her clothes so drenched they stuck to her skin, whereas *he* hadn't even broken sweat.

Retrieving her sports holdall from the rear of the court, she tucked her racquet inside, slung it over her shoulder and walked towards him extending her right arm. They shook hands awkwardly, a sporting gesture between two old friends that seemed formal and somehow inappropriate.

Jo was so out of breath she could hardly speak. 'Return match later this week?'

Stamp nodded. 'Suits me.'

'I'll see if the court's available on my way out and confirm by text.'

'Actually, I need a word. You up for a quick drink on the way home?'

'Can't, sorry. Wish I wasn't, but I'm tied up.'

What had seemed like a good idea at the time now felt like a chore to Jo. It had been a long day. Much as she liked Ron Naylor, she'd just as soon cancel their arrangement, go home and sink her aching body into a hot bath. She loved the quaint little place she'd rented at the coast. She'd always wanted a traditional Northumbrian cottage overlooking the sea and now she had one. Adorable it was too.

Pity Kate wasn't there to share it.

Taking in the clock on the wall, Jo missed the rejection on Stamp's face.

'Actually,' she said. 'I'd better get a wriggle on.'

'Anyone I know?' he asked. 'Or is it a secret?'

Jo shook her head as she made her way off court. 'Detective Super I used to work with.'

A twinge of regret edged its way into her thoughts. If she was honest, she missed Naylor and the rest of Northumbria Police's Murder Investigation Team, Kate Daniels in particular. Finding out that her ex had moved on with a local artist – the delectably gorgeous Fiona-bloody-Fielding – Jo had thought it best to cut and run. But had she acted hastily? Not only had she failed to get Kate out of her head, but the research job at the prison was a bloody disaster. It bored the tits off her most of the time.

There: she'd *finally* admitted she'd made a mistake.

'Hello?' Martin Stamp waved a hairy hand in front of her face. 'Earth to Jo . . . I said it's a woman's prerogative to be late.'

Jo gave an emphatic: *No!* 'It's also impolite to keep people waiting.'

'C'mon,' he pleaded. 'Half an hour? It's about Em.'

Why didn't that surprise her?

'Please,' Stamped begged. 'I'm seriously worried about her.'

'Don't be, Martin. She won't thank you for it.' Jo made a move for the door on legs so weak she could hardly stand up, her anger boiling over as she walked past him. 'And stop playing the bloody hero, why don't you?'

'What's that supposed to mean?' he yelled after her.

Ignoring the question, Jo entered the eerie corridor. This part of the prison was deserted at night. She didn't want to talk about Emily behind her back. She was a good mate to both of them. It would feel like a betrayal.

Stamp caught up with her, barring her way as she reached the shower-room door, demanding an explanation for her throwaway remark. His behaviour reminded her of what he was like before he grew up – an immature hothead. It also brought to mind her late ex-husband: easy-going one minute, petulant the next.

Her eyes flew to the door handle on which Stamp had a vice-like grip.

'Move please, Martin.'

He stood his ground, refusing to budge. 'Not until you tell me what you meant.'

'Can your ego stand what I have to say?'

He didn't answer.

Jo was *really* pissed now. Bullying was her pet hate. Controlling men a close second. She'd put up with an abusive husband and had vowed never to be a victim again. 'You want the truth or the toned-down version?'

Still no response.

Her sarcasm wasn't helping. She calmed herself, tried talking some sense into him. 'Martin, I know Emily has leaned on you big-style since Robert died, but you're rushing her. She's not ready for another relationship. Don't pressurize her. Keep supporting her by all means but be sensible about it. Do the decent thing. Accept that you can't take up where you left off two decades ago.'

'Who said I want to?'

Jo tried not to snigger. 'I'm a lot of things but blind isn't one of them. Believe me, I know what I'm talking about. Recapturing a lost love is *never* that simple. It takes time and patience, only one of which you appear to have. Emily's not going anywhere, so why the rush?' She glanced again at the door handle. 'Now, are you planning to let me in there, or shall I call security?'

But Stamp was sulking, unwilling to let the matter drop.

Jo tried again. 'Look, all I'm saying is give the woman some space!'

'We're talking at cross purposes here . . .' he insisted. 'I do have feelings for her, of course I do, but this isn't about what I stand to gain. It's more a question of what she might lose.'

'Meaning?'

He scanned the corridor. 'Not here—'

'Oh, for God's sake! Cut the melodrama.'

Jo fell silent as a group of off-duty prison officers left the gymnasium. Instead of heading towards the two of them, they turned the other way, pulling their coats on as they headed for the main exit, shouting their goodbyes. She felt like calling after them, telling them she would walk out with them, but thought better of it. They would misinterpret her actions. By morning it would be all round the prison that she and Stamp had been fighting.

As they disappeared through a double door, Stamp opened the shower-room door and pushed her inside.

'Get off me!' Jo yelled. 'What the hell is wrong with you?'

'Shh, keep your bloody voice down!' Stamp put his ear to the door and listened before continuing: 'I can explain everything. Please, Jo . . . meet me at the pub and hear me out.'

Jo's pulse raced.

No point screaming. The officers were long gone.

'I told you, I'm *busy*,' she said. 'Now get out of here.'

Stamp wouldn't release the door.

'Martin, stop it! You're freaking me out.'

'I'm sorry . . .' He let go of the door handle, shifting his hand to her forearm. His touch made a shiver run down her spine. Responding to the fear in her eyes, he spoke again. 'Jo, don't be scared. Please . . . accept my apology. I don't know what came over me. That was totally out of order—'

'Damn right it was.'

'I said I'm sorry!'

Jo liked Martin but he was beginning to unnerve her.

Despite his apology, his eyes were like two black pools, devoid of any emotion. Looking down at her arm, she tried to shrug his hand away but he wouldn't let go. His fingers had closed around her wrist so tightly his knuckles were white. He just stood there, a weird look on his face that made the hair stand up on her neck. She had to get out of there. *Fast.*

16

Armed with the knowledge that her victims hadn't been buried at the same time, Kate headed back to Alnwick station. It was cold and dark outside. It had stopped snowing but heavy footfall had made the pavements all grey and slushy. Not that it mattered. Now that the enquiry was up and running she'd be spending much of her time inside.

An old man was struggling to cross the road. Offering to help him over, she got the brush-off. Ignoring her outstretched arm, he muttered something about managing by himself for eighty-odd years – or words to that effect – waved her away with his cane and shuffled off, mumbling under his breath.

With neither the time nor the energy to care whether or not he made it to the other side, she walked on, a dozen separate actions competing for attention in her mind. Naylor was nowhere in sight when she reached the incident room. The rest of the team were exactly where she'd left them – except Hank, who'd shifted to a desk near the window.

He was eating a chicken wrap and washing it down with Coke, a newspaper spread out in front of him. Kate was worried about him. Since his marriage hit the rocks, he'd let himself go. He'd been drinking and smoking more than usual, eating out to avoid going home. Not taking care of his health had become a habit of late, and it was beginning to show. She'd bullied, coaxed and pleaded with him to stop the rot, but may as well have been talking to the wall.

Well, if he wanted blocked arteries, so be it.

Sensing a presence, he looked up.

Seeing her standing on the threshold, he rose from his seat and lumbered over to greet her. He seemed tired today, more so than usual, but she knew his lethargy was down to inactivity rather than the size of his waistline. All day she'd felt much the same. Having little to occupy their minds when they were used to working at breakneck speed hadn't been easy to take. Kate was restless too, knew exactly where he was coming from.

'Any news?' He binned the wrap packaging in a wastepaper basket.

'Some, but don't get too excited.' She draped her coat over the nearest chair. 'It looks like we're in for the long haul on this one. Has the guv'nor gone for the day?'

Gormley nodded, licking Caesar sauce from his fingertips. 'He's got a conference call with Bright scheduled. Then he's off to get himself spruced up for a night out with you-know-who . . .' He sniffed at the air and screwed up his face. 'You changed your perfume, boss?'

Kate grinned. 'Wanna slap?'

He smiled back. 'Just making an observation.'

He was right though. She stank to high heaven. Every pore on her body seemed to ooze disinfectant and chemicals. The sickening, overpowering stench of death was in her nostrils too.

She looked at her watch.

It was past teatime and her tank was empty.

She nodded towards the rest of the squad. 'Have they all eaten?'

'Fed, watered and ready to go,' he told her. 'And there's something green and boring in the fridge for you too.'

'OK, briefing in ten. That's everyone. No excuses.'

Picking up the overnight bag she carried in her car in case of emergencies, Kate vaulted the stairs two at a time to the rest room on the floor above. She took a hot shower, a touch of jealousy creeping into her thoughts over Naylor's dinner date with Jo. She'd been sorely tempted to accept his invitation to join them. But how could she? Especially when she and Jo were not on the best of terms right now.

With no time to indulge that thought, she got dressed quickly. Repacking her bag, she stowed it in a free locker, then reverted to type and went back to work. By the time she walked into the incident room, Hank had prepared the team for a full briefing.

Kate ate while she brought the team up to date with Tim Stanton and Abbey Hunt's findings.

Or lack thereof.

'I have an observation to make,' she said. 'Bamburgh's like a lot of coastal villages in that it's not a place you come upon by accident. In my humble opinion, that could be highly significant.'

'It's not on the main road, if that's what you mean,' DS Robson said.

'Exactly my point, Robbo. To get there you need to leave a major north–south border route. I'm pushing the scientists for a time of year when the burials might've taken place. In the meantime, I want checks on all hotels, guest houses and holiday rentals for anyone staying in the area during 2001 and 2006. That's everyone, leisure guests or business. I want names. And I don't give a monkey's if we have to copy every database in the area to get them.'

'Are we releasing this to the press?' Lisa Carmichael asked. 'They've been on the blower already from both sides of the border.'

'Good question. The answer is no. Let's be clear here . . .' The SIO scanned the faces of her team, making sure they were all paying attention. 'What we have is two bodies of young girls: one approximately ten years old, the other fifteen. The ten-year-old has been buried about ten years, the fifteen-year-old about five. From a media point of view, we found two bodies on a beach. I want no hint or suggestion that those girls were buried at different times. Nothing I've told you leaves this room. If you get asked any awkward questions you say we're doing random checks, building a profile of people visiting the area. I'm particularly interested in regulars.'

Kate's eyes searched the room and came to rest on DC Maxwell. 'Neil, you're on missing persons. You're looking for kids who went AWOL in the relevant years and a couple of months either side. Got that?'

Maxwell answered with a nod.

'That's a very precise timeline, isn't it, boss?' The question had come from DC Brown. He blushed as heads turned in his direction. 'I mean, can we really be that certain? Look at them!' He pointed at the murder wall where crime scene photographs of the two victims were pinned side by side. 'If we're out by a year we'll be wasting our time, won't we?'

'You've obviously not met Abbey Hunt.' Hank slipped into cowboy drawl to make his point. 'She don't make no mistakes, boy! Pity anyone who suggests she do.'

Everyone laughed.

The next question came from Maxwell. 'With regard to missing persons, you want me to concentrate only on our force area or what?'

'For the time being, yes. Then, depending how you get on, we widen the search gradually. I suggest we start with neighbouring forces: Lothian and Borders, Durham, Cumbria – in that order. Maybe North Yorkshire too. We go national after that, if necessary.' She waited as he scribbled a note to that effect. 'I want to be informed each time you intend to redraw the search boundaries. It's important to keep control and let everyone know where we're at.'

DCs Brown and Carmichael were sitting next to each other as usual, so close it surprised Kate that their hips hadn't fused together. They had joined the force in the same intake, had come to MIT as a pair. And what a great pair they were proving to be. An inseparable combination, they were complete opposites in terms of skills and personality. Brown was Daniels' obs man. Quite a shy lad with the patience of a saint, he was highly skilled in surveillance techniques. Carmichael was an all-rounder. Technically savvy, an outgoing, gregarious detective with bags of confidence – an officer who could turn her hand to anything, pretty much.

'Lisa, I want a trawl of the database: all suspicious incidents in and around Bamburgh the last fifteen years. Liaise with the back record team for that. Andy, concentrate on known offenders, any MO that remotely mentions dressing victims up. That's it, guys. I declare this enquiry officially underway.'

17

The Railway Inn wasn't far from the prison. It was a typical farmhouse conversion with a cosy wood-burner and photographs of a past association with horse racing adorning the walls. The lounge was almost empty. Not surprising on such a grim night. Jo Soulsby and Martin Stamp had taken their drinks to one corner of the lounge so as not to be overheard by the four regulars standing at the bar, all men. At least one of them was a prison officer, a tall skinny guy with two cute border terriers fast asleep on the floor at his feet.

Jo's glass of red wine was divine, if a little chilly, a bit like the atmosphere across the table. Stamp was silent now, staring into his pint as if it held the answer to his problems. He'd fallen over himself to apologize to her. It turned out he'd been to see Walter Fearon when he had no authority so to do and in her opinion no damned right either.

She wanted to clear the air but was still wound up about his weirdness in the prison corridor after their squash game. To make matters worse, Naylor was due at any second. If *he* got wind of their little spat, policeman or not, the gloves would be off in the car park.

Jo didn't want that.

Feeling like one half of an argumentative married couple, she scanned the empty tables around her. Other locals would pop in for the last hour, their way of showing support to the landlord for keeping the only pub in the village alive. The prison officer at the bar was watching her, casting the occasional glance here and there, maybe even the odd comment to the others if the smirk on his face was anything to go by.

She looked away, avoiding his eyes.

'You've overstepped your brief,' she told Stamp.

And he had: flashing his impressive credentials in order to infiltrate the medical wing; convincing the late shift that it was in their patient's best interests to be seen by a psychiatrist, sooner rather than later, following his suicide attempt. Getting Fearon to open up and, in so doing, feeding his sick fantasies.

Pushing her wine away, Jo took a deep breath and tried to calm down. She'd been angry with him ever since he made his move to step into Robert McCann's shoes so soon after his death. But now she had more reasons to add to the list. His rough treatment of her was unforgiveable. He'd also blatantly poked his nose into Emily's professional life. That was both patronizing and unfair.

And still he didn't answer.

'I mean it, Martin. I'd like to believe you're just looking out for her, but she doesn't need or even want your protection.' She wasn't getting through. 'When she finds out she'll be bloody furious—'

'Hold on a second! Didn't she ask for our input only this morning?'

'Yes, but—'

'But nothing! As far as I'm concerned, her request justifies my actions. I just stopped by and had a little chat with him, that's all.' He took in the group at the bar and leaned closer, lowering his voice a touch. 'This kid is dangerous and un-predictable.'

'I know. I heard you the first time!'

'And he's obsessed with Emily.'

'You think I don't know that? I work at this prison too, remember?' She eyeballed him across the table. 'Sorry to state the obvious but, apart from me, she's the only woman he sees. His fascination with her must be seen in that context.'

'Does that extend to the screws?'

'Excuse me?' Jo was utterly thrown by his remark.

Stamp eyeballed her. 'I see the way they look at her.'

Jo's mouth fell open. 'I can't believe you said that out loud. Martin, *listen* to yourself! You're the one who needs help. You're acting like a jealous prick.'

He took a long slug of beer, glaring at her over the top of his glass. He'd embarrassed himself and made her feel un-comfortable.

No wonder he wanted to see her outside of work.

'OK, OK! I admit it,' he said, buckling under the intensity of her gaze. 'I'm crazy about her. I blew my chance once. If anything were to happen to her now I'd never forgive myself. I'd lose her all over again. I'm not having that, Jo. And I'm certainly not going to apologize for wanting to make her happy. This inmate, Fearon, he's—'

'A manipulative freak is what he is.' Jo almost laughed. 'Wake up, man. Ninety-nine per cent of men in prison are sexually frustrated. That's hardly news, is it? She's gorgeous and they're locked away from females! Most straight males in there will have fantasized about her at one time or another.

Why should Fearon be any different? Do you seriously think that passed her by? You heard her this morning. She's hardly written him off as a pathetic loser, has she? She knows precisely how dangerous he—'

'She doesn't know he slit his wrists in order to get close to her, does she?'

Jo stopped ranting. 'He said that?'

'He didn't have to. It was written all over his face. Like it or not, she's vulnerable now. Look, I know what I'm talking about. I think it would be best if she ceased working with him, at least for the time being. And I think you—'

He checked himself, didn't finish what he was going to say. Whatever it was, Jo wanted to hear it. 'Going to patronize *me* now?' she asked.

'I wouldn't dream of it.' He was blushing.

'Go on, I'm sure you could manage if you try *really* hard.'

He ignored the wind-up. Changing the subject, he pointed at her glass and asked if she wanted a refill. She declined, told him what she wanted was an explanation.

'Emily trusts you, Jo. You're her friend. You're also a Home Office psychologist—'

'What's that got to do with anything?'

'You could easily take over Fearon's supervision. No one would bat an eyelid, least of all the Governor.'

'It's not the Governor that concerns me.' Jo glared at him across the table, regretting her decision to bring him along while she waited for Naylor. Even though Stamp had scared her, she wanted to get to the bottom of what was making him act so out of character. Now she wished he'd piss off and leave her be. She leaned forward, picked up her wine and swigged it back in one mouthful. She needed another – but not with him.

He narrowed his eyes. 'Oh, *I* see.'

There he goes again. 'What? What do you see?'

'Female pride is over-rated, Jo. Don't let it get in the way of good judgement.'

'You're a nobber, Martin. And don't waste your breath, because the answer is still no. You've got *no* right to even suggest I get involved. Just think through what you're asking here. If I took over Emily's case, what signals would that send to Fearon, not to mention the rest of her clients, and the prison staff, since you brought them into it? Her authority would be totally undermined. She'd be finished. I won't do it.'

He climbed down a bit. 'No one's questioning her professionalism, or yours.'

'Oh really? Then give us both some credit.'

'I am!'

'Are you?' Jo's hackles were up and it showed.

Stamp exhaled loudly. He wasn't done yet. 'You don't get it, do you? Fearon seriously believes he's special to her. Can't you see how risky that is? You do know she's the *only* reason he hasn't asked for Rule 43?'

Now Jo was listening.

That particular regulation meant complete segregation from other inmates. Many sex offenders sought to hide behind it, preferring to spend their whole prison term living in solitary confinement rather than face the wrath of the mainstream population – and for good reason. Even the most vicious of their number couldn't fight every thug who fancied chancing their arm. The saying 'safety in numbers' wasn't true in this case. Jo had to concede, Stamp had a point. Fearon's life inside would certainly have been easier if he'd chosen the segregation unit over B-wing.

The hiatus was enough to convince Stamp that he'd won Jo over.

'Now do you get it?' he asked smugly. 'Fearon would rather be bullied for being a nonce by every inmate in that prison than not see Emily on a daily basis. The fact that she's been away for so long has made him all the more determined. She needs warning that—'

'No. You need warning!' Jo bit back. 'If you seriously believe the two of you have a future together, I'd advise you not to take that tone with Emily. Robert never would have. And mark my words, if you ever lay a hand on me again, I'll call the law.'

The pub door opened and Naylor walked in.

Conversation over.

18

Kate was really unsettled. Not because she wasn't dining with Jo and Naylor when she damned well ought to be – although the thought had crossed her mind – but because something elusive had been niggling away at her subconscious for the past hour. Something to do with the case she just couldn't get a handle on.

Detective Chief Superintendent Philip Bright's voice sounded hoarse down the line. He'd insisted she field all media enquiries herself, show the public that her team were working flat out to identify the victims, reassure them that resources were being allocated commensurate with the severity of the gruesome find at one of the county's major tourist attractions. In reality, the DCI had half a dozen officers, no forensics or intelligence and bugger all else to go on.

The upside of that was, the press would be similarly stumped.

Handling journalists and television correspondents was a skill Kate had cultivated during her time in the CID. After years of practice, she had it down to fine art. Under her former guv'nor's guidance she'd discovered how useful the media could be to an SIO with a little give and take. But with huge resources at their disposal they also got in the way on occasions, appropriating information from potential witnesses before the police got to them. It was a dead cert that they had already started digging into her case. It wouldn't take a genius to work out that the archaeologists involved in research in and around Bamburgh Castle lately would be their first port of call. Thankfully, Carmichael had got in ahead of them and project leaders had given assurances that they would refrain from talking to the media until after they had spoken with the Murder Investigation Team.

One less problem to worry about.

'You blitzed the missing persons, I take it?' Bright asked.

'Doing that now, guv.'

'Any knowns with a similar MO?'

'Looking into that too,' Kate said.

'Is that a euphemism for "wind your neck in"?'

Hank Gormley made a face, stifling the urge to laugh out loud. Bright was no fool. He'd hand-picked them both years ago, was single-handedly responsible for their collective wisdom when it came to the detection of major incidents. Unfortunately, having achieved his ambition to take charge of the CID, like Naylor and other senior detectives, he was missing the cut-and-thrust of running enquiries himself. As a result, he couldn't resist the temptation to stick his nose in occasionally.

A phone rang loudly in the background.

Kate willed him to answer it. 'You want to get that, guv?'

'No, I bloody don't. That's what they pay Ellen for!' He yelled without covering the speaker. 'Ellen? ELLEN? Jesus Christ!'

The phone rang twice more and then stopped.

Bright lowered his voice again. 'Sorry, Wonder Woman has

disappeared. I was about to say the Crime Intelligence Unit have done some checking. I can tell you for a fact there are no incidents nationally where two girls went missing together, not since the Grantham enquiry.'

He was referring to a case that had dominated TV screens for months a few years ago: two lovely young girls wearing their favourite outfits, arms linked as they posed for the camera after a gathering to celebrate a family birthday. After tea they had gone to the park. They were never seen alive again. The bodies of Caroline Johnson and Amy Prentice had been dumped in Whatton – eleven miles east along the A52 from where they went missing. An offender named Stobbart was later apprehended.

Daniels swore under her breath.

Bright hadn't been given vital information.

Falling short of his expectations made her angry. Over the years she'd learned to be prepared. Whether it was a face-to-face meeting, a full-blown press conference or a telephone conversation she always, *always* went in sure of her facts and took nothing for granted. It paid not to piss off the head of CID. And yet she was suddenly on the back foot, steeling herself for an ear-bashing from the man himself.

'Sorry, guv. I thought you knew—'

'Knew?'

'About the timeline . . .' She rolled her eyes at Hank. As SIO, it was her responsibility to keep their former guv'nor informed of all major developments in a case as high profile as this, and she would have done had Naylor not indicated that he'd take care of it. She chose her words carefully so as not to sound like she was trying to shift the blame. 'Your conference call with Detective Superintendent Naylor—'

'Didn't happen.' Bright paused. 'Why? Something I don't know?'

'Our victims were buried years apart, guv. Chances are, they didn't go missing together unless the ten-year-old was abducted, killed and preserved for at least five years. Can't see it, can you?'

Bright said nothing.

Kate looked out of the window and quickly changed the subject. 'What's the weather like your way, guv? It's a complete white out here, otherwise I'd head back to town. I need stuff urgently for the MIR. Alnwick isn't well equipped to deal with major incidents, something I hope you'll put right now you know about it.'

'Say the word, it's yours.'

'Appreciate that, guv.'

'Don't mention it. Email your request in the morning. I'll see you get what you want. In the meantime you stay put, you hear me? The weather is atrocious. The A1 is already down to one lane. Not a gritter in sight. I don't want you driving round the county in this. And if you have to go out, take Hank along.'

Kate glanced at Gormley.

Their old guv'nor was worried about her driving in the snow. Hardly surprising: he'd lost his wife in a horrific car crash on the M25 in a spate of heavy rain. The articulated lorry they were following jack-knifed during an overtaking manoeuvre, practically wiping out the passenger side of his car. Stella Bright hadn't died right away. She'd spent several months in hospital and several more in a wheelchair before fading away completely. Bright remained tormented by the experience and still struggled with survivor guilt.

'Don't concern yourself, guv. The crime scene is as far as I'll be going tonight. We'll take my car, not *his*. That means it's entirely legal, full of diesel and running like a dream. I have a blanket, a medical kit and a shovel in the boot in case of emergencies, plus Hank. We'll be as safe as houses.'

Bright told her to keep him posted and rang off abruptly.

It was a dig certainly, one she didn't deserve, but she wasn't complaining. Hank made a joke about her falling from grace. But in her head she was at the crime scene with two skeletons lying side by side. And then it hit her, the thing that had been playing at the back of her mind since the briefing.

'Pearls . . .' she said. 'The victims were *both* wearing pearls.'

19

Officer Kent eyed the inmates on free association, unhappy that his SO had rostered him for another night shift, punishment for his outburst against Fearon.

On one side of the cavernous room, laughter drifting through an open door – the television room. Nearby, a group of four inmates were playing cards, generally having a laugh, egged on by a gaggle of supporters. To their left, other inmates sat writing letters home or reading books. The rest were banged up in their cells by choice, keeping their heads low and their hopes high for early release, a privilege afforded for good behaviour and a clean prison record.

It was a different story on the other side of the room.

Wing bullies Saunders and Jones weren't going anywhere fast. Both were serving twelve for the attempted murder of a drugs rival, neither making any attempt to mend their ways. They had collared the pool table and were clearly in cahoots over something. Odds on, it wasn't about turning the other cheek during their long stay at Her Majesty's pleasure.

Saunders wasn't your stereotypical bully: no shaved head, battle scars or visible tats. A Mancunian just turned twenty, he had boy-band looks and pulling power too, if his mailbag and cell wall were anything to go by. He had no less than four different women on the go, two of whom had spawned the next generation of gangsters, none of whom had an inkling of the others' existence.

Yet.

Kent could feel an anonymous letter coming on.

Saunders looked innocent enough. But beneath his pretty-boy image an evil bastard lurked. He took great pleasure in hurting people – including his harem, if he felt so inclined. Jones on the other hand fit the profile of an inner-city thug perfectly. He was hated and feared throughout the establishment by staff and cons alike. He had bad skin, a mean mouth, stood no taller than five three. What he lacked in height, the vicious little shit made up for in immorality. Like Saunders, he enjoyed inflicting pain. Simply put, he was a very nasty piece of work.

Kent's fellow officer nodded towards the pool table. 'What's their sketch?'

'Something unsavoury, by the looks.' Kent scratched his crotch. 'Any intel from security?'

'Kiddin', aren't ya? The snouts wouldn't dare.'

'Search team find anything?'

'Not a damn thing. Dogs never even got a whiff.'

'Figures.'

Both officers fell silent.

Saunders and Jones had a foolproof operation running on the inside just like they did on the out. Prison or not, it was business as usual for them. They carried out their evil deeds secure in the knowledge that they wouldn't be grassed up, stashing their drugs and weapons in other mugs' cells, absolving themselves of blame should the screws get lucky. Consequently, any associated punishment doled out by the governor didn't touch them. Instead it passed down to the weaklings whose sentences kept getting longer and longer.

For Saunders and Jones, cooperation was key.

Not many refused this pair.

None did so a second time.

They grinned at one another, aware that they were under scrutiny. Neither gave a fat rat's arse. They would make their move when they were good and ready. Not before. They had all the time in the world.

Taking his shot cleanly, Saunders made the pocket and high-fived Jones.

Game over.

Two prisoners waiting to take their turn moved forward. Then stepped away again when Saunders blanked them out, setting up the triangle for another game like he owned the place.

'I need a crap.' Kent's colleague tapped his radio. 'Yell if you need me.'

Kent nodded, his eyes continually scanning the association room.

No sooner had his fellow officer disappeared than the atmosphere in the room changed. Tension was building. A shifty look passed here and there – mostly in Jones' and Saunders' direction. Inmates were fine-tuned to recognize trouble. A few were packing up their stuff in readiness to retire; odd behaviour, given the fact that their free association period had another half-hour to run.

It had been a quiet week so far: not many fights, no riots, no security alerts. Other than Fearon's shenanigans that morning, it was boringly normal considering the scum contained therein. A situation too good to be true, Kent figured.

It wouldn't last.

Jones was lying across the pool table, one leg outstretched behind him, his tongue touching his upper lip in concentration as he eyed the balls on the table. Alerted by the sound of keys jangling in the corridor beyond, he abandoned his shot and stood up, shifting his gaze from the green baize towards the wing gate.

A nod to Saunders was almost imperceptible.

Kent had seen it.

The radio pinned to his chest announced that an inmate was being escorted on to the wing. Kent glanced at the gated entrance, receiving a nod of acknowledgement from the escort as he came into view.

A shove in the back helped Fearon on his way.

The escort gave the thumbs-up sign: transfer of prisoner complete.

Relocking the gate, he turned away, his boots echoing in the corridor as he disappeared from sight. Exposed and alone, Fearon remained at the gate for a while. Looking pale but otherwise unscathed from his antics in the shower block, he stood there taking in the scene, checking out the territory. He was a lot of things: stupid wasn't one of them. Like the duty officer, he sensed trouble the moment Saunders reached for his pool cue.

Kent didn't move. Just sat back in his chair, keeping one eye on the toilet door, one on the situation. This could all turn nasty in a heartbeat. He was a lone member of staff on the wing now.

He looked at Saunders . . .

The toilet door . . .

Saunders . . .

The toilet door . . .

Still no sign of his fellow officer.

How long can one crap take?

Any minute now that door would open and his colleague would reappear.

But it didn't.

He didn't.

Then, suddenly, it all kicked off.

Saunders smashed his cue into Fearon's gut as he walked past the pool table: payback for having been locked in his cell for most of the afternoon. Doubled up in pain, Fearon hit the deck. Saunders dragged him violently to his feet, kneeing him in the groin, gobbing in his face.

Kent glanced at the toilet door.

No joy.

A glob of spittle slid off Fearon's broken specs and down one cheek as he tried to remain upright, his steel-grey eyes burning into his attacker, a clear warning that this wasn't over. Saunders hit him with the cue again, this time full in the face, blood spurting from a cut lip. Winded and bloodied, Fearon made no attempt to fight back. Glaring at the screw being paid to protect him, he sloped off to spend another night alone in his cell.

Kent smiled.

No more than the cunt deserved.

20

The smell of fried bacon hit the DCI as she left her room and headed down two flights of creaky stairs. It was still dark outside. And cold. *So bloody cold.* The B & B's ancient central heating system was struggling to cope. It had limped into life before six, the pipes gurgling and banging beneath her windowsill. The shower was inadequate too. The water ran hot one minute, cold the next, dribbling from the shower head. Thank Christ she hadn't washed her hair.

Kate had just come off the phone with forensic scientist Matt West. What he'd had to say had thrown up more problems than it solved, leading to a drain on precious and finite resources, financial as well as physical. His words echoed in her head as she entered the breakfast room.

It was an oblong room with a deep bay window at one end. Surprisingly, three of her team had beaten her down. Hank was busy eating his bodyweight in saturated fats. Robson was texting, Brown reading last night's *Evening Chronicle*, both still waiting to be served. They were obviously hung-over and seated at the largest of three tables in the room. No sign of Maxwell or Carmichael yet, but so far no civvies. The detectives had the room to themselves.

It had been past eleven-thirty when Kate turned in the night before. The rest had stayed on, a chance to spend some down time together, something they rarely did outside of the odd retirement bash. Lengthy shifts were hardly conducive to socializing beyond their working day. So they milked it for all it was worth when it did happen.

Wondering what time they'd eventually got to bed, Daniels was delighted to think that the owner of the B & B might also have been awake half the night.

If her guests couldn't rest, then why should she?

Hank looked up from his food. 'Sleep well, boss?'

'Like a baby,' she said.

'Really?'

'No! My bed had lumps in it. It squeaked every time I turned over. The duvet kept slipping off and when I ran to the' – she made inverted commas with her fingers – 'shower, I could see my own breath it was so damned cold in my bathroom. You?'

'He did. I never.' Robson stopped texting, pocketing his phone. 'Forget what I said about the bairn yesterday. I'll take Callum as a room-mate over Hank any day of the week. The missus sent a text. Can you believe it? Little bugger didn't wake 'til six. The very first time he's slept all night in nearly *two* years and I'm playing house with a snoring pig.'

Gormley laughed and yawned at the same time.

He handed Kate a menu as she sat down beside him, directly opposite the other two. The stench of second-hand beer across the table almost took her breath away. That too was par for the course. CID officers away from home tended to work hard and play even harder. Thankfully their powers of recovery matched their appetite for alcohol. With a good breakfast inside them it would be game on, as usual.

The door opened and Carmichael appeared. 'Wish I'd brought some warmer kit.' Her voice had dropped an octave. 'Whose idea was it to stay in the B & B from hell?'

'Er, that would be yours!' Hank grinned. 'Looking a little shabby this morning, Lisa. Sit down before you fall down.'

Shivering as she approached, arms wrapped around herself, Carmichael slumped down in a chair, chucking her room key on the table, knocking over the salt. Not bothering to pick it up, she scowled at the others, her sunny personality nowhere in sight.

'What a dump!' she said.

'Morning!' a cheery female voice behind them said.

Carmichael held her tongue as a woman of indeterminate age arrived in the breakfast room: grey-blonde hair cut short, very little slap, a red pinny over boyfriend jeans. She had an order pad in her hand and a big smile on her face, a hint that she was happy to have her premises full in mid-winter with paying guests who wouldn't argue the toss when it came to settle up at the end of the day – ones unlikely to give her any grief during their stay.

Kate didn't imagine that was a given.

There were some glum faces round the table.

Robson requested kippers, Brown a full English, Kate poached eggs on toast, Carmichael a bacon sandwich on white bread with brown sauce to go with it. Gormley ordered more coffee, adding the words 'fresh this time'.

Putting down his knife and fork, he pushed his plate away.

'So what's up?' He was looking at the SIO.

'Up?' Kate was aware of all eyes turned towards her. 'Other than this place, you mean?'

'I've seen that look before. It usually means business. I'm guessing you got hold of Matt.' Gormley glanced at his watch. 'What pearls of wisdom did our eminent scientist have to impart at this ungodly hour?'

Daniels raised an eyebrow. 'If this case wasn't so sad, that might've been funny, Hank.'

'Blimey,' he said. 'That bed *was* lumpy.'

A chuckle went round the table.

Two fresh pots of coffee arrived along with a shamefaced DC Maxwell. The DCI asked the waitress if there were any other guests staying. She wasn't astounded to hear that there weren't. Returning guests in this B & B was a stretch, even for her imagination. Requesting some privacy, she waited until the woman had taken Maxwell's order and cleared the room before speaking.

'It won't surprise you to hear that the pearls found on our victims were not real. They were plastic fakes. Cheap imitations, like poppers kids play with. You know the ones I mean: male and female on either end, the type that snap together to make a chain?'

There was a nod of heads around the table.

'Not lesbian chains then?' Maxwell quipped.

Hank Gormley nearly spat out his coffee.

Too tired to respond, Carmichael focused her attention on her boss. She may have been feeling down in the mouth but her mind was still very much on the job. 'Any identifying marks on the pearls?' she asked.

Kate shook her head. 'Unfortunately not. But I can say they aren't identical. According to Matt, one set are well made but contain a high level of toxic additives that would never be allowed in present-day manufacture. The others are contemporary; chatty imitations of the first, but with no obvious health-and-safety risks. I've asked him to fax a photo to the incident room and provide a section of both for comparison. We need to identify the manufacturers and distributors ASAP.'

The comment drew a collective groan around the table.

'Sorry, guys, but that's just how it is.' Her eyes fell on DS Robson, the team's statement reader. 'Robbo, you're on missing persons today.' Kate turned to Maxwell. 'I'm sorry to change your brief, Neil. I want you on the train to the forensic science lab as soon as you've eaten.' She thumbed out the window where snow was beginning to fall again. 'You're not driving down in this and we can't risk the post. Hank will run you to Alnmouth station after breakfast. There's a train at 7.47 that will get you into York at half nine. You can either hop on a train to Harrogate and take a taxi the rest of the way or get a taxi from York direct. It's up to you.'

'That's hardly fair, is it?' Carmichael blurted out. 'It'll take him most of the day to get there and back, longer if there happens to be the wrong kind of snow on the tracks. Any old excuse and he'll be gone for a fortnight!' She flushed up and shot a hacky look at Maxwell, who could hardly contain his joy. 'How come *he* gets a couple of extra hours' kip while we're all slaving away?'

Carmichael really *was* in a bad mood. It wasn't like her to whinge about who did what, even less to be so grumpy first thing in the morning. Whatever the reason behind her attitude, she did have a point. On the face of it, Maxwell had scored an easier day than most.

For a moment nobody spoke.

Kate put down her toast. 'The answer is in the question, Lisa. British weather and British Rail is a lethal combination. It might not be such a cushy number when you come to think of it.' Maxwell's joy melted away. 'You're not on your jollies, Neil. I want you back here tonight. No excuses.'

Carmichael brightened instantly but she didn't look good. *Serve her right for drinking with Hank.*

Kate moved on. 'The interesting thing in all of this is the significance of the pearls to the sick bastard who killed those kids. That's symbolism, plain and simple.'

'For what?' Brown was frowning at the DCI.

'I've no idea,' she said. 'We find out why, we find him.'

21

During her compassionate leave, a temporary replacement had been drafted in to cover Emily's caseload. She didn't know the woman personally but it soon became apparent that she'd done the bare minimum and no more. Case-notes were unfiled scrappy bits of paper, referrals left untouched, parole reports either deferred for her return or awaiting her countersignature. There was a shedload to do and it would take her ages to sort out the mess.

She was standing at the window looking out over the prison grounds. The sky was almost Mediterranean blue. She wondered what Rachel was up to today, whether she'd decided to go back to college and pick up where she'd left off when Robert died, carry on with the media studies he'd been helping her with.

Emily hoped so.

A digital radio was playing gently in the background, tuned to Radio 4, the station she always listened to as she made the most of her lunch hour. It was a quiet time when protocol demanded the suspension of all prisoner movement, a time to get on with stuff without fear of interruption, a time to relax.

The golden hour.

In theory, at least.

Except . . .

And Emily didn't know it yet . . .

One prisoner had other ideas.

Unobserved, Walter Fearon stood outside her door, eyeing her through the narrow strip of security glass, his eyes focused on that great arse and shapely legs as she stood with her back to him, gazing out of the window. He couldn't stop thinking about yesterday, wondering what had been going through her mind as she knelt beside his naked body in the shower room.

Emily turned from the window, took a few paces to a grey filing cabinet that stood in one corner of the room, and began rifling through the contents of the bottom drawer. With her attention otherwise engaged, he pushed open the door and moved across the threshold.

Sensing a presence, Emily turned round expecting to see a colleague, a prison officer, anyone but him. Her scalp tightened as the hairs on her head stood to attention. Her legs grew weak, her mouth dry. Fearon said nothing, just loomed over her. He was much larger and more powerful than she'd realized. Or was it just in her mind that he'd taken on a Jack Reacher type stature, all 6'5", 250 pounds of him? Only difference was, Fearon was real, not some fictional creation – a force for evil, not good – a young man who oozed ill intent.

She noticed fresh injuries: a split lip, a black eye.

It was difficult to judge his mood or see the expression in his eyes through the filth on his spectacles and one cracked lens. She couldn't decide which was the more chilling: seeing his scary eyes or not seeing them, and therefore not being able to read them.

She cleared her throat. 'What are you doing here?'

Her voice sounded tremulous, even to her.

Fearon didn't move a muscle or give an answer. His breathing seemed laboured as he stood there defiantly, both arms freshly bandaged. Emily swallowed down her fear. What was he doing there? What was he thinking? Did she even want to know the answer to either question? Was he eking out the time he had left? Just how much time *did* he have left? And what damage was he capable of inflicting before it expired?

Emily glanced at the clock on the wall above his head: 12:35. Lockdown was still fifteen minutes away.

He wouldn't be missed until the head count.

'You're supposed to be at lunch.' Emily was trying to mask the anxiety in her voice. She could see from his smug expression that her efforts had failed.

'I gave them the slip,' was all he said in return.

Emily couldn't afford to show fear. But years of training hadn't equipped her for this. Everything she knew about working with dangerous prisoners deserted her then. Adrenalin surged through her body. The answer came to her in a flash. In the event of a threat, the hostage-negotiating team had instructed her to take a non-confrontational stance.

Sit down . . . put a barrier between you.

Somehow she found her seat. She was now inches from the red alarm button mounted on the wall behind her. If she hit it now the troops would come running. But Fearon was close enough to grab her and she didn't want that. The mere thought of his hands touching her made her skin crawl.

Everything she knew about him scrolled across her mind like some bizarre, evil slideshow. Stamp had warned her how dangerous he was. That he'd faked a suicide attempt for no other reason than to draw her closer. *A crime waiting to happen,* or words to that effect. *An unhealthy obsession. Keep your distance, Em.*

And he wasn't the only one to think that way.

The prison medic had said the same thing.

Why would Fearon do that?

What was he up to?

He'd gone to great lengths to be in the wrong place at the wrong time. This visit was no accident. Was he planning to take her hostage? She could not – would not – allow him to intimidate her. Just how she managed it she wasn't sure, but when she spoke again her words were measured, her voice calm.

'There'll be trouble if you miss the head count, Walter. You'll lose days.'

'Saunders and Singh are scrapping.' He grinned. 'All the screws are busy.'

Emily held his gaze. 'Officer Kent will come looking, you know that.'

The implied threat of Kent hadn't worked.

Fearon took a few steps forward, a grin spreading across his face. He looked even more sinister exposing a chipped front tooth, the result of his latest altercation. No charges had been brought. For all Fearon hated Saunders with a passion, he wouldn't grass him up and there were no witnesses. Even

Kent, the lone officer present at the time of the assault, claimed he hadn't seen a thing.

Sure he hadn't.

'I need to see you,' Fearon said.

'You know the rules. Make an application in the morning.' Emily's tone was harsh. Her words hung in the air between them. Fearon's casual attitude and total disregard for the trouble he was in alarmed her. 'Did you hear me? Go on! Get back to the dining room before you land yourself in even bigger trouble.'

'Yes, miss. Sorry, miss.' He was mocking her now.

After what seemed like an hour, he turned and walked away without another word. Rooted to the chair, Emily blew out her cheeks. For a moment, she couldn't move. Her legs were shaking beneath the desk, her heart pounding in her chest. When he was out of sight, she raced towards the open door.

Fearon winced as the door slammed shut behind him. He waited outside, still as a statue, with his spine pressed hard against the wall. A smile lit his face as a key turned in the lock, followed by the sound of Emily's footsteps returning to her desk. Chancing his arm, he took a quick peek through the window and was rewarded by the sight of her fumbling for the phone, hands shaking so badly it was all she could do to hold it.

She was well spooked.

Power coursed through his veins. He'd craved that feeling since the first time he set eyes on her. He'd been wondering how she'd react to him once they were alone, with no screws hanging around on the other side of the door. In a couple of weeks he'd be released and they could be alone together again, outside of this stinking hellhole. Somewhere warm and cosy, where they could get better acquainted. He'd make sure of that.

Not long now.

She'd seen him in all his glory. The least she could do was return the favour.

Her voice sounded muffled through the door. 'Ash?'

Pure terror.

'Ash?' It came out like a sob.

Silence for a long while.

Fearon took another peek. He was right. She was weeping. One shaky hand holding the phone, her free hand over her mouth now, trying to keep control, but failing miserably.

Class.

He hadn't even touched her and yet it was as if he already had the ligature round her neck and was applying pressure, watching her eyes roll back in their sockets.

'Yes, I'm here . . .' Emily recovered, her distress replaced with rage. 'Mind telling me what the fuck is going on? Fearon just left my office . . . He bloody well was! I nearly shit myself.'

As the alarm bell blasted out, Fearon walked away, unperturbed.

Life inside wasn't *so* bad.

22

Day two of the murder investigation had been full on. A sustained information-gathering exercise had begun in earnest with no sign of hangovers from the team or strops from Carmichael after being late to bed and suffering a poor night's sleep. In the incident room, heads were down, focus exclusively on the job with one aim in mind: to catch those responsible for the unlawful deaths of two little girls.

Kate sucked in a breath and let it out again.

Even with all her years of experience, she was at a loss with this one. She'd contacted the National Crime Faculty requesting a trawl of their database for cases involving bodies buried in sand. It was a long shot, but worth doing.

In the meantime, the DCI had to face facts . . .

Without victim identification, she was totally screwed.

In the absence of any other evidence or intelligence, the crime scene was all she had. Time and again, her mind kept returning to that stretch of dunes. Bamburgh beach was a body deposition site – no more, no less – and, because of the long interval between death and discovery, there was no way of knowing if it was also the attack site, the murder site or just a convenient burial site.

But that was just it . . .

The site wasn't convenient – not by a long chalk.

Glancing at the murder wall, Kate forced herself to repeat the mantra that all was not lost. At the morning briefing, she'd actioned several lines of enquiry that were, if not exactly bearing fruit, at least throwing up a few possible leads. If the burial site couldn't help her, maybe offender profiling might. Jo Soulsby wasn't around to help with that, but after a trawl of the PNC a few local persons of interest had come up.

Two paedophiles in particular had been thrown in the hat by Brown as worthy of attention. This in turn had created a series of other actions for their outside team to deal with. These two individuals were nut-jobs with a bent for dressing their victims up. Along with other relevant data, Brown was now adding their names to the murder wall in thick red pen. They must be traced and, guilty or not, suffer the inconvenience and indignity of closer examination.

Tough.

In the SIO's opinion, they were both volunteers.

She wondered if they had any links to the village of Bamburgh. Brown had no knowledge of any thus far, so Kate moved on to Carmichael. Her trawl of incidents in and around the area confirmed only what the team already knew to be the case. The pretty coastal village wasn't exactly the crime capital of Europe. As expected, there had been very few criminal incidents recorded during the relevant years. Lisa was scraping the barrel with only a couple left to check.

It wasn't looking good.

Undeterred, Kate asked her to go back further still.

What was it about Bamburgh that disturbed her so?

A crime scene was key to any SIO. But in this case it didn't have the potential to tell her much. Or did it? As she returned to her office, her mind drifted to the view from the dunes: *Holy Island*. When she'd climbed up from the beach with Gormley yesterday and turned to face the sea, her gut instinct had been that the burial site might in itself be significant. That thought had remained with her ever since. Now she mulled over what might have motivated an offender to bury his victims in that particular spot. Had religion played a part? Or was there some other reason connected to the significance of the location? Maybe one of the archaeologists working on the Bamburgh Research Project could help.

She raised an action on her computer, allocating the task to Lisa Carmichael.

Unlocking the bottom drawer of her temporary desk, Kate pulled out a list Robson had compiled earlier. His efforts had given her a few leads – all of them sad. Missing children whose parents had been in limbo for years. For the parents of these two girls, the waiting was nearly over. Closure was on its way.

Kate gazed at the ceiling, her thoughts in turmoil.

The delivery of a death message was a task that came with every new incident. She wondered how long it took for hope to die. How long before parents came to accept the fact that they would never see their offspring alive again? In her mind's eye, she saw her hand poised in mid-air and felt a stranger's pain in that split second before she knocked at the door and gave news too awful and depressing to contemplate.

It never got any easier.

She doubted it ever would.

23

In the en suite washroom attached to her office, Emily turned on the cold tap, cupped water in her hands and washed her face. She was calm now and beginning to realize that her reaction to Fearon's unscheduled visit had been over the top. She'd worked in a prison long enough to have taken it in her stride, not made such a drama out of it. It was a situation she'd rather not repeat, that much was true, but she was angry with herself. Thanks to Stamp, she'd immediately jumped to the conclusion that she was in danger. Consequently, that was the only thing on her mind the whole time the inmate was standing in her doorway.

It was bloody ridiculous.

Emily was still looking in the mirror as the sound of running footsteps echoed in the corridor outside.

Stamp appeared in the doorway, sheet-white and out of breath.

'He didn't touch you?'

Emily dried her face on a towel.

'Did he?'

'No, he didn't.'

'Come here.' Stamp opened his arms for a hug.

Emily's feet remained rooted to the spot. 'Don't fuss, it was just one of those things.'

'It was a fuck-up that could have cost you d—'

'Drop it, Martin!' She was angry now. 'It was no one's fault. Ash is doing his best with limited staff today. A fight distracted them. Fearon was only missing for a few minutes. It was no big deal.'

'What the f—'

'Keep your voice down!'

Stamp moved towards her but Emily stepped away.

She wanted him to go and told him so. 'I've got a lot to do and so I imagine have you.'

He didn't move. 'I'm just looking out for you, Em.'

'I know that.' She let out a big sigh. 'I'm not trying to push you away but I'd appreciate some space. Just back off a bit, give me time to settle in. Can you do that for me?'

'If that's what you want,' Stamp said caustically, his frustration bubbling to the surface.

Emily softened. He was like a big kid sometimes, wanting to play the knight on the white horse, stamping his feet because she wouldn't let him. She pulled a funny face, frowning like a clown, making light of the situation, trying to get him onside. It had always worked when she was married. Robert could never stay cross with her for long. He would burst out laughing and within minutes they would be friends again, unable to recall what had made them angry in the first place.

Stamp was having none of it.

Sitting down, he glared at her like a spoilt child. They were now engaged in a game of blink first.

She threw him a crumb. 'Will you go if I promise to holler when I need you?'

He said nothing but the ice began to melt.

'Hey, don't let's fight. Finding my way again was always going to take time, Martin. We both knew that. It's been a tough couple of days. To be honest with you, I'm struggling to remember who the hell I am right now. Please tell me you understand. If you don't, I'll be cross for the rest of the day, tomorrow and possibly even the day after.' She managed a grin. 'Rachel's not the only one in my family who knows how to sulk.'

He raised his hands in a gesture of surrender.

Emily smiled warmly. 'There is one thing you could do for me . . .'

'Name it.'

'I'm concerned about Rachel. She's still not coping and I'm too close to be objective. I know she's difficult and, let's face it, not your *greatest* fan, but will you talk to her?'

'I thought you wanted me to butt out of your life.'

'Don't be like that.' Emily put on her begging face.

'I can't see the point,' Stamp said. 'She flew off on one last time, practically accused me of seducing you. If I remember correctly, she made her feelings crystal clear. I'm no bereavement counsellor, Em. That isn't my forte. So I'd rather not, if it's all the same to you. Why don't you ask Jo?'

'I would, but she has issues of her own right now.'

Stamp made a face. 'Jo's second name is *Issues*.'

It was obvious to Emily that there had been a falling out between her colleagues, but she was too wired to indulge in speculation. Besides, she had a rough idea it involved her and she didn't want to get into that.

She tried again. 'You've been around Rachel a lot since

Robert died. I did think about asking Jo, but I thought a male might connect with her better. I know it's a lot to ask after all I said but she really needs help. I'm just not getting through. She's hiding things from me, Martin. Every time I tackle her, she storms off. I'm at my wits' end. We may be flesh and blood but I have no idea what she wants.'

'Can you bring Robert back?'

'Don't be spiteful.' Emily glared at him.

'I'll think about it.' He got to his feet. 'That's the best I can do.'

Emily watched as he walked away without a backward glance.

24

Maxwell was late. His away-day at the forensic science lab had turned into a 'mare, just as Daniels had predicted. Apparently the journey from hell was too kind a description. After an initial short delay at Newcastle Central Station, everything had gone swimmingly until the train stopped and sat in the middle of nowhere for the next two and a half hours.

No heating in the carriage.

No refreshments.

No power: full stop.

'And no frigging explanation either,' he grumbled, rubbing his upper arms to get the circulation going. 'First the guard asks us to disembark, then to board again. We were on and off that many times I lost count. You should've seen the older passengers, the mothers with kids – it was chronic. By the time we eventually got going again and limped into York, the train was nearly three hours late.'

Even Lisa Carmichael was showing signs of sympathy.

'The return leg wasn't much better. I thought I was home and dry 'til my cab got stuck in the snow.' Maxwell was so blue it looked as though he would never thaw out. 'I walked the last mile.'

'Job done though, eh?' Lisa was trying her best not to

laugh. 'Grab yourself a hot shower. Give us the samples and I'll make sure the boss gets them. She's just next door.'

Maxwell shivered, his teeth still chattering. 'I handed them to the exhibits officer downstairs. Grey-haired guy, don't know his name.'

'He's a copper,' Hank said drily. 'He's bound to have grey hair. Most likely spends all his days trying to work out if he's got enough years in so he can leave before he's sixty-bloody-eight.'

'I'd pack it in now if I could afford it,' moaned Maxwell. 'After the day I've had.'

'Do me a favour!' Carmichael again. 'Sitting on a train all day is hardly night shift, is it? Besides, what the hell would you do if you left? Take up golf? You're not exactly the sporty type, are you, Neil?'

'I'm sure I'd find something.' Maxwell gave her a lecherous once-over and got a black look in return. He made light of it with a joke. 'Maybe I'll ask for a transfer to the Tweet Squad.'

Hank looked bewildered. He wasn't into social networking.

'I was playing with this on the train—' Maxwell held up his new iPhone. 'It may have passed you by, Sarge, but every area command in the country is now on Twitter.'

'Are you serious?'

Maxwell nodded. 'Unfortunately. I'm sure the public will rest easy in their beds once they know you can join an online forum to discuss policing in the twenty-first century.'

'What the hell do they put on there?' Hank was sure this was a wind-up.

'Bloody allsorts.' Maxwell blew on his hands. 'A hit and

run, a nasty arson, appeals for information on every bloody incident and accident, at least one request for help in tracing a sex offender . . .'

'Thought that was our job.'

'So did I,' Lisa joined in. 'But Neil's right. You can even, wait for it, *ask a cop a question* . . . oh yes you can!'

'I'd like to ask one.' Daniels' voice sounded behind them. 'Gimme the link and I'll ask why they're not out there locking people up.'

They hadn't noticed her re-enter from the side room she'd commandeered as her office. She'd been in there for several hours, cogitating, having ordered the team to leave her be unless there was any significant progress to report.

'I couldn't agree more, boss,' Maxwell said. 'Pound to a penny, some arsehole will get off at court because they've been outed on Twitter. That's not what it was designed for, in my humble opinion.'

'What was it designed for?' It was a serious question from Gormley.

Lisa laughed.

There was no answer from Maxwell either: he was too busy telling the DCI what an awful day he'd had. He got no sympathy.

Eventually the gathering dispersed. It was time to knock off. Kate sent them back to the B & B, intending to join them as soon as she'd viewed the samples collected from the forensic science lab. As she made her way downstairs she was still reviewing the day's events in her head, chewing over the possible significance of Bamburgh and why it had been chosen as a burial site.

On the floor below, she pushed a buzzer on the exhibits room counter and waited for a response. After signing for two separate evidence bags, she opened them up and laid the samples out, checking the labels to see which body they'd been taken from. The sample from the most recent victim was exactly as Matt West had described it: a small section of very cheap, popper-type imitation pearls made of extremely hard plastic. The pearlescent effect was not a coating but an integral part of the manufacturing process. Kate returned them to the bag. The second sample was similar. But these pearls felt waxy to the touch. They were also much softer than the first sample, coated to look like the real thing. Some of the coating had worn away, exposing white plastic underneath.

Her heart began to race.

A rare stroke of luck?

She'd seen an identical set before.

25

Day three of the murder investigation, 12 February. Skipping breakfast, Kate headed straight to the incident room hoping for some quiet time before the others got in. The samples she'd received from Matt West had set her imagination off and running. Holding them in her hands the night before had triggered a strong childhood memory, one that bothered her so much she'd called Gormley and told him she wouldn't be coming back to the B & B. Instead she'd jumped in the car and driven home to check out a hunch.

On arrival at the incident room, she set about preparing for the morning briefing. She'd already decided that she would hold off mentioning the pearls until she'd had a chance to develop her theory. No point raising expectations only to have them dashed if it didn't work out. Instead she busied herself recording her thoughts about the scene in large capital letters on a whiteboard which she placed in a prominent position where everyone would see it.

An hour later, the team were assembled and gathered around her, wanting answers.

'Where are we with scene issues?' she asked.

Blank faces stared at her. Heads shook, shoulders shrugged.

'OK, why Bamburgh? You want a place to bury a victim there are easier sites to pick. Ones where you won't see a

Labrador attached to some dog-walker every fifteen minutes. There are deserted strips all along this coastline where you'd not run into another living soul. So why that particular stretch of beach, in full view of the castle and Holy Island? It has to be significant.'

'The girls might've been trafficked from abroad, come in on a boat under cover of darkness—'

'Five years apart?' Kate eyeballed Maxwell. 'I considered that too, Neil, but then discounted it. If they were DOA, they'd have been dumped at sea. No, those bodies were carefully placed. Whoever buried the first victim returned to the exact same site five years later to bury the second. To be that precise, bearing in mind this was before everyone started carrying phones loaded with GPS navigation apps, you'd have to pace it out from a fixed position – the castle or car park. I'd be inclined to suggest the latter. The castle is quite a hike inland over rough ground. It would've been too risky. If a local happened to see someone arriving by boat and acting suspiciously, they'd probably jump to the conclusion they were smuggling drugs or burgling the castle – it's happened before, remember? – and the first thing they'd do is phone the law.' She focused on Robson. 'How we doing with missing persons, Robbo?'

'Not good. You have the full list, boss. The fact that there are no local kids missing makes the burial site more significant, not less, in my opinion. As you pointed out, it's a detour from any major road. Whoever we're looking for travelled across open countryside and woods, both of which are a damn sight more accessible than Bamburgh beach, and much less risky.'

'Unless they were already in the area,' Kate reminded him.

'There's no evidence of that. As I said, we have no reports of kids missing locally.'

'That's assuming they were reported missing in the first place,' she continued. 'For obvious reasons, not all kids are. Check with social services and education for any cases where kids were taken out of school without prior warning. You never know, we might just get lucky.'

'I'm on it already, but it'll take time.'

The DCI turned to Carmichael. 'Lisa, why Bamburgh? Tell me *you* have something more for me.'

'I'm still struggling, to be honest. Bamburgh's such a quiet place. Very few suspicious incidents recorded in the village. The odd complaint here and there, mainly kids messing around, barbecues on the beach and such. Couple of fights. Nothing serious. Nothing we haven't already looked into and dealt with.'

'All right, go back and cross reference each incident with every B & B and hotel on our list. And don't forget the action for the Research Project team. I'm hoping they might help us. What about house-to-house? They come up with anything?'

'Sergeant Yates says not. His team are knocking on doors, but the information they're getting is sketchy for the times you specified. Some hoteliers' books were full, others not. There was plenty of availability in winter but pretty much full house throughout the summer months. You know what that means . . .'

Daniels did indeed.

She and Jo had once gone camping near Keswick on a typical Bank Holiday weekend. It began raining not long after they arrived. Within hours, the campsite was knee-deep in water that had drained off the surrounding hills. They'd packed up their stuff and driven around in a desperate attempt to find alternative accommodation. Every hotel and B & B for miles around was full to the gunnels. Tourist Information couldn't help. The last person they spoke to suggested a cousin who lived on a farm and took in paying guests occasionally. *Cash only, mind – she doesn't take cheques or cards.* Carmichael was right. In the leisure industry, the black economy was rife; a sobering and depressing thought for a DCI trying to find out who was or wasn't in the vicinity at the time her victims were buried.

'These two paedophiles,' she asked, 'what's the story with them?'

'There's only one still in the frame, boss,' Brown said. 'I just had it confirmed. The other is no longer with us—'

'As in deceased, or moved away?'

'Dead. Vigilante group mashed his brains to a pulp four years ago. The Ricky Nichols enquiry, remember?'

Kate nodded.

How could she forget?

As murder investigations go, it had been a difficult one to crack. Locals had zero sympathy for the victim. Disgusted with the paltry sentences handed down by the judiciary, they preferred the permanent removal of paedophiles from their midst. By whatever means. There had been plenty of eye-witnesses to the killing, but none who were willing to come forward. Most were extremely hostile to the police, seeing them as defending the rights of dangerous sex offenders instead of protecting innocent kids. As far as they were concerned, it was a case of good riddance to bad rubbish. If they'd had their way, Ricky Nichols' killers would have been given a medal instead of a prison sentence.

'Doesn't mean he wasn't responsible for our offences,' Daniels said. 'Raise an action to have him eliminated. What about the other one?'

'We're still trying to find him.' Robson flipped open a small notebook, removed a photograph and handed it to her. 'John Edward Thompson. Thirty-eight years old. Last known address: Claymore Place, Blyth.'

Kate was staring at the photograph. Thompson's mugshot showed a man with vacant eyes. A prominent birthmark the colour of port wine spread from his right eye down his cheek.

'What did he do?' she asked.

'Dressed his last victim in an adult nurse's uniform. She was just thirteen. He subjected her to serious sexual assault – buggery, to be precise – for which he got four years. She lived, but has since attempted suicide three times.'

'Jesus!' Gormley shook his head, his jaw bunching. 'Don't you want to feel *his* collar?'

'Is there anything else to put him in or out?' the DCI asked.

'Hard to say. He's a bit of a traveller, by all accounts. Not in the Romany sense – he just moves around a lot, dosses down wherever he can.'

'How come?' Brown cut in. 'I thought scum on the sex offenders' register had to have a permanent address.'

'His brief appealed on grounds of a human rights violation,' Robson explained. 'His name was removed. He's not come to our notice for any offence in a decade or more. Last time was October 2001. He spent a night in custody at this very station for possession of Class A. Magistrates committed him to Crown. He did time for intent to supply from May 2002 to November 2005. Got out early. Good behaviour, would you believe?'

'That puts him in then,' Gormley said.

'I want a TIE action out for him right now,' Daniels said.

'Because?' It was Robson who'd asked the question. He was curious to know what had prompted her decision to take such drastic action, focusing their efforts on this particular individual. A Trace, Implicate or Eliminate action was a very big deal, one that involved a family tree, an associates' tree, the compilation of every bit of information ever written about the offender – going back to his birth, if necessary – in order to put him in or out of the frame.

Her pause was like a big question mark.

'Because we've got sod-all else,' she said finally. 'Because, like Hank, I want to make his life hell. And because I say so – need I say more?'

The squad were ecstatic. A TIE action usually had that effect.

Suspect number one coming right up . . .

26

Kent was in a foul mood. Punishment for going AWOL during lunch was usually swift – a few days on the block was the norm – but in Fearon's case it hadn't been as harsh as it ought to have been.

No, siree.

Having put the fear of God into Emily McCann on her second day back at work, the fucker had escaped the long walk to the Governor's office. And that was down to her. When security had rushed into the wing, batons drawn, the silly cow had insisted she didn't want to make an issue out of it.

'He's been through a lot lately,' she said.

With the day shift standing around gawping, waiting to see what action he'd take, Senior Officer Ash Walker had no choice but to disagree. It wasn't something he could let go, he told her, not without imposing some form of penalty, else they'd all be at it. But after a long discussion in his office – a closed-door job – he'd acquiesced and the psychologist got her way. Kent was furious. It was nepotism, plain and simple: the SO clearly had the hots for her.

Half an hour later, Kent was summoned to Walker's office and consigned to the great outdoors to supervise a group of offenders on litter-picking duty outside C-wing, Fearon included. It was no more than a slap on the wrist for mis-behaving. The nutter would be laughing his cock off.

Well, he'd see about that.

Kent was standing at the gable end of C-wing, shoulders hunched, his breath clearly visible in the icy air. Debris was being blown across the prison grounds. His skin was red raw, his nose dripping like a tap. Blowing on his hands, he stamped his feet, his temper boiling over. He couldn't feel his extremities.

Just who was being punished here?

Resentment bubbled up inside Kent. He watched like a hawk as Fearon edged his way along the wall. Unaware that he was under scrutiny, he was shoving litter into a black plastic bag he could hardly hang on to in the gusty wind. Somehow he'd managed to wheedle his way into Harrison's favours. Although the Principal Officer normally left the selection of offenders' duties to lesser mortals, he'd person-ally intervened to select Fearon's employment within the establishment.

Unheard of.

Wing fucking cleaner, no less!

A warm and cushy number he didn't deserve. God knows how the bastard had swung it. Wouldn't surprise Kent if the nonce was doing a little trading, giving the PO a regular blowjob in return for such a big-ass favour. Whatever the sketch, it meant the fuckwit was in Kent's face all day and every day. No one argued with Harrison's little arrangement. The PO had justified his decision on security grounds, telling wing staff it was the best way to keep a close eye on Fearon. Keep your friends close . . .

Bollocks!

There had to be more to it than that – not that Kent would ever find out. Right now, he didn't care. He was too busy freezing his fucking ass off guarding this working party. The only upside: Fearon was as cold and miserable as he was.

Kent had a shovelful of muck in his eyes but didn't dare turn his back for fear of losing control of the cons under his supervision. If that happened, *he'd* be the one for the high jump.

Already on a final warning, he couldn't afford that.

No sooner had he filed that worrying thought away than an argument broke out between Jones and Singh. Just a bit of pushing and shoving at first. Then Jones waded in. Fists flew, feet too as he put the boot in good and proper. His language was choice. Singh, who was about the same height but less powerfully built, went down hard and curled up in a foetus-like ball in order to protect his head. Knowing that Jones was a racist pig who wouldn't stop unless forced to, Kent moved in to break it up.

The moment his back was turned, Fearon made a run for it. Within seconds, he was round the side of the building and out of sight. Moments later, a siren sounded and HMP Northumberland was plunged into a full lockdown.

27

Kate Daniels couldn't concentrate. Despite freezing temperatures, the weather had improved sufficiently that the local kids were out in force. A game of basketball was going on below her office window, punctuating her thoughts with the constant clatter of the ball hitting the backboard of a net attached to the house across the street, followed by the roar of laughter and occasional bad language between teenagers having a bit of fun. She'd been good at netball as a girl, even played for her county once upon a time.

Part of her wished she could join them.

'You look like you're somewhere else,' Hank said as he walked through the door.

She nodded toward the window. 'Just listening to the exuberance of youth. Wishing I was their age with nothing better to do than throw a ball around, take the piss out of my teachers and smoke behind the bike sheds.'

Gormley smiled. 'It's not like you to reminisce.'

He was right – it wasn't – but she'd been doing little else the last few hours. Even during the morning briefing she'd been replaying her trip home last night. After a nightmare journey, she'd gone into her study to face something she should've faced ages ago but hadn't had the guts. Standing on a chair, she'd opened up an overhead cupboard and lifted out a shoebox. Then she'd sat cross-legged on the floor, staring at the three-letter-word written neatly on the side: MUM.

Registering the faraway expression on her face, Gormley asked, 'You feeling OK? You look a bit pale.'

His boss nodded, trying to drag herself into the present. But a memory a quarter of a century old sucked her in again. Kate touched her hair. She could feel her mother's hands gently lifting it off her face as she prepared the birthday girl for her party. Transported back in time, she remembered the cake with ten candles on it standing proud on the table, the feel of every brushstroke as her mother wove her hair into a plait and tied it with a yellow ribbon to match her party dress. The same yellow ribbon Kate had used to secure a shoebox containing her mother's precious keepsakes following her death.

And now, in her head at least, she was in her study, untying it again.

Breathe . . .

In her mind's eye, she raised the top off the box and peered inside: a parcel of letters, some old photographs, various items of cheap jewellery, a folded silk scarf. Lifting out the scarf, she peeled away the corners as if her actions might cause the delicate fabric to disintegrate in her hands. Wrapped inside were two sets of rosary beads, her own and her late mother's. Placing them beside her on the floor, she drew the scarf to her face, inhaling deeply, allowing the memory of her mum's scent to engulf her.

'You sure?' Hank asked. 'You don't look too good.'

Kate managed a nod. Reaching into her pocket, she pulled out a string of plastic pearls almost identical to the ones recovered from their ten-year-old victim. She handed them to Gormley. 'Very like our samples, am I right?'

He examined them for a moment. 'Looks that way. Where d'you get them?'

'Home . . .' she said. 'My home.'

He didn't understand. Why would he?

'They belonged to my mum – a gift from my paternal grandmother. They must be forty or fifty years old. As soon as I saw the exhibits Neil collected yesterday I knew I'd seen some just like them.' She pointed at the pearls, the pearlescent paint missing in places. 'I was allowed to play with those as a kid, but was told to keep them safe. Don't suppose I ever questioned why. I certainly got the impression that they were special somehow.'

'Special?'

'Yes . . . no, I don't know, Hank. I've been racking my brains all night, trying to remember, but I just can't.' Using her index finger, she tapped her right temple. 'The answer is in there somewhere, but it's evading me. I have this feeling that these pearls might have a past connection with an area not so far away from here.'

'Now you've lost me.' Gormley sat down.

'Have you never wondered how a miner's daughter like me was born and brought up so far away from a pit village?'

He shook his head. 'Thought never crossed my mind.'

'It's odd though, yes?'

'S'pose.'

'My family haven't always lived in the Tyne Valley. On both sides they were miners going back generations. Mum was from Durham, my old man was Ashington born and bred—'

'That's only twenty miles away—'

'Exactly. It's a bit of a long story . . .' Kate waved Hank to the seat across the desk and waited while he made himself comfortable. 'My old man inherited his cottage from an uncle he never even knew he had – a childless widower. He was an engineer by all accounts, an entrepreneur who started his own business and did rather well. My father's inclusion in his will came as a complete surprise. He'd not long married my mum, but he was already down the pits by then, earning OK money, enough to feed and clothe them at any rate. He wanted to sell the cottage on, but Mum wouldn't hear of it. She persuaded him to keep it and carry on work-ing, using it only for holidays. They didn't move in until I came along. Not many miners had their own homes and none were mortgage free, so when the pits closed they were better off than most.'

'Nice uncle.' Gormley held up the pearls. 'You sending these off for comparison?'

'I certainly am.'

'You going to ask your old man about them?'

Kate grimaced. 'Do I have a choice?'

Taking an envelope off her desk, she wrote instructions on the front and held it open. Hank dropped the pearls inside. She stuck it down, hoping her father would shed some fur-ther light on what had made the pearls an heirloom to be passed on. A little local knowledge could go a long way.

Picking her mobile off the desk, she dialled his number, wondering if he'd be home from his weekly visit to his favourite haunt. He was an avid reader of political thrillers, a founder member of a reading group that met at Corbridge Village Hall, and a staunch supporter of the 'Save Our Libraries' campaign.

His phone rang out unanswered.

She looked at her watch. It was almost one. The meeting ought to be over by now.

The voicemail kicked in. At the tone she left a message: 'Dad, it's me. Can you call me when you get this? It's very important. Thanks.' Hanging up, she made a mental note to call him later. But before she had a chance to pocket her mobile, it rang in her hand.

It was him.

Her father didn't bother to introduce himself. There was no friendly greeting. No: Hi, how you doing, love? No explanation as to why he'd ignored the phone a moment ago, merely a curt and frosty: 'Is something wrong? You said it was important.'

Kate glanced around her, hackles rising.

The incident room was busy. Phones were ringing: always a good sign that information was beginning to come in. Civilian staff were tapping away at their computers, updating HOLMES. The rest of her team were too engrossed in what they were doing to pay her any heed.

She went back to her call. 'I need to see you. Will you be in later?'

'You're coming here?'

She didn't bite. She'd not set foot inside his house for a good while. Not since their last major blow-up. *When was that?* There had been so many. She was too wired to recall.

'I'm in Alnwick, Dad. Not sure what time I can get away, but I'll be there – probably late afternoon or early evening, depending on the weather and traffic. Is that OK?'

Ed Daniels agreed it was and promptly rang off.

28

Emily hadn't heard the fracas going on a hundred metres away. The first she knew of it was when the alarm sounded. Word that a prisoner was missing from a working party spread like wildfire. No one told her which prisoner it was, but a full security alert was now in operation and a search was ongoing close to the perimeter fence, the obvious place to start looking for an escapee.

Kent and his working group had been bundled into the Governor's office and were being questioned by the head of security. Unconcerned, Emily got on with her work.

So deep was her concentration, the tapping noise hardly registered at first.

It was irritating more than anything. It sounded as if it was coming from below ground: probably the ancient plumbing, unable to cope with radiators turned up high after the sudden drop in temperature.

The noise stopped and Emily went back to making notes in a case file. When the tapping resumed, she put down her pen and looked around, trying to identify the source.

The clock above her office door moved forward a notch.

It was nearly quarter to four and already getting dark.

She went to the window and looked out in the half-light beyond . . . and shrank back as Fearon's face suddenly appeared, pressed hard against her window, flattened and distorted, a menacing expression in his eyes.

That was it. She'd had enough of his nonsense.

By the time the litter-picking party were led back to C-wing, Emily and Walker were waiting by the entrance, ready to intercept them. Despite the fact that he was bringing up the rear, Fearon clocked them from way down the corridor. He never took his eyes off Emily as he shambled along towards her, a smirk on his face.

Walker pushed his key into the wing gate and turned it.

He glanced at Emily. 'Want me to deal with him?'

'Thanks, Ash, but this is something I need to do for myself.'

'OK.' Reluctantly he nodded for her to proceed. 'If he gives you any lip, though, he's mine.'

'Fair enough.'

Jones was first in, top dog as usual. He obviously knew what had happened because, as he passed Emily by, he smiled and said: 'Shall I do him, miss? Say the word and I'll stick him in the showers.'

Ignoring his remark, Emily glared at Kent. There was only one way Jones could have found out what had gone on outside her office window. It had to have come from one of the prison staff, and it wouldn't take a Mensa member to work out which one. Jones grinned, pleased to have witnessed obvious aggro between two people he hated with a passion. He moved off as Singh caught up with him, his right eye all puffed up, a dribble of blood on his chin.

When SO Walker asked if he needed medical attention, Singh shook his head.

'What happened, Ajit?' Emily asked.

Singh's eyes flitted past them.

Emily looked over her shoulder.

Jones was standing a little way off – eyes fixed firmly on Singh – his powerful arms crossed over his chest, his tongue pushing out his left cheek, an unspoken message writ large on his ugly mug: *Grass and you're dead.*

Singh's voice was hardly audible. 'I don't want no trouble, miss.'

'That isn't an answer,' Emily persisted. 'I asked you a question.'

'I slipped. Please, miss, you have to believe me.'

'You sure about that?'

The inmate couldn't look her in the eye.

And who could blame him, with Jones looking on? The poisonous shit was enjoying his moment. Laughing at them. He could afford to do as he pleased. Unlike Singh, he wasn't getting out early. He had nothing to lose. Emily asked the SO to remove him immediately. Walker nodded to one of his men, the fittest of the bunch if his physique was anything to go by. The young officer sprang into action, helping Jones along with a sharp shove in the back.

Emily waited until he was out of sight then turned to Singh. 'I have your parole decision.'

He searched her face optimistically.

Smiling, she held up a thumb. 'You deserve it.'

Punching the air in celebration, the inmate rushed off to pass on the good news to his personal officer, the member of staff who'd supported him throughout his sentence and rec-ommended the granting of parole. Emily turned. Fearon was being held beyond the wing gate, his face streaked by the shadow of the bars. As Emily beckoned him inside, Kent released his grip on the prisoner's arm. Fearon shuffled forward, shoulders hunched, head bowed, pretending he was sorry for what he'd done.

Unmoved by this show of contrition, Emily stepped in front of him, blocking his entry. 'Try that again and I'll take you to the Governor myself. What on earth did you think you were doing?'

Fearon's glasses were so plastered with filth it was hard to see the message in his eyes.

Ash Walker turned to the psychologist. 'Want him on report?'

'Damn right.' She moved aside, allowing Fearon to continue on his way. As he passed her, she added, 'And if he tries to make an application to see me, it's refused.'

Fearon's step faltered.

He'd overheard. He was meant to. As he turned to look at Emily, her mind was made up. *If he wanted war, he'd get war. Two could play at that game.*

29

An owl hooted, disturbed by tyres on gravel, as the Q5 swept to a halt outside a five-bar gate. Keeper's Cottage lay nestled in a woodside clearing at the end of a long narrow driveway. Typically Northumbrian, the single-storey, stone and slate former gamekeeper's cottage stood alone.

There wasn't another house for almost three miles.

Cutting her headlights, Kate Daniels leaned against the headrest, letting her tired eyes become accustomed to the dark, taking a moment to compose herself before getting out of the car. In her time as a police officer she'd interviewed murderers and rapists. Chased armed robbers through crowded streets with sirens screaming. Hunted down the most evil drug dealers, even gone undercover, putting her life at risk. Nothing fazed her. But the prospect of meeting her father had reduced her to a small girl who was about to be denied pocket money.

To put it mildly, she was dreading the encounter.

Taking a long, deep breath, she hoped her luck was in tonight. She was counting on her father providing vital information that would take her enquiry in the right direction. Problem was, in order to drag it from him she'd first have to step into a happy world she'd buried long ago.

And so would he.

The familiar smell of a real coal fire floated in the air as she got out of the car. Though she had no key, she didn't think to knock. Residents in this part of the world felt no need to lock their doors to keep intruders out. Even at night. Even after a double murder in the village church a couple of years ago that had shocked the community to the core. Open house was a way of life here. It had been for hundreds of years. It would take more than a depraved killer to change that.

Kate pushed open the door. By the sounds of it, her father was making himself busy in the tiny scullery at the rear of the house. Not wanting to startle him, she called out as she approached along the narrow hallway.

'I'm not deaf!' he grumbled as she walked in. He didn't look up from the dishes in the sink. 'There's tea in the pot. Probably stewed now, but don't blame me. It was fresh when you drove up.'

Kate hadn't thought she'd been sitting outside that long.

Putting her briefcase on the floor, she unhooked a clean mug from a peg on the wall and took a carton of milk from the fridge. She'd drink his tea, not because she was thirsty but to keep the peace. As she poured it out, she noticed two of her favourite chocolate biscuits laid out on a plate on the kitchen bench, a nice reminder that her father had a heart. But then he went and spoiled the moment by walking away.

She found him in the living room. He was standing with his back to a roaring fire, waiting for her to explain herself. Kate sat down, apologized again for disappointing him on his birthday, then tried to steer the conversation away from her failure in the good daughter contest. 'This is an odd question,

Dad, but do you remember a string of pearls I played with as a little girl?'

His frown was a major disappointment to her.

Hoping she hadn't wasted her time driving all this way, she tried again. 'I seem to remember Mum telling me that Grandpa gave them to her.'

'Grandpa?'

She gave a little nod.

When she was a youngster, to avoid confusion, her maternal grandfather was referred to as Pops, her paternal grandfather as Grandpa. Her father didn't speak for a little while. He seemed sad all of a sudden but his melancholy didn't last long.

'Your grandpa would've given her the world if she'd asked for it,' he said. 'He loved your mum. Maybe the pearls were your nan's.'

Sadie Daniels had died young, long before Kate was born. But still . . . there was a story to the string of pearls she'd found, she was certain of it. Before leaving the office she'd sent them off for analysis, requesting comparison with those recovered at her crime scene.

Searching her father's face, she took care not to lead him. 'They weren't real, Dad. They were plastic. The type you pull apart and snap together. You know the sort I mean? Kids' stuff.'

A flash of recognition crossed his face.

'You remember them, don't you?'

'Every miner's daughter got a set back then. The boys got a football.'

What on earth was he on about?

Her father was one of four boys.

For a long while he said nothing. He just stared at the floor, considering. Kate, seeing he was upset, struggled to understand the cause. Eventually, he raised his head. Picking up on her confusion, he swallowed hard and sat down beside her. Taking a deep breath, he began speaking.

'I had a twin sister . . .' The words caught in his throat. He paused: a moment of inner torment that seemed to last for ever. Kate didn't pressure him. She could see how the memory grieved him. She didn't touch him either, knowing it would push him over the edge. 'Her name was Mary,' he said. 'She died when we were four. Hit and run.'

Kate couldn't believe she was hearing this for the very first time. Then a conversation with her mother jumped into her head. Before she was born, her parents had agreed that if they had a boy her mum would choose her name, a girl and her father would. He chose the name Mary but then changed his mind when registering her birth, an action he'd never fully explained to Kate's mum.

Now she knew why.

Mary Daniels.

It didn't sound right.

Her father's face was pained by the memory of his dead sister. Kate felt sorry for him. He'd lost all the women in his life: his mother, sister, wife, *her.* As an only child, she was the sole surviving female, the only one capable of carrying on the family name. *So, it was curtains for clan Daniels.* Another guilt trip he could lay at her door.

'I'm so sorry, Dad. I didn't know.'

'Makes no odds now . . .' He looked at her accusingly. 'Your lot were next to useless when it happened. That's what my dad told me, anyway. The police never did find the person responsible.'

God! Why did he always blame her for everything?

'What did you mean when you said everyone got a set "back then"?'

'The Coronation,' he said.

'So that would have been 1953?'

'The Miners' Welfare organized street parties to celebrate. A few sandwiches and cake, that's all. But the weather was atrocious and most were moved inside. It tanked it down. The roads were all flooded, but we didn't care . . .' Ed Daniels' mood lifted momentarily. 'Aye, it was a grand day.' Then his eyes were empty again. 'Mary was dead within the year.'

30

Emily McCann was pleased to be home, a gin and tonic in her hand, her feet up in front of the fire after a long hot bath. Then the phone rang: *the prison*. Fearon had caused a lot of trouble during the day – and enjoyed doing it – but he was now extremely agitated, according to officers watching over him. Alone in his cell on the punishment block, he'd flown into a rage, begging for writing materials on which to scribble down a grovelling apology, rapping on the cell door so hard he'd opened the wound to his right wrist, drawing blood.

'Oh, he's sorry all right.'

Not because he scared me, Emily thought. *That's what turns him on.*

'He's sorry because I'm angry with him . . . Well, tough.'

She listened as the officer explained his dilemma. Fearon had woken the rest of the cons. There was bedlam on the wing and he needed to restore calm. Appeasing one prisoner was the best way to do it. Fearon wanted assurances that she'd see him next morning.

'OK,' she said. 'Give him what he wants if it'll shut him up. You guys have a hard enough job without having to put up with that all night.'

They said goodnight and rang off.

Emily returned to the sofa and tried to unwind, but she

couldn't help thinking about Fearon, imagining the state he was in. She'd told him time and again that he was a reckless hothead. Not her fault if he didn't listen. There'd been times when her sessions with him had been so difficult that she'd found it necessary to debrief with another staff member afterwards. Though each session lasted no more than an hour, she always emerged feeling wrung out. Completely and utterly exhausted. Sometimes it took several hours before she could clear her head of the despicable images he painted.

The clock struck the hour.

Rachel had left no note to say where she'd gone or what time she'd be home. Wondering where she was, Emily got up and threw a log on the fire. She poured herself another drink and sipped it absent-mindedly as she tried to process the day's events, specifically Fearon's behaviour and the risk he posed. She shuddered, picturing the smirk on his face as he sat in her office chair, relishing her unease as he recounted what he'd put his victims through, flirting with her while describing every morbid detail.

Pathetic: *she was old enough to be his mother.*

But therein lay the problem . . .

Fearon had never been interested in girls his own age. He seemed incapable of a loving relationship with anyone. It was all about power with him: sex too, but with an element of fear ever present. Horror even. His penis was a weapon, an instrument of terror. That was what made him so dangerous.

His victims were all forty plus. Emily didn't need Stamp to tell her that. She knew fine well what Fearon was up to. According to Ash Walker, he'd been gutted when she'd suddenly disappeared from work after Robert died. He'd taken her absence personally. Couldn't eat. Couldn't sleep. Talked about her constantly, as if afraid she'd left him and would never return.

By the time she'd heard about that, Emily was in a place too dark to realize the significance. Too numb to care. Robert was dead and that was all she could think about. But then things had taken on a sinister twist. After he'd cut his wrists, Fearon had openly admitted he'd done it to get her attention: *Because you don't love me any more.*

Emily shivered.

Just how deluded was he?

She hadn't shared that conversation with anyone, not even Jo Soulsby. And certainly not Stamp. That would have been guaranteed to set him off. He was right about one thing, though: Fearon had a dangerous and deep-seated obsession with older women. He'd turned his focus on her and she'd have to watch her back.

As she drank the last of her gin, her eyes drifted to Robert's picture on top of the piano, smiling at her as he sat astride his bike. He was not a handsome man on the outside but he'd had a big, big heart. He'd loved her with a passion.

Emily suddenly felt guilty.

It had only been a few months since he'd passed away and yet she'd been tempted to let Stamp into her life. Her desire to overcome loneliness was strong, her urge to have sex even stronger. She didn't care that Rachel might disapprove – or anyone else, for that matter. She wanted – needed – to feel alive again. In her head, she could almost hear Robert's voice . . .

Knock yourself out, babe! I just want you to be happy.

She wiped a tear from her cheek, her sadness turning to anger. The prison staff had been sloppy while she was off work. Fearon had obviously overheard them talking about her loss. The day before yesterday, he'd woken up in the prison hospital and told her it was the best day of his life when he heard the news that her old man had croaked. *She must be gagging for it now*, he'd told himself.

The ramblings of a deranged mind. But all the same . . .

She'd fled the ward in tears.

Bile rose in her throat as she recalled his joy. Her fury didn't end with him. Prison staff had no business discussing her in the presence of men like Fearon. They should've kept their mouths shut.

Well, maybe Emily couldn't turn back the clock, but she could and would make a stand. It was time to show Fearon who was boss.

She'd told him once that every action resulted in a reaction and today she'd proved it. Never in his worst nightmares had it occurred to him that she might push him away. But that was exactly what she'd done. Much to SO Walker's obvious delight: a brief respite from Fearon was like a day off, so high maintenance was he.

No doubt Kent had been pleased about it too, *the bastard*.

Emily sighed.

Fearon could barely handle being banged up in solitary overnight – what would happen if they moved him to another wing when he got out? What if she didn't keep her promise and refused to see him tomorrow? The day after? The day after that? In his present state, he'd surely flip.

With only a couple of weeks to go till his release, time was running out. If *she* didn't work to correct his behaviour in the final days of his sentence, who would? If she managed to get through to him, it might just save another woman's life.

Much as she would have liked to wash her hands of Walter Fearon, she wasn't ready to give up on him just yet.

31

Kate climbed into her car and reversed at speed off her father's drive, eager to get back to the incident room at Alnwick station. Her father had seemed OK when she left him. She'd hung around a while, to make sure. Buoyed by the information he'd provided, she'd called ahead, telling Carmichael to fire up that computer of hers and find out all she could about Ashington Miners' Welfare . . .

'I need a contact, Lisa. And I need it yesterday.'

'For what, boss?'

Explaining about the pearls she'd found in the shoebox at home and what she'd discovered since with her father's help, Kate asked Lisa to find a local historian. By the time she arrived at the office, Carmichael had located one and sent a Traffic car to fetch him to the station. Chris Ridley had been given a cup of tea and briefed that the SIO was on her way.

'Good to meet you, Mr Ridley. I'm DCI Kate Daniels, Murder Investigation Team.' Kate extended her hand and received a firm handshake from the spritely and switched on septuagenarian. 'Thanks for coming in at such short notice. I won't keep you a moment longer than absolutely necessary.'

The old man sat down. Told her he was happy to help in any way he could. His son had joined Lothian & Borders force, was now a DCI himself with a formidable reputation for solving complex cases. She didn't know the officer, but she'd heard good things of him and told Ridley so.

'In my job it pays to know the competition,' she said.

Ridley grinned proudly.

'I need your help to solve a puzzle . . .' She sat down beside him. 'But before I get into that, I must stress that this is extremely sensitive. What I'm about to tell you cannot leave this room.'

'Goes without saying,' he said.

Hank, who'd kept the old man company while they waited for the DCI to return, considered him thoroughly trustworthy, an assessment Daniels agreed with wholeheartedly. With a family member in the force, he understood the exigencies of the job, the need to keep information confidential.

'We're dealing with the recent discovery on Bamburgh beach,' Kate said. 'You probably heard about it.'

'Yes, terrible business.'

'It's pretty grim.'

Mr Ridley took off his reading specs. He peered across the room, squinted at the murder wall, specifically at blown-up photographs of both victims: bones, skulls, the lot. Had the images been more than skeletal remains they would almost certainly have been covered up. Obviously, Hank hadn't thought it necessary and Kate was satisfied that his call had been right on this occasion.

She cleared her throat to regain his attention. 'Items of children's play jewellery were found on both victims,' she said. 'It's imperative that I trace where it came from.'

'There are two victims?'

'Unfortunately, yes.'

'I hadn't realized—'

'Thing is, I'm struggling to identify the jewellery. As a result of enquiries elsewhere, I've been led to believe that there may be some connection with the Ashington area around the time of the Coronation.'

'Which is where I come in.'

'Exactly.'

Chris Ridley was intrigued. 'In what respect?'

'Let me show you something . . .' She handed him a photograph of the pearls.

The old man put his specs on and studied them carefully, then looked up, waiting for her to explain their relevance.

'I've been told that local youngsters may have been given imitation jewellery like this as a remembrance gift at a celebratory party financed by the Ashington Miners' Welfare in 1953.'

'That's true, some were . . . I had no kids of my own at that stage, but I do remember the parties the Welfare put on . . .' He glanced at the murder wall. 'Is that how long they've been there?'

'No. Despite their condition, they were buried within the last decade.'

'Oh, I thought—'

'You said *some*?' Kate interrupted. 'You mean, not all girls got a set?'

'That's correct. I seem to remember the miners themselves chose the wee gift their kids would get. It wasn't one big party for the whole community, you understand, but a series of street parties. Not every kid got the same. Some girls got tiaras, some got pearls. The boys all got footballs.'

'So I hear. That's an odd choice, isn't it?'

'What do you mean?'

'Didn't the boys want a themed gift too?'

'You mean a sword, a crown, something royal to mark the occasion?'

She nodded.

The old man chuckled. 'Unless you could play a bit, you went down the mines in those days, pet. What would you choose?'

The term 'pet' made Hank Gormley smile. No offence was meant by it and none was taken by the DCI. It was a term of endearment a man of Ridley's age would automatically use in this part of the world, without consideration of the title, rank or status of the female he happened to be talking to.

'Bobby Charlton signed for Man U about then, didn't he?' Hank said.

The historian grinned. 'Young lads like me thought that was far more exciting than a change of monarchy. Bunch of Philistines, we were. Some round here still are.' His eyes lit up. 'But he's Sir Bobby now, isn't he? It might tek us a while, but some of us Ashington lads get there in the end.'

'You're a big fan, I take it?' Kate said.

'Of Bobby? Not many round here aren't . . .' Ridley winked at Hank, dragging him into the conversation. 'I can see your sergeant here agrees with me.'

'I do indeed.'

'Aye, they broke the mould after Charlton and Robson. Charlton especially. He was – and still is – a canny lad, just like his uncle before him.'

He was referring to Jackie Milburn, ex Newcastle United

and England centre forward – known affectionately as 'Wor Jackie' – undoubtedly Ashington's most famous son.

Kate quickly changed the subject, ending Chris Ridley's trip down Memory Lane. 'Is it possible to say how many children we're talking about?' she asked.

'Off the top of my head, no . . .' The historian paused for thought, then frowned. 'Geography determined which miners' children went to which parties. If I'd had kids, they'd have gone to the one for folk living on the two Victorian terraces close to Ashington town centre. A couple of my fellow miners are still alive. We were the lucky ones. A lot died of lung disease, sadly.' He looked again at the photograph of the pearls. 'I can make enquiries, if you'd like. Shouldn't be too difficult. There'll be a receipt somewhere, no doubt. Every penny had to be accounted for, much like Police Federation funds. The Coronation celebrations would have been well documented at the time.'

'That would be very helpful,' Kate said. 'This is an important line of enquiry. Can you give us a rough estimate of how many sets of pearls were given out?'

'Coronations don't happen every day of the week,' the old man reminded her. 'It was a rare treat. Not too many though, I don't think. Only kids of ten years and under would have been given them.'

The DCI hoped he was right. Her own set of pearls had been handed down the generations. Because they belonged to a relative who had died soon afterwards, they held a special significance to her family. She suspected that many more – probably most – would've been regarded as junk and thrown away.

'I'll be honest with you, Mr Ridley. If we were talking about pearls in their thousands, that would be hard for us. Less than a hundred, still difficult. A couple of dozen and we're in business. We need to trace the recipients or their descendants, irrespective of whether or not the pearls are still in their possession. That way I can rule them in or out of our investigation.'

'I understand.'

'To your knowledge, did many people actually keep them? Do you recall anyone in your family hanging on to Coronation memorabilia?'

The old man shrugged. 'My wife's not a hoarder, pet. If we had any, they'd be long gone now, I should think. But I'll ask around, see what I can find out.'

Kate's eyes scanned the incident room. It was late and therefore quiet; phone traffic negligible, civilian staff long gone. Directing the old man to an empty desk with a phone in one corner of the room, she encouraged him to use his local knowledge and ring round his acquaintances to find out more. His expertise had given her a mini breakthrough.

Suddenly, things were looking up.

32

Emily removed the green silk scarf from around her neck and put it down on the edge of her desk. Whoever had decided to turn the heating up overnight had gone totally overboard. It was a mild morning and stifling in her office. Not the kind of atmosphere she wanted while dealing with a round of prisoner applications that covered a variety of issues: bad news from home, a spat with another prisoner, a Dear John letter, a ploy to avoid work. There could be umpteen reasons an inmate would request an appointment with her.

Pouring herself a large glass of water, she took a drink, then pushed a button on a small desk fan. It whirred into action, sending ribbons dancing in a cooling flow of air. Having finished her daily list, Emily summoned Saunders and gave him the benefit of her advice. His bullying had to stop. The only leverage she had over him was an education course he was desperate to sign up for. He'd been accepted once before but had been so disruptive in the first few weeks he'd been thrown out on his ear. Staff had since refused to lift the suspension.

Knowing how much it meant to him, Emily thought she might change their minds if – and it was a *very* big if – she could demonstrate an improvement in his attitude. Perhaps education would yet prove the catalyst for a change in his behaviour. He'd got good grades at school. According to social enquiry reports, he'd even had aspirations to start his own business. Unfortunately for his local community, that business involved drugs, which in turn required muscle, which was where Jones came in.

It was downhill from there on in.

Well, Emily reminded herself, *I'm the muscle now.*

'Tell you what,' she said. 'You do something for me and you have my word I'll return the favour.'

Saunders didn't reply.

'I thought you were a businessman,' Emily looked him square in the eye. 'Call it a transaction of mutual benefit. I have something you want. Your good behaviour is the means to pay for it. Stay out of trouble for the next six months and I'll see what I can do. Do we have a deal?'

He glared at her, resentful. His charm offensive had failed, and that didn't happen very often where women were concerned. Finally he gave a resigned nod. She dismissed him and he left the room, yanking open the door, leaving it wide open. Almost immediately, Walter Fearon appeared in the doorway, rubbing the top of his right arm with his left hand. He looked awful, his eyes ringed by dark circles, his hair sticking up at odd angles. He wasn't the only one to have had a sleepless night. She had too: Rachel hadn't come home until 3 a.m.

'What's wrong with your arm?' Emily asked.

'Nothing.'

'What do you want, Walter?'

'I've come to apologize. I've got something for you.'

Emily thought about last night, specifically the argument

she'd had with herself after the officer rang and told her how distressed Fearon was. Could she live with herself if she wrote him off as a no-hoper? Despite the risk he posed to her personal safety, she felt duty-bound to listen. He was only twenty-one. Years of abuse had turned him from helpless victim to high-profile perpetrator. He needed therapy in spite of himself. It would be totally unprofessional to turn him away.

She pointed at a chair. 'Sit down.'

Fearon did as he was told. He fumbled around in his trouser pocket, making her nervous. When she picked up her phone, he panicked, thinking she was about to have him removed. Withdrawing his hand from his pocket, he placed a tightly folded and slightly crumpled piece of prison-issue paper on her desk.

'It's for you, miss.'

'An apology?'

He bowed his head, eyeing her over the top of his filthy specs.

She spoke into the phone. 'Walter Fearon is in my office . . . I know I did, but I changed my mind . . . yes, thank you.' Emily hung up, her eyes drawn to the scruffy note in front of her.

She didn't touch the paper. Instead, she got up and went to her filing cabinet to retrieve his prison record. Feeling his eyes on her back, she opened the manila folder and retraced her steps, flipping through the case-notes until she came to the last entry. Only when she was seated across the desk from him again did she look up, coolly returning his gaze.

'Seeing as you're here, we may as well discuss your release,' she said. 'A hostel place has been made available to you. I'm sure you know why. You obviously can't go home, and your local authority have refused to house you. I don't mean to labour the point, but that leaves you with no other option: it's a hostel or the streets. You'll receive a travel warrant to get you there. Do you have any questions?

He didn't respond.

He was too busy eyeing her hair as it wafted slightly in the breeze from the desk fan, his eyes taking in every feature, every blemish with that same constant and persistent gaze that had unsettled Emily since her return to work. She was fighting the urge to cringe from his stare when, over his shoulder, she saw Ash Walker in the doorway. The old Emily would have taken offence, but she knew the SO meant well. He was there for her protection – *Just in case Fearon kicks off*, as he'd told her on the phone a moment ago.

That was a nice way of putting it.

Emily gave nothing away as she cast an appraising eye over the inmate. Not including yesterday's prank, he'd spent a total of thirteen days on the block for breaches of discipline while he'd been inside. He'd also missed out on privileges such as parole and home leave. Like a lot of other young men in there, he had bugger all to go home to.

It wasn't Fearon that Emily worried about. It was the women he might come into contact with. She shuddered at the thought of the damage he was capable of inflicting before his next term of imprisonment.

'Close the door on your way out,' she said.

Fearon was trying to act cool but his non-verbal behaviour was giving him away. He was visibly seething having been dismissed: his jaw bunched, the grey eyes flashed behind his spectacles, and his fists were clenched so tight his knuckles had turned white. The tirade that followed was vicious but short-lived.

Glancing over his shoulder, he clocked the SO loitering in the corridor. Fearon got to his feet and left the room without another word, pushing past Ash Walker on his way out.

'Everything OK?' asked the SO, popping his head round the door.

Emily nodded.

'Well, if he gives you any more grief—'

'I'll be sure to let you know.'

'You made any decision about Kent?' Walker asked. 'Whether to make a complaint, I mean.'

'No, not yet, Ash. Despite the fact that I think he's an arse, I'm prepared to give him the benefit of the doubt. The problem is, he's avoiding me. That'll be down to Harrison.' She managed a smile. 'I'm persona non grata as far as the PO is concerned.'

'Join the club,' Walker said.

'Anything you want to tell me?' Emily looked at him, inviting him to speak up, but he remained silent. She still had no clue what issues might be bothering Kent, but now was obviously not the time to question Walker about it. Maybe Stamp was wrong . . . Maybe Walker had nothing to tell her and she'd just have to drag it out of Kent herself. 'I'm sorry, I shouldn't have asked. I don't want to compromise your relationship with him.'

Closing her door quietly, the SO left her to her work.

Emily wrote Kent's name in her diary, a reminder to catch

him later. He could refuse to see her, but she'd at least offer him the opportunity to discuss his attitude. Who knew? Maybe he'd surprise her and accept some well-meaning advice.

Her eyes landed on the note Fearon had left on her desk.

Reluctant to touch it without gloves on, she took a pair out of her drawer and slipped them on. Teasing open the folded sheet of paper, she braced herself for the drivel it might contain. If it was an apology it would be badly spelt and lacking punctuation. He'd sent her notes before. His writing was barely legible, school being the one institution he'd managed to avoid. He'd run away at ten, never to return. When Emily read about that in his prison file she'd suggested a literacy course. He laughed, telling her he'd learned so much more on the streets than he ever could in a stupid classroom.

She read the note: *I wil lern too controal meself miss. I'll stop hurtin wimon if you give uz 1 last chanse. Carnt do that if you send me away can i?* He'd signed his name and added a kiss. Beneath the message there was a mark on the paper. Emily stared at it for a very long time. It was in the shape of a heart. A red heart.

And it was written in blood.

33

Kate Daniels gave Detective Sergeant Robson the TIE action on John Edward Thompson and a couple of DCs to help him with it. As he set to work, she received a phone call she'd been waiting for. Local historian Chris Ridley had been as good as his word. What he had to say sent a ripple of excitement through her.

'At least one set of pearls are still in existence,' he said. 'I spoke to a lady called Pauline Watson. She'll wait in for you to collect them.'

Kate scribbled the address down as he read it out. It wasn't far away, off Ashington High Street. The news made her heart sing. Another set of pearls meant a three-way comparison.

'Any idea how many sets of pearls were purchased in 1953?' she asked.

He'd done some checking and her luck was in. Only eighteen sets of pearls had been given out by Ashington Miners' Welfare, a surprising statistic in her opinion.

'Why so few?' she queried. 'There must've been scores of kids at those parties.'

'There were. But, as I suspected, most miners' daughters wanted a diamond tiara like Princess Elizabeth was wearing that day.'

'Thank heaven for little girls, eh?' the DCI said.

'It looks like you're *in business*,' Ridley said, quoting her words from the day before. 'I should warn you that there were actually twenty purchased. I couldn't say what happened to the others – probably thrown away after the event or taken home by welfare staff for their own kids to play with.'

A small discrepancy, but still: the odds were in her favour.

'Don't concern yourself, Mr Ridley. You've been a great help to us.'

He agreed to send a list of names and addresses. Thanking him, Kate put down the phone and waited for the email to drop into her inbox. *Bless him.* In the subject box, Ridley had entered TOP SECRET in large red type. Selecting the message, one of several dozen unopened emails, she clicked on the print icon and called Maxwell, asking him to retrieve it from the general office.

'Do a job on it right away. I want those miners and their descendants traced. I'm not arsed how long it takes, just make sure it's done. Drop everything else I've given you.'

His silence was like a groan.

Kate grinned. Intuitive was something this particular DC had never been. Consequently, he found himself lumbered with much of MIT's donkey work. 'I know it's a tedious job, Neil. But you're good at that when you put your mind to it. Every office needs a plodder. You happen to be mine. I'll devise a pro forma and let you have it later. Any complaints, spit 'em out now.'

He didn't need telling twice.

Maxwell was lucky to be in the squad at all, having come close to being sacked after pissing her off on a previous enquiry. *Water under the bridge now.* As far as she was concerned, it never happened. They understood each other perfectly. She knew he'd come good in the end. The promise of overtime seemed to satisfy him. As an added bonus, she excused him from the afternoon briefing and put down the phone.

Daniels kept the briefing short and to the point. It was more an update of the day's events, an impromptu meeting earlier having covered pretty much everything else. As the team disbanded, she caught Gormley's eye. 'Don't disappear, Hank. We need a word.'

He blushed. 'Am I in trouble?'

'No, you idiot! Why? Have you done something I should know about?'

'Always.' He made a face. 'What then?'

'This Ashington link. It's not a definite. At best, it's a maybe. But I'm going to follow it through because it's the only maybe we've got.'

'Sounds like a plan to me. What do you want me to do?'

'Later . . .' She looked at her watch. 'I'll call you in ten.'

A civilian indexer approached with a tray of coffees.

Daniels grabbed the sole mug of black, headed straight to her office and shut the door with the intention of devising a pro forma questionnaire for the outside team, one that would illicit the information she required.

Picking up a pen, she listed relevant questions: particulars of each child recipient of the pearls, parents, siblings and extended family too. With genealogy currently in vogue, Kate figured that some family trees might already be available to give her a starter for ten. If not, the Murder Investigation

Team would have to produce their own. Either way, the details would need to be verified from at least one other source.

Ten minutes later, as satisfied as she could be that she'd nailed the questionnaire, she rang Gormley telling him what she'd been up to, asking him to join her in her office to go over it in case she'd missed anything.

'You might want to speak to Jo first,' he suggested. 'I know she's not part of the squad any more, but I'm sure she'll give us the benefit of her advice. An offender profile would come in handy right now. Might even prompt other lines of enquiry.'

'Good idea . . . you want to chase that up?'

'Don't you?' he asked.

'I'm delegating.'

'Oh, it's like that, is it?' He sounded as if he was smiling.

'No, it's not like that!' She mimicked him. 'I'm busy, that's all. I've got Naylor to see, Abbey Hunt to chase up, Forensics and God knows—'

'OK, OK, I didn't ask for a list of reasons. One would've done.'

'Cheeky bugger! Get in here now!'

Within seconds, Hank was walking through her door trying to hide the grin on his face. Soon after, they were forming a plan of action. Without giving the game away to the Ashington miners or their families, Daniels wanted to establish whether any of the pearls were, or had been, still in existence within the last decade. She was particularly interested in finding out if any family had a direct link with Bamburgh, either now or in the past. More importantly, she wanted to know what had happened to the pearls.

'Want my opinion?' Gormley asked.

'Always.'

'I think you're pissing in the wind.'

'Thanks for the vote of confidence.'

'You know what kids are like,' he said. 'Some of those pearls will have been lost in the street the day they were received or thrown away the day after. They could've been lifted from the rubbish after the event by anyone. It's sixty years ago!'

'Doesn't mean we can ignore it as a line of enquiry.'

'OK. I think you're wasting your time, though.'

'I heard you first time.' Kate brushed a hair away from her face. 'That's why it's so important to get this right from the get-go. The outside team need to be asking a set of predetermined questions. We decide what those questions will be. Then we can log the information and hopefully avoid having to re-interview at a later date. That way, the target families have no opportunity to change their story or conceal things from us. You know as well as I do that first responses tend to be closer to the truth than those given after folks have time to think—'

'The element of surprise, Dr Watson.'

'It's vital we keep the upper hand, if that's what you mean.'

Hank leaned across her desk to the phone and picked up the receiver.

He held it out to her. 'You going to call Jo, or shall I?'

Kate narrowed her eyes. She was about to say something when the door opened and Brown walked in, a police-issue radio in his hand. 'Control room for you, boss. Pete Brooks just had a shout from uniformed inspector 7534. He spotted

John Edward Thompson in Morpeth. Suspect came out of a shop, spotted 7534 and did a runner. The intrepid inspector gave chase. It's still ongoing.'

Kate grabbed the radio.

She held up a thumb to Brown and he left the room as Brooks' voice hit her ear, repeating almost word for word what she'd just been told. The officer chasing Thompson was an ex DS looking to get back to the CID following his promotion out of the department. He was someone Daniels had a lot of time for. A fearless soul, he wouldn't think twice about taking off in hot pursuit of any suspect. He wouldn't wait for backup either. He'd just get stuck in. Brooks had once done the same thing and wished to God he hadn't.

The radio crackled . . .

'Thompson pursued west along Market Street, down to Old Gate and over the bridge,' Brooks said. 'If you want to get somebody there, he's running north on High Stanners now . . . I'll keep you updated.'

'Put a call out, Control. See if any squad member is anywhere near Morpeth.'

Moments later, Carmichael's voice came over the radio. 'That's affirmative. I'm travelling south down the A1, taking the A192 down Pottery Bank and Newgate Street. Awaiting further instructions, over.'

'Good girl,' Kate whispered under her breath.

'He's still running!' Brooks again. 'He's down by the river now, travelling north, 7534 in pursuit. Suspect quite a way in front – seems he's fit as a butcher's dog. Looks like he's heading for Borough Woods. Sorry, we've got no helicopter; it's down in Houghton-le-Spring. They'll shout if they get freed up. Your DC on Milford Road now, she might be able to head him off. I've lost contact with 7534. Stand by . . . I'll try and raise him.'

Gormley was off his seat, pacing, waiting for news.

Brooks' voice: '7534 from Control: what's your location?'

No response from 7534.

'Control to 7534. Repeat, what's your location, over?'

Nothing.

Shit! Daniels wondered what was going through Brooks' mind right now. About five years ago he'd been badly injured when an offender he was chasing turned, aimed a shotgun and blasted his lower legs at point-blank range. Although he could no longer work outside, he'd still wanted to be a copper. A job in the control room was marginally better than going off on a medical pension. He was good at it too. He knew the force area like the back of his hand. He also had excellent knowledge of officers on the ground. What's more, he cared what happened to them. He was – not to put too fine a point on it – the very best radio operator there was.

Even so, the SIO could feel his anxiety as he waited for an update.

Pressing the transmit button on her radio, she said: '7824 to 7534, please respond.'

Still nothing.

'*Anyone* got sight of 7534?' She was getting worried.

A couple of Panda drivers who'd joined the hunt both gave worrying negative feedback. 'Sorry, boss. No word from 7534. Nope, can't see him. Hang on . . . member of the public pointing towards the river. I'll get back to you, over.'

'Hopefully, he's slapping the cuffs on Thompson,' Kate said, muting the radio.

Hank nodded. 'Failing that, they're scrapping and he's lost his radio in the drink.'

Kate unmuted the radio: 'Keep me in touch, Control.'

'Will do.' The radio went quiet. When it sounded again a minute or two later, there was a note of triumph in Brooks' voice: 'Contact with 7534 re-established. He still has sight of him, boss. Suspect has turned left/left by the river. Now crossing Price Street. Could be planning to go via Mitford Road and Dogger Bank, or he might double back into Morpeth.'

'I'm on Mitford!' Carmichael yelled. 'Someone else can take Market and Bridge Streets.'

'We've got him.' Gormley sat down, a wide grin on his face. 'She'll be with them any second now.'

'Boss?' Brooks again. 'Boss . . . shit!'

'Fuck!' The cup rattled on Kate's desk as Gormley slammed his fist down. 'The silly bastard's lost him.'

'Yep, 7534 has lost him . . .' They could hear the disappointment in Brooks' voice. 'He's a bit . . . hang on . . . yeah, lost him Mitford Road/Dogger Bank area. We think he's gone towards the school . . .'

There was another short pause as Brooks asked for an update from officers on the ground. None were any the wiser.

'OK, everyone. Thanks for trying,' Daniels said, trying to conceal her frustration. 'Pete, give me details of his last position and direction of travel. Carmichael's in plain clothes in an unmarked car; she's probably our best chance of spotting him now. If he sees a uniform or a Panda he'll just leg it again.'

'Yep, last seen Pottery Bank Wood, travelling north . . . 7534 is on the line now. He knows Thompson well. Says he hangs out with an associate named Terence Watts in the Stobhill area. He's suggesting he may have been trying to run in the opposite direction to lay us off the scent. He'll find the address and let you have it, soon as the poor bugger gets his breath back.'

'OK, everybody, stand down. Keep your eyes peeled and report to Control the moment Thompson makes another appearance.'

The radio went dead. Kate looked at her thwarted DS. 'No sweat, Hank. We'll give him an early morning knock at his mate's house, pick him up there.'

Hank looked at his watch. 'Fancy getting out of here? I need some air.'

34

It wasn't difficult to achieve serenity under blue skies and brilliant sunshine on a long stretch of deserted beach. Emily had come here a lot with Robert. When he died, she stopped. There were too many ghosts. Too many plans for the future and promises made. Memories that reminded her of how much she'd lost.

Only when Rachel started lashing out at her had she returned, partly to get away from her daughter, mainly to clear her head and talk to her late husband in peace. Life went on here: birds flew, the sea pounded the shore and the view across open water changed constantly as light rose at daybreak and faded at dusk. Here she finally began to grieve . . . and, later, to recuperate.

Jo Soulsby was a few metres in front of her. She seemed preoccupied today for some reason, deep in her own thoughts as she moved along the water's edge, sturdy Hunter wellies on her feet. She stooped to pick up Nelson's ball and lobbed it into the surf. The Labrador raced off in pursuit, returning seconds later to drop the ball at her feet for round two.

Emily selected a smooth white pebble and popped it into the pocket of her Barbour jacket. She'd suggested the trip to the beach because she needed to distance herself from HMP

Northumberland, put things into perspective before they got out of hand.

She'd thought that sharing the details with Stamp would help. Turned out, that was a big mistake.

The moment he heard about Fearon's latest escapade he'd launched into a lengthy I-told-you-so lecture. She tried tuning him out, trying to focus on the smooth pebble in her fingers, but when stress-relief tactics failed to do the trick she rounded angrily on Stamp, telling him that she was well aware Fearon was a threat, one she couldn't afford to ignore. Nevertheless she wasn't about to let him intimidate her.

'At least put him on report,' Stamp pleaded.

'I can't do that.'

'You mean you won't.'

'OK, I won't. I encouraged him to write his feelings down and now he has. I can hardly go running to the Governor because I don't like the content. Besides, I'd rather know what's going on in that mind of his.'

Kent and another prison officer jogged by, heading in the opposite direction. They were both wearing iPods so no words were exchanged. But they acknowledged Emily with a nod as they ran by.

'Have you spoken to *him* yet?' Stamp asked. He was referring to Kent.

'Ash already asked me that,' Emily replied. 'He gave Kent a gentle nudge in my direction yesterday but he's been avoiding me like the plague all morning. The words bury, head and sand spring to mind.'

'Makes two of you then,' Stamp sniped.

Jo had overhead. She turned to join them, her glare

warning the psychiatrist to back off. 'Kent will have to see you eventually, Em. It's either that or take unpaid leave, I heard. I'm not sure what the circumstances were, but I gather he's had a lot of trauma in his life.'

'So I understand.' Emily looked at Stamp, hoping he'd bite. He didn't.

Turning back to Jo, she said, 'Martin knows all about it but doesn't think it's his business to tell tales out of school. It's obviously something quite personal. Apparently, Ash knows too. I made a half-hearted attempt to raise the matter earlier, but he didn't open up either.' Emily rolled her eyes. 'I didn't push it for fear I might jeopardize his relationship with Kent. To be honest, I'd rather get it from the man himself.'

Jo watched as Stamp carried on walking, obviously in a sulk. Whatever was going on between him and Emily, she didn't want to be part of it. It was childish and stupid and it was getting her down. She threw the ball along the beach, trying to keep the dog out of the water in the vain hope that he'd dry off by the time they returned to her car.

As he bounded ahead, two figures emerged from the dunes to her left – one male, one female. They walked towards the water's edge, then turned right, striding purposefully, heading straight towards her. Both suited and wearing sunglasses, they looked like an FBI detail or a clip from a Madness video – except there were no baggy trousers in sight.

But then . . .

Emily had seen them too. 'Isn't that . . . ?'

'Kate and Hank. Yes, I think so.'

I know so.

Jo swallowed hard.

This was going to be tricky.

There was nothing she could do to avoid the encounter. Kate had spotted her now, her step faltering as the realization dawned. Seconds later, they were face to face for the first time in a long while. Jo noticed Kate's hair was a touch shorter and a little lighter than when they'd last met. She looked tanned and healthy, as if she'd taken a winter holiday. Jo ventured a guess at whom she might have gone with.

Fiona-bloody-Fielding in all probability.

They kissed – a peck on each cheek – Kate's distinctive perfume affecting Jo in ways she hadn't thought possible any more. After a moment of awkwardness, Hank shook hands with Stamp and introduced himself before turning to Emily. He hadn't seen her since her bereavement. As he stepped forward to offer his condolences, her eyes filled with tears, one of which sat like a tiny balloon on her lower lid until gravity made it fall on to her cheek. Giving her a big bear hug, he held on until she'd regained enough composure to pull away.

Putting an arm around her shoulder, Jo told Hank it was good to see him. She meant it. She'd missed him. She'd missed them both.

'Likewise.' He smiled. 'We're heading for a jar after work. Fancy joining us?'

'Thanks,' Jo said. 'But Martin and I have a squash game arranged.'

'That's OK,' Stamp cut in. 'We can play anytime.'

Jo shot him a look. 'What, and deprive me of the chance to get my revenge?'

It was obvious to everyone that she was making excuses.

Hank glanced sideways, urging Kate to say something. She didn't flinch but must've felt the intensity of his stare burning a hole in her right cheek. He looked back at Jo. 'That's a damn shame, because we –' he waved a hand to indicate himself and the DCI – 'could use your help. Isn't that right, boss?'

'Don't worry about it.' Kate's smile nearly cracked her face. 'There are other profilers.'

'That's not what you said earlier!' Hank gave her a *what-are-you-like?* look.

There was an awkward pause. After a moment, Jo said she had the time now if Kate was up for it. Glancing at Nelson – approaching fast, ball in mouth and covered in sand – she advised Kate to keep moving or she'd need a change of clothes. Kate kissed Emily, said goodbye to Stamp and told Hank to bugger off and get some exercise. Clearly he'd pushed his luck.

35

They walked for a while, side by side. Jo was silent for the most part, Kate the opposite. She was overly chatty, anxious too, it seemed. She talked about Nelson, how big he'd grown, the atrocious weather, every damn thing, eventually asking after Emily and Rachel McCann.

Jo told her they were struggling, Emily in particular.

'Aren't we all?' Kate said.

'Not like Em is. She's on another planet at the moment.'

'She has a right to be, doesn't she?'

'It's not just Robert. Rachel's being a royal pain in the arse. That girl needs a reality check, if you ask me. Her father would have been furious at the way she's treating Emily.'

Looking up and down the beach, Jo took in a long deep breath of fresh air. Apart from Hank, Emily and Stamp, there wasn't another living soul to be seen in either direction. The surf was pounding the shore, great white waves rolling further and further inland before being absorbed into the sand. Both women loved this part of the Northumberland coast.

Picking up Nelson's ball, Jo lobbed it down the beach, watching as he raced after it. He was more like a whippet than a Labrador. 'Something bothering you, Kate?'

'I was about to ask you the same thing. You've got something on your mind, I can tell. Does it have anything to do with Martin what's-his-name?'

'That's very intuitive. How did you know?'

'He was cool towards you. Is there some history between him and Emily that I'm not aware of? He didn't seem to like it when Hank gave her a hug.'

'You spotted that?' Jo threw the ball again.

'I'm a detective. Is something going on between them?'

'In his dreams.'

'Oh? They seemed quite close to me.'

'They're not.' Jo turned towards her. 'Well, they are . . . Let's just say he wants to move their relationship on to another level.'

'Talk about crap timing!'

'You're telling me. Actually, that's not all. There's this weirdo in the prison giving her a whole load of grief. It's more than a crush, Kate. He's obsessed with her. Martin knows about it and he's taken it upon himself to play the hero. He's going about it the wrong way too, undermining her in the worst way possible.'

'So tell him.'

'I have!'

'Then do it properly next time. Has it occurred to you that Emily may need his help?'

Jo pulled a face. 'She doesn't know what she wants.'

'And you do, I suppose.'

'I think so, yes.' Jo paused and turned to face her former girlfriend. She looked a bit uncomfortable as she changed the subject. 'I *was* going to call you. Really I was.'

'So what stopped you? Battery ran out on your mobile?'

The profiler ignored the jibe.

'Personal or professional call?' Kate asked. 'I don't like to presume we're still mates.'

'Don't be like that. You know we are. We'll always—'

'Mates return calls, keep in touch.'

Now it was Jo's turn to blush. 'I thought you, me and Emily might go out and eat sometime when she feels up to it. Recapture a little of the old days. Have some fun. She needs her mates around her while she gets back on her feet. You remember how to have fun, don't you?'

It was a dig, one Kate didn't deserve. She was in the middle of a murder enquiry and didn't have time to socialize, friend or no friend. Jo knew that. She back-pedalled quickly, apologized for asking, melting away the tension between them. Kate promised to call her if she found a window of opportunity in her busy schedule . . .

'But only if you promise to pick up the phone,' she added. 'Where are you living now?'

'How did you know I'm not at home?'

Kate didn't answer.

'You staked out my place?'

'We don't stake out places in the UK. We keep obs on them. I might've called round once or twice. You should get a neighbour to pick up your mail more often and dump some stuff in your rubbish bin, close the curtains now and then. The house *looks* empty – it's a dead giveaway. Where did you say your place was?'

'I didn't . . .' Jo hung her head, avoiding eye contact. Her face was flushed when she looked up. 'I rented a cottage at Low Newton-by-the-Sea. I'm sorry.'

'Nice . . . I'd love to see it.'

'Thought you were too busy?'

'There are some things you make time for.'

To cover her embarrassment, Jo looked at her watch, her smile fading as she realized the time. 'Look, I've gotta go.' She didn't look happy about it.

Picking up Nelson's ball, she began to walk towards the car park.

Kate fell in step. 'You love the new job then?' She was being ironic.

'Is it that obvious?'

'To me it is. I told you it would be pants, but you wouldn't listen.'

'I should have,' Jo said. 'There's no point denying it. The research project doesn't quite fire my jets like the incident room used to. Bad call on my part. Stamp doesn't give a shit about the project either. He's too busy chasing Emily.'

'Want to come back?' Kate asked. 'To work with us, I mean. Position's still vacant.'

Jo gave a half-smile. 'Naylor already asked me that.'

'And what did you say?'

'I said I'd think about it.'

'And will you?'

'Depends.'

'On what?' Kate pulled up sharp, wanting an answer. It didn't come. 'Are we OK, you and I?'

Jo looked off into the distance. It was the six-million-dollar question she'd been asking herself for weeks. Could she go back? Could they? Should they? She didn't answer, just turned away and kept on walking.

36

They had hardly said goodbye when the text came in. Kate reached into her pocket. Instead of pulling out her phone, she pulled out her car keys. Handing them to Hank, she told him to go on ahead and wait for her in the car. As he set off along the narrow winding path through the dunes, she turned towards the advancing sea, her eyes dwelling on the dramatic scenery as she accessed the message she suspected was from Jo.

It was.

DID YOU WANT TO TALK ABOUT THE CASE OR NOT?

Kate smiled. *About the case. About them. About any bloody thing so long as they were talking and she had Jo's ear. She wasn't arsed what the topic was.*

Glancing along the strip of sand to her right, she caught sight of Jo about seventy-five metres away. She was making her way slowly off the beach, head bowed, her sole focus the phone in her hand.

Seconds later, she was gone.

On the fringes of the dunes, Kate sat down on a tuft of rough grass. She was about to respond to the message when a second text arrived in the light blue chat box beneath the first.

WHAT'S THE STATUS OF THE ENQUIRY?

Daniels keyed a quick reply: NOT ON THE PHONE. CAN YOU GET AWAY FROM THE PRISON FOR AN HR OR TWO THIS PM?

S'POSE.

I CAN MAKE AN OFFICIAL REQUEST IF THAT WD HELP.

NOT NECESSARY. ANY EXCUSE AND I'M GONE FROM THERE.

OK. ASK FOR ME @ FRONT DESK. I'LL COLLECT YOU.

I STILL HAVE A KEY.

NOT TO ALNWICK NICK YOU DON'T!

DOH! I FORGOT. WILL I BE SHOT FOR NOT HANDING IT IN?

Daniels grinned. I'VE ALREADY TOLD BRIGHT YOU'RE COMING BACK.

There was a short pause: GIVE ME AN HOUR.

Jo made it to Alnwick Police Station a few minutes earlier than expected and was escorted upstairs by someone who happened to be entering the station at the same time. She looked amazing in a figure-hugging navy suit; shirt unbuttoned a touch, high-heeled boots – a complete contrast to the dog-walking gear she'd been wearing at the beach.

She sat down beneath the windowsill.

Kate looked outside.

The sun had disappeared and it was beginning to cloud over. More heavy snow was forecast. By the looks of the sky it wouldn't take long to arrive. It meant a longer stay at the B & B for the whole team, a thought that didn't exactly fill her with joy. She was about to ask Jo a question when her office door opened and Hank walked in, a mug of tea in his hand.

They got straight down to business.

Jo agreed to work up a profile in an unofficial capacity and was briefed on the case. The more she knew, the better equipped she would be to make a judgement on the type of perpetrator they should be looking for. The only thing Kate omitted was the fact that she had a suspect in her sights.

In truth, there was no hard evidence against John Edward Thompson beyond the knowledge that he was local to the area and liked to dress his victims up. So what if he'd legged it when confronted by a police officer earlier in the day? That didn't mean he was a candidate for a double murder. They would have to wait until he was picked up to determine that.

'I requested a comparison on the kids play pearls,' she concluded. 'We may have got lucky with the provenance of—'

'So soon?' Jo was surprised.

'Rush job. Plastics expert just confirmed a positive match on all three sets.'

'Three sets?' Jo asked.

Kate explained about her own set of pearls. Her hope that they might be a match for those found on Nominal One – the unidentified child who'd been in the ground the longest – and those supplied by a local woman who claimed to have received hers on Coronation Day 1953.

'Their manufacture and composition is identical,' she said, before rewinding slightly. 'Given the killer's return to the crime scene, it goes without saying that the burial site is crucial. That much was obvious from the moment the second body was unearthed. We're assuming the offender might have lived or holidayed in Bamburgh at some time in the past.'

'Do you still have a beat bobby there?' Jo asked.

Kate shook her head. 'There used to be a police house in the village, but it's now in private hands. These days it's just a case of someone doing a drive-through to show the flag occasionally. Once upon a time we'd have gone to see the collator. By the time he'd had a fag and made himself a cuppa, he'd have recalled every last incident and told us, "I know what this is about . . ." And we'd have been in possession of stuff it would take us months to assemble nowadays.'

'But you have super-duper computer systems.'

'They're only as good as the person who inputs the information,' Hank told her. 'Good indexers are hard to come by.'

'He's right,' Kate said. 'If you use HOLMES in the way it was intended, following all its rules and conventions, then it's a fabulous tool. But free-text searches don't actually work very well. If the terms are too broad, you get too many responses. It's like Google: key in the wrong search criteria and you're screwed. I've raised an action to trace all officers who've been stationed in, or had responsibility for Bamburgh in the past. I'm hoping to jog a memory or two.'

'Retired officers too, I take it?' Jo said.

Hank nearly inhaled his tea. 'That'll not be hard. There'll only be three of them in the last half-century. Once they get in there, you need a shoe horn to get them out. Salty Sam was there for twenty-odd years that I know of!'

Jo chuckled. 'Who's Salty Sam?'

'Tell you over a pint sometime.' He paused. 'You miss having a laugh with us, doing something worthwhile, don't you?' He didn't look at Daniels and therefore had no idea that she'd tuned him out. 'We miss having you around, Jo. Well, personally I can take you or leave you. But Kate does. Don't you, boss?'

'The Coronation was a long time ago . . .' Kate was thinking out loud rather than addressing the others. 'Even if the offender was a kid in 1953, he'd have to be over fifty-eight years old by now, if my maths are correct. What do you reckon, Jo?'

Gormley sighed, exasperated with her insensitivity.

'What?' Kate realized she'd missed something.

Hank was already staring into space.

'Forget it,' Jo said. 'Wasn't important.'

'Will someone tell me?'

Jo carried on as if she hadn't heard her. 'I don't think you're looking for an elderly male.'

'What makes you say that?' Hank asked.

Now they were tuning Kate out.

'I think it'll be someone much younger,' Jo said. 'The offspring of a recipient of the pearls, or someone who'd been given them to play with, as Kate was.'

'But therein lies our problem,' Kate butted in. 'If we're looking for a descendant of a female recipient, wouldn't it be a woman? I mean, what man would want to hold on to a set of cheap plastic pearls? I'm not ruling out a female offender altogether, but I don't believe a woman was responsible, do you?'

Gormley gave an emphatic: 'No.'

'Me either,' Jo said. 'But I agree that after the crime scene those pearls are the most significant clue to follow. It can't be a coincidence that the victims were wearing similar jewellery. Logic would suggest it must mean something to the killer.'

'Yeah, but what?' Hank asked. 'Our crystal ball isn't working today.'

'Your guess is as good as mine,' Jo said. 'The more we talk

about this case, the more inclined I am to think it might involve an act of devotion.'

Hank's interest grew. 'Like a sacrifice, you mean?'

'God, I hope not,' Kate said. 'We've got enough to cope with.'

'Sacrifice is not a word I'd care to use,' Jo said.

'But you wouldn't rule it out?' Gormley pushed.

'Or in,' Jo countered. 'Not yet anyway.'

'What word *would* you use?' Words like *tribute* and *homage* barged into Kate's thoughts. 'Are you suggesting the crazy bastard is somehow marking his respect?'

'Nah,' Gormley screwed up his nose. 'People lay flowers to mark respect, not dead bodies!'

'Not if they're completely unbalanced,' Jo reminded him.

Running the scenario in her head, Kate picked up her pen and wrote: *MO searches: crimes involving any kind of devotion/ sacrifice.* She looked at Jo, still trying to come to terms with such an outlandish theory. 'You think these murders were triggered by the long-term effects of separation? A permanent one? A death?'

'Possibly.'

'Blimey, you two are fun to be with.' Hank looked at the SIO. 'How d'you make that leap?'

'I've been around Jo long enough to have picked up some tips.'

'Oh yeah?' He grinned. 'What tips would they be?'

'Shut up and concentrate, Hank! There's a clear parallel here. This is beginning to make sense to me. My pearls were kept for that very reason.' Registering Jo's confusion, she added, 'Long story – my father's twin sister died shortly after receiving them – I won't bore you with the details.'

'I didn't know Ed had a sister!'

'Neither did I, until yesterday. We already know that the death of a family member can be completely devastating, psychologically speaking. Remember Makepeace?' She was referring to a previous murder case where a man had taken revenge several years after the death of his only daughter. 'Would it make a difference if the bereaved person was very young at the time?'

'Why?' Jo asked.

'No reason.'

'Then why ask? Jo pressed her.

'It has no bearing on the case,' Kate sighed. 'Or maybe it does . . . My dad lost his twin sister when he was four years old. It's a wonder he remembers her at all. Instead of dealing with it, he buried it. I'm talking figuratively, not literally. You should've seen him when he was telling me about it. All these decades later, it's obvious that he still hasn't come to terms with it.'

'It's not uncommon,' Jo said. 'I'm not talking about your father in particular, but kids who lose significant family members can become completely detached, unable to form bonds like the rest of us. The human psyche is complex. Some people withdraw. In extreme cases – rare ones, thankfully – it can lead to the equivalent of mental meltdown. The majority internalize it—'

'And the minority?' Hank asked.

'A tiny percentage may say and do things the rest of us would find abhorrent. A killer's motivation isn't always fuelled by hate, Hank. Love is as powerful an emotion. In this context it's twisted love, but love all the same. For some, the trauma of losing a loved one is so strong they are driven to kill.'

'Like Nilsen, the Muswell Hill Murderer,' Hank offered. 'Weren't his crimes sparked by loss?'

'It's true Nilsen claimed his grandfather's death sowed the seeds of his psychopathy, but he was a necrophiliac, murdering his victims to feed – no pun intended – his fascination with corpses. I don't buy his explanation for killing those young men—'

'I agree,' Kate said. 'He was a sexual predator offloading his guilt.'

'I take it there was no sexual element in this case?' Jo queried. 'You never mentioned—'

'We can't tell,' Kate said. The room descended into silence for a while. Then she spoke again. 'Maybe we *are* looking for someone exactly like my old man, an adult who was a child when they lost a female family member, someone who later inherited her stuff. Think about it: the demographic of Bamburgh is white, middle class, wealthy . . . elderly. Stop me if this seems too much of a long shot.'

'No, I think you're on the right track,' Jo said. 'As far as I'm concerned it's highly plausible. A female recipient dies and the pearls are a reminder of that person – a beloved mother or grandmother perhaps? You said yourself the victims were dressed in adult clothing.'

'We'd assumed that was done to put us off the scent. To conceal the fact that the victims were kids.' Kate's focus shifted to Jo. 'Maybe we were wrong! Maybe the killer dressed his victims up to look like an adult to replicate the person he'd lost. It's worth a trawl of parish records, a cross-reference to the names of miners our outside team comes up with.'

Her words hung in the air. The notion that Bamburgh Castle or Holy Island – two of the most revered places in Northumberland – could be some kind of macabre monument to murder stunning them into silence.

37

After her lunchtime stroll, Emily finally got her shit together and came to a decision. With a young man like Fearon under her supervision there was no room for ambiguity. Determined to confront him, once and for all, she made a beeline for Ash Walker's office and told him of her plan.

Reluctantly, the SO agreed to excuse the prisoner from work so she could call him up and deliver a stark ultimatum: Fearon must agree to an intense concentration on his offending behaviour before release or Emily would break off all contact. There was no point seeing him otherwise.

Emily felt better for having taken control. To her amazement, Fearon didn't argue. He listened intently to what she had to say, nodding in all the right places, offering his consent, trying his best to convince her he had the capacity to change.

But did he?

Emily stared at him pointedly. 'I'm serious, Walter. You need to address these issues if you're going to stay out of prison. Do we have an agreement or not?'

'Yes, miss.'

'For what it's worth, I think your choice is spot on. The alternative is to spend the rest of your days in places like these. That's not what either of us wants, is it?'

Fearon shook his head. 'I just don't like—'

'What? What don't you like?'

'Talking about that sort of stuff, miss. Not with you.'

Emily eyeballed him. 'It's never stopped you before.'

'Are fantasies the same as dreams, miss?'

Already, the facade was gone.

He was laughing at her.

'Stop wasting my time! You know full well what fantasies are. You wrote about them in your little note, didn't you?'

Fearon bowed his head and then raised it again. In that split second, he'd morphed from a manipulative and slightly edgy character to a young man on the edge of insanity. It was as if someone had flicked a switch. Emily had witnessed such behaviour changes in other inmates but never in him. She was beginning to wonder if he was borderline schizophrenic – an unsettling thought.

'It happened again last night, miss.'

He seemed to be looking through her, not at her.

'What did? This is no laughing matter, Walter. If you're not going to take this interview seriously, you can get back to your—'

'I took her away this time . . .' His eyes were like ice as they fell on the belt round her waist, on the keychain hanging from it. 'When she wouldn't have sex with me, I strangled her with a thick silver chain.'

Emily felt sick as the words spilled from his mouth. On and on he went, deeper and deeper into a world that existed only in his imagination. A world of sexual deviancy that was both sickening and menacing. The psychologist listened hard. The filth he was spouting didn't fit his profile. He was talking about a young girl now, not an older woman. Nothing he said bore any relation to his previous crimes. At least, none she could identify. Until . . .

The truth hit her like a brick.

He was talking about Rachel.

How she managed to get him out of her office, Emily wasn't sure. Next thing she knew, she was tearing down the main corridor, retching as she ran, ignoring the curious glances of inmates mopping the floor. Trembling violently, she reached the wing gate, her hands fumbling with her key pouch in her panic to get out of there. Sweat ran down her face and stung her eyes as she groped for the bars, trying to stay upright.

Faintly aware of footsteps getting closer, Emily looked over her shoulder convinced that Fearon would be standing there laughing at her. The prison chaplain smiled. Patiently, he stood aside, waiting for her to unlock the gate. When she didn't, he stepped forward and did it for her. It was then he noticed her keys dangling from the belt around her waist, her fists clinging on to the bars as if her life depended on it.

'Emily?' he said. 'Are you unwell? Do you need help?'

She ignored him and pushed through the gate, hearing him call after her as she raced down the corridor. She had to catch Stamp before he finished for the day. *She just had to.* He had a meeting planned in Newcastle at three o'clock. Her heart was pounding as she ran as fast as she could across the open ground, her legs heavy and uncooperative, as if she was running through mud. It seemed like another world on A-wing, adding to her confusion as she tried to find Stamp.

An officer pointed her in the right direction.

Finally she came to a halt, staring at a door marked: *Interview in Progress.*

Emily took a deep breath and turned the handle. A monster of a youth hauled himself off his chair as she entered the room. Pulling out the now vacant chair, he politely offered it to her. Frozen to the spot, she just stood there, waiting for Stamp to get rid of him. The psychiatrist made an excuse and quickly ushered his interviewee from the room.

Emily sat down.

She was too numb to cry.

For a moment she said nothing. Then her words came tumbling out in an avalanche of expletives, interspersed with sobs. Stamp listened intently to what Walter Fearon had said to her and didn't interrupt. He let her finish and then calmly gave his take on things. It wasn't remotely what she expected, let alone wanted to hear.

Why wouldn't he listen?

Wasn't she making sense?

She tried again – but still he didn't get it.

'Oh, how many more times?' Emily was yelling but she didn't care. She stood up and began pacing the room, wringing her hands as her frustration boiled over. Stamp was her friend. Her only support since . . . *Christ, why wasn't he listening to her?* 'It wasn't mind games, Martin! He described Rachel to a T – he even described our home.'

'Emily, please sit down. You're not thinking rationally.'

'Oh that's rich, coming from someone who not ten minutes ago was warning me to watch my back. You were right, OK? Fearon *is* a viable threat. I should've listened to you—'

'No! Can't you see he's winding you up?'

'He's done that all right.' She sat down and then stood up again, palming her brow. 'I wanted to punch the little shit.'

'He's enjoying himself—'

'And I'm playing into his hands, is that it?'

'You answered your own question, Em.'

'I suppose you think it's totally illogical.'

'I do. You're so careful to keep your private life private. There are no pictures of Rachel in your office. How could he possibly know?'

'I don't know how! But he does!'

Joining her near the window, Stamp gave her a hug. She didn't resist. It felt good to lean against his chest, to feel strong arms around her, a hand gently stroking her hair. He led her back to the chair, left her for a moment and returned with a tumbler of water and tissues. He wiped away her tears, then sat down beside her and held her hand.

'Do you trust me, Emily?'

She sniffed. 'What's that supposed to mean?'

'Do you?'

'Of course I do.'

'Good . . .' Reaching into his pocket, he took out his mobile phone, dialled a number and waited for the ringing tone. Handing her the phone, he smiled. There was only way to allay her fears.

38

Rachel McCann wiped her hands and took the pan off the stove. Switching off the radio, she picked up the phone and answered with a cheery hello. No one spoke but she could hear background noise, doors banging in the distance.

The prison.

Crossing one foot over the other, she leaned against the kitchen bench and looked out through the open window. The sun was shining. The snow on the lawn had almost disappeared, but on the driveway it had compacted under the weight of her father's four-by-four. It was like an ice rink out there.

Rachel sighed.

The line was still open but her mother was obviously not yet free to speak. It was hopeless trying to have a sensible conversation while she was at work. Invariably they would be interrupted by a prisoner, an officer, a more important call. Even her poor dad had taken a backseat where her mother's job was concerned, though she'd probably never admit it – certainly not now.

'Mum? Is that you?' Placing the phone in the crick of her neck, Rachel turned away from the window to stir the contents of the pan. A man's voice reached her ear. Muffled.

Urgent. Whispering? Pound to a penny it was Martin Stamp. 'Come on, Mum! I haven't got all day!'

She was about to hang up when her mum spoke. 'I'm here, Rachel. Sorry, love—'

'Why should *you* be sorry? You weren't the one who flew off on one last night.'

'Forget it, darling. I have.'

Rachel felt guilty then. She had her mother's looks but her father's fiery temperament – and boy had she let rip. All because Emily had pointed out the dangers of binge drinking when she'd come home late, having consumed her body-weight in alcohol: double vodkas to drown her sorrows, ginger ale to take the taste away.

Vic was buying. What did she care?

'You OK, Mum? You sound a bit down.'

Rachel knew whose fault *that* was. Not only had she lied to her mother about where she'd been last night, more especially who with, she'd woken with a stinking hangover and hadn't managed to rouse herself in time to see her off to work. Consequently, they hadn't made up. Rachel resolved to put that right the minute she got home.

'You're pissed off with me, aren't you?' Rachel said.

'What? No! Makes you say that?'

Rachel smiled. Her mother always asked a question when faced with one she couldn't or didn't wish to answer. 'You are still angry, I can tell.'

'I'm not, I just thought I'd check in while I'm free.'

'Hardly free, locked up in there all day.'

Emily laughed. 'It's my job!'

Her attempt at humour was forced . . .

Something was up.

Rachel didn't pry.

'Just how much alcohol *did* you drink last night?' Emily's tone was jokey.

'Not that much,' Rachel lied. When her mother asked how she was feeling today, she said she was fine. That was a lie too. She was definitely not fine. Her head felt like someone was banging a drum in there. And that wasn't all. Someone – she didn't know who – was creeping around outside. She'd just seen their shadow cross the interior wall. As her mother made out that all was well, Rachel did the same, glancing along the hallway and laughing under her breath at her own paranoia.

Burglars didn't usually knock.

Rachel hadn't heard, nor could she see his familiar red van. But, in all probability, it was the postie. In this remote part of Northumberland it wasn't unusual for him to deliver mail this late in the day after a period of bad weather.

Besides, he knew the doorbell was iffy.

Her mother's voice again. 'Have you been out today?'

'No, I didn't feel like it. Not *today*. I'm making a cake for Dad's birthday.'

'That's nice . . .'

'You don't mind . . . if we still celebrate, I mean?'

'Course not, silly!'

Another tap on the door . . .

'Gotta go, Mum.'

'Rachel . . .'

'Yes?'

'I won't be late tonight, love. I need to pick up some stuff in the village on my way through and then we can do the river walk before it gets dark, if you feel up to it. Do us both good. Sound like a plan?'

'You mean it?'

A lump formed in Rachel's throat. They hadn't done that since her father died. Emily had spent so much time down there with him, sitting with him, watching him fish, she hadn't been able to face it.

The doorbell drowned out her mother's response.

'Ta, Mum. See ya later!'

'Who's at the door?'

Too late: the phone went down.

Emily was left hanging, a monotonous dialling tone summing up just how she was feeling. She sighed. Whoever it was, Rachel obviously hadn't been concerned. She'd have heard it in her voice if that had been the case. Returning the mobile to Stamp, she thanked him.

'For what?' he asked.

'For listening.' Emily looked away.

She was deeply embarrassed for having panicked over Fearon. Grateful that Stamp hadn't said or done anything to make her feel worse. There were no told-you-so lectures. No digs. No attempt to persuade her to take more time off. Emily suspected that was down to Jo Soulsby's intervention. She didn't need either of them to tell her she'd returned to work too early. That much had been obvious since day one.

There . . . she'd finally admitted she was struggling.

When she turned to face him, Stamp was fastening the top button of his shirt. He winked at her, straightened his tie and stood up. Slipping his jacket off the back of his chair, he put it on in readiness to leave. Bending over the table, he scooped up his papers, stuffed the lot into a worn leather briefcase and picked up his car keys.

'Sorry, Em. I've got to run. I'm late as it is.'

Emily glanced at her watch. *Two twenty-five.* 'Shit! I'm late too!'

'Aren't you leaving early?'

'Yes, but I've got a training course to run first!' Emily caught his arm as he made for the door. 'You will drive carefully, Martin?'

Stamp dropped his head and kissed her on the nose.

39

Leaving Hank Gormley in her office, Kate walked Jo to her car. She watched as the profiler opened the tailgate of her Land Rover Discovery, leaned in and attached a choker chain around her dog's neck. Nelson leapt out on to the pavement, straining on the leash to reach a bit of rough ground at the side of the station.

Jo led him towards it to have a quick pee.

Kate followed them. 'You going straight back?'

'No . . .' Jo pulled the dog away from a half-eaten burger someone had tossed under a bush. 'I'm supposed to be in town at a meeting. Only I'm here with you instead.'

'Thank you. Hope it hasn't put you out.'

'No. It was my pleasure . . .' Jo was smiling. 'I'm seeing Martin later for a bite to eat. He can fill me in on what I missed. Thought I'd pop home first and pick up my mail. A close friend warned me my security is pants.'

'Shame, I was half hoping I'd get an invite to that cottage of yours.'

Jo yanked the dog's chain. 'Didn't think you'd be interested.'

'I love Low Newton-by-the-Sea!'

'That's not what I meant and you know it.'

There was an intense moment of sadness as they stood on

the grass facing one another, not knowing what to say. A passing police car tooted its horn. Kate didn't see who the driver was but waved anyway. When she turned back, Jo was staring at her with those pale blue eyes, her hair hanging loose around her shoulders, her expression serious. She broke the silence. But what she said wasn't what the detective wanted to hear . . .

'It wouldn't work second time round, Kate. Let's face it, it would never be the same.'

'How will we know if we don't try?'

'I do know,' Jo said. 'Anyhow, you've moved on.'

'Says who?'

'I seem to recall a certain artist.'

It was like a slap in the face. During the last case they had worked together, the two of them had argued – just as they were doing now. Thinking there was no hope of ever getting back with Jo, Kate had spent the night with Fiona Fielding, only to discover a voice message from Jo next morning asking her to give their relationship another go. Later, when Kate got home, a handwritten note had been pushed through her door.

I guess I have my answer was all it said.

Bad timing didn't quite cover it.

'That was your fault,' Kate said.

'It always is . . .' Jo bent down to remove Nelson's choker. When she stood up, her hair was a mess, as if she'd just rolled out of bed. '*I* wasn't the one ripping her clothes off, was I? Let me see . . . no, I think I'd have remembered. And I wasn't the one making mad, passionate love to her either. Stop me if I'm getting warm.'

'It wasn't like that.'

'Wasn't it?' Jo gave a wry smile.

'I'm not denying I slept with her,' Kate corrected herself. 'But I didn't make love to her. Not in the way you mean. It wasn't like that.'

'You're telling me it was a quick shag?' Jo countered, a smirk crossing her face. 'Sure it was: so quick it lasted the whole night.'

Kate felt ridiculous standing in the street talking about something as personal as a night she'd spent with an artist she barely knew. She wanted to reach out to Jo, reassure her that it was a one-off. Tell her that sex with Fiona was good but it wasn't great. Not like it was between the two of them. But that would have been a lie. Fiona was bloody amazing in bed, a woman with an insatiable appetite for all things carnal. There was so much Kate wanted to say, but what was the point? Jo had made her mind up and she was powerless to change it.

Since their separation, their feelings for one another had become complicated. It was as if they could only function with other people around them. The minute they were on their own, the barriers went up.

They were two grown-ups acting like children.

But if they were arguing it meant they still cared.

40

Jo got in her car and drove off without another word. With no arrangement to meet again, Kate returned to the office in a foul mood. Hank was still there, helping himself to her coffee. He made her one too and then sat down, taking an open bag of cheese and onion crisps from his pocket.

'Low fat . . .' He grimaced. 'They taste rank.'

'So bin them,' she said.

'No need, I added salt. They're better now. Want one?'

Kate laughed even though she felt like crying.

He was too busy with his snack to notice her eyes filling up. Recovering quickly, she did her usual and immersed herself in work. On this occasion, it was a long list of items she wanted to tackle at the evening briefing. By mid-afternoon, they were ready for a break. Yawning, Hank leaned back in his chair and stretched his arms above his head, grinning as if he'd won the force lottery.

She asked what was so amusing. Her own sense of humour had gone walkabout. He said something facetious about all being well now that the Dream Team was back in action, which she didn't find in the least bit amusing or comforting. Getting up, she drew down the window blind, a message to outsiders that they were not to be disturbed.

Gormley made a face. 'Am I in for a bollocking?'

'In a manner of speaking.' She didn't attempt to mask her anger as she sat down. He was treading on very thin ice interfering in her private life and she told him so. He'd stage-managed a meeting with Jo in the name of work. That wasn't on. 'I didn't raise the issue on the way home from the beach, but it's time I did. So keep it buttoned, eh? If I want your input, I'll ask for it.'

'What's up with you?' He made a meal of looking over his shoulder. 'There's no one else here, Kate—'

'Your point being?'

'My point being, there's no need to go off on one. A blind man on a galloping horse could see you missed having her around.'

'So you took it upon yourself to arrange a meet?'

'How the hell did I know she'd be on the . . . beach.'

Kate rolled her eyes. *What-do-you-take-me-for?*

Gormley knew he'd been rumbled. 'She told you, didn't she?'

'About you meeting her in Alnwick yesterday? Yes, she told me.'

'Now that *was* pure chance, I swear.'

'I don't doubt that for a second.'

'So what's the problem? It's what you wanted, right? Seeing her again, I mean.'

'Since when do you know what I want?'

'Oops! Sorry, my mistake. I thought I did.'

Kate glared at him stony-faced. It was ridiculous arguing with him when he was acting in her best interests. She should be thanking him, not berating him, allowing her pride to get in the way. If she carried on like this, she'd have no one to confide in. She should apologize at once.

'Knock you back, did she?' Hank said before she could open her mouth.

'Excuse me?' Now he really *was* taking the piss. 'You're hardly in a position to play Cupid, are you? Maybe you should get your own house in order before organizing mine.'

He just looked at her. Inscrutable. 'Y'know what? You can be an arsy cow sometimes. But you're dead right. Aren't you always? I've made a complete bollocks of home life. Julie and I are about as far apart as we ever were. Ryan hates my guts. Even the neighbours can't stand the sight of me. That's why I thought I'd spread a little sunshine your way. But hey!' He held up his hands. 'I'll stay out of your business in future, no need to ask twice.'

Kate swallowed her guilt.

She could see she'd hurt him. She ought not to have dragged his marital problems into their silly spat but she was too prickly to apologize. He thought he was helping. She thought he'd gone too far. End of. It was as well *their* relationship was strong enough to survive a difference of opinion. He was her number one fan; her professional partner as opposed to her personal one. He'd forgive and forget before the day was out. She couldn't believe they were having a go at each other. Still, she wished she could take back what she'd said.

Jo would laugh if she knew they were fighting over her.

Sending him off to brief the team, Kate left the station without telling him where she was going, something she never ever did. She needed some time alone – time to get her focus off Jo Soulsby and on to the job. Time to cool down. The best way to achieve that was a visit to the morgue.

41

Dark clouds threatened to dump their load across Northumberland as Emily left the prison with an errand to run. It was something she should've done long ago; something far more important than some arsehole rookie officer showing off to his mates during her training course.

Two young officers had really got up her nose. They were being charged with the containment of some of the most serious sex offenders and yet they were behaving like adolescent schoolboys. The victims of those sex offenders deserved better. Angered at the suggestion that women were a bunch of cock-teasers who deserved what they got, Emily had displayed photographs of beaten and murdered women, real crime scenes where the victims had been horribly disfigured.

That made them pay attention.

As her presentation came to an end, her mind drifted to one sex offender in particular, more especially his threat to commit murder. A horrible thought kept gnawing away at her subconscious – one she could hardly bear to contemplate. It was Fearon's preoccupation with *her* that had put her daughter's life at risk.

Rachel was safe now, but for how long?

Today's events had put things into perspective. From this moment on, her daughter was her one and only priority.

Handing in her keys at the gatehouse, Emily felt drained and exhausted as she accepted her tag in return. Her head ached after the seminar, the first in a series of six in-depth discussions she was scheduled to carry out over the coming weeks. Hopefully it would do some good, challenge idiotic notions like the ones she'd come up against this afternoon. That sort of thing couldn't be overlooked, let alone tolerated, in or out of the prison environment.

Checking underneath Robert's rusty old Defender before she got in – force of habit drilled into her by security staff – Emily put on her seatbelt and turned over the engine. The vehicle sounded like a tractor but she couldn't bring herself to part with it. She put it in gear and moved off, desperate to catch the hardware store in Felton before it shut up shop for the day.

Fifteen minutes later, she pulled up outside. A sign on the door said CLOSED but a light from the window offered a glimmer of hope. She tried the handle.

No joy.

She peered through the glass in the door. The shop was a veritable Aladdin's cave, crammed with all kinds of gadgets: pots, pans, brooms, items and equipment for every conceivable use. The owner was hunched over his counter, balancing the day's takings by the looks of it. A poster behind him screamed: **HOLLER IF THERE'S SOMETHING YOU NEED THAT I DON'T SELL!** That was the type of shopkeeper Reg Hendry was, why he'd survived where others had failed, why he was still in business in a village this small. But he was as deaf as a stone and hadn't heard her knock.

Emily knocked again, harder this time.

The old man looked up, walked round the counter to unbolt the door, a bell tinkling as he pulled it open. He couldn't afford to turn good customers away even though he'd been open since eight o'clock that morning. He stepped aside to let her pass, following her gaze as she scanned the untidy shelves, so many items it was hard to distinguish one thing from the other.

'Something pacific you were after?'

She tried not to laugh. Reg was a master of the malapropism.

'I need some locks,' she said. 'Bolts too, if you have any.'

'Window or door?'

'Both. I was hoping you could advise me.'

'Expecting a break-in are you?' The old man had hit a nerve. He noticed Emily's concern but pretended he hadn't. 'Best if I fit them, eh? No extra charge.'

'Would you? That would be really kind.'

'I'll nip out tomorrow. Afternoon OK with you?'

Emily nodded. 'I'll pop home from the prison and make you a cuppa. Hang on! Isn't tomorrow your half-day?'

'Every day's a half-day at my age, flower.' He dropped his voice to a conspiratorial whisper. 'I never could refuse the ladies, but don't tell the wife.'

42

After a brief visit to the morgue, Kate got in her car and drove around for a while, needing time to think, time to calm down after her spat with her favourite DS. Time to call Jo. She'd already tried her twice. She was about to try again when her mobile rang.

Hank.

'You speaking to me yet?' he asked.

She smiled. 'No.'

'That's what I thought.'

Robson interrupted at the other end. It sounded urgent. Hank asked her to hold on. He didn't bother covering the speaker and she heard every word that passed between them. Pete Brooks from the control room wanted to speak to her urgently but her phone was engaged and he couldn't get through. Something about her suspect, John Edward Thompson, a.k.a. JET – due to his initials, she assumed, and not because he could run like a bastard when cornered by the police.

'Boss?' Hank was back.

'I heard,' she said. 'Hanging up now.'

Maybe, just maybe, this could be the break she'd been waiting for.

*

Pulling on to the drive of her isolated cottage, Emily couldn't fail to notice the open garage door. It was an engineering enthusiast's garage, full of assorted tools and motoring memorabilia, including a bookshelf crammed with Robert's old car manuals. Not one but two of his treasured motorcycles stood side by side, both of them polished to perfection.

Rachel was nowhere in sight.

Emily's eyes fell on her front door. The wonky knocker. The peeling paint her late husband had said he'd fix but never got round to. It was the threshold over which he'd lifted her on their wedding day – the best day of her life – the door to their future life together. That door now stood slightly ajar . . . a sight that scared her witless.

Frozen to the Defender's seat, she was unable to summon up the courage to move. Unable to do anything except listen to Fearon's threat running through her thoughts. She'd lost her husband. She couldn't lose Rachel.

Get a grip, she told herself.

He's in a cell.

In a prison.

Under lock and key.

But still . . .

Her eyes slid over the kitchen window where Rachel would've been standing when they spoke an hour and a half ago. There were no lights on inside. *Unusual.* Flanked on either side with a copse of trees, the north-facing cottage required illumination, even during the daytime, even in summer. There was no movement anywhere. With her heart in her mouth, Emily dialled Kate Daniels' number.

*

The DCI picked up. Pete Brooks came on the line. 'Got something for you, boss. Report just in from Bamburgh. Man resembling the description of your suspect, John Edward Thompson, on the beach, acting in a suspicious manner according to the caller.'

'Suspicious?'

'He's lighting candles, boss.'

'What makes you think it's him?'

'Witness claims he has a deep red patch on his face.'

Kate did an immediate U-turn and put her foot down on the accelerator. 'Have you sent anybody?'

'Yes, 3465 is on his way. Ten minutes before he can get there, mind.'

'Nobody nearer?' Kate had been driving around aimlessly and now she was forced to check road signs in order to get her bearings. According to what Brooks was telling her, no one else was closer. No CID. Not even a dog handler. She was on her own. 'No sweat,' she replied. 'Put a call out for any of my squad in the vicinity to meet me there. If I break the law, I'm about five minutes away.'

'Hank's on his way too,' Brooks said. 'ETA, more like twenty.'

'Tell him not to bother. He's miles away and I'm not waiting. Put me on talk-through with 3465 – Hank too if he insists on following me. No offence, but in his current mood he's not going to listen to you. I'll be coming in north of the castle, Pete. I'll head for the car park and walk south along the beach. Tell 3465 to make his way from the south end near Armstrong Cottages. I know I'm going to get there first. Who made the call?'

'Couple walking their dog.'

'Are they still on the line?'

'Negative. The guy was anxious to get his wife home.'

Shit! Daniels did a quick head check. The streets were almost deserted. It was after kicking-out time for schools. Fortunately for her, the weather was naff and doing its bit to keep pedestrians inside. The few folk that were around were in cars, not on foot. 'When did you receive the call?'

'Just before I called Hank.'

'Right, speak to them again. I want full details before I hit the beach.'

'You sound like a navy seal, boss.'

Kate laughed out loud as a million questions ran through her head. She rattled them off one after the other. 'What's our guy wearing, Pete?'

'Description the witness gave was sketchy: jeans, parka jacket, white trainers.'

'Where were they? Where was he, exactly?'

'They were on the beach walking their dog. He was kneeling on the ground just below your crime scene. He turned and looked at them, then pulled his hood up – she says trying to cover his face. That's what triggered the alarm.'

'Was the man alone?'

'Affirmative.'

Daniels' speedo was climbing, trees flashing by on either side of the road. 'And he was still there when they left the beach?'

'I believe so.'

'OK, keep me updated. Find out how many vehicles were there. Did they see anyone else? Did they see how he made his way there? Did they see him before he lit the candles or afterwards? I want the whole SP.'

She rang off.

Driving on, she knew she had a decision to make before she left the car. She had two choices: wait for backup or go it alone. In reality, there wasn't any call to be made. Back in her uniform days, when she'd faced the possibility of confronting a group of arseholes in a pub armed with glasses, knives or guns, that had been the time to start worrying. In her present situation it was just a matter of one suspect on a beach and a colleague only minutes away.

Piece of cake.

She knew Thompson's record inside out. The offences he'd committed – what she believed he might have done – the kind of person he was. A soft shit in all probability. Offenders against children invariably were. He was evil if he'd killed those girls, but Kate couldn't allow herself to think that he might kill her too. If she lost her bottle every time she faced danger, she might as well hand in her warrant card now. Assuming Thompson was involved, the way she saw it, he could run but he couldn't fight. She could fight *and* she could run.

She had the upper hand.

The phone rang.

'Control here, boss. I've spoken to the witnesses. They're pretty shaken up. They reckon the man they saw seemed anxious. They don't know if he had a car. They didn't speak to him, just buggered off. They don't remember any vehicles in the car park or recall seeing anyone else. And you were right by the way: Hank wouldn't listen. He's on his way.'

Of course he bloody is.

'I'm two minutes away. Coming off Church Street . . . now heading for the car park at the end of The Wynding . . . hold on . . .' Her eyes scanned left and right as she drove into the car park. 'No vehicles in the north car park. Uniform 3465, I want you at the south car park, near the castle. Keep your eyes peeled for vehicles.'

'3465: message received.'

The DCI rang off.

Party time.

Emily hung up. She couldn't wait any longer for Kate to get off the phone. Opening the Defender's door she climbed down, her feet sliding on the icy incline as she walked toward her cottage. She listened. No sound beyond that of the countryside. The security light came on as she neared the doorway.

Twenty feet.

Deep breath.

Ten.

There was mud on the step but no sound from within.

Unheard of.

When Rachel was home, music usually filled the house.

Reaching up, Emily eased open the door trying not to make a sound. Her heart was banging in her chest. She didn't know what she expected to find. She didn't dare think about it. Her sensible self was telling her to stop all this nonsense. But the mother in her couldn't push away the image of Fearon in her office, nor wipe away his ugly words.

Then she saw them . . .

Muddy footprints. Too large to be her daughter's.

The sight made her gasp.

In the hallway now, she was able to see into the living room. Everything appeared normal. Except . . . one of the photographs of Robert had been turned so it was facing the wrong way. Other than that: nothing untoward. But as she crept into the room, her hand flew to her mouth as saw the broken vase on the floor, its scattered flowers wilting in the heat in the room.

A smear on the floor caught her eye.

Blood.

Kate raced from the car. As she ran down on to the beach, two scenarios played out in her head. Thompson could either run or stand his ground. What action would she take if he stood there? Would she kick him in the balls or keep her nerve, excuse herself politely and ask what he was doing there?

Riding a motorbike had taught her a lot. She'd learned to prioritize every second of every mile of every journey. At each hazard, she had a call to make. Depending what action she took, it could hurt, it could hurt a lot, or it could kill her.

Coppers made those calls all the time.

On a scale of one to ten, the fear factor she was facing was probably a five. It wasn't a six. She had no idea if a weapon might have been used to kill the girls buried on the beach. If she had, that might have nudged it up the scale to a six or even a seven. But based on the knowledge she had – and Jo's theory that the killings might have been a twisted act of devotion – it was a definite five. In any case, she couldn't hang around to ponder what ifs.

By the time she reached the beach she was breathless, the

phone in her pocket now connected to Hank's, her earpiece in. Though she wasn't particularly dressed for it, she began jogging on the spot. Glancing to her right, directly below her crime scene, she saw a figure crouched down, a hood obscuring his face.

At this distance she couldn't tell if it was Thompson.

'I can see him, Hank. About a hundred metres away.'

She did a few stretches, never taking her eye off her target. Then began to jog up the beach towards him.

Seventy metres . . .

Sixty . . .

Fifty . . .

Transfixed by the sight of blood on the floor, Emily hadn't heard the front door close quietly behind her. It was more a sense of a presence that made her swing round. Rachel was standing at the front door in work clothes, a pair of her father's wellington boots over mud-caked jeans, her face red with exertion, hair tumbling down, a badly applied plaster on her thumb.

'I'm sorry about that, Mum . . .' She was looking at the mess on the floor. 'There was no super-glue in the garage. I was trying to find some in the shed, but the top was glued on and I couldn't get it off.' She stared at Emily, a worried look on her face. 'What's wrong? You look awful.'

Emily's smile felt forced as she tried to cover her distress. For the second time in a matter of hours she felt very silly, standing there listening to her own heartbeat. Thank God she hadn't been able to get hold of Kate Daniels.

*

Thirty metres, twenty, ten, and still the target hadn't moved. But then . . . Kate stopped suddenly as the man hauled himself off his knees and glanced in her direction.

'It isn't Thompson,' she said. 'Control, I repeat: it is *not* John Edward Thompson. Officers attending the scene near Bamburgh Castle don't break your neck. It is not Thompson.'

'Shit!' Hank swore under his breath. He sounded both disappointed and relieved. 'Boss, that doesn't mean he's not the arsehole we're looking—'

Kate hung up.

The man looked at her oddly as she walked up to him. She was tall but he towered over her. Close up, she was able to properly see the whites of his eyes, the fresh grazing to his forehead and cheek, healed over with a dark-red scab.

She'd made the right call.

'May I ask what you're doing here, sir?'

'I'm just paying my respects to the lasses they found.'

She wanted to tell him to pick up his ring of pathetic candles and sod off. Outpourings of grief by complete strangers made her blood boil. What the fuck was he waiting for, a television crew?

If her guts were anything to go by, the whole damn thing was a total waste of time. But the witnesses who rang the control room had clearly been spooked by his behaviour. As soon as they told their friends and neighbours, fear would spread. She'd have to eliminate the idiot from her enquiry now, whether she liked it or not. He'd have to answer a number of questions, give samples and, if possible, account for his movements at the time her victims were buried.

Although at the moment that was yet to be determined and, according to Abbey Hunt, it might never be.

'You have knowledge of what happened here, sir?'

'No, of course not!'

'You sure about that?'

'Yes! What's it to you anyhow?'

'Can I have your details please?'

'No, you can't. What d'you want them for anyway? Who the hell are you?'

'I'm the one asking the questions, sir.' The DCI held up ID. 'This area is the scene of a serious offence. We're anxious to trace people who have knowledge of what happened here. You're telling me you don't, and that may well be the case. But you must realize that I now need to satisfy myself of that.' She pointed at the candles. 'That kind of thing really isn't helpful. People think it's suspicious and ring the police. Then someone like me has to turf up here and speak to the likes of you. See what I'm getting at?'

The man blushed.

He was a dead ringer for Thompson: height, build and stature, but no birthmark. Pete Brooks had heard about his suspicious behaviour, taken down a description, put two and two together and made five. It happened. No one's fault. It could so easily have gone the other way.

Kate took a pen from her pocket. 'Now, I'd like your full details if you don't mind.'

'And if I do mind?'

'I'd take the easy route if I were you.'

The man scowled, gave his name, age and date of birth, his address and occupation.

'Do you have any identification on you? Bus pass, driving licence?'

'I ride, I don't drive. That's how I got this.' He pointed at his head. 'Some tosser in a lorry decided to cut me up a week past Wednesday. Thanks to him, I'm on the Pat and Mick.'

The DCI wasn't interested in his sob story. 'Anything else that'll confirm your identity?'

The man patted the back pocket of his jeans. He handed over a crumpled gas bill, telling her that if she cared to walk him home there was plenty of stuff to verify that he was who he said he was.

Pulling out her phone, Kate rang the control room. When Brooks came on the line, she reeled off the man's details: 'Sydney Curtis, 2 Cottage Row, Bamburgh. Age and date of birth as follows . . . Do a check on him will you, see if he's known?'

'I'm not!' Curtis said.

'Shut it!' Kate warned.

Brooks was back. 'Nothing known or recorded, boss.'

The DCI took in Curtis' smirk. 'No NFAs or matters pending?' she asked.

'Correct,' Brooks said. 'Nowt on the PNC at all.'

Thanking him, Kate hung up just as a pint-sized uniform police constable ran out of the dunes and down the beach towards them, baton drawn. She gave him a look that stopped him in his tracks and muttered, 'Fuck's sake you idiot, put that thing away!'

43

Heart still in her mouth, Emily hugged her daughter and held on for a very long time. Her thoughts were in turmoil as they stood in the middle of their living room, a spilled vase of flowers on a wet cream carpet, Fearon's threat playing like a mantra in her head, filling her with alarm and making her question her sanity. And still she couldn't write it off as a load of crap. The sick bastard had been so precise. So convincing. Did he have access to information about her? How could he?

Emily didn't know.

She wanted things to go back to the way they were before a quirk of fate ripped her world apart. They were a family of three, not two – and so happy – the perfect couple with the perfect child, a string of hopes and dreams stretching far into the future. Now all she had left was a bloody big empty space. The black hole sucked her in, deeper and deeper, as each day passed.

She was angry too.

Her husband hadn't been fighting for his country or saving a drowning child when he died. There was no freak accident. No act of God. No terrible weather event had taken him away. A dodgy aortic valve had caused him to collapse while running a half-marathon.

How stupid and pointless was that?

The phone rang in the kitchen.

Leaving Rachel to clear up the mess on the floor, she walked away to answer it. It was Jo Soulsby, wanting to know if she fancied a drink. Emily declined, reminding her what day it was.

Jo suggested an alternative, meeting Kate later in the week. 'If she can drag herself away from that job of hers.'

'I'd like that,' Emily said.

Mention of Kate brought to mind her frantic attempts to contact the DCI by phone. In turn that led her thoughts back to Fearon. 'Jo, did Martin tell you there was another incident at the prison today?'

'Incident?' Jo said.

She hadn't been told.

Before Emily could say more, Rachel arrived in the kitchen looking for a dustpan and brush, preventing further discussion of her mother's latest confrontation with the prisoner from hell.

'My office or yours?' Emily opened the cupboard under the sink, took out a bottle of carpet cleaner and handed it to Rachel, hoping Jo Soulsby would take the hint on the other end of the line. 'Tomorrow morning any good for you?'

'Rachel's there, right?'

'Correct!'

'Nuff said. See you tomorrow, Em.'

The line went dead.

It was perhaps as well she couldn't talk freely. Emily was done talking about Fearon and far too exhausted to go over it again. Maybe she was jumping to conclusions. Now she came to think about it, the prisoner had merely described a younger version of herself. It stood to reason that any daughter of hers would possess similar physical characteristics. As for their home, Fearon wasn't local but he knew what a traditional Northumbrian cottage was like. It was an educated guess – nothing more – and she had done exactly what Martin hinted at – played right into his hands.

By the time Emily and Rachel were ready to go for a walk, the sun had come out. It often did that, this near the coast late in the afternoon. They didn't have far to go. Their tiny cottage was blessed with four acres of land, including five hundred metres of fishing rights on the River Coquet, which rose in the Cheviots and meandered through Northumberland before discharging into the North Sea – a journey of around forty miles.

A keen angler, Robert had fallen for the property as a young man. He used to fish there with the son of a former owner. He particularly loved the bend in the river, the way it bubbled and danced over the bedrock. When the cottage came on the market, he'd snapped it up, consulting with Emily only after the event, hoping she'd love it too. That evening, he'd taken her to a pub in Walkworth, bought a bottle of wine they could ill afford and sprung the news on her . . .

'We've got to have it, Em. It's not massive but it's big enough. It's well built. It has land. It's in a fabulous location. And . . .' He looked at her, *really* looked, like he wanted to get her into the sack. In that moment, time stood still. They were the only customers in the bar – the only couple on the planet – two people madly in love, eyes for each other and no one else. Robert lifted his glass and said the magic words: 'The Stint is a great place to raise a family.'

She loved the name: *The Stint*.

He was right too, except the big family never materialized. For reasons that baffled them both, more so their GP, Emily conceived only the once. It wasn't for lack of trying either. They didn't need a baby-making excuse to rip each other's clothes off. But neither did it matter all that much. If fate chose not to grant them a second child, then that was OK by them. They'd been blessed with a precious daughter.

'She's enough,' Robert always said.

And she was.

44

Kate Daniels was exhausted. It had been a bummer of a day so far. Hours and hours of purgatory: a suspect found, then lost; an argument with Jo; a bust up with Hank after he'd made his mouth go; an idiot lighting candles near her crime scene who turned out to be nothing more than a voyeur. Consequently, she had no enthusiasm for the briefing.

The squad looked jaded too, but as the meeting progressed it soon became apparent that things were about to get a whole lot worse. For starters: the pearls. During the day, Robson had discovered that Kate's set, and those found on the first victim, were manufactured prior to the Coronation by a company that had ceased trading in the mid-seventies. That was bad news because the line of enquiry could go no further. Worrying too because whoever put them on the child had gone out of his way to recreate the exact same scenario with his second victim.

'OK, it's not the end of the world,' Kate said. 'But if we can't find the supplier, then the house-to-house team needed to get a wriggle on with that list of recipients I asked for. Anyone know how they're doing?'

No one spoke.

A phone bleeped. Hank went for his pocket. 'I'll have a

word with Yates first thing in the morning,' he said, before accessing the message that had just come in.

'Where are we with the other set of pearls?' asked the DCI.

Brown had an apology written all over his face as he raised a hand at the back. A serial note-taker, he flipped a few pages before answering her question. 'They're bog standard, boss. Cheap, mass-produced rubbish manufactured in the States. They're sold in several chain stores and in vending machines too. Y'know, where you put money in and get a toy inside a plastic ball? They're still current and available over the Internet. I talked to one of the main suppliers. They're shipped to Europe and right across the USA, distributed to craft shops and toyshops all over the knot end. Chances are we'll never trace them.'

Another dead end.

'Well, well!' Hank raised his eyes from his phone, specifically from his inbox. An email marked urgent had come in from the forensic science lab. 'It seems the pearls aren't the only thing our victims had in common.'

Everyone looked at him.

He held the phone up. 'Report from Matt West. The shoes have now been forensically examined. They're also old and bore the same manufacturing label.' He caught Kate's eye. 'But don't get too excited. You ever heard of Philby & Son on Prudhoe Street?'

'Where the hell's Prudhoe Street?' Carmichael asked.

'Before your time, Lisa,' an old detective at the back said. 'It was pulled down years ago. Philby & Sons was a cheap shop, bit like Farnon's, another establishment you young 'uns won't have heard of. It was in a grid of streets near the

Haymarket bus station. The arse end of Eldon Square Shopping Centre.'

'So where does that take us?' Kate was looking at Hank now. 'Can we get a familial DNA match from shed skin in the shoes?'

He shook his head. 'Apparently not.'

Kate's shoulders dropped. Matt West was an expert in his field. If it had been remotely possible to extract a sample of DNA she knew he would have. 'So how does it help us?' she asked.

'The shoes were well worn. And here's the thing . . .' Hank glanced at his email. 'The wear pattern was almost identical. The scientists are sticking their necks out here, but they say, quote: they belonged to the same person in all probability. Both were worn down on the left inner heel.'

'Mother of the offender?' Kate suggested.

'That would be my guess.'

'Sounds like Jo's theory was right,' DS Robson said.

'Looks that way. What else we got?'

Kate had just come from a meeting with Abbey Hunt. The anthropologist had completed her tests and was now certain that the years she'd given them to work with – 2001 and 2006 – were spot on in both cases, but she couldn't be any more specific than that. Her best guess was a winter burial. As for dental records, she'd lucked out there too. Nominal 1 had perfect teeth. Nominal 2 had all her permanent molars and some decay but no restorative treatment that might assist with identification.

'Not everyone has a dentist,' Brown said. 'NHS or otherwise.'

Carmichael stuck her hand in the air. 'What about broken bones?'

'A well-healed fracture of the right tibia on the fifteen-year-old,' Kate said.

Gormley was about to say something when a phone rang on the desk nearest to him. Picking it up, he listened for a moment and then interrupted Kate, holding up the phone. 'Gerry Offord, front desk, for you – and before you ask, I did remind him to hold all calls. You want it on speaker?'

Kate nodded. Offord was big mates with Brown, a man who wouldn't dream of disturbing a Murder Investigation Team in full flow unless it was important.

'This had better be good, Gerry. You know I'm busy.'

'Apologies, ma'am. I'm holding an urgent call from North Yorks Major Incident Team. I'm assured you'll want to take it.'

'Says who?'

'The SIO, I assume—'

'You assume? Did you verify the ident?'

'He sounded genuine enough—'

Kate rolled her eyes. 'If I said I was the tooth fairy, would you believe me too?'

Offord went quiet at the other end.

Detectives in the room were grinning. It might not be written down in the *Front Desk for Dummies Manual* but it was standard procedure in their department to verify a caller's identity before entering into any detailed conversation. Many a detective had been caught out by unscrupulous arseholes claiming to be someone they were not in order to feed the twenty-four-hour news.

It pained Kate to think that people would go to such

lengths to obtain information on murder cases never intended for release to the press or wider public. Even more worrying, the thought that an offender might get the upper hand just so some tosser could make a name for him or herself with a front-page scoop in a newspaper.

Sloppy gits like Offord made for a very leaky sieve.

'Did they ask for me by name?' she asked.

Offord sidestepped the question, telling her the DCI's name was Munro.

'Male or female?'

'Male.'

'OK, put him on.'

A voice came on the line. 'Apologies for the interruption to your briefing, but I have an unsolved level 1 case from '99. Similar MO to yours. Young girl, disposed of in a woodland grave, dressed in adult clothes.'

'Where are you?'

'My office.' He began to reel off a number.

Kate cut in before he could finish: 'Call you back.'

She hung up, pointing at Carmichael's computer monitor. 'Lisa, police almanac. Look him up: MIT, North Yorks, DCI Munro. Fast as you can. The rest of you, take a break. Quick one, mind – I want you all here by the time I've finished this call.'

As Carmichael began typing, the team made their escape. Some headed for the loo, others out on to the fire escape for a quick fag break. As Kate waited for confirmation of Munro's ID, his voice replayed in her head. It was measured, calm, the accent more Cheshire than Yorkshire, she would've said. She thought he was on the level. For a start, he hadn't called his murder incident a 'cold case', a media term she hated. And he hadn't made out he was some kind of hero on a quest. He sounded a lot like Bright.

He sounded the real deal.

Carmichael picked up her phone and started dialling. The phone was answered straight away. She asked for Munro, first name Gordon. The man she was speaking to said that was him. Asking him to hold for her SIO, Lisa glanced at her own tired DCI. 'This is him, boss. Line two.'

Picking up the handset, Kate said: 'I have one question.'

'Which is?'

'Was she wearing any jewellery?'

'What kind of jewellery?'

'Pearls, Gordon. Was she wearing any pearls?'

45

Emily glanced at Rachel as they walked. She hadn't said a word since they'd left the house. Probably wanted to be alone with her own thoughts on what would have been her father's forty-eighth birthday. Or was she mulling over how spooked *she* must've appeared earlier? Maybe she was waiting for an explanation, a chance to bring the subject up.

Emily would lie rather than burden her with that.

In single file, they negotiated a difficult section of riverbank that had fallen away in places, eroded by heavy rain. Once past the obstacle, Rachel paused, her eyes drawn to a tall figure casting his line from the centre of the river beyond their boundary fence.

The landowner lifted his head, tipped his cap and carried on feeding his rod.

Although filthy rich with an estate covering hundreds of acres, he was so like Robert in many ways, a thoughtful neighbour they had known for years. And, like Robert, he was completely at one with his surroundings. The two of them had liked nothing better than to while away their days hunting or fishing together. Often out until dusk, they would come up to the house, crack open a beer and share their stories until the early hours.

Good times.

*

'I'm going back to college tomorrow,' Rachel said. Emily's heart leapt. It was the news she'd been hoping for but never imagined would arrive, especially not today. 'And I want to learn to ride too – a motorcycle, I mean.'

'I don't know about that, love.' Emily felt instantly sick.

Rachel's wish to ride was hardly unexpected. She'd grown up on bikes, in a sidecar as a kid, on the pillion when she was old enough. She'd also seen many accidents over the years, some fatal, one a very close friend of the family. She knew the risks. But the idea scared her mother, even though she rode herself. It was on the tip of her tongue to say no when common sense prevailed. She couldn't allow her anxiety to colour every decision she made about her daughter.

'It isn't as easy as it looks, y'know, darling.'

'You managed.'

'I had a good teacher.'

Emily wished she hadn't said that. But Rachel was too engrossed with their neighbour to react. As he cast his line again, Emily experienced a sudden flashback. In exactly the same spot on the riverbank, Robert had hooked a fish. Looking over his shoulder, he'd called out, 'Rachel! Come and see!'

A four-year-old raced towards her father, her chubby little legs obscured by long grass, her ponytail bobbing up and down as she ran. Watching her father land the fish, Rachel started to cry, gently at first, then in huge sobs. Big blobs of water fell from her dark lashes, soaking her T-shirt. Seeing her unhappy face, Robert lifted the fish from his net, put it back in the water, hugging her close as it swam away.

'No more tears.' He pointed at the disappearing fish. 'He's starting a new life, see?'

'No more tears, Mum.'

No more tears . . .

Rachel's adult voice pulled Emily from her daydream.

'C'mon here . . .' Rachel tucked her hand inside the sleeve of her fleece jacket, took out a tissue and wiped the side of Emily's face. 'Tell me, Mum. What's wrong?'

Emily could find no words.

'Is it because it's Dad's birthday?'

Emily shook her head.

'It's me, isn't it?' Rachel said.

'No!'

'What then? Look, I know it's hard for you too. You don't have to hide it from me all the time, or tiptoe around me. I'm a big girl now. I'm getting there all by myself.'

Emily put her arm around Rachel. 'Darling, learning to ride won't bring him back.'

'I know that! I do . . . I'd just feel closer to him, that's all.'

At that very moment, so did Emily. It was as if Robert was standing there with them creating that all important watershed when they could finally turn the corner. The fighting would stop now. Things would return to normal. Emily could feel it. She smiled at her daughter. Maybe learning to ride was exactly what she needed.

46

Kate's emotions were in turmoil as she put down the phone. Her team were back from their mini-break, bringing with them not only the whiff of cigarettes but coffee, crisps and chocolate bars from the vending machine recently installed in the bait room. It made her realize how bloody hungry she was.

No one had eaten since lunchtime and it was too late to catch a restaurant in the market town of Alnwick. That was the way it was in the country. Different if you worked in the Met. Still, nobody minded. They would most probably make up for it at breakfast.

All heads turned in her direction, keen to get the lowdown on a call that was so important it had stalled the evening briefing.

'And the upshot is . . . ?' Gormley put down his coffee.

Kate shook her head. 'No pearls, but get this – according to Munro, our friend Thompson was interviewed at length in connection with his enquiry.'

Maxwell nearly choked on a Cadbury's Twirl.

'Bingo!' Robson said.

Kate didn't respond, at least not in such enthusiastic terms. On the face of it, this new information had raised the stakes on an enquiry that could turn out to be the most difficult of her career to date. Her victims were, not to put too fine a point on it, a little less fresh than was normally the case. It was far too soon to jump to conclusions about Thompson. But she had to admit the link intrigued and excited her.

Picking up a glass of icy water Carmichael had thoughtfully placed on the desk beside her, Kate sat for a moment dwelling on the conversation with the Yorkshire SIO. Specifically on how his information impacted on her planned operation to detain and question her only suspect. Often it was good to tell an offender they were being arrested on suspicion of a major crime – whether or not it was murder – particularly if the evidence against them was circumstantial, as it still was in Thompson's case.

The question she was asking herself was: how would it benefit her? Would she gain by putting the suspect under pressure from the outset? Or should she arrest him on suspicion of some minor offence and see where that took her before wading in with the more serious matter? She was sure she could come up with something if she tried real hard. *Breathing, for example.*

In the end, she decided to play it by ear and make that call when the time came. She ordered everyone back to the B & B, intending to grab a few hours' sleep herself and then accompany a squad of uniforms to the address supplied by the uniformed inspector who'd given chase that morning. He seemed to have his finger on the pulse of all wrongdoing in the area in and around Morpeth. She wanted to be there during Thompson's arrest and detention for further questioning, but sharing her intention with the squad turned out to be a mistake.

Brown, whose speciality was covert observations, immediately jumped up. Volunteering his services, he offered to take a pool car and head straight over there. While the town slept, he would lay in wait for the offender to appear. The job was right up his street, he told her. He was practically begging.

How could she possibly refuse?

His suggestion galvanized the squad.

Feeling left out, Gormley and Carmichael said they would get up too, negating the need for uniforms altogether. Reluctantly, Kate agreed. After a long shift, the Murder Investigation Team were weary, yes. But they wanted to get stuck in and move the investigation forward a notch. Doing something practical to make that happen was a good place to start.

47

Arresting someone in the middle of the night isn't hard. Operationally, the most effective time for kicking doors down had always been four a.m., the theory being that the prigs inside would either be stoned or pissed on the cocktail of their choosing, therefore in a deep sleep, oblivious to the world around them.

When her alarm rang out, Kate dressed quickly in a pair of jeans, knee-high boots and a North Face fleece jacket to keep out the cold. Though she'd had less than four hours' sleep, she felt alert and ready for action, buoyed by the adrenalin coursing through her veins. The others were waiting in the foyer as she crept downstairs trying not to wake their host.

They all piled into her car and drove off into the night.

A few moments later, Kate rang Brown. 'Any sign of Thompson?'

'No, boss. But he's in there, I can smell it.'

There was a collective chuckle in the car. The Q5 turned on to the A1 heading south and picked up speed. Brown was right. You could sense if a house was occupied or not. If their intelligence was as good as they hoped it was, this particular address housed John Edward Thompson and his mate, Terence Watts.

The DCI gave an ETA and rang off.

Gormley and Carmichael had little to say during the twenty-minute journey. Kate assumed they were playing the forthcoming operation in their heads – as she was. They weren't expecting violence. Neither Thompson nor the offender he was dossing with had any assault convictions. Thompson's own brand of aggression was only ever directed at defenceless young girls.

Was he capable of murder?

Parking a street away, she radioed Brown asking him to meet DC Lisa Carmichael at the rear of the target property in case the offender made a break for the back door. Herself and Gormley would cover the front. They didn't want any bother. The quicker they got in, the quicker they got a result. The element of surprise was a copper's best friend. And that was exactly how it went down.

Using a battering ram he'd borrowed from the station, Gormley smashed his way into the house, hitting the front door so hard it flew off its hinges and landed at an angle on the deck beyond. Trampling it flush to the hallway floor, he rushed forward into the house shouting: 'POLICE!'

Following close behind, Kate shone her torch to find the light switch.

Bleary-eyed, shocked and obviously intoxicated, Thompson and his mate didn't know what had hit them. They looked ridiculous, standing in the bedroom of the ground-floor flat in underpants, their milky-white bodies shivering in the cold night air that was blowing like a hurricane through the missing front door.

'Who's gonna pay for me door?' the tenant complained.

'What door?' Gormley checked behind him. 'You haven't got one.'

'You fucking bastard! I'm getting on to me MP!'

'Calm down, Mr Watts,' Kate said. 'You should've opened up.'

'Eh? I was fucking asleep!'

'Sorry, mate. We did knock . . .' Tongue in cheek, Gormley glanced over his shoulder as Carmichael and Brown joined them in the room. 'Anyone knock on this lad's door?'

'I did,' they said in unison.

'Aye, with a feather, mebbies!' Watts bit back.

'John Edward Thompson, I'm arresting you on suspicion of murder . . .'

'Eh? You're kidding, aren't ya?'

'Does my boss look like she's laughing?' Gormley said.

Ignoring them both, Daniels rattled off the rest of the police caution. Then she sent Brown to fetch the pool car he'd parked around the corner out of sight. She was keen to get Thompson out of there and back to the station. There was no way the little scrote was parking his skinny arse on the seat of her new Q5. He was shitting himself, panicking now he'd realized what he was being arrested for.

Pointing at some strides dumped on the floor beside the rumpled bed, Kate told him to get dressed. Then she turned her attention to Watts, who was already climbing into his own jeans.

'Not you,' she said. 'Just him.'

Watts gave her a load of lip.

'Oh, you want to come too?' she said. 'That can be arranged.'

He decided to leave it.

Good choice.

Now they could all go back to bed.

48

There was hardly another car on the road. Carmichael drove, with Thompson in the rear, flanked on either side by Brown and Gormley, all the while complaining that they had got the wrong man.

'Yeah, yeah,' Gormley said. 'We've heard it all before.'

'It's true! Dunno who got croaked but it wasn't me, I swear!'

'You ever clean your teeth, mate? Get a wash?' Gormley held his nose and opened the rear side window. 'You reek of stale sweat and cheap booze.'

'He's right, you do,' Brown said. 'You'll never get a lass if you don't smarten yourself up.'

'You just pulled me from my pit, man. What d'you fuckers expect?'

'Must've been all that running you've been doing,' Brown said, his tone serious now. 'Hope you know that's an offence.'

'Eh?' Thompson looked at DS Gormley. 'What's this divvi on about?'

'Yeah,' Brown said. 'Like you don't know.'

'Know what?'

Gormley played along. 'You should listen to the officer. It's now an arrestable offence to run from the police, contrary to the Morpeth Town Police Clauses Act. It's a new piece of legislation. Rubber-stamped by the Tories only last week. Surprised you and yours haven't heard of it. Maximum three years if found guilty. Looks like you're going back to the pokey pal.'

Thompson had no idea they were talking rubbish. For someone who'd been in and out of jail all his life, he wasn't very savvy where police humour was concerned. He really ought to have known he was being had.

Carmichael turned on to the A1 heading for the nick. Flooring the accelerator, she pushed the car to the limit on empty roads. As Thompson realized they were travelling north he began to whinge. 'Piss! Where you taking us, man? I've got no cash on us, have I? How the fucking hell am I going to get home?'

'Who says you're going home?' Brown said.

Thompson wound his neck in.

Fifteen minutes passed and then he started again as they neared the outskirts of Alnwick, panic setting in. He kept repeating over and over that he was an innocent man. 'Whatever you think I done, I never!' he said.

Carmichael reversed the pool car up close to the cell-block wall. Daniels was already there waiting. She overheard the prisoner protest his innocence as she opened the car door. Hank got out first. Holding on to Thompson's arm, he heaved him out too, at the same time giving the SIO a little shake of his head, letting her know the suspect had said nothing in the car to implicate himself in any offence.

'So why run?' Daniels asked.

'You've got a warrant out for us.'

'No shit!' Gormley laughed as they frogmarched Thompson

towards the back door of the station. 'He's lying, I checked. You're locked up, matey. Time for a nice warm cell. Don't worry, you'll feel right at home.'

'No! Listen will ya!'

They stopped walking.

'You have one chance,' the DCI said.

Thompson hesitated. 'I thought there might be a warrant. I lost count—'

'OK, you blew it!' Daniels yanked him nearer to the door.

'OK, OK! There's no warrant. I lied about that, but I'm not lying now. I lifted the fucking coat I had on. That's why I ran. When I walked out the shop I saw Arsehole of the Empire, the uniform gadgie, standing right by the front door, so I legged it. I swear to you, I'm telling the truth!'

'Where'd you ditch the coat?'

'In the woods, where d'you think? So when I came out I didn't have the same description as when I went in. I'm not entirely stupid, am I?'

Kate didn't want to admit it – even to herself – but his explanation made sense. She marched him into the nick, handed him over to the custody sergeant for processing, telling the officer to bang him in a cell to await his fate. Too drunk to interview was the official excuse for leaving the sod to sweat.

49

The prisoner was lean and strong, not an ounce of fat on him. He had a six-pack worthy of a professional footballer. He worked on it too. Every minute he got the chance. Kent had had enough of watching him pump iron in the state-of-the-art gym it would cost the tax-paying public five hundred quid a year to match.

Where was the justice in that?

He despised this one more than most. Not because he spent hours in the gym preening in front of a mirror, then shuffled back to his cell like he didn't have the strength to fight his way out of a paper bag. Or because of the offence that brought him to the prison in the first place. There were worse sexual deviants under lock and key at HMP Northumberland. Neither was it because he had a thing about women – though clearly he had – particularly those in authority. It was because he was a creep: period.

As a wing cleaner, Fearon was right there every time a skirt stepped foot inside the gate. Kent had hidden in the shadows on numerous occasions observing him observing them – psychologist Emily McCann especially. The arsehole was besotted with her.

Kent felt his anger rising as he thought about McCann. She had never been *his* greatest fan. There'd been a time when they got on OK, but recently she'd been making that lovely mouth of hers go. Now he was on the back foot, his PO and SO demanding that he get his shit together, insisting that a little chat with her could do him some good.

He sniggered.

Other way round, more like.

Pity her sympathies lay with the nonce.

Kent looked around him. There were eight inmates exercising in total. As usual, Saunders and Jones had collared the elliptical trainers. Three others were on treadmills – two walking, one running. Singh was lifting weights on a flat bench behind them while his partner took on water.

The room stank of sweat.

Fearon was lying on the deck, a hard vinyl mat beneath his body. He was working through a gruelling series of sit-ups that would make a fit man weep, a thin veil of sweat on his upper lip but no sign of effort on his face. Kent couldn't plant one on him in full view of everyone. He decided to bide his time, wait until his colleague's back was turned before making his move.

And there it was.

As Fearon got up off the floor, Kent seized his opportunity to take a pop at him. It was like punching a brick wall. 'Grab your kit and come with me!' he said.

Hearing the commotion, his colleague looked round, nonplussed. 'What gives?'

'Nothing I can't handle.'

Over the officer's shoulder, Saunders and Jones were pissing themselves laughing having witnessed what had taken place. The rest of the cons had seen it too, but they looked away, minding their business. Fearon wasn't popular.

Kent tensed.

Only one prisoner could cause him any trouble and the little twat was fast approaching, a complaint already forming on his lips.

Time to head him off at the pass.

'Looking forward to going home later, son?' Kent's eyes held a warning.

Ajit Singh backed off.

'Thought so.'

Job done.

Placing Fearon in an arm lock, Kent hauled him out through the gym door, yelling at his oppo to keep his eye on the others. The corridor beyond was empty. For a moment, he wondered if he'd bitten off more than he could chew. If the lad turned on him now he knew he'd be in trouble despite his combat training.

'Stand still!' he bawled. 'Or I'll break your fucking arm.'

He would too, the mood he was in.

Fearon went limp. Raising his head, he eyeballed the screw, a look of sheer hatred passing between them. Despite the damage he could do, Kent was willing him to kick off. Any excuse to get stuck into him for real. But Fearon was too clever to fight with a member of staff so close to his release date. His present sentence couldn't be extended, but a new assault charge would queer his pitch good and proper, putting paid to his plans to visit Emily McCann. So he just stood there, showing no emotion, good or bad.

Drawing his arm back, Kent hit him again, in the stomach

this time, bringing up some of his breakfast. Expecting some form of retaliation, he stepped away, lifting his fists ready to defend himself. Wiping vomit from his bottom lip, Fearon smiled as SO Walker rounded the corner.

Game over.

For now . . .

The walk to C-wing was long and silent apart from two pairs of boots squeaking on the highly polished floor and Fearon's gym shoes padding along beside them. SO Walker led the way, having listened to Kent's explanation as to what had taken place outside the gym. He hadn't asked Fearon for his version of events, merely invited Kent to escort the prisoner to his office for, as he put it, 'a more detailed conversation'.

Kent knew he was in for some stick. Not in front of Fearon. The two officers went back a long way and, whatever the story, Walker would never undermine one of his own with a prisoner present. As the nonce assumed the position on one side of Walker's desk, the SO walked round behind it and sat down.

He didn't look happy.

Closing the door, Kent moved forward and stood to attention, shoulder to shoulder with Fearon, ready to blag his way out of a tricky situation. He didn't want to deceive his SO, but what other choice was there? This time he'd gone too far. His job was on the line.

Ash Walker sat in his chair, his eyes shifting from man to boy and back again, searching their faces for the truth.

Kent's jaw was so fixed he thought it might lock. Though his own gaze was trained on the wall opposite, he could feel the SO's eyes boring into him and wondered which one of the two he was going to believe. He relaxed then. *If in doubt, close ranks.* That was how it was. How it had always been. Uniforms backed each other up. No question.

No contest.

'Assaulting an officer is a very serious breach of discipline,' Walker said. He picked up a pen, opened an A4 incident log, looking directly at the inmate. 'Mind telling me what happened again? Just for the record. I've heard one explanation, now I'd like yours.'

He waited . . .

'C'mon! You're always making your mouth go, Fearon. Now's your chance to put the record straight.'

'I never touched him. I was going through my training programme. I got up and he elbowed me for no good reason.' Placing his left hand on his right side, Fearon winced. 'I think he bust a rib too. He's always on my case. You know that as well as I do. Check your logbook if you don't believe me. See how many times I've been to see the Governor on his say so. It ain't on. Know what I'm saying?'

'You're alleging Officer Kent singles you out for special attention?'

'Yeah, I am.'

'I see. He makes your life hell for the fun of it?'

'Yeah, exactly!'

'And Ms McCann too, I suppose? Is she part of this conspiracy?'

Fearon clammed up.

'Why would either of them do that?' Walker asked. 'You sure it isn't the other way round?'

'I never done nowt to him, man. He's making it up. He's a fucking psycho! Everyone knows what he's like.'

'Oh, so now I'm part of the problem.'

'No, sir. You ain't got eyes in the back of your head. I understand that, dunni? But I got rights too, y'know . . .' Fearon looked to his right. 'I want this wanker off my case.'

'Shut it!' Walker glanced at his log, his pen poised to record the incident. There was a moment of silence while he considered what action to take. 'I've had about enough of you, Fearon. You've been a pain in the arse since you arrived on this wing, not just to my staff but to Ms McCann and everyone else you come in contact with. I've put up with your antics long enough. Maybe you need a change of scenery.'

'No!'

'Excuse me? Did I say you had a choice?'

A look of panic flashed across Fearon's face. 'Don't move me, please, sir. I take it back. I'm the problem, not Officer Kent. I swear I won't make no complaint. I ain't moving wing, man. No way!'

Kent fought hard to keep a straight face.

The nonce was almost begging.

Ash Walker crossed his arms over his chest and sat considering his options. Kent could read his mind. The prison was full to capacity. Moving Fearon out would mean moving some other poor bugger in; one who probably didn't deserve, let alone want, to shift. Movement for movement's sake upset the status quo. The resulting disruption would cause a ripple effect throughout the prison. They all knew that. Besides, what wing PO would be daft enough to accept the agitating bastard?

Kent wanted to laugh his cock off.

He was home and dry.

The SO pointed at Fearon. 'You piss me off one more time and you're transferring, you hear me?' Fearon nodded, even said thanks. Walker looked at the clock above the door and said, 'Fulham–Chelsea are on Sky tonight at eight o'clock. Shame you'll miss it. Now get out of here before I change my mind. This incident never happened, you got me?'

Another nod from Fearon.

But he didn't move quick enough for Walker's liking. 'I said GET OUT!'

Dragging his feet, Fearon trundled out, slamming the door behind him.

'Keep your eye on him today and bang him up early,' Walker said. 'Straight after his evening meal.'

Kent turned to leave.

'No, Bill. Sit down. We need a word.'

Kent remained on his feet. He knew what was coming: another lecture, another pep-talk, so much sympathy he was drowning in the stuff. He was sick of it – sick of working with nonces like Fearon – sick of every damn thing and everybody: Fearon, Harrison, McCann, even Ash Walker, now he came to think of it.

'You're due some leave,' Walker said. 'Take it!'

'No thanks.'

'I'm telling, not asking. Get on the phone and arrange it.'

'Not my style, boss.'

'Fuck's sake! Then go and see Emily. She'll help you, I know she will.' Walker dropped his voice a touch as a work party of inmates were led past the office. 'Look, I understand it's difficult for you, but you can't lose your rag with the cons and expect to get away with it. It's not on, you hear me?' Walker sighed loudly. 'Consider yourself on a final.'

Kent headed off.

'And, Bill . . . ?'

Turning as he reached the door, Kent waited.

'Don't mess with him, or me,' Walker said. 'You'll end up losing.'

50

Concentrating on a minor theft and forgetting the arrest for murder was a decision Kate Daniels was comfortable with for the time being. John Edward Thompson obviously thought his luck was in when she handed him over to spend a night in the cells. According to the custody sergeant, he'd cooperated during the charge-room process, insisting that he neither required nor wanted a solicitor present. He'd been no bother during the night; not a peep from him, in fact.

Interesting . . .

She was observing him on CCTV.

He was sitting at a table chewing his nails. He looked dishevelled, having slept in his clothes. His hair was greasy and stuck to his scalp and he could do with a wash. No wonder Carmichael was keeping her distance by the door. What interested Kate most was the fact that Thompson seemed unconcerned about being held in custody overnight. Then again, why should he? He knew the drill. He was an old hand now.

Time for a little chat.

In interview, he stuck to the same story. He'd run because he'd been shoplifting, nothing more. Daniels now knew he was telling the truth, having sent Gormley on a mission to recover the coat, which was right where Thompson told them it would be. What's more, Hank had identified it as coming from the shop from which their suspect had done a runner. *Probably had his DNA all over it.* Shop security had even provided CCTV that showed a hint of a police uniform at the front door.

'Told ya!' Thompson smirked.

He was getting cocky now – a bit too cocky – and it made the DCI's heart sing. In her experience, if you told someone you were arresting them for murder and they hadn't done it, they did one of three things: they went berserk, put up a wall of silence or screamed for their brief and made an official complaint. Thompson had done none of these things.

So why hadn't he made his mouth go?

They had broken his door down in the middle of the night, hauled his arse to Alnwick, and taken the piss out of him unmercifully. And yet he'd taken the lot on the chin without kicking up a fuss. In her mind, that meant only one thing. He didn't want to draw attention to himself or his previous offending because he had something to hide.

That something was probably serious.

'It looks like you're going to prison unless you help us.' She eyeballed him across the square Formica table, pausing a moment, allowing him to sweat. 'If I were you, I'd use my loaf. You may well have proved beyond reasonable doubt that you ran from us because you were thieving. But if you cast your foggy mind back to last night, I didn't arrest you for theft in the first place, did I? That other matter hasn't gone away.'

'Shame . . .' Carmichael tutted. 'Not so clever now, eh, pal?'

The put-down hit home.

Thompson's bravado disappeared and he asked for a brief.
Carmichael grinned. 'You hear something, boss?'

'Don't think so.' Daniels glanced at Thompson's custody
record. 'Oh look! At 0440 hours the suspect declined a solicitor. See here?' She pushed the record across the table, using
her index finger to point to a specific entry. 'The custody sergeant has even signed his name right there next to it in case a
judge should want to see it too.'

'I changed my mind,' Thompson huffed.

'Tell you what,' Daniels said. 'You help me and I'll forget I
ever saw that CCTV. How does that sound to you?'

She and Carmichael had called up Thompson's police
record earlier. Years ago he'd dressed a couple of young girls
up in adult clothing before abusing them. He'd stopped short
of killing them, but he'd left them in a terrible state: degraded
and traumatized, unable to sleep, fearful of men. He'd
snatched one of them from her home in broad daylight while
her mother was in the garden hanging out her washing.

Walked right in through the front door.

That took nerve.

It was one of two reasons he'd come up as a possible
suspect. The other was that he'd gone to prison in May 2002
and come out again in November 2005, which meant he was
capable of having committed both offences that fell within
Daniels' timeframe, such as it was. Since the enquiry began,
the SIO had been asking herself why the long interval between
victims. The obvious conclusion was that the offender had
been locked up and therefore unable to commit an offence in
the intervening years.

Thompson's incarceration spanned the gap perfectly.

When questioned in connection with Munro's enquiry, he'd insisted he was living and working on the Continent from August 1995 to September 2001. *So what?* A cheap flight from Spain was no barrier to murder. Relaxed border controls within Europe meant passports were rarely scanned – another change in the law that made the job of murder investigation teams across the globe more difficult. He could've been back and forth a hundred times without being detected.

A TIE action had never put him out of the North Yorks enquiry but neither had it put him in. With no hard evidence to implicate him, he had been released. Munro's frustration over the phone was palpable. The DCI was nearing retirement and wanted to detect this one before he handed in his warrant card. Kate totally understood how that would eat away at him. Major incident teams throughout the country faced exactly the same issues on a daily basis. Staff had to pick up and drop actions and incidents, constantly re-evaluating and feeding their priorities. As a result, some cases were left undetected, marring the end of a fine career. She hoped that wouldn't happen to her.

51

Ash Walker was waiting for Emily at the entrance gate, feet crossed over one another, arms folded, his back against the wall. He'd removed his tie and put on a civilian jacket to disguise the fact that he was a prison officer who was technically still on duty. It was the done thing if uniformed staff ventured out at lunchtime in public.

It hadn't worked.

The white shirt, dark strides and black boots were a dead giveaway. His whole persona screamed prison service personnel.

It had been a while since they had seen each other outside of the perimeter fence – a few months at least – certainly before Robert passed away. The last occasion was probably someone's leaving do or possibly a retirement bash. There weren't the facilities to celebrate such events on site. For obvious reasons, alcohol was strictly forbidden.

It was a stunning day outside: cold and crisp, clear blue sky and bright winter sunshine. They took Walker's Renault and had the road to themselves. The pub they were heading for was handy for the prison – only fifteen minutes along narrow country lanes – but it was not one of Emily's favourites, it had to be said.

Walking through the door transported her back in time.

To describe the place as tired was being kind. The decor was drab and old-fashioned. The lounge hadn't been redecorated in ages. Smoking had been outlawed years ago, but the heavily embossed wall fabric still retained a slight whiff of nicotine.

Gross.

'You certainly know how to spoil a girl,' Emily joked.

Walker winked at her. 'You better believe it.'

There was no hot food so they ordered a sandwich and a beer, then retreated from the bar, taking their drinks with them. At a table near the door, Walker pulled out a chair for her. Ignoring the seat he was offering, Emily sat down with her back to the window, giving him the sea view in the distance.

Lifting his pint, he saluted her.

They clinked glasses.

Walker took a long drink, set his glass down on the table and wiped a line of white froth from his upper lip with the back of his hand. He looked troubled today, hence the invitation to lunch at such short notice.

Emily thought she knew what was coming.

'You going to tell me what's on your mind?' she said.

Walker grinned. 'Am I that transparent?'

'It isn't every day I get invited to such a prestigious venue for lunch.' Smiling widely, Emily looked beyond him. There were few customers in the bar. No prison staff. She figured that was the reason he'd chosen to bring her here. 'What's bothering you, Ash?'

'This'n'that.'

'A euphemism for Bill Kent, I presume.'

'He needs your help, Em.'

'So everyone keeps telling me.'

'To be honest, I don't even know why I'm bothering when he won't help himself.'

'He's still digging his heels in?'

'I'm working on him.'

'I hope he's worth it.'

'I don't expect you to believe me, but he wasn't always such an arse. Thing is, the idiot will lose his job if we don't get him on track. He's already on a warning. If he steps out of line again I'll have no choice but to put him on paper. If I do that, the PO will have to do something about him whether he likes it or not. That won't make you very popular with Harrison either, will it?'

'I can't make Kent talk to me.'

'True. But as I said, he has his problems.'

'We all have our cross to bear.'

'That's a bit harsh!'

Walker stopped talking as the barman, a frail-looking man with sallow skin and whisky breath, arrived with their sandwiches. He eyed them suspiciously – as if new customers were something to be feared and not encouraged – then shuffled to the bar and disappeared out back somewhere, presumably for another slug of Bells or a Marlboro.

'Will you stop talking in code now?' Emily said.

'I hate to lay this on you, Em. I know you're not in a good place at—'

'This isn't about me! So tell me what's on your mind and be done with it.'

Walker finally caved in. 'Bill Kent had a daughter when I

first met him. Early on in his service she disappeared. She went off to school one day and never came home.'

'God! How old was she?'

'Ten . . .' Walker paused. 'A murder investigation was launched, but the police never found her body.' He looked past Emily, his eyes finding the horizon. 'This business up the coast is taking its toll on him.'

'I bet it is. How long ago was this?'

'It must be close to ten years.'

Emily's thoughts turned first to her friend Kate Daniels and then to Stamp and his evasiveness over Kent and his problems. She felt guilty that her preoccupation with Fearon and her own daughter's safety had prevented her following up on Kent's strange behaviour.

'Has he been in touch with the police locally? I know the SIO personally.'

'I don't know. He won't talk to me.'

Emily went quiet. This was beginning to make sense to her. Maybe Stamp had been cagey because he was counselling Kent in an unofficial capacity. Maybe that was his way of taking the heat off her.

She shared that thought with Walker.

He shook his head. 'I doubt it. They're not on the best of terms.'

'How so?'

He put down his sandwich. 'Long story.'

Emily folded her arms and said nothing, waiting for him to elaborate.

With a sigh, Ash obliged. 'We were all three working at Coleby Prison back then. There was a huge investigation. The hunt for Sophie went on for months. Several of Bill's colleagues were questioned, Martin Stamp included.'

'Martin? I never knew.'

'Stamp was furious. Allegations were rife. Lots of names were bandied around. Bill himself was obviously high on the list of suspects.'

'Poor bugger . . .'

Emily meant that. Having a child go missing was every parent's worst nightmare, one she'd contemplated only yesterday. If that parent then fell under suspicion, she could imagine all too well the devastating psychological effect it would have on them. There would always be those in the community who believed there was no smoke without fire. And now that bodies had been discovered close to Kent's workplace, the rumour-mongers would be at it again.

A horrible feeling crept over her.

When Stamp arrived at HMP Northumberland, he'd not divulged a past connection to Kent or any other prison officer there. Fair enough. Maybe, as Ash said, they didn't get on. But she'd known him back then. Even though they parted after university, they had never lost touch. So if he'd fallen under suspicion when Sophie Kent went missing, why hadn't he mentioned it?

'Where is Coleby?' she asked. 'I've never heard of it.'

'It closed down a year after Sophie went missing. Staff members were dispersed around the country. Kent and I ended up here. At the time I thought it might help him, y'know, moving away. Not that you ever get over something like that.'

'Especially when there's no body, no burial, no closure.'

'Exactly! I know you think he's a prat, but take my word for it, he was a good bloke before all this.' He shook his head, looked at her. 'I swore I wouldn't say anything, but I thought you should know.'

'Where did Martin go?'

'What do you mean?'

'You said you and Kent moved here.'

'Oh . . . I seem to think he went to Ashworth for a time. Not sure after that. I never saw him again until he landed his current job.'

'He should have told me – about Kent, I mean.' Emily had something more to add, but in view of what had been said already, she knew that now wasn't the time or place to bring it up. Walker, however, picked up on her reticence and asked what was on her mind. She hesitated. 'I don't miss much that goes on around here, Ash.'

'What did you hear?'

'Just that Kent had another go at Fearon. You promised me it wouldn't happen again.'

'I know, but there was nothing I could do. There was an incident in the gym. Fearon came off worse.'

'Is that the official version?'

'That's not fair, Em.'

'I'm sorry, I apologize. You didn't deserve that. I'm angry with him, not you, in spite of what you told me.' Emily picked up her beer and took a drink, meeting his eyes over the rim of her glass. 'So how did you get to know about their latest altercation?'

'Right time, right place. I just happened to walk round the

corner when they were sizing up to one another. Kent maintains Fearon threw the first punch.'

'Yeah, well, he would, wouldn't he? I can see you have your doubts.'

'I made a few discreet enquiries. Kent's duty partner claims he saw nothing. He had his back turned, apparently. And before you say anything, I know that sounds very convenient. All the same, for what it's worth, I believe him.'

'I'm hearing a but.'

'I found a witness. Ajit Singh claims Kent struck the first blow. He said the attack on Fearon was totally unprovoked. He won't make a statement to that effect and, to be perfectly honest, I didn't want to push him.'

'Can't blame him, can you? He's hardly going to rock the boat on discharge day.'

Walker checked his watch. 'He'll be on the bus home now.'

Emily's mobile rang.

She took it out of her bag and checked the display.

It was Reg Hendry's wife.

'Shit!' She'd forgotten about her home security. Reg was probably at the house, wondering where she was. 'Mind if I take this, Ash? It's important.'

Shaking his head, Walker picked up his sandwich and bit into it.

'Vera? I'm so sorry . . .' Emily listened. 'Oh no! Is he going to be OK? No, not at all . . . you tell him he's to stay right where he is until he's better . . . No, I promise you. Next week is fine . . . OK, yes . . . yes, will do. Give him my love. I'll call you soon.'

She hung up.

'Problem?'

'The old guy who owns the hardware shop in Felton was supposed to be doing some work for me at home today. Apparently, he's fallen and hit his head. Nothing too serious, but the doctor has confined him to barracks for a couple of days to be on the safe side. I was supposed to be meeting him at my house, but when you asked me to join you for lunch I clean forgot. Poor old boy is knocking eighty.'

'Anything I can do? I'm a bit younger than that and a dab hand at DIY.'

Emily declined. It was a kind offer but it could wait. Her cottage was empty now. Rachel wasn't at home today. She was safely ensconced in college as planned. Suddenly, the lock thing didn't seem so urgent.

52

Detective Superintendent Ron Naylor wasn't looking where he was going as he left the MIR. He ran headlong into Hank Gormley at the door, the mobile in his hand crashing to the floor. Gormley stepped back, apologizing for the collision even though it wasn't his fault.

'What's up, guv?' he asked.

'Ask your DCI!' Picking up his phone, Naylor examined the screen before lifting it to his ear. The line was dead. He cancelled the call, put the mobile in his right trouser pocket and sloped off down the corridor, leaving Gormley none the wiser and a tad bewildered.

Kate Daniels and Naylor were best buddies. On top of that, the Super was always so calm, so easy-going. Hank couldn't remember the last time he'd seen him riled. Wincing as the double door slammed shut at the end of the corridor, he turned on his heels and pushed on into the incident room.

Kate and DC Lisa Carmichael were sitting together by an open window, a pile of paperwork and handwritten notes spread out on the desk in front of them. They both looked spent. An afternoon giving John Edward Thompson a police agenda interview had obviously taken its toll.

He wandered over to join them.

'Who died?' he asked.

Neither one spoke as he pulled up a chair and sat down.

Getting to her feet, the DCI wandered aimlessly away.

'Fine!' Hank huffed. 'What the hell is wrong with everybody?'

'Difference of opinion,' Carmichael replied without looking at him.

'About?'

Lisa glanced up. 'The Chief was on to Naylor earlier, suggesting we convene a press conference. Naylor mentioned it in passing. The boss was having none of it. She told him straight. They had words. He stormed out. End of.'

'Ah.' Now Hank understood.

There were things about the Bamburgh case the public didn't need to know. Kate wanted to keep it that way. It wasn't her style to stir up a media frenzy in order to make the police look good. Or take credit in front of the force logo, telling everyone how harrowing it was for the team to have witnessed a burial site containing the remains of two young girls. She hated all that showboating stuff. It was bollocks anyway. Murder detectives were paid to witness these things. *That was their duty.*

'Don't blame her,' he said finally. 'Anyway, why bother? We've got fuck-all to tell them.'

'S'pose.' Yawning, Lisa rubbed her upper arms. 'I'm cold.'

'No "suppose" about it.' Hank got up, closed the window, then sat down again. It was already pitch-black outside. 'Kate's the one who'll take the flak if information falls into the wrong hands. She has to be careful around the media and people like Thompson. It's a fine balancing act, one you'll have to implement yourself one day.'

'She's good at it too.' Carmichael yawned again. 'Through-out the interview, Thompson hung on her every word. If you ask me, he was getting off on all the attention. Cocky little git.'

'That's always the danger with paedophiles. You can't share stuff with them in case they tell fellow abusers who may also be involved in the offence you're investigating. You can't let it slip why they're in the frame.'

'How d'you mean?'

'Think about it, Lisa.' He looked at her pointedly. 'Once he realizes it's because he dresses his victims up, that knowledge reveals something about the enquiry. And none of us want that.'

'Oh, I see what you mean. Got any paracetamol?' she asked. 'My head's throbbing.'

'Ask Sicknote.' Hank was referring to Maxwell.

Massaging her temples with the middle finger of each hand, Carmichael glanced around the office. Maxwell was nowhere in sight. 'Two hours we were in there with Thompson. He denied any connections with Bamburgh.'

'He would. Doesn't mean there aren't any.'

'This whole case is a 'mare,' Lisa said glumly.

'No-victim-ID cases always are.'

'We went through every bloody thing: antecedents, family tree, turned his criminal record inside out. Nothing. His custody record puts him in *and* he has contacts with the area and the former mining community. But the clever shit was quick to point out that so does everyone else who comes from Blyth.'

Hank studied Lisa. His protégée looked very pale. He wondered if she was coming down with some bug or other or if it was due to lack of a proper night's sleep. There was no point telling to her to bugger off to the B & B and get her head down for a couple of hours. She'd rather stick pins in her eyes.

'Don't fret, Lisa. If Thompson is guilty, we'll get him. The TIE action will expose any holes in his story. It'll never be put to bed until the enquiry winds up. In my view, he's in for both or he's out for both. It's not likely he's working with anyone else.'

'How can you be so sure?'

'I can't. Some paedophiles are very well organized. But I don't think Thompson has the bottle—'

'He abducted a kid from her own front room! What would you call that?'

'We'll see. For the time being we need to concentrate on the periods he was inside. With any luck we'll identify our two victims and home in on exactly when they went missing. Only then can we hope to prove if he's in or out.'

Daniels was back. She'd washed her face and combed her hair, made herself look a bit more presentable. She put a hand in her pocket and then handed a couple of pills to Carmichael.

'How you feeling now?' she asked.

'Better. Hank's been holding my hand, figuratively speaking. He's convinced me that things may not be as grim as I was beginning to think they were.'

'Has he now?' Daniels' face brightened noticeably. Hank was good with young detectives, especially when the chips were down. That's why she'd chosen him to mentor Carmichael.

Same reason she'd selected him as her number two all those years ago. "Bout time he did some work around here."

'Ouch!' he said. 'You kiss and make up with the guv'nor?'

'Might have.'

'Did you?'

She grinned. 'What do you think?'

'Good! I can't stand seeing a grown man cry.'

They all laughed.

'So,' Hank said. 'At the end of the day all we've detected is a theft.'

'I had three choices,' Kate sighed. 'Charge him, bail him or release him.'

Gormley didn't have to ask. He could see from her face that John Edward Thompson was long gone.

53

Appalled by what Walker had told her at lunch, Emily had gone looking for Kent with a view to offering her help without letting on she knew about his daughter's disappearance. But all afternoon he'd kept his head down, even volunteering to supervise a creative writing class taking place in the prison library, a dull duty for someone who'd never read a book in his life. It was obvious he was ignoring her.

C'est la vie!

She'd done all she could. Time to go home.

Emily hurried to her car. It was freezing outside but a beautiful evening. The night sky was inky black, the stars brighter than she'd seen them in a long while. Turning out of the prison car park she rang Vera Hendry to check on her husband's progress and let her know there was no rush for him to act as locksmith.

The news wasn't good.

Since his fall, Reg had been complaining of extreme dizziness. Further examination by his GP revealed a swelling of the optic nerve. Suspecting a slight bleed on the brain, the doctor had ordered the old man to Rake Lane Hospital to undergo a CT scan. The situation wasn't life-threatening but it wasn't good either for a man of his age.

Determined not to dwell on another miserable newsflash,

Emily drove on, arriving at The Stint around fifteen minutes later. The place was in darkness. She let herself in, stooping to pick up junk mail from the hallway floor. It was the first time in ages she'd come home to an empty house. It hadn't occurred to her how awful and isolating it must've been for Rachel since she'd taken the decision to return to work.

Emily lit the wood-burner, prepared dinner, made the beds and stuck some washing in. As she re-entered the living room to check on the fire, her eyes were drawn to the wall above the hearth where two framed photographs took pride of place. Both were of Robert. In one he was fishing in the river at the bottom of the garden. In the other, he was standing beside his Land Rover Defender, a rifle cocked over his arm, an old black gundog by his side. She remembered taking the photo, poking fun at him, telling him he looked like an advert for the BBC programme, *Countryfile*.

Miss you, Rob.

Swallowing down her grief, she went to the window and looked out. The lane outside was empty. Emily checked her watch. Six fifteen. As she raised her eyes, the headlights of a single-decker lit up the tree-lined road beyond her garden wall. Only half-expecting it to stop outside, she was nevertheless disappointed when it didn't. Rachel rarely managed the early bus from Newcastle.

She'd be on the next for sure.

Emily was about to turn away from the window when a police car took the brow of the hill at speed, its blues and twos flashing. She watched it get closer . . . and was horrified when it turned into her driveway, its tyres crunching on a mixture of gravel and ice as it came to a sudden stop.

A policeman got out, putting his cap on as he climbed from the vehicle. With her heart in her mouth, Emily edged ever so slowly into the hallway. A blurred profile appeared through the frosted panel of her front door. A flood of mixed emotions ran through her head. She couldn't see the officer's expression but she could feel the seriousness of his visit like a heavy vibration through the door.

What was he waiting for?

As he tapped on the door, Emily remembered that the bell was iffy. She didn't move for what seemed like an eternity. Then, lifting her arm, her hand froze in mid-air as she reached for the latch. She withdrew it again, staring at the blurred shadow of her unexpected visitor, as if leaving the door closed would save her from a fate worse than death.

A knock this time: harder and more businesslike. A face pressed to the glass peering in at her. She took a deep breath, lifted the latch and pulled the open door. The officer was tall, maybe six-three, around forty years old, pale blue eyes framed by fair lashes and intelligent brows. He had what her mother called good suit shoulders, straight not slouched, that filled his pristine uniform perfectly.

Emily tried to speak but no words came out.

Removing his hat, the policeman stowed it under his left armpit. 'I'm looking for Ms McCann?' he said.

'You found her.' Emily's voice caught in her throat.

He pointed into the hallway. 'Could we talk inside?'

'Of course . . .' Stepping back to let him in, a sense of dread wrapped itself around Emily as it had the day a policeman turned up at the prison without warning to inform her of Robert's sudden death. She offered this one a seat but he remained standing, his eyes searching her face, forming impressions, making judgements.

What the hell for?

'Do you know why I'm here, madam?' he asked.

How could she? Confused, Emily only managed a shake of her head.

'Did you come straight home from the prison?' His tone was flat.

How come he knew where she worked? 'Yes, why?'

'What time did you leave?'

Emily shrugged. 'A little after five-thirty.'

'Can you be more specific?'

'I'm sorry, I can't. It was around then, I couldn't say for sure.'

'You seem rather nervous.'

Emily felt hot. She had a good right to be nervous. There was a policeman standing in her living room asking her ridiculous questions and she didn't know why. Her answer obviously wasn't satisfactory and he wanted more. She glanced at her watch. 'It was no more than half an hour ago. I've not been long in. What's all this about?'

'Any contact with anyone since you left?'

'No, yes. I called a friend. Why is that important?'

'We were alerted by prison staff—'

'About *what*? I don't follow. Has there been an escape?'

He didn't answer.

Did he think she'd assisted an offender to get away, willingly or otherwise?

'Officer?' she pushed.

'No, madam. There's been no escape.' His expression was like a reprimand. 'I'm here for the keys. Where are they?'

'Oh shit!' Now she understood.

Feeling like a kid who'd been caught stealing, Emily looked down at the key pouch on her waist, the realization dawning. Leaving one of Her Majesty's Prisons without handing in her precious keys was tantamount to treason. One of the most serious breaches of security it was possible to make. Potentially, every lock on every gate and every cell door would have to be changed unless the authorities were satisfied that it was purely accidental.

A grovelling apology was in order.

'I feel such an idiot . . .' Unclipping the keys from their chain, Emily handed them over. 'Please assure the Governor they've not left my person or passed into the wrong hands. I'm so sorry.'

'It's easy done, I imagine.'

'It's not, actually. Gatehouse security is usually very thorough. I can't believe I wasn't stopped as I passed through. I've been a bit preoccupied of late.'

'Yes, I heard about Mr McCann. I'm sorry . . .' Checking his watch, the policeman made a note in his pocketbook. Looking up, he asked, 'Have you had any visitors at all since you got home?'

Emily shook her head.

'Stop anywhere on the way?'

'No.'

'You mentioned phoning someone. May I check your phone?'

Emily got her bag and handed over her mobile. Accessing her calls list, the officer wrote down Vera Hendry's number, asking her who it belonged to. She told him about the old lady, pleading with him not to worry her unnecessarily, explaining that her husband had been admitted to hospital that afternoon. He made the call, noted down his findings, and then called his control room telling them he was now in possession of the keys and that he was satisfied – as far as it was possible to be – that it was a genuine oversight on Emily's part.

Ending the call, he held the keys up to Emily. 'I'd better get these back where they belong.'

Repeating her apology, Emily showed him out. It would be up to prison security to determine whether any further action was required. She couldn't care less. Compared to what was going through her mind when the policeman arrived, the keys going AWOL didn't even come close. It certainly wasn't something she'd lose sleep over.

She sighed.

The only emotion she was feeling right now was relief. As long as Rachel was safe, Emily was bulletproof. Nothing else mattered. Waving as the policeman reversed off her driveway, she wondered who had told him about Robert. There were too many people discussing her business and she resented it.

The traffic car sped off the way it had come. Watching its tail lights disappear over the hill, Emily put on her coat and walked down her garden path to the main road to wait for Rachel, grateful that in the countryside the bus would stop anywhere to let its passengers off. A few seconds later, it flew right by.

54

Twenty-two miles away, Kate Daniels parked her car in the fishing village of Low Newton-by-the-Sea, one of her favourite places along the North Northumberland coast. Taking a bottle of red from the passenger seat, she climbed out, feeling a rush of pleasure as she scanned her surroundings.

Breathing in the fresh salty air, she admired the starry sky, the moonlight dancing on water, the waves crashing on to the shore. Jo's rented cottage was situated a spit off the beach. Picture perfect, it sat at one end of a single-storey white-washed terrace with a small porch out front. No wonder she'd chosen to live here.

Jo was a little unkempt when she answered the door, as if she wasn't expecting company and had just pulled her grey knitted dress over her head and hadn't bothered to comb her hair afterwards. She was barefoot, her slim legs wrapped in footless tights, toenails painted a deep shade of plum that matched her lipstick perfectly. The neck of her dress was pulled a touch too low at one side revealing a hint of pale lacy underwear.

'Come in quick before you're blown away.' She straightened her dress, wriggling her body into it, hopping on one foot to adjust one leg of her tights. 'As you can see I'm running a little late, sorry.'

'No need to apologize.' Kate stepped inside.

'Emily phoned. She had a visit from one of your lot. I think it gave her a bit of a fright.'

'Problem?' Kate took off her coat.

'You could say that. She left the prison with the bloody keys!'

'Oh dear.'

The smell of burning candles and the crackling of logs hit Kate's senses as she walked into the living room. Handing Jo the wine, she kicked off her shoes, the warm glow of the fire making her feel right at home. Her eyes scanned the tiny space her ex had made her own in the short time she'd lived there. It was really cosy and she told Jo so.

'It's basic but comfortable.'

'It's a whole lot more than that!' Kate said.

There was an awkward moment between them, a beat of time as they abandoned the present in favour of the past. Getting a bolthole at the coast – somewhere they could escape the rigours of life in the fast lane – had been high on their agenda when they were living together. Low Newton-by-the-Sea was their place of choice and the small cottage fit the bill perfectly.

'It wasn't intentional, Kate.' Jo looked away, embarrassed. 'It was the only one-bedroomed cottage available this close to the beach, I promise you. I needed it for Nelson. I didn't do it to hurt you. You know I'd never—'

'Hey! Don't worry about it. I'd have done the same in your shoes.'

'Liar!' Jo smiled nervously, relieved that Kate wasn't about to make an issue of it. 'Come on, I'll show you the rest.'

The tour didn't take long. This was not a family pad. You could fit the whole cottage into two rooms of Jo's permanent home – a Jesmond town house not far from Newcastle. There was a double bedroom, a shower – no bath – and a galley kitchen at the rear with stunning views over the shoreline of Newton Haven. And then they were back in the living room where they began. It had enough space for a two-seater sofa, a flat-screen TV, a square dining table, two chairs and little else. To the right of the fire was Nelson's bed. He was curled up in it fast asleep, next to a huge, empty, log basket.

Jo's eyes fell on the very spot. 'Shit! I forgot the logs. Supper's on the stove. Can you give it a stir while I pop out a sec?'

Kate offered to go.

'It's fine,' Jo said. 'There are steps down to the log store. You're liable to break your neck if you're not used to it. Help yourself to a drink. There's a bottle breathing on the kitchen bench or soft drinks in the fridge if you prefer. I know you don't partake on a school night. Won't be long.'

Kate took three steps into the kitchen.

The cast-iron pot on the stove had no ladle. She called out, 'Where will I find the—?'

Too late: the front door slammed shut.

Her phone rang: *Hank*.

She didn't answer. He was more than capable of holding the fort for a few hours without bothering her with trivia. Besides, he was the one hell-bent on getting her and Jo together. Now she was here, Kate had no intention of running out. If the matter was urgent he'd leave a message.

There was a selection of spices and herbs in the first

drawer Kate tried. In the next one along, she found a wooden spoon. Dipping it into the sauce, she helped herself. Licking her lips, she smiled. Jo always forgot the pepper. Finding some in a wall cupboard, she added a little and was about to put it back when something struck her as odd: a small framed photograph laid face down on top of a row of tinned tomatoes. Hidden, she suspected, from *her* prying eyes.

Lifting it down, she saw why.

It was a happy snap of the two of them, taken a couple of years earlier on a beach that was, quite literally, two paces beyond the kitchen wall.

She didn't pack light then.

Hearing the front door opening, Kate quickly replaced it.

They ate as soon as supper was ready: linguine with a sauce Jo had conjured up from nothing, a few fresh ingredients she had in the fridge, some oregano and olives thrown in, a green leaf salad. To go with it, German sunflower bread steeped in extra virgin olive oil, rubbed with roasted garlic cloves.

Kate couldn't remember enjoying a meal more.

Passing on the wine, she poured Jo a glass, watching her tuck into her pasta. It felt unsettling being in the same room with her when they hadn't seen each other socially for months. Eating with her, especially in candlelight with soulful music filling the air, required a level of intimacy she'd missed since they'd split up.

'I'm stuffed,' Jo said, pushing her plate away.

'Me too . . .' Kate put a hand on her stomach to labour the point. 'That was delicious, above and beyond considering I invited myself along at such short notice.'

'You always were pushy.'

'I never heard you complaining.'

Nelson snorted, making them both laugh, taking the heat out of the conversation. His body twitched. He opened one eye and then closed it again. Rolling over on to his back, he splayed his legs out giving them an eyeful of what Hank Gormley would refer to as his Gutiérrez.

'God!' Jo laughed. 'He's such a slut. You want dessert?'

Kate blew out her cheeks. 'No room.'

'Me neither.'

They cleared away the dishes together, replenished their glasses and returned to the living room where Jo stoked the fire and joined her guest on the sofa. Panic seized hold of Kate. This was the point of the evening when the small talk was over and they would turn their attention to her murder case, safer ground for both of them. But the photograph she'd found in the kitchen kept edging its way into her thoughts. She wanted to mention it, to ask Jo why she'd felt the need to conceal it. Instead, she said nothing – fearful of spoiling the moment she was hoping still might come.

They talked about the case. Then, to Kate's surprise, the conversation drifted to more personal matters, the good fun they had enjoyed at home and at work in the preceding years. Relaxed and happy, Jo pulled up a footstool and turned off the standard lamp, plunging them into the past and the room into semi-darkness.

In flickering candlelight, Kate reached for her hand, began stroking it. When Jo didn't pull away, she leaned across and kissed her gently on the lips. There was no resistance – no words exchanged – just an intense closeness between them.

Caught up in the moment, Jo responded, tentatively at first, then with an urgency that surprised and excited her former lover.

Kate groaned as her mobile rang.

Jo pulled away, her expression a mixture of embarrassment and annoyance.

Kate let the phone ring out, cursing Hank. She knew it would be him. *Who else would it be?* When it stopped, she kissed Jo again. This time her whole body responded. Altering her position, she straddled Kate, a mischievous grin spreading over her face, eyes on fire.

'We've a lot to thank him for,' she said.

Kate felt a pang of guilt.

Crossing her arms, Jo took hold of the hem of her dress, peeling it off in slow motion. Dumping it on the floor, she unclipped her bra, causing it to fall from her shoulders. The sight of her naked flesh took Kate's breath away. Her pale breasts were full, her dark nipples enormous. She smelled wonderful. Her skin was soft, her back warm from the fire.

'If you stay the night—'

'*If?*' Kate pulled a face. 'Where else would I be staying?'

'There's no bacon and egg in my fridge.'

'I'm not on Dukan. Give me toast.'

'No bread, sorry.'

'Stop talking.'

They kissed again.

A mobile rang. Jo's this time.

'Shit, shit shit!' She grinned at Kate. 'I'm ignoring that!'

'You sure?'

'Fuck's sake! Course I'm sure . . .' Easing herself forward, Jo whispered in Kate's ear: 'Don't make me wait. I've missed you so much.'

'You drive me mad,' Kate said.

Jo's desperation had always been appealing. If she was up for sex, she never held back. The woman was shameless and totally uninhibited. Kate ripped off her shirt as the mobile died, leaving only the sound of pounding waves outside, the odd crackle of firewood, her own heartbeat.

Two seconds later the house phone rang. They both tried to ignore it but the answer machine kicked in. Emily McCann's voice pushed its way into the room. She was very distressed. 'Jo, if you're in, please pick up. It's Rachel. She hasn't come home!'

Grimacing, Jo shut her eyes.

Kate sighed.

The magic had gone.

55

Jo sat in silence. The atmosphere in the car was grim. Words seemed difficult for both of them following a scramble to get dressed. Kate's eyes were fixed on the road ahead. Jo couldn't fathom what the hell was going through that level head of hers.

Were they a couple again? Just good friends? What?

Was that even a good idea? Jo wondered.

Her thoughts drifted back to when she'd ended it between them.

Kate was a terrific person, an attentive lover, but ambitious to a fault. Her work came first. Always had. Still did. And now, Jo was asking herself, what had changed? Nothing, was the truthful answer. Not a damned thing. A little red wine might have brought *her* guard down on this special day but their romantic evening would most probably have been a one off.

Maybe Emily had done them both a favour.

In Alnwick, Kate slowed the car, pulling up outside the nick. She put the handbrake on but left the engine running, signalling her intent not to hang around, relieved that the journey had come to an end.

Well, that made two of them, Jo thought.

Jumping out, she held on to the door, preventing Kate

from driving away. 'Call you tomorrow?' she asked. A nod was all the reply she got.

Kate put the car in gear. 'Will you explain to Emily?'

'Of course.'

Kate gave a weak smile in lieu of thanks.

She needed no excuse to avoid getting involved in Emily's latest drama. Incident room personnel had sent texts asking her to get in touch as a matter of urgency. Hank had called several times, twice in the last half hour. Their persistence probably signalled more bad news: another death, another family in distress. Jo hoped not, for all their sakes. Shutting the door, she waved Kate off and then went inside.

Emily McCann was seated on a hard wooden bench in reception, her coat wrapped up in a ball beside her, elbows resting on her knees, head in hands. A tan leather bag lay open on the floor, a pack of tissues spilling out. Sensing a presence, she looked up anxiously. It was obvious she'd been crying. Her face was all puffy and red, a telltale smudge of mascara beneath her right eye. She was still dressed in the clothes she'd worn to work. She seemed to have aged ten years since the afternoon.

'Thank God!' she said. 'Maybe you can talk some sense into them. I've been here for ages and no one's taking any bloody notice of a word I've said.'

'I'm sure that's not true,' Jo said.

'The PC I saw is not much older than Rachel. You'd think he'd understand. And when I insisted on seeing a detective, someone in authority who's over eighteen, he took offence and the shutters went up.' Emily looked past Jo to the entrance. 'Where's Kate?'

56

The name caught Kate's eye as soon as she entered the MIR. She didn't need telling that there had been a major break-through in the case. It was writ large on the murder wall beneath crime scene photographs of the more recent victim. It was her sole focus. The longer she looked at it, the bigger it became. It was like looking through a camera lens, zooming ever closer. Carmichael's handwriting. Black marker. Capital letters. Neat script, around three inches tall. A simple name. Two words: **_MAXINE O'NEIL_**.

'She's busy, Em. Really busy,' Jo said. 'The incident room have been calling nonstop.'

Jo was used to making excuses for Kate. She'd lost count of how many engagements she'd cancelled because Kate had been called in to work. Never off duty was a clichéd term but it was also a true reflection of the working life of a detective. Emily knew that to be the case. Even so, her disappointment was plain to see.

Jo sat down, changing the subject. 'Tell me what happened with Rachel.'

Emily's bottom lip quivered at the mention of her daughter's name.

Jo put her arm around her. 'I can't help if you don't talk to me, Em.'

'She didn't come home. Something terrible has happened, I know it has!'

'You can't possibly—'

'I do!'

'Emily, listen to me—'

'I gave the copper a recent photo, the names of Rachel's friends, but he's wasting his time. I already rang round everyone.'

Jo looked around. 'Where's the officer now?'

'Officer?' Emily's expression hardened. 'Don't make me laugh.'

The desk sergeant looked up from her paperwork. Jo smiled – a forgive-her-she's-upset kind of smile – trying to keep her onside. Turning to Emily, she dropped her voice and said, 'Em, you need to calm down. You're not going to get anywhere if you don't. Where is he?'

'Making calls.' Emily looked over her shoulder. 'What's taking so long? I told him Rachel's not one to run off—'

'That's not strictly true though, is it?'

'Excuse me?' Emily bit back. 'Whose side are you on?'

'It's not a question of sides. She's gone missing before—'

'That was years ago, a schoolgirl prank and you know it. You know Rachel! She's a responsible adult now!' Emily paused, then swung round as Jo's gaze shifted to a point over her shoulder. The PC she was waiting for was standing right behind her. Emily glared at him. 'Well? What are you waiting for? *Now* will you take a missing person report?'

*

Carmichael nudged Hank Gormley's arm, tipping him off that their boss had arrived. Kate was standing in the doorway, her eyes focused on the murder wall. She'd changed her clothes and done her hair, had on a little more make-up than usual. She looked stunning.

Gormley left the others to greet her. 'Where the hell have you been?' he whispered. 'We've been trying to contact you for hours. I was about to call the police.'

Ignoring the jibe, Kate walked further into the room, side-stepping his question with one of her own. 'What is this? DNA match?'

'Yep. Maxine O'Neil. Fifteen years old. One of four children to Suzanne and Graham O'Neil. Missing since around 11.30 on Tuesday, 12 February 2006. Last known sighting at a bus stop on the A1079, five miles north of Hull.'

'Seen by who?'

'Passing motorist. School teacher who knew her well.'

'Male or female?'

'Male. They're not allowed to pick up students, so he drove right by.'

'Allegedly,' Robson said as he approached.

'Why weren't they both at school?' Kate queried.

'Half-term,' Gormley said.

Kate met his eyes. 'How seriously was her disappearance taken at the time?'

'Not very. It was treated as a misper, in view of her age.'

Kate noticed Lisa Carmichael's disgust. She understood it too. If the girl had been five or even ten years old they would have been on it like a rash. But that wasn't necessarily the case for fifteen-year-olds. Chances were they had gone off with a boyfriend or just decided they'd had enough of their parents and run away. All of those things came into play when deciding who to believe and how to proceed. However, now she was a murder statistic, all that was about to change.

57

'We need to talk some more,' the PC said.

'Fine!' Emily pointed at Jo. 'I want her to come too.'

'No problem.' The PC unlocked a door to an interview room and stood back, checking Jo out as she followed Emily into the room. All three took a seat, the policeman placing a scruffy reporter's notepad on the table between them. He cleared his throat. 'You should listen to your friend, Mrs McCann.'

'No, you listen to me!' Emily said. 'You may as well, because I'm not going to be put off. Thousands of kids go missing every year in this country. I know what I'm talking about, OK?'

'You just said Rachel was a responsible adult.'

Jo looked at her friend. 'He's right, Em. You can't have it both ways.'

Emily looked wounded.

Despite the fact that he was the only one with any authority in the room, the PC appeared intimidated by her outburst. He chose his words carefully, acknowledging that of course people of Rachel's age went missing every day but pointing out that more often than not they returned unharmed within a few hours or days.

'Why?' Emily was off again. 'Why would Rachel go missing?'

'You tell me,' the PC said. 'Boyfriend you don't approve of, perhaps?'

Emily's cheeks flushed, her eyes darting to Jo for support.

Knowing there was some truth in that, Jo said nothing. Emily had suspected a clandestine relationship for weeks. That said, Jo understood her reluctance to rubbish her daughter to the police. Only last night, mother and daughter had apparently reached an agreement: Emily would stop treating Rachel like a kid and in return, Rachel would resume her studies and start keeping regular hours.

Would she suddenly go back on her word?

'Why won't you listen to me? I already told you what I think has happened.' Emily looked at Jo, a plea for help. 'I've told him about Walter Fearon, the things he said. Please make him understand or get hold of Kate. Do *something*.'

'Who's Kate?' the PC asked.

'She's a DCI with a bit more oomph than you,' Emily said.

'Emily!' Jo apologized to the officer then turned to her friend. 'C'mon, Em. You're doing yourself no favours.'

Emily combed a hand through her hair, her face pained with distress, tears welling up in her eyes. 'I'm sorry, honestly I am. It's just . . . I want my daughter back.'

'This young prisoner,' the PC queried, 'he's someone you both work with?'

'No.' Emily wiped her eyes. 'Just me.'

'I'm aware of him,' Jo said quietly. 'He's a piece of work.'

Emily confirmed that with a nod. 'I know it sounds crazy, but he's obsessed with me. That might appear odd to you given my age, but older women are his thing. He's not been getting his own way lately and I think he's done something awful to Rachel just to get back at *me*. I've been giving him a hard time over his behaviour in prison.'

The officer was looking directly at Jo. 'Do you agree with Ms McCann?'

His question was a lowballer designed to divide and conquer. A clever tactic when he was on the back foot. He was beginning to piss Jo off.

Where the hell was Daniels when you wanted her?

'I agree that he's a very dangerous young man,' Jo said.

Her failure to commit herself wasn't lost on the other two.

'He's making that up though, surely,' the policeman said. 'I mean, he's in prison, right? He's not going anywhere.'

'Yet!' Emily said.

'He's due out imminently,' Jo explained. 'Which is why Emily is so distraught.'

'And I have every reason to be,' Emily said. 'It may have passed you by, but sex offenders often work in pairs. That obviously didn't appear in your police entrance exam!'

'Has it occurred to you what day it is?' the PC asked, ignoring the dig.

'Day?' Emily looked puzzled.

Jo knew what he was getting at. His question felt like a slap. Taking hold of Emily's hand, she gave it a gentle squeeze. The physical contact produced a sudden flashback: Kate stroking her hand and ripping off her shirt in a candlelit room.

A lot can happen in an hour.

'It's Valentine's Day,' Jo said gently.

Emily looked away in a flood of tears.

Jo focused on the officer. 'Emily's husband died a few months ago. Were you aware of that?' she asked pointedly. The PC clearly was. 'Then perhaps you'll understand why she can't bear to let her daughter out of her sight. Hardly surprising she's beside herself, is it?'

The PC blushed. 'Rachel's mixed up too, I gather.'

Jo resented the inference that Emily's state of mind was not good. But the way she was acting, it was hardly surprising the policeman would take that view. She certainly sounded like she was losing it.

'Enough to harm herself?' the PC asked.

'No.' Jo shook her head. 'Rachel would never do that.'

'No way!' Emily snapped. 'I'm her mother! I should know. She hasn't run away, or thrown herself under a bus. I told you, this offender described her to me, he described the house where we live.'

'How come?' the PC asked. 'Did you talk to him about—'

'No! Why would I? I have no idea how he knows. He just does! Please, I'm begging you. Take me seriously before it's too late.'

Jo realized there wasn't a lot the officer could do. It was obvious he thought that Rachel had gone off with a mate. She hadn't been missing long and, by her own admission, Emily had already done what the police would do under the circumstances: contacted all Rachel's friends, the college, etcetera. Although he was under pressure to offer Emily some small crumb of comfort, at least show some sympathy for the woman's plight, behind his eyes there was a steely determination Jo had seen so often in Kate Daniels when she was about to deliver bad news. A sucker punch was on its way.

58

Core members of the Murder Investigation Team were sitting in a semi-circle in the centre of the incident room, lights dimmed, no civilian personnel present. DC Lisa Carmichael looked as though she wanted to punch someone. It was an appalling state of affairs but, like it or not, age had a bearing on how any police force dealt with missing children.

'Hank, you up for driving to Hull?' Kate took in Gormley's nod. 'Maxine O'Neil's parents need telling and I'd like to be the one to do that before they find out from some arsehole blabbing to the press. Who spoke to Humberside?'

DC Maxwell raised a finger.

'What enquiries were made?' the DCI asked. 'How far did they take it?'

'That's difficult to say. The parents maintained she was a lovely kid. Not the type to go off on her own. There was no fight. No argument beforehand. Others said different.'

Kate's interest grew. 'Go on.'

'There were rumours,' Maxwell said.

'Kind of rumours?'

'Information from her mates that there was another side to her.'

'The school bike, you told us,' Carmichael made a face.

Maxwell shot her a look. 'Humberside's description, Lisa. Not mine.'

'Sounds like yours.'

'Yeah, well it wasn't.'

'Oi! Cut it out, you two! Look, we're all tired. But we need to focus, now more than ever.' Kate's eyes were on Maxwell. 'And the upshot was?'

'They did what they could but their enquiries came to a dead end.' His face flushed as he realized his choice of words might've been better.

'Did they do a reconstruction?' Kate wanted to know. 'Because if they didn't, we might need to.'

'Not sure.'

'Find out. Lisa, phone Humberside. Let them know we're on our way. I want the missing-person form and the file faxed up here immediately. I want you lot to grab a couple of hours' kip at the B & B and then come straight back here. I expect a broad antecedent history by the time I return. Any links with this area, any links with Bamburgh in particular. OK, that's it. You know the drill.'

'So I'm wasting my time then,' Emily glared at the young PC.

'I'm not saying that, and I can see how distressed you are. But we've got to wait a while before we proceed further.' The PC glanced at his watch, his eyes darting to Jo as he looked up. Then he turned his attention to Emily. 'It's barely eleven o'clock, Mrs McCann. She's only been gone a few hours. You're far better going home. If Rachel isn't there by morning, by all means, contact us again. Why don't you give her another call now?'

'I've phoned her umpteen times and got no answer,' Emily wailed.

'Did you know she'd not been in college this afternoon?'

Emily gave a resigned nod.

The PC flipped his notepad open. 'And did you also know she'd called her friend Susan Myers at four o'clock?'

'Did she? Susan never mentioned it to me.'

The PC shrugged. 'According to her, you never asked.'

'No,' Emily said. 'I don't suppose I did.'

'Miss Myers was in a lecture when the call came in. She wasn't able to pick up but it was definitely Rachel's number. She read it back to me . . .' The officer shifted his gaze to Jo, then to Emily. 'Your daughter has a new boyfriend, Mrs McCann. His name is Vic.'

Emily went quiet.

It was the killer blow Jo had been waiting for. She squeezed Emily's hand. The PC might be very young but he was pretty switched on. Given the fruits of his enquiries he had good grounds to doubt Emily's version of events. Maybe he was right to do so. Rachel had been stroppy, secretive, and downright disobedient of late. She'd come in drunk several nights running since her mother had returned to work. Was it any wonder she wasn't thinking straight? Her story sounded far-fetched, even to Jo.

Making arrangements to meet their Humberside colleagues early next morning, Daniels and Gormley grabbed their coats and left the incident room for the long drive south.

'You got the sample?' she asked.

Gormley patted his jacket pocket and nodded his head.

'I'll have to ask the girl's parents about the pearls whether I like it or not, and a whole lot more besides . . .' As the DCI pushed through the door into the corridor her mobile rang. Cursing, she took the phone from her pocket, pressed to answer and lifted it to her ear.

'DCI Daniels,' she barked. 'What is it? I can't talk now.'

'Can you call me later then?' Jo asked.

'Oh, sorry. Actually no, yes . . . maybe, I don't know.' A thought popped into Kate's head. 'Hold on!' She grabbed Gormley's arm, stopping him in his tracks, not bothering to cover the speaker. 'Wonder if Munro knows about Maxine O'Neil?'

'He's bound to,' Gormley said. 'You want me to ring him before we set off?'

'No, it's OK, I have his number in here.' She pointed at her phone with her free hand. 'C'mon, you can bell him on the way.' As they left via the rear exit, Jo's voice was drowned out by the din from a passing ambulance. 'Sorry, Jo. Didn't catch that. What did you say?'

'I said, that'll be a no then.'

'What's that supposed to mean?' Kate pressed her key fob and the lights on the Q5 blinked as the door locks clunked open. She climbed in and started the engine. 'Hey, look, I'm sorry. Something's come up. I'm flat-out here.'

'Fine!' Jo's voice filled the roomy interior of the Q5. 'Sorry I bothered you.'

'Don't be daft . . .' Kate hadn't figured on a public row. But as soon as she turned her key in the ignition, her mobile had switched to the hands-free system. She tried to ignore the heat of Gormley's eyes on the side of her head and the sarcastic remark that followed, an observation about Jo being in a strop and laying the blame at *her* feet. Resisting the temptation to rip into him, Kate said, 'Take no notice of Hank. Just believe me when I tell you it's important.'

'It always is,' Jo said. 'Shame you care more for the dead than the living.'

Kate winced. 'How is Emily?' she asked, sheepishly.

The dial tone hit her ear as Jo put down the phone.

'Great answer,' Kate muttered, pulling away.

'Mind if I ask you a serious question?' Hank said.

She looked at him. 'Fill your boots.'

'Do all dykes argue 24/7?'

Kate didn't know whether to laugh or cry.

59

They made good time. Even managed to snatch a few hours' shut-eye at a hotel in Beverley, the East Yorkshire market town closest to Maxine O'Neil's home. Carmichael woke Kate Daniels shortly before six to advise that the missing-person file had an important note attached. Anyone with information should seek out PC Ailsa Richards, a community liaison officer at the town's police station.

'She has close links with the family,' Carmichael said. Her voice sounded thick, the result of another late night and very early morning. 'She was the first to attend when Maxine went missing. I managed to catch her going off duty an hour ago. She'll stay on and meet you there at seven.'

'Thanks, Lisa. Anything else?'

'No, not yet.'

'Call you later then.'

Hanging up, Kate rang Gormley's room to make sure he was up and about, then jumped in the shower and joined him for breakfast. There was no way either of them could face the day without fuel. They ate in silence, neither with any real appetite for food – much less for informing the dead girl's parents that they would never see their child again.

Kate wondered if the O'Neils were the type to leave their daughter's stuff untouched, as was often the case when children went missing. She'd known cases where Christmas and birthday presents had lain unopened for years. One family kept a burning candle in the window the whole time, a beacon of hope they firmly believed would guide their loved one home to them.

It didn't.

That depressing thought matched the weather outside. A veil of dense fog shrouded the outskirts of Beverley, making travel difficult. What little traffic there was on the road appeared out of nowhere like dark smudges on a white canvas, rendering headlights useless as drivers picked their way cautiously along.

They were late getting to the nick but PC Ailsa Richards was waiting in reception when they arrived. She gave them the hard copy of the missing-person file, confirming that she'd sent a copy electronically to Carmichael. Then they adjourned to a quiet office where they could talk without fear of interruption.

Ailsa Richards was about twenty-five years old, shorter than the average copper, with fair hair cut in a bob. She had an interesting face, a slightly crooked nose that had obviously taken a beating at some point. Her eyes were the colour of cornflowers, the left one with a green fleck in it the DCI couldn't stop staring at.

She sat down, gestured for the other two to do likewise and then focused on the Humberside officer. 'I understand you're close to the O'Neil family, is that correct?'

PC Richards nodded. 'Yes, ma'am.'

'Are you properly involved with them, or is that a load of bollocks?'

'Ma'am?'

'Drop the ma'am, Ailsa. No offence intended, but people write things on forms that aren't true sometimes.'

'Not in this instance, I can assure you.' Richards stood firm. 'I'm not sure how you deal with things in Northumbria, but here in Humberside we try to do things right. I promised the family I'd keep them updated of any developments, big or small, good or bad. I've kept my word, visiting every three months for the past five years, never missed once.'

'That's good to hear.' Kate meant it. If she was any judge of character, this officer was not only truthful, she had balls. She liked that. 'I hope you understand my need to be sure. This is going to be a difficult day for everyone involved. The family don't need a fuck-up and neither do I.'

The PC didn't flinch.

Daniels studied her closely. It was important to see the whites of her eyes and work out how well or ill-equipped she was to deal with something as sensitive as a death message. To an outsider, they were all much of a muchness. But to anyone charged with the task of delivering them on a regular basis, there was a world of difference. The death of an elderly relative was often half-expected; the sudden death of a young person was deemed somehow worse; in the case of a road accident, an element of bad luck came into the equation. Most people understood and came to accept that eventually. But the deliberate, violent and senseless deaths, the ones where murder was involved, those were another matter entirely.

And then there was the worst type of all.

On a sliding scale of one to ten, the kind of death message

Kate was about to deliver was in a league of its own. The O'Neils had waited five long years to hear news of a much-loved daughter. It was hard to imagine how they had coped, every single day dragging painfully on to the next, keeping themselves going by clinging to the hope that Maxine was out there somewhere. Living a new life – happy, even.

'The O'Neils have other children?' Gormley asked.

The PC nodded. 'Two boys and a girl.'

'How old?'

'Twelve, nine and five.'

'Mrs O'Neil was pregnant when Maxine when missing?' Kate queried.

Another nod. 'Seven months.'

The DCI glanced at Gormley, an unspoken message passing between them. From the look of him, his antenna had raised just as hers had. They were both remembering an enquiry they had worked some years ago where the victim's father had turned to her for sex when his wife, the girl's mother, was heavily pregnant. The girl threatened to go to the law, so he silenced her for good, concealing her body in the bottom of a chest freezer under legs of lamb and pork chops.

'Who'll tell them?' the PC asked. 'You or me?'

'Depends on how you feel about that.' Kate looked at Richards. When she made no comment, the DCI made an observation: 'You know them personally, I don't. But I can't have you getting upset. If you're going to do that, it's best that I tell them.' She paused, allowing her comment to sink in. 'Do you usually ring before you visit?'

'I didn't used to, but . . .' Richards looked away.

'Let me guess. Every time you went to the door, every time

they saw a Panda in the street, they were shitting themselves, right?' Richards answered with a nod. Kate noticed the green fleck in her eye twitching slightly. 'Well, as soon as they see me and DS Gormley they'll know.'

For a moment, no one spoke.

'I'm tempted to say if you want to do it, you do it, and if you look like you're going to bottle it, I'll interrupt. Question is: have you done it before?'

The PC shook her head.

'Then this is no time to start, Ailsa. There'll be difficult questions to answer. In situations like these you can't afford to pull your punches. There are no mistakes to be made, get me? I can see you don't want to do it and that's perfectly fine. There's no shame in that. How about I do it? I know you've been up all night but it would really help me out if you were on hand to pick up the pieces when I leave. Are we agreed?'

'Thanks, boss.'

'C'mon then, let's get it over with.'

60

At the end of her fifth consecutive nightshift, PC Ailsa Richards looked shagged out as she climbed into the Q5 and rode up front with Daniels. Gormley took the back seat, the missing-person case file open on his knee, speed-reading as they made their way through the back streets. The fog hadn't lifted any. They could hardly see a hand in front of their face as they skirted the edge of town. There was nothing to recommend being out and about.

Even less the reason for their journey.

'So, Ailsa . . . what is it you're not telling me?' Kate turned left and then glanced at her brooding passenger. 'You have something important to say, I'd like to hear what it is.'

Gormley offered to pass Richards the file to refresh her memory.

She waved it away, telling him she didn't need it. There wasn't a detail in there she hadn't been over a million times already. It was clear she'd taken a personal interest in the case and the Northumbria detectives were keen to hear why.

Kate tried to draw her out. 'Tell us about the O'Neils.'

'They're a big Catholic family and lovely with it. For what it's worth, I don't think they have anything to hide.' Richards peered through the gloom, then pointed towards an upcoming junction. 'Take a left here, and then the second exit off the mini roundabout. That's if you can see it, boss.'

Kate took the turning. 'Who raised the alarm?'

'Suzanne, the girl's mother.'

'Odd timing, I thought. Eleven-thirty at night I could understand, but in the morning?'

'Maxine had slept over at a mate's house the night before she went missing. She was a gifted musician and a brilliant dancer with an important audition at eleven the next day. She'd spent years practising. It was a chance in a lifetime – not exactly *X Factor*, but not far off. She had big ideas for such a little girl. Suzanne hadn't wanted her to stay out that night, but her father thought it might relax her to be with her mates. In the end, they let her go. When she didn't return the next day, Suzanne called us.'

'What's *he* like?' Hank asked.

'Graham? He's a nice bloke and a fantastic dad. He's had to be . . . Suzanne isn't the most stable since Maxine went missing.'

'File states he was at work at the time,' Hank said.

'Clocked in at seven, out again at eleven when his wife rang with the news.'

'There's no dispute about that?' Kate asked.

'None.'

'What about the teacher? What's his name?'

'John Butterworth.'

'Was he absolutely sure it was Maxine he saw at the bus stop?'

'Yes. He knows . . . knew Maxine very well. He taught her music in the third year. Knowing what a big day it was for her, he gave her the thumbs up as he drove by. She waved back but glanced anxiously at her watch. He automatically checked the clock on the dash. It was nine forty-five. There was a bus due in five, plenty of time before her interview. Otherwise, he said, he would have stopped, rules or no rules.'

'The bus driver was traced?'

'Yes. No one got on or off at that stop. At least four passengers corroborated his evidence.'

'Did you check the whole of Butterworth's journey?' Kate asked.

Richards nodded. 'His alibi checked out.'

Kate looked sideways. 'You figured he needed one?'

'Someone did. There was a five-minute window in which the girl went missing. In my opinion, she was taken against her will, and by someone she knew.' Richards pointed out the window. 'It's left here, boss. Actually, no, if we go that way we might end up in a hole. There are roadworks down there. Take the next one instead.'

The DCI cancelled her indicator. 'What made you think it was someone she knew?'

'Everyone I spoke to was agreed on one thing: there was no way she'd have got into a car with a stranger. Besides, it's a busy road. If she'd been dragged into a vehicle kicking and screaming, someone would've seen it happen. There were other things too. Apart from the music thing, Suzanne and Graham say she was happy at home. She adored her siblings and was excited about the new baby—'

'With respect, Ailsa, all families say that.' Hank was playing Devil's advocate.

'Left here?' Kate asked.

Richards nodded.

'We were told Maxine was sexually active,' Hank said. 'Was she?'

'No more than the rest of us, Sarge.' Richards had made herself blush. 'She had the world at her feet and was hugely popular with the boys. She was fifteen! Of course she was experimenting. Hell, we've all been there – least, I have.'

'You must've been very young in service when this happened,' Kate said.

'Nineteen. I'd been in less than a year. It was the most important case I'd worked on up to that point. Still is. Consequently, it meant a lot to me.' Richards paused, keeping her eyes on the road ahead. After a second or two she said, 'Can I talk off the record, boss?'

Here it comes.

'Be my guest,' Kate said. 'But I'll be straight with you, Ailsa. If you tell me something case-related, there's no guarantee I won't repeat it. There's too much at stake.' She pulled up at a red light. It was important to get the unofficial as well as the official version of events, to build a picture of what had gone on back then. She could see that Richards was in two minds whether or not to trust an SIO from another force.

She needed a little nudge.

Kate looked at her. 'You told me earlier you do things right. Well, there's never been a more important time to do that than now. This is a murder investigation, Ailsa. I need your help.'

'I struck up a relationship with Graham and Suzanne. They trusted me, always asked for me personally if they rang the station. My then sergeant cottoned on. He was a lazy git. The shift called him Olympic Torch because he never went out.' Richards wasn't smiling. 'He's retired now. Anyway, he encouraged me to get involved with the family. When he found out Maxine wasn't a virgin he made a judgement error, in my view. All of a sudden she was labelled as some promiscuous little slag who liked to put it about. One up from a prostitute.'

'Let me guess . . .' Kate moved off as the lights changed. 'He lost interest?'

'In a word, yes. He refused to take her disappearance seriously. I disagreed vehemently and fell out of favour. He accused me of getting too close to the family, marked me down for it too, the bastard. I never told anyone this but I became a bit obsessed with the case. I took the file home, even spoke to Maxine's mates on the QT when I was on patrol—'

'And when you were off duty too, I bet.'

The PC refused to be drawn on that. 'Some of the kids were sixth-formers, a couple of years younger than me. I got on well with them. No one suspected Maxine was going to do one. Run away, I mean. But I couldn't find any evidence to get the case upgraded to an abduction—'

'Sounds like you're wasted in uniform,' Kate said.

Ailsa's face lit up. 'I'd swap with you any day of the week.'

'You'll get there,' Kate said. 'If you want it enough and stick in.'

'Not with a black mark on my record, I won't.' Richards tried to keep the bitterness from her voice. 'Anyway, my sergeant suggested that the kid had run away because she couldn't face the pressure of the audition. He persuaded

Suzanne to take part in a TV appeal. You know the type: *If you don't want to ring us, get in touch with someone: relative, friend, police officer. Tell us something about yourself that only you and us will know. We're not angry with you. Just come home . . .'*

Richards sighed. 'It was a load of bollocks. All the local TV and radio stations covered it. Graham was furious. He could see that it was counter-productive, taking everyone's eye off the ball, making out Maxine had run away and letting the police off the hook in one fell swoop. He suspected something awful had happened to her, but Suzanne wouldn't have it. She seized on the idea that Maxine had fled from the threshold of fame.'

'And since then?'

'The family have survived. Just. Suzanne has clung on to the ridiculous belief that her daughter is out there somewhere. But now we know she isn't . . .' Richards went quiet for a moment. 'There's one thing I don't understand, boss.'

'Fire away.'

'Didn't you recover *two* bodies in Northumberland?'

'My DC tell you that?' Kate asked.

'No, I saw it in the police bulletin.'

'Really? I'm impressed. And, yes, we have two bodies.'

'We only had one missing girl,' Richards said. 'I checked.'

'There's information about the case we've not yet released.' Kate eyeballed her Humberside colleague. She seemed like an honest soul, someone she could confide in. 'I'm going to trust you to keep your mouth shut, Ailsa. If you don't, you'll have me to answer to. Is that understood?'

'Perfectly.'

'This is going to sound odd, but was there any mention in the file of pearls?'

'Pearls?'

'Kids' fake jewellery.'

'No.'

'Sure?'

'Positive.'

''Kay . . . forget I asked you that.'

Again, Richards pointed through the window. 'This is it, boss. Number twenty-four.'

Kate pulled up in the quiet street next to a semi-detached local authority home. Curtains drawn. Lights on upstairs and down. She imagined the family round the breakfast table, going about their business, getting ready for work or school. Radio tuned to a local station, kids arguing over the last piece of toast or whose turn it was to use the bathroom.

Normality.

'Right, you two. Mobiles off.'

They got out of the car and walked up the narrow path in single file. It seemed to take for ever to reach the front door. Ailsa Richards rang the bell and stepped aside. Kate swallowed hard. Heard a female voice from within. The hall light went on. An indistinct shape appeared through the glass panel. The DCI couldn't be sure, but the figure seemed to falter as it neared the door and then pick up speed again.

Her stomach churned as the chain came off and the door edged open. Predictably, the woman knew as soon as she set eyes on them. A strangulated wail cut through the foggy street as her legs gave way and she collapsed in the doorway in a heap, her heart breaking as the truth hit home.

61

Daniels liked PC Richards. She hadn't put a foot wrong all morning. She'd taken the O'Neil children to a neighbour and then done her level best to comfort the family while the SIO delivered the sad news. A newsflash on the radio had already alerted them to the find on Bamburgh beach. The O'Neils had been dreading a knock on the door ever since.

Kate gave them a moment alone.

Richards made a pot of tea, then they all sat down around the kitchen table surrounded by cereal bowls, unfinished glasses of juice, abandoned packed lunches and school bags – much as the DCI had imagined while walking up the garden path.

The relationship between Maxine and her parents had been recorded on the missing-person file as natural but Kate could take nothing for granted and asked the question anyway.

'It's important to be sure,' she said.

Mrs O'Neil confirmed that her oldest was their natural child.

Graham O'Neil asked why they wanted to know.

'In order to be one hundred per cent certain it is your daughter,' Hank explained. 'I'm afraid we need to take samples for comparison.'

Suzanne O'Neil seized on this, her focus shifting from the DS to the DCI. 'So you're not absolutely sure it's Max? How dare you come here then?'

'We've carried out tests,' Kate said gently. 'We are as sure as we possibly can be until we compare your DNA with hers . . .' She paused, taking in the reaction of both parents, checking that they fully understood. Mr O'Neil appeared resigned. But his wife was still clinging to the vain hope that the police were somehow mistaken. The DCI felt compelled to disabuse her of that. 'For the purposes of identification it would be helpful to know if Maxine ever broke any bones at all.'

'She broke her right leg once, quite badly. She thought it might stop her dancing but . . .' Mrs O'Neil's voice trailed off as she realized she'd just confirmed what all three officers already knew. She extended her hand and found her husband's, her words catching in her throat. 'When can we see her?'

It was the question Kate had been dreading.

According to Ailsa Richards, Mrs O'Neil was already on strong medication for depression, a condition that had deteriorated the longer her daughter had been missing. There was no way she was up to seeing the remains. An image of Bamburgh beach jumped into Kate's head. She wanted to describe the location to the grieving couple. It was a crime scene, yes. But Maxine had been buried in a place of beauty and solitude, not some ugly, smelly back yard or council tip, a ditch off a main road like other murder victims. However, it was not appropriate to do that now. In time, they would visit the site and see for themselves. Perhaps they would find some consolation in that.

Kate liked to think so.

She felt like pleading with the couple – *save yourselves the distress* – but they just stared at her, waiting to be convinced.

'I appreciate how distressing this is for you, but you need to know that Maxine has been buried in sand for probably the whole time she's been missing.' Kate chose her words very carefully. 'If you'd like me to, I can tell you what her body looks like. But you must bear in mind that whatever I say could never prepare you for what you would actually see. You are Maxine's next of kin and you have every right to a viewing. I'd never prevent you from doing that. But I'll be upfront with you: I strongly urge you not to.'

'You're saying there's no body to see?' Mr O'Neil said.

Kate gave a little nod. 'I'm so sorry.'

Mrs O'Neil shuddered violently and swallowed back vomit.

Her husband put his arm around her and spoke gently as he turned to face her. 'Suzanne, I don't want to do it. Please, don't force me to. There is nothing to be gained from it. I want to remember Maxine as she was. We all do. We've got the little 'uns to consider now. Besides, you know it'll make you ill.'

'I think that's very sensible.'

Mr O'Neil palmed away his tears. 'When will we know? For sure, I mean?'

'It'll take a day or two to compare the samples.'

'But it's a formality, you say?'

Again, Kate nodded. 'I'm sorry, sir.'

'Do you want to see Maxine's stuff?' her father asked.

'DS Gormley will call back later, if that's OK.' Kate was

desperate to check Maxine's journals, notepads, school books, diary, any documentation that might lead to her killer. But first the couple needed a few hours alone. 'In the meantime, I'll make sure you are assigned a Family Liaison Officer, someone who'll keep you posted on all developments as and when they occur.'

'Can't Ailsa do it?' Mr O'Neil asked.

'She'll be helping DS Gormley with enquiries. We need her local knowledge – she's been a great help to us so far. We have specialist officers on hand to assist you and Mrs O'Neil at any time of the day or night.' The couple appeared to accept that. They were both close to tears again but trying to be strong. It was all proving too much for them. It felt like an insult asking the next question, but it had to be done. 'Is there anything else I can do for you before we proceed with the samples?'

Graham O'Neil pulled himself together. 'Don't think badly of us, Inspector, but there isn't a room for you to search as such. Maxine shared a bedroom with her sister. It was traumatic enough when she went missing without the daily reminder of her things lying about, especially for our younger children. After a while we decided to pack her stuff in boxes. It's all in the loft, if you want to see it.'

'I understand. DS Gormley will take care of it. Don't you worry about that.'

Taking buccal swabs from the mouths of parents within an hour of telling them their daughter was dead was a job Kate found abhorrent, one she'd avoid if there were any other way. Unfortunately, there wasn't. When she was done, PC Richards stepped forward, asking for a quiet moment with the family.

The DCI and Gormley gave their condolences and with-drew to the car.

The fog had lifted slightly but the improvement in the weather wasn't nearly enough to raise their spirits. It was such a dull, grey morning – such a gloomy, sad street. Kate couldn't shake the image of the photograph mounted on the wall in the O'Neils' living room: Maxine centre stage during a local school production with everything to live for.

Such a bloody waste.

'Hank, I'm going to bugger off back to Northumberland and leave you here to run things this end. I'll get Lisa to drive down and join you. Stay as long as it takes. Make sure you get an FLO out here to the family right away. I want you to scour those boxes. See if you can find an address book or some-thing. I want you to examine every page in every book. Ask around. I don't think Twitter was up and running when Maxine went missing. Facebook was. Did she subscribe to it, or any other social networking site? She was an entertainer, so chances are she did. I'm looking for a connection with anyone we already have in the system. I'm thinking John Edward Thompson in particular.'

'I take it you want everybody re-interviewed?'

She nodded. 'Starting with the teacher.'

Ailsa Richards walked down the path, head bowed as she approached the Q5. Her face was ashen. She was physically upset as she got in, pulled the door to and strapped herself in. She was exhausted too. Who wouldn't be after a twelve-hour nightshift . . . and then some? With no time to indulge her distress, Kate turned over the engine and pulled away.

'You did well in there,' she said. 'I've known detectives with years of experience bottle it because they had personal history with the family.' The young PC didn't comment. After a moment of consideration, Daniels spoke again: 'I was going to send my DC down here to work with Hank on this. But I have a better idea. How would you like a temporary secondment to my Murder Investigation Team?'

Richards tired eyes lit up. 'Really?'

'Why not? It was your incident in the first place. You have local knowledge and I, sadly, have no clue of where the offence was committed. Northumbria has invested heavily in this case. We'll obviously be the prime mover, even though our area may be nothing more than a disposal site. It's a linked incident now. So, until we know where those kids were killed, we remain the lead force. I'd be grateful if you'd consider it.'

The young officer took no persuading.

Kate made the call immediately, asking to speak to Ailsa's supervision. After a brief exchange, it was agreed that Richards could act as liaison between the forces for a few days, seconded to Daniels' team.

'Only a few days?' Kate queried, pulling a face, Ailsa hanging on her every word. 'OK, if that's the best you can do, it's better than nothing . . . Of course I'll put it in writing – in triplicate, if it makes you happy.' She gave Ailsa the thumbs up, then caught Gormley's eye in her rear-view mirror. 'Hank, soon as you're satisfied I want you back in Alnwick.' She glanced at their new recruit. 'How are you fixed at home, Ailsa?'

'Fixed?'

'You got commitments, pets, kids?'

'You kidding? I wouldn't even have to cancel the milk.'

'Win win.' Kate winked at Hank in the mirror. 'Bring her too then, Hank.'

'I thought her guv'nor said a few days only?'

'I've decided she'll be indispensable,' Kate said.

62

The journey north was trouble free. Not so, the grovelling apology to Jo when Kate found out that Rachel McCann still hadn't resurfaced. It had been twenty-four hours since her last contact with anyone – the phone call to her college friend, Susan Myers, at four o'clock the previous day.

'Did Emily ring round her friends again?' she asked.

'Of course she did.' Jo sounded pissed.

'And?'

'Either they know nothing or they're not saying.'

'What do we know of the boyfriend? Vic, did you say his name was?'

The mobile signal was weak. Jo's voice came and went. 'Her friends don't . . . a clue. They aren't . . . he exists except in Rachel's imagination.'

'Maybe he doesn't.' Putting her foot down, Kate passed a lorry with an unsafe load, a flapping tarpaulin no longer securing a cargo of second-hand furniture. 'It wouldn't be the first time a girl invented a boyfriend to impress her mates. I did it myself once. Rachel's unhappy, Jo. She's missing Robert. Maybe Vic is her way of keeping her father alive.'

'Oh, so you're a psychologist now!'

'Don't get arsy with me. You asked my opinion: I'm giving it to you.'

Three cars on the inside lane indicated to pull off the motorway at a service station. Kate looked at her watch, her stomach rumbling a plea for food. But the stench from a nearby pig farm made her plough on without stopping. There would be time enough to eat when she got back to the station. Hopefully by that time Robbo would have both food and progress to impart.

'I didn't mean to get at you,' Jo apologized. 'I'm feeling guilty, that's all. I've known for ages that Rachel was being difficult. Hell, I've even witnessed it on occasions. I just didn't think it was my place to interfere. I gather Stamp tried and wished he hadn't. So I did sod-all and now . . .' She sighed. 'Emily's in a right state.'

'It was obvious she wasn't coping,' Kate said.

'Oh, that's *very* helpful.'

Kate ignored the dig. 'Did you stay with her last night?'

'I offered, but she wasn't having any so I went home. When I got to Low Newton I rang her, only she didn't pick up. I drove over there early this morning and she wasn't in. One of the locals said he'd seen her acting weird. He stopped and asked if she was OK but she wouldn't talk to him.' Jo sighed loudly, her words spoken in monotone almost, evidence of how desperate she was. 'I don't think she realizes what an impression she's giving out. I mean, a lone female standing on a bridge in tears. I gather the local man thought she was about to jump. She was still there when I found her. She'd been out searching. I don't know what she expected to find, but she just can't conceive of Rachel eloping with a boyfriend, Valentine's Day or not.'

Right now, Valentine's Day seemed a world away to Kate.

So much had happened since their brief encounter at Low Newton-by-the-Sea. None of it good. 'Look, I'm an hour away,' she said, trying to take the pressure off Jo. 'Leave it with me, I'll try and get hold of her. See if I can talk some sense into her.'

'Would you?'

'I just said so, didn't I?' Kate needed the distraction like a hole in the head. But having spent time with the O'Neil family, missing girls were high on her agenda at the moment. No matter how busy she was, she couldn't turn her back on a friend in need. 'It might not be in person, but I will talk to her. Is she at home now?'

There was silence on the line.

'Don't tell me she's at work?'

'Against my advice,' Jo said. 'And with a ridiculous notion of tackling Fearon—'

'She can't do that!'

'I don't mean she's going to ask him about Rachel – give her *some* credit! She wants to keep him close in the vain hope that he starts mouthing off and inadvertently gives away a clue as to where she might—'

'Vain being the operative word. Does she have any idea how crazy that sounds?'

'She doesn't care. She just wants Rachel home safe.'

By the time Kate reached Alnwick station, Rachel McCann's disappearance was all round the nick. As she entered the stairwell, heading for the incident room, she overheard snippets of conversation that made her very angry. A police constable was standing on the ground-floor landing making fun of the 'weirdo' who'd come in to report Rachel missing.

She hung behind, grinned at him. 'Give her the brush-off, did you?'

The PC grinned back.

Smug bastard.

'Sure did!' he crowed. 'Silly bitch was chuntering on about some DCI from the Toon being a personal friend – like *that* was going to make a difference.' His face went red as he saw the reaction of those he'd been mouthing off to. His audience retreated quickly, leaving him to face the music.

'Listen to me, you lazy git. I'm the DCI from the Toon you just referred to. So get your arse out there and look before I land you with a blue form! I'm not telling you because I know the family socially or because Rachel McCann is a decent lass – I couldn't give a shit if she was the chav from hell! You treat her mother with the respect she deserves. You hear me?'

'Yes, ma'am.' He could hardly bring himself to look at her. 'But can I just say in my defence—'

Her glare cut him dead.

He tried again. 'Ma'am, the girl was in touch with a mate of hers. I didn't think—'

'You got that right! Has it never occurred to you that a clever offender might use the victim's phone to call someone in order to *create* the impression of normality and throw us off the scent? Given that most of her friends are at college, at that hour in the afternoon there's a strong likelihood they'll be in a lecture and therefore unlikely to pick up.' He opened his mouth but Kate waved him away in disgust. 'I'm not interested in your poxy excuses – just piss off out of my sight!'

*

The Murder Investigation Team were hard at it when Kate walked in, still livid with the dickhead in the corridor. There was no recent activity recorded on the murder wall. No identity for the second victim. No news: period. She went straight to her office and shut the door with the intention of contacting Emily. But as she pulled her mobile from her pocket, it rang in her hand.

Gormley had worked quickly. He'd already re-interviewed John Butterworth, Maxine O'Neil's teacher, the only witness to see her standing at the bus stop before she went missing, a split second observation as he drove by that may or may not have been accurate. He'd been labelled as the last person to see her alive and was therefore the most appropriate witness to start with.

'Does his story hold up?' Kate asked.

'Yep. Drove the route myself and checked his movements on CCTV. His car was seen leaving Beverley at the time he gave in his original statement. He had an appointment at a private dental clinic four miles away. Their security camera captured him arriving – a few minutes early, according to the receptionist. I timed the run and there would be no time to abduct the girl and conceal her, unless he had her hidden in the boot while he was sitting in the dentist's chair.'

'How did he come across to you?'

'Genuine, I'd say. Really upset when I told him we'd found her body. Visibility was good that morning. No fog, like we had here this morning, no parked cars obstructing his view of her standing there.'

'And the bus driver?'

'One hundred per cent convinced that she was not at the

stop as he drove by. He's adamant on timings. His evidence is, or should I say was, corroborated by witnesses on the bus at the time. I've yet to trace them all. Some have moved but I've got Ailsa on it. The bus driver knew Maxine, by sight not name, often picked her up at that stop and dropped her close to her home. It was and still is his regular route.'

'Damn!' Kate had been hoping for some discrepancy between what the witnesses were saying now and the statements obtained at the time. But Gormley quickly ruled that out. 'OK, keep on it. Anything else I need to know?'

'Nah. I've got a list of witnesses who came forward at the time, those who used the road regularly. I'll work my way through them in case our boy is among them. But it'll take some time. It's the main east–west route used by thousands every day, so there's a good few to get through.'

'Have you been to the scene of the last sighting?'

'Yep, it's a long straight road. Not much vegetation to hide in. It seems likely she was taken by car. Whether she was taken by force or accepted a lift off someone she knew is the million-dollar question. Any news on Rachel?'

'No. I'm about to call Emily. Speak later, yeah?'

'Yeah . . . give her my love.'

63

Over the days that followed, Emily combed the area, posting Rachel's picture at all points in local villages, stopping people in the street to ask if they had seen her. No one had. She kept ringing Kate in the incident room, frantic for news. At night she sat in her daughter's bedroom, alone and distressed. Office hours she spent on B-wing, trying to act as if it was business as usual, as if she wasn't watching Fearon's every move, hoping he would betray himself with some careless word.

On the morning of 19 February, Rachel's twentieth birthday, there was a light tap on her door. Kent put his head round, fatigue written all over his features. He was working a split shift and wanted to talk.

Emily was about to turn him away, but how could she?

She beckoned him in.

Stepping inside, he shut the door behind him. Even as he approached her desk he appeared to be having second thoughts. Declining the offer of a seat, he stood to attention on the other side of her desk, feet slightly apart and hands behind his back. Understandably nervous.

'Maybe this isn't such a good idea, under the circumstances,' he said.

'Bill, relax . . . I'm paid to look after the work force as well as the residents.'

'Yeah, but now is hardly appropriate, is it?'

Emily knew he meant well. She appreciated his kindness but didn't want his sympathy. 'It's as good a time as any,' she said. 'The word appears to be out. You know what it's like in here. I haven't had one single application all morning. Either the inmates' lives have miraculously improved or they've heard the rumours that my Rachel is missing.'

Kent pulled out a chair and sat down. His personnel file was on her desk. She'd skimmed it once or twice over the last few days but couldn't bring herself to read the whole sorry tale of his daughter's disappearance. It just made her own personal drama that much more terrifying. Rachel hadn't been in touch or contacted any of her friends. That meant one of two things: either she didn't want to be found or . . .

Don't think that way.

'I know exactly what you're going through.' Kent managed to acknowledge her vulnerability and their common ground without actually mentioning his own daughter's disappearance. Emily didn't blame him. She could see how difficult it was for him – for both of them. He looked like a torn soul. Like he'd been to hell and back. 'When it happened to me, I . . . well, let's just say it's not something you ever get over. It does help to talk about it . . . not that I've been doing much of that lately.'

And still he hadn't uttered his daughter's name.

Without realizing it, Emily let her guard down. It was as if she'd crossed to the other side of the desk: therapist turned patient. She talked about Rachel openly, told him how lost she was without her, insisting vehemently that she hadn't just run away. Emily had talked about nothing else for days, sounding off to anyone who cared to listen. She'd even appeared on local radio, appealing for information. There had been a groundswell of support from neighbours and community leaders. Everyone had been kind. At the very least, she knew that eyes and ears were alert to any news. Thanks to Kate's intervention, an experienced female sergeant, Jane Lowther, was now on the case.

'Emily?'

The sound of Kent's voice pulled her back into the room.

'I asked if there was news. From Sergeant Lowther or the SIO?'

A sinister thought popped into her head. Kent no longer looked like a man on the edge of the abyss. Why had he chosen to come to see her now? She doubted it was to talk about his problems. He'd never wanted to before. He seemed much more interested in discussing hers. She'd been so caught up in her own problems that she'd readily obliged. She couldn't remember a damn word that had passed between them in the last hour. And that unnerved her. Suddenly, she was wary of him. Maybe he was digging for information, checking to see whether the police were taking her daughter's disappearance seriously.

Maybe he was involved.

64

Kate Daniels swore under her breath and stared at her warbling mobile phone. How in God's name anyone expected her to evaluate a case and field calls at the same time was beyond her. One more interruption and she knew she'd start yelling. Snatching up the phone, she gave her name and rank, trying her very best to keep the annoyance from her voice.

'Kate, I need to talk to you . . .' Emily's tone was urgent, her voice hushed as if she didn't want to be overheard. 'I know you're busy but it's important. I think it is, anyway, I'm not sure.'

'Is Sergeant Lowther not on duty?'

Emily ignored the nudge to take her problems elsewhere. 'I didn't ask. This is something *you* need to hear.'

'OK, I'm listening.'

For a moment there was silence.

'This is off the record, OK?' Emily explained she didn't want to get anyone into trouble. 'Kate? You still there?'

Looking up at the ceiling for divine inspiration, Kate wished she had a quid for every time she'd heard that. In her early days in CID there used to be a red phone – *the Bat Phone* – in the incident room for 'off-the-record' calls. Only trusted informants were given the number, and when answering the Bat Phone detectives just said 'hello' or recited the number, keeping it all strictly unofficial – no mention of rank or name. But those days were long gone. Besides, Emily wasn't an informant. She was a mate.

'This sounds like it's going to take a while. Can you hang on a second? I've got someone with me but I'll send her away.' Kate made a 'sorry' face to Carmichael and covered the speaker. 'We'd get more peace and quiet in Sarah's Café. Gimme five, will you?'

Lisa got up and left the room.

Kate waited until she'd shut the door. 'All clear, Emily. What's the problem?'

'There's an officer on my wing who has issues with Walter Fearon, the inmate I told you about. This man's daughter went missing in suspicious circumstances . . .' Emily hesitated. 'She was the subject of a murder enquiry, Kate.'

'How old was she?'

'Not very old . . . ten, I think.'

Alarm bells rang in Kate's head. Her thoughts shot to the morgue, to an unidentified girl reduced to bones, a grotesque grinning skull, a set of sandy pearls around her neck. Picking up her fountain pen, she asked, 'Do you know her name?'

'Sophie Kent. Her father, Bill – full name William George Kent – was questioned, along with other males known to the family. No charges were ever brought.'

'How long ago was this?'

'Ages, several years at least. I'm not exactly sure.'

'And they never found her?'

'No, they never did. I have to tell you, I didn't hear it from Kent. His SO told me in confidence a few days before Rach went missing—'

'And you didn't think to tell me before now?'

'I'm so sorry, I didn't think.'

Kate had to work hard to keep her temper in check. 'Tell me about the officer.'

'He was advised to consult with me. *Ordered* might be more accurate – he was given no choice in the matter. He's been victimizing one of the inmates at every opportunity and threatened with the sack if he doesn't lay off. He's been avoiding me like the plague – until about an hour ago, when he knocked on my door and asked to see me.'

'That's good, isn't it?'

'Maybe, I don't know. We talked for a while and . . . well, I felt uncomfortable around him. He didn't talk about his problems. He seemed more interested in mine. He may just have been curious. Look, I know this sounds paranoid, but I got the distinct impression he was fishing for information.'

Emily was moving as she talked, pacing up and down by the sounds of it. Kate sensed there was more to come. 'How did he know Rachel was missing?' she asked.

'Are you kidding? Everyone knows. I've been on the bloody radio, haven't I? Look, I don't want to accuse anyone of anything.'

'You said that already. Is that why you waited several days before calling me?'

'No! I'm sorry, OK . . . I did hesitate, that's true – for good reason. I could be out by a mile. If Kent is entirely innocent, he's gone through a terrible trauma and I don't want to add to that. It would help if . . .' Emily paused: an icy silence for a split second. 'Kate, I need to know if his name has come up in your enquiry.'

'Hang on! This guy turfs up at your door giving you lots of sympathy and that makes him suspicious?' Daniels' office door opened. Irritated, she waved the intruder away and carried on with her call. 'Did Kent mention his daughter at all?'

'Kind of, in a roundabout way.'

'Either he did or he didn't.'

'He said he knew how I felt. I took that to mean he'd experienced the same thing. I didn't push it or let on that I knew his situation. How could I? I'd promised his SO that I'd treat what he'd told me in the strictest confidence.'

'That's the problem with off-the-record, Emily. It ties people's hands.' Daniels had a nasty feeling in her gut. There was something wrong with the picture. She didn't have a clue what it was, but she sure as hell wanted to find out. 'He never mentioned his daughter once? Are you absolutely sure about that?'

'I'm . . . I don't know.'

'Emily, think very carefully before you answer my next question. Is Fearon the only inmate Kent has a downer on?'

'Why?'

'Is he? Does he give anyone else a hard time?'

'I've had no other complaints.'

'Fearon's offences: do they involve children?'

'No.'

'Could they . . . potentially?'

'What do you mean?'

'Just answer my question.'

'I guess, but it's not likely. He's into older women.'

'Isn't that what paedophiles do when they want to target children? Make friends with their mothers, I mean. See what

I'm getting at? Why is Kent so down on Fearon? Because he's a sex offender?'

'Yes, well, that's what I assumed . . .' More pacing at the other end. Kate could hear the distress in Emily's voice as she tried to explain her concerns and put her point across. She was failing in that regard. 'What if he's a sex offender too? What if their antagonism towards one another is nothing but an elaborate hoax to fool people into thinking they're the worst of enemies?'

'You're suggesting they're in cahoots, jointly responsible for Rachel's disappearance? No, Emily, I'm not buying that. When I had dinner with Jo last week she talked about Kent, not by name, and without mentioning his daughter's disappearance. I don't imagine she knows about that or I'd have heard about it before now. It was his inability to curb his temper she was angry about; "a despicable animal" – those were the exact words she used to describe him. She said he'd beaten Fearon on more than one occasion.'

'So?'

'Sex offenders acting together don't beat each other up.'

'Unless Fearon had stepped out of line. He's not the easiest person to control. If he's a threat to Kent, that could explain it, couldn't it?'

The DCI didn't answer.

'Please listen to me, Kate. I checked Fearon's record against Kent's personnel file. HMP Northumberland isn't the only thing they have in common. The inmate spent a short time at HMYOI Wetherby when he was fifteen years old. Kent was on secondment there for part of that sentence. I'm begging you, please tell me whether he's already under suspicion.'

'You know I can't do that, Emily.' Kate wished she could. The internal phone rang. 'Damn! Leave it with me, Em. I've got to go.'

'No, wait! Walker said Kent was upset because of what happened on the beach at Bamburgh. Can you at least confirm whether he has or hasn't come forward in relation to the bodies you recovered there?'

'No, I can't. I'm sorry.' Robson stuck his head round the door and mouthed Bright's name. Kate nodded at him. 'OK, I'm hanging up now, Em. My guv'nor is screaming for me. I need to be somewhere. Rest assured, I will look into this. You were right to come forward. It might be important.'

'You promise?'

'Promise.'

'Thank you.'

'Don't thank me. You do realize this man could be entirely inno—'

'Kate, I'm not going mad.'

'I didn't suggest you were. But you've been under a lot of stress lately. It's hard to keep a clear head with Rachel missing. If Kent *is* the father of a murder victim, I wouldn't necessarily expect him to contact the incident room or turn up here. Even if it happened ten years ago, we'd have taken samples from him. The minute a match was found, we'd have been on to him like a shot to inform him that his daughter had been located, and probably to take a closer look at him.'

'Have you identified your victims?' Emily asked.

'Don't ask me that. I can't say any more.'

The line went dead.

65

The prison gymnasium was noisy with the clatter of equipment and multiple conversations taking place as officers used their break time to get some exercise. Senior Officer Ash Walker lay on his back on a bench lifting barbells, his jaw bunching as he extended his arms for the final time. He liked to stay in shape but his ability to haul heavy weights had diminished in recent years. He'd have to consider switching to something that put less strain on his body.

'I'm done,' he said.

Kent took the strain of the bar, placing it on its cradle, throwing his sweaty senior officer a towel. Walker sat up, his stomach muscles impressive for a man of his age. Draping the towel around his neck, he hauled himself off the bench and rubbed his hands together, sending a plume of chalk high into the air.

'What time is it?' he said.

Kent looked at his watch. 'Time we weren't here.'

They moved to the changing rooms, stripped off and took a quick shower.

Kent hardly said a word as he donned his uniform, though it was obvious he had something weighty on his mind. Assuming it was his daughter, Walker didn't pry, hoping Kent would tell him of his own free will. When it didn't come, Walker felt duty-bound to intervene.

'How did it go with Emily?' he asked.

'A bit of a role reversal, if you want the truth.' Kent buttoned up his shirt.

'How d'you mean?'

'She's losing it, boss.' Kent made a screwing motion with his index finger against his forehead. 'And you think *I* need help? Jesus Christ, I couldn't get a word in edgeways. She's convinced Fearon is behind her daughter's disappearance, did you know that? Totally barking, if you ask me.'

Walker didn't comment.

'What?' Kent scoffed. 'You think it's possible?'

'Did I say that?'

Kent stood for a moment, head on one side, as if Walker had defended the theory and he was weighing both sides of the argument. 'You could have a point. Nonces stick together, don't they? Maybe he has someone on the outside doing his bidding. Stranger things have happened.' Pulling on his jacket, Kent gave the SO a wry smile. 'If I had the hots for her, I'd tear the little shit apart 'til he squeals.'

'Everyone, drop what you're doing and gather round!' Kate Daniels didn't have to ask twice. The look on her face was enough to tell the Murder Investigation Team she had something important to say. 'I've just received information that the father of a missing ten-year-old is working down the road at HMP Northumberland. His name is William Kent. The girl's name is Sophie. So, why didn't I know about it? It should've been flagged up.'

No one spoke.

'Well?' she pushed.

Robson's face was flushed. 'There's no DNA match to any missing kid on the database.'

'I still don't like it . . .' Kate's unease was reflected in the rest of her team. *If a mistake had been made with the DNA, this could be a vital lead.* 'Pull the file. Get me everything there is on the father and the names of anyone who was hauled in under suspicion.'

'Did Kent come forward?' Carmichael asked.

'No, but you can't read too much into that, Lisa. Neither did the O'Neils, remember? Innocent parents fear asking the question when they can't face knowing the answer. Besides, he knew we had her DNA, so in the event of a match we'd contact him. No, this information came from Emily McCann. She's in a bad place now and acting as mad as a box of frogs – but that doesn't leave this room. Clear?'

There were nods and murmurs of: 'Yes, boss . . . crystal . . . understood.'

'Good. I gather Kent was interviewed at length, along with a number of others. I want to know who they are and whether any of them has form. If they so much as dropped litter, especially in the vicinity of Bamburgh, I want to know about it . . .' Kate pointed at Carmichael's computer screen. 'Lisa – ten-year-old females, missing, presumed dead – get the list up now. Make sure Sophie's on it. I don't trust computers, even ours. If there's a glitch, she might've been missed.'

Carmichael practically broke into a run. Tripping over a loose wire in her rush to get to her desk, she arrived a lot quicker and a little less elegantly than she'd anticipated, snagging her tights in the process and swearing loudly. Ignoring derisory comments from her colleagues that she was a hopeless Health & Safety rep, she logged on to her computer, pressed a few keys, then sat eyes glued to the monitor as the page loaded.

Text popped up on screen and she tapped a few more keys.

'Fuck!' Her face paled.

'Don't tell me she's not on it,' Kate said.

'She is . . .'

'But?'

'She's from East Yorkshire, boss. If I'm not mistaken, she was taken from a village not far from Beverley. Geography was never my strongest subject, but I know that area because my mum was brought up there. If I'm right, it's a stone's throw from where the O'Neils live.'

No one said a word.

Kate leapt from her seat, joining Carmichael at the computer as the others gathered round. It wasn't a Eureka moment exactly but, in her considered opinion, it was unlikely to be a happy accident either. Sophie Kent was the same age as their un-ident *and* went missing from the same county as their second victim *and* her father just happened to be working in the wilds of Northumberland less than thirty clicks from the burial site.

The atmosphere in the room was suddenly charged with electricity.

Kate's eyes found Maxwell's. 'Neil, get Hank on the phone.'

'I just spoke to him, boss. He was heading out for dinner.'

'I don't give a shit if he's being knighted – do it!'

Scooping up the nearest phone, he made the call, handing

her the receiver as soon as Gormley picked up. Kate rapidly brought him up to date and said she'd email all the relevant information, asking him to stay on in Yorkshire for a few more days and make discreet enquiries at his end. 'And don't chew while I'm talking to you, Hank. It's very rude!'

Detectives earwigging the conversation smiled at one another.

'Have you got plenty cash?' the DCI asked.

'Yeah, no worries,' he replied.

'OK, I'll cover your Xs and overtime as soon as you get back . . .' She could almost hear him grinning as he thanked her. 'Let me know if there's anything else you need. And tell Ailsa I'll clear it with her supervision. Her input is going to be more important than ever now. You think she'll agree?'

'Are you kidding? She's my new best friend.'

Kate hung up.

In the dead of night with the prison locked down and only a skeleton night shift on duty, Walker instructed a security officer to join him in the wing office, requesting that he bring his sniffer dog along. Minutes later, the pair arrived.

The German Shepherd, Flash, was the pride of the dog section. While Walker briefed his handler on the search they would be conducting, Flash sat looking up at him, a long pink tongue lolling from his mouth, an elastic string of saliva dripping from the end of it on to the highly polished floor.

'No names, no pack drill, *capisce*? I just want to drag the bastard out of his pit and turn his cell over.' Although there was no one else in the room but the two men and a dog, Walker lowered his voice conspiratorially: 'By the way, this

operation never happened – until I say otherwise. Understood?'

'What operation?'

'Good man.'

'What we looking for anyway?'

Walker glanced at the dog. 'He'll know when he finds it.'

Taking a green silk scarf from his pocket, Walker put it to
the dog's nose. Flash sniffed at it enthusiastically, his tail
going back and forth at such a speed and with such force that
it was drumming on the office wall. He was ready to go to
work.

SO Walker checked the cell landing. The coast was clear.
Stopping outside Fearon's cell door, he lifted the flap and
peered inside. The occupant was fast asleep – as still as a
corpse. Walker unlocked the door, allowing his security colleague to step inside. The officer shone a torch around walls
covered in bare flesh, then directed the beam into the inmate's
eyes and kept it there.

No sodding response whatsoever.

Seconds later, Fearon blinked and turned his head away
without waking.

Giving him a dig with a size-ten boot, Walker commented
on the stench of stale sweat in the room, pushing open the
tiny cell window to let it escape. The temperature plummeted.
Hearing voices, Fearon sat up, using his hand to shield his
eyes from the harsh light, giving his jailers a load of abuse for
disturbing his sleep, asking what the time was.

'Shut it!' Walker said.

The security officer loosened his grip on Flash.

More terrified of the dog than the screws, Fearon lifted his knees to his chest and scrambled to the corner of his bunk, pulling the covers around him for protection, his eyes showing real fear. Warning him to remain still and calm, the dog handler spoke a few words of encouragement, telling his canine partner that they were good to go. But Fearon wasn't having any. He struggled as he was dragged off his bunk and dumped unceremoniously on the floor, leaving his gonads hanging loose from torn boxer shorts, a source of added curiosity for the dog that brought howls of laughter from both officers.

'Get that fucking thing away from me!' Fearon was yelling now. 'And shut the bastard window. It's fucking freezing in here.'

Yanking the prisoner out on to the landing, Walker held on to him with a vice-like grip, advising him to button his lip while the dog did what he was trained to do. Guided by his handler, Flash covered every inch of the floor, including under the bed and round the toilet bowl, two favourite hiding places for contraband items smuggled in by prison visitors.

Fearon fixed his gaze on the SO. 'What you looking for, man? I've got nowt!'

Walker ignored him.

'Oh, I get it. This is Kent's idea, right? Told you the bastard's got it in for me!'

One or two prisoners were banging on their doors now, yelling at them to keep the noise down. Walker urged the dog handler to step on it before the whole damn prison woke up.

Flash leapt on to the bunk, burying his nose in the rumpled grey blanket, grabbing the pillow between his teeth.

Then he lifted his leg and peed on the bed – something the search dogs often did in cases where the personal hygiene of the inmate was dodgy. This led to more verbals from Fearon – but not for long. He ceased whining as the dog began barking and pawing frantically at the collection of porn by the head of the bed. It had picked up the scent of something.

66

A hand trembled. Emily was half-dressed, standing in her living room, holding a copy of a photograph Walker had just discovered in Fearon's cell. The SO had come straight there on his way off duty to hand it over personally. 'It was hidden behind a picture on his wall.' He could hardly look at her. 'I'm sorry, Emily. It looks like you were right about him all along.'

Staring at the photocopy in disbelief, Emily's heart was banging in her chest, her worst fears realized. She and Rachel were the subjects in the photograph, the image taken in their cottage garden just weeks before Robert's death. Looking up, her eyes met Walker's, an unspoken plea for answers. He stared back at her, a mixture of embarrassment and sympathy. She wanted to slap him hard for not offering her the level of protection she deserved within the prison environment.

His wing. His responsibility.

She held on to her anger.

'What drove you to search his cell?' she asked.

'Does it matter?'

Of course it mattered.

Emily wanted to thank whoever it was. It was nice to know that someone was looking out for her. Walker's body language was revealing. He looked out of the window, an avoidance tactic if ever she saw one. If it wasn't his own idea, then whose? Had Stamp intervened on her behalf, called in a favour from night-shift security? He was big mates with the principal officer in that department. Or was it Jo? Few officers at the prison would turn her down.

'Well, was it Martin or Jo?'

'Neither.' Walker didn't offer an alternative.

Emily's stomach lurched as she realized there could only be one other name in the hat. Guilt washed over her. She owed Bill Kent a big apology. She'd fingered him to the police and, in so doing, had probably kick-started a catastrophic chain of events that might cause him a lot of unnecessary grief. She'd have to undo that immediately, apologize to Kate Daniels for wasting her precious time.

Fair enough.

At least everyone would now understand that her fears were legitimate. Perhaps they would start to take her allegations seriously, stop treating her like a deluded attention-seeker with a tendency toward paranoia.

'Was it Kent?' She knew the answer before Walker had a chance to nod. 'But how, Ash?' She tapped the photo. 'The original of this was in my desk, out of sight. Please tell me Fearon hasn't been in my office unsupervised.'

'He's a wing cleaner, Em.'

Emily held her tongue, ran a hand through tangled bed hair, her lips pressed tightly shut to stop herself from breaking down. She looked at him accusingly. 'Have you been listening to me at all? I thought that you of all people . . . How could you? Knowing how that creep feels about me! How could you let him in there?'

Walker wouldn't meet her eyes. He knew he'd let her down and had no answer. Emily asked him to leave. She wanted him out of her house so she could ring Kate and explain how wrong she'd been and what had happened during the night. Shutting the front door, she listened as Ash drove away, then sank to the hall floor and wept. There was a bomb in her head and Fearon had just lit the fuse.

67

It was still early – 6.30 a.m. – Kate Daniels' thinking time before the squad got in. She'd arrived half an hour ago and was so intent on studying the murder wall, concentration etched on her face as she took in key facts that set her pulse racing, she never heard the door to the incident room open or the sound of footsteps approaching.

'Penny for them?' said a familiar voice behind her.

Jo was standing in the doorway with her coat on, briefcase in hand. Ordinarily, a wonderful sight first thing in the morning – or at any other time – but for once the DCI didn't want to see her. It wasn't that she resented the intrusion into her working day. It was because of what she'd scribbled on the murder wall a few moments ago, an aide-memoire as she tried to make sense of what she knew and decide where to go next, jottings she didn't want Jo to see.

Too late.

Jo was already taking them in, making judgements on the mini diagram facing her. Next to her unidentified victim, Kate had placed a big question mark and written Sophie Kent's name and the date she went missing. A dotted horizontal line led across the murder wall to a second, even bigger question mark, another name. Clear evidence of the SIO's thought processes, a fairly convincing demonstration that, in theory at least, she strongly suspected she'd found her second victim and may even have identified a third.

Jo couldn't draw her eyes away from that third name: *RACHEL MCCANN.*

A phone rang on someone's desk.

Ignoring it, Kate continued to stare at the murder wall. She'd set Munro's 1999 case aside, unable to establish a link. There was dressing up, but no pearls, nothing to suggest they were the work of the same perpetrator. Not so for the three facing her. Assuming they were linked, she didn't need crime-pattern analysis to determine the connections. The similarities screamed at her in thick red pen: Sophie Kent – aged ten – missing since 11 February 2001; Maxine O'Neil – aged fifteen – had suffered the same fate on 12 February 2006; Rachel McCann – aged twenty – missing since 14 February 2011.

As she reviewed the information, she drew up a mental list:

Mid-February abductions.

Five years apart.

Five years difference in age.

An anniversary of some sort?

What the hell is going on?

Jo's eyes were empty of emotion. Without saying a word or getting upset, she took off her coat, threw it over the nearest chair and placed her briefcase on the floor. Then she walked toward the murder wall, picked up a whiteboard marker, adding seven words of her own: *Five years, victims' ages, pearls, Bamburgh, Valentine?*

'You read my mind,' Kate said. 'I'm sorry you had to see that.'

'Don't worry. None of it will go any further. Not even to Emily . . .' She hesitated, a tremor in her voice. 'Especially not to Emily.'

'Actually, it was Emily who tipped me off in the first place – without realizing the significance, obviously.' Kate pointed at the murder wall. 'I've been over and over this since I got in and I just can't ignore the fact that these cases may be linked. I don't know as yet where that leaves Rachel, but we're definitely on to something.'

Jo's voice was flat. 'When will you tell her?'

'Emily?' Kate sighed. 'When I have more than supposition to go on is the short answer. There were several suspects for Sophie Kent's abduction. My priority now is to do a job on them, both here and in Yorkshire.' She turned her head away, an attempt to avoid eye contact. She didn't feel able to heap even more bad news on Jo by telling her that her long-standing friend and current colleague, Martin Stamp, was among them.

When she turned back, Jo was putting her coat on. 'If you need a hand—'

'I'll call you. It might be a while though. There are cross-checks and countless searches to be done. I need to establish where the suspects are now. If anyone who was interviewed then has walked across the same county at the same time, I want to know about it. If they're already in the system, I'll know I'm on the right track.'

Another nod from Jo. 'And if you get any hits?'

'I'll TIE-action all of them.'

Jo understood the term – *Trace, Implicate or Eliminate.* 'You look worried.'

'I am. I don't want a Yorkshire Ripper scenario. Sutcliffe was interviewed several times about five-pound notes and size of feet and the police did fuck-all about it. I want these men questioned so I can work out what the tale is.'

'Do yourself a favour. Take Rachel out of the equation, at least in your head. If you don't, it'll be too much of a distraction, preventing you from doing what you do best. Just find the bastard that took her. You've uncovered a huge link here: dates, prisons, girls buried here that went missing in Yorkshire. Now all you have to do is work out what it all means.'

68

Daniels was unavailable on the incident room number, so Emily rang her mobile and left a text message she couldn't pretend she hadn't received:

> KATE, I'M SO SORRY. I WAS WRONG ABOUT KENT: RACHEL'S DISAPPEARANCE HAD NOTHING TO DO WITH HIM. HE'S BEEN TRYING TO HELP ME. I FEEL TERRIBLE FOR HAVING DRAGGED HIM INTO THIS. PLEASE FORGET WHAT I SAID ABOUT HIM. STUFF HAS HAPPENED. IT'S FEARON. DEFINITELY. PLEASE GET IN TOUCH WITH ME OR SERGEANT LOWTHER ASAP FOR A FULL EXPLANATION.

Kate sighed.

She'd already had words with Jane Lowther and knew exactly what had taken place at the prison in the early hours. Emily wasn't coping. *Hardly surprising.* She was living on a knife-edge, clearly not thinking straight. And she was wrong about Kent. Somewhere along the line he was involved in all this. Daniels was sure of it. She texted a reply, choosing her words carefully: DON'T CONCERN YOURSELF, EM. ANY CONVERSATION WE HAD IS CONFIDENTIAL TO THIS OFFICE.

There was no way she could tell her of the covert operation being carried out. Not at this stage at any rate.

Maybe never.

*

On the floor below, Sergeant Lowther welcomed Emily to the station and led her to the same interview room where she'd given a brief statement that her daughter had gone missing to a slip of a lad pretending to be a detective.

Was that only six days ago?

It seemed like for ever to Emily.

Lowther appeared professional and businesslike. She was around forty years old, six-two if she was an inch, with wavy blonde hair, worn short and brushed straight back, just touching her uniform shirt collar. She reminded Emily of South African actress, Charlize Theron. She had high cheek-bones, a generous mouth and eyes that could kill at a hundred yards . . .

They were looking directly at Emily.

Before either of them had a chance to say anything, there was a gentle knock at the door. The young PC who'd seen Emily the first time she'd come into the station stuck his head in. He smiled at her, apologized for interrupting, and warned Lowther that psychiatrist Martin Stamp was insisting on joining them.

'Apparently Mrs McCann is expecting him, Sarge.'

Emily was expecting no such thing but nodded her consent when Lowther looked at her pointedly. She figured that a little moral support wouldn't go amiss right now. Still crushed by the find in Fearon's cell, she wanted answers. With his complete disregard for authority, Stamp would help her get them should she meet resistance from the police a second time.

Lowther nodded at the PC.

The rookie disappeared, closing the door behind him.

Under the female sergeant's steady gaze, Emily began to fidget, trying her best not to prejudge the outcome of Fearon's police interview. But a sinking feeling in the pit of her stomach increased in intensity as the seconds ticked by. Desperate to hear what had gone on, she imagined him drooling over Lowther, eking out the time he was in her company, playing his games. Enjoying another ludicrous fantasy, acting the innocent all the while.

Sick fuck.

The door opened and Stamp was shown into the room.

Leaning across the table, he shook hands with Lowther and introduced himself. *Charm personified.* He was good at that. Except, on this occasion, the woman on the receiving end wasn't having any. He sat down next to Emily. Taking her hand, he squeezed it gently, giving her a little smile of encouragement as he apologized for keeping her waiting. So convincing was he, Emily began to wonder whether she had asked him along after all.

'I won't beat about the bush.' Lowther's eyes were on Emily. 'I'm afraid I have nothing positive to tell you. Walter Fearon no replied his way through most of his interview. I wish I had better news, but I don't believe in giving people false hope. As it stands, there is no evidence to link him with Rachel's alleged abduction.'

'*Alleged?*' Stamp scoffed. 'What the hell do you mean by that?'

Lowther glared at him.

'Surely the photograph proves—'

'It proves nothing,' Lowther said. 'Unless his prints are on it.'

'They're not?' Emily's voice was barely audible. She'd been in her job long enough to know what was coming. 'He swears it was planted in his cell, right? Well, he would do, wouldn't he? An offender's default position, wouldn't you agree?'

'She's right,' Stamp switched his focus to Lowther. 'Like claiming they slipped in the showers when they get beaten up. You're not buying his crap, surely?'

Lowther's eyes held a warning. 'Let me be quite clear on this. The photograph was not wiped clean. There are prints on it, but none that belong to the offender in question. In the absence of evidence, my hands are tied. I'm afraid I cannot authorize his further detention.' Pausing for breath, she opened the manila folder she was holding. Then she levelled her eyes at the psychiatrist, watching his reaction as she carried on talking. 'He claims any number of people had access to his cell in recent days, yourself included, Mr Stamp.'

'That's—'

'I'm not finished,' Lowther cut him off. 'Fearon gave me a long list of visitors to his cell, an even longer list of those with access. Including Officer Kent, who I gather has a serious, well-documented and long-standing attitude problem, and Senior Officer Walker, who ordered the search without reference to the duty security SO. Strange behaviour in the middle of the night, wouldn't you both agree? And you, Mrs McCann – you have keys, do you not?'

Neither Stamp nor Emily had an answer to that.

Lowther was on a roll. 'There are others: his personal officer for one; the discharge officer; Principal Officer Harrison;

even the prison chaplain. You see my problem here? You've got to admit he has a point.'

'He wouldn't know the truth if it ran up and bit him,' Stamp said.

Emily looked at the floor.

Lowther was right. Cell doors were often left open. In the days leading up to release, it wasn't unusual for a range of professionals to sign off on an inmate with a one-to-one pep talk. Hell, she'd done it herself often enough. No. Without his prints on the photograph, there was no way they would make the theft stick.

Her disappointment was not lost on Lowther. 'I'm so sorry. Whether Fearon is involved indirectly in your daughter's disappearance, I'm afraid I cannot say. But DCI Daniels has asked me to assure you that she is looking into the other matter you mentioned.'

Stamp glanced at Emily, his expression a mixture of surprise and bafflement.

'Other matter?' he said.

69

What a waste of an SIO's time. Kate Daniels slammed down the phone. She'd spent the best part of an hour arguing the toss about cross-border money with her counterpart in the East Yorks force. One of her victims was abducted from there. Two, potentially. One or both may have been killed on their patch. And yet the divvi she'd been speaking to wasn't bloody interested.

Well, she'd see about that.

Ordinarily, she'd rather die than let some officious prick get one over on her. But, on this occasion, she had more pressing matters to attend to. Like her job; her real job, not the horrendous pile of admin that came with it. Naylor would sort Yorkshire out and, if he couldn't get through, her former guv'nor would. There would be hell to pay if Bright got involved.

That image made her feel all warm and fuzzy inside.

Taking a deep breath, she extracted her ID from her computer, slid it into its leather pouch and stood up, ready to meet her team. They had spent the morning reviewing the original investigation into Sophie Kent's disappearance, trying to establish whether she was indeed their second victim. The most worrying fact was that, along with four prison officers, all adult males known to the girl, Martin

Stamp had been questioned in connection with her disappearance.

With that thought lingering in her head, Kate left her desk and wandered into the incident room to find everyone waiting for the briefing to start, Jo Soulsby among them. Naylor had given permission for her to be there. She'd assisted them many times and had always been the first point of call if they needed the opinion of a criminal profiler. But her inclusion in a formal briefing at a critical stage of a double homicide made it official. She was back – if only in a part-time role.

That warm feeling again.

The DCI's eyes were drawn to a second visitor present. Sergeant Jane Lowther was perched on the edge of Brown's desk, the two of them deep in conversation. She'd promised to liaise with the Murder Investigation Team following her interview with Emily McCann.

She stood up as Kate approached.

'Hello, Jane.' The DCI gestured for Lowther to sit. 'Thanks for joining us. How did Emily McCann take the news?'

'She was pretty stoical, given the circumstances. She's a lovely woman.'

'Yes, she is . . . I understand Martin Stamp was present when you interviewed her.'

'Yes, ma'am.' A flicker of doubt crossed her face.

Kate pounced on it. 'Problem?'

'Not exactly. I'm fairly sure she wasn't expecting him, that's all.'

'What? He turned up here unannounced?'

'According to the desk sergeant.' Lowther gave a little shrug. 'Emily hadn't mentioned he was on his way.'

'Interesting. What did you make of him?'

'Good-looking nowt.'

Kate grinned. Lowther was a woman after her own heart. No point in beating about the bush. 'I take it you didn't warm to him?'

'Not a whole lot, no. Don't ask me why. He was pleasant enough, but he got a bit arsy when I told them Fearon had blanked me out during questioning. Are they an item then?'

'Just good friends.'

In her peripheral vision, Kate noticed Jo turn to face them, a mixture of annoyance and puzzlement on her face. Like Emily, she had no idea as yet that her friend and colleague, Martin Stamp, might be implicated in a serious offence. It was time to share the unpalatable truth.

'Can you excuse me a second, Jane?' Kate said. 'I have some beans to spill.'

She moved towards Jo with the intention of having a private chat before the briefing began. But she hadn't gone two paces when Carmichael walked in, a big smile on her face, and intercepted her.

'Jane tell you about the photograph debacle? Sounds like a smokescreen to me, boss. They're all in it together!' She grinned and continued, loud enough for the whole room to join in the joke: 'It's like four weddings and a funeral. Only we have four prison officers and a psychiatrist in the frame!'

Jo's face was a picture as she spun to face Kate. 'Mind telling me what's going on?'

70

There was little air in Principal Officer Harrison's office. Emily McCann was finding it hard to concentrate after her unproductive meeting with Sergeant Lowther. Of course Fearon denied taking the photograph. Did anyone expect him to admit it?

Pulling at her roll-neck sweater, she scanned the faces of the department representatives crammed into the room: Harrison, the wing probation officer, the chaplain, Kent, Stamp. Their lips were moving but their conversation was drowned out by two words whizzing round in her head in perpetual motion, driving her insane.

Alive . . . or *dead*

Rachel must be alive.

Emily had to believe that. The alternative was too painful to accept, too awful to contemplate. She'd convinced herself that she'd have known if that were not the case. Now she was having doubts. Robert had been dead for two hours before she found out. There had been no special sign, no feeling of doom or dread the day she received the news.

The day her world collapsed.

Back then, had anyone asked whether things could get any worse, she'd have laughed in their face. But they had. And now she was drowning. Trapped between her professional conscience at work and her private hell at home. The world was crumbling around her and she felt powerless to do anything about it.

'What preparations are in hand for Fearon's release?' Harrison asked.

His words cut through her. *He had to be joking.* He wasn't seriously suggesting that Fearon was still getting out, not after all that had happened in the past twenty-four hours? Christ, only a matter of hours had passed since the police hauled him in to be interviewed on suspicion of collaborating in the serious offence of abduction.

Fuck's sake!

Harrison was looking at the probation officer, asking if she had any further comments. When the woman shook her head, Emily rounded on her, urging her to speak up against the injustice of Fearon being allowed out while he was under suspicion in an active investigation. The probation officer was a parent too. If anyone ought to understand the grim reality of the situation, surely it was her. Besides, she'd been friends with Emily for years, even before they came to work at the prison.

Her eyes said otherwise.

There was a mixture of concern and sympathy, but Emily could tell she didn't have her full support.

'Tell them!' she exploded. 'Please . . . what's wrong with you?'

'I'm sorry, Em. You were the one dead against parole. There's nothing we can do now except trust hostel staff to do their jobs and guide him in the right direction when he returns to Sheffield. He's done his time. Short of the Home

Secretary's intervention, he walks in three days whether you agree with it or not.'

'And so he should.' The chaplain shifted his gaze from the probation officer to Emily. 'We all know how you feel. And we sympathize, truly we do. But I for one believe that Fearon has learned his lesson. He's a changed young man since I first saw him on reception. He has become a regular member of the congregation and he's promised to go straight when he gets out—'

'Bollocks!' Emily's face was white with anger. 'The despicable loser's found religion and God has forgiven him, is that it? Well, that's OK then. We'll just pat him on the head and send the bastard home, shall we?' Emily glared at him, hating everything he stood for, wanting to rip that white collar from his throat. 'Don't you understand? He's a vile, dangerous lowlife. And one of his cronies has my daughter!'

'You don't know that, Emily.' Harrison's tone was sympathetic but his eyes also told a different story. 'Where's that professional integrity of yours? It wasn't long ago you were lecturing the rest of us on prison protocol, how all inmates deserve fair treatment. Isn't that so?'

'That was before—'

'That's enough!' Harrison cut her off, demanding that she calm down or leave.

'No, you calm down, Ted. I'm not having this—'

'Emily, please!' Stamp was staring at her lap. 'You'll make yourself ill.'

Emily looked down. Her knuckles were white, her fists clenched so hard that a drop of blood had trickled on to her skirt from the cut her fingernails had made in her palm. Hot, salty tears ran into her mouth. She wiped them away with the back of her hand.

This wasn't happening.

'Doesn't my professional opinion count any more?' She wanted to scream out loud but could hardly breathe. Fearon was involved in Rachel's disappearance, she was sure of it. He was clever and manipulative and a lot of other things. Not like Emily, whose words were all jumbled up. Her argument sounded incoherent even in her own head. 'Can't you see . . . Fearon's a risk . . . not just to my Rachel but to the public generally. We should be protecting them!'

'Hallelujah!' Harrison said. 'We have ourselves a convert.'

'With all due respect, sir. Emily has a point.'

The comment had come from Kent. It wasn't like him to speak out, especially not in opposition to his principal officer. Harrison bristled. Stamp said nothing. Not a damned thing. Did he agree with them? Was he too gutless to press for something to be done? He'd had plenty to say to Lowther. For all the good it had done.

'Please,' Emily said. 'Will none of you help me?'

'I'll take no further part in this fiasco.' The chaplain picked up his belongings and got to his feet. 'Walter Fearon deserves to be treated like a human being, and I for one believe his remorse is genuine.'

'No!' Emily was begging now. 'He doesn't know the meaning of the word remorse. He's a manipulative psychopath. Can't you see?'

'Which is why release on licence should've been considered when we had the chance,' the probation officer repeated. 'Parole was always the lesser of two evils, but I was shouted down. By you, Em, as I recall. So now he walks, with no external control over his behaviour whatsoever. There is nothing we can do at this point. Our hands are tied.'

The chaplain stood up. 'You know where I am if you need me, Emily.'

She told him to shove it and he walked out.

71

Jo Soulsby was visibly shocked by what she'd learned in the briefing room. In all the years she'd known Martin Stamp he'd never mentioned being questioned by the police about Sophie Kent's disappearance.

'Doesn't that strike you as odd?' Kate asked. 'Honestly?'

They had retired to her office at Jo's suggestion, to take 'a few moments alone for a quiet word'. Kate expected a row for not having warned her before Carmichael blurted out the news, an awkward situation for both of them with the entire squad looking on. With the benefit of hindsight, the DCI was forced to accept that she might have handled it better.

'Let's not condemn him just because he kept it to himself,' Jo warned. 'You've miscalculated before – well, Bright did – and I ended up inside. He was wrong then. You're probably wrong now.'

The dig was entirely justified.

A couple of years ago, Jo had fallen under suspicion and spent time in custody, wrongly accused of her ex-husband's murder, pilloried in the media, her name splashed across every newspaper and TV screen, her reputation in shreds. It took ages for the press to leave her be, even longer to put the experience behind her.

'Don't *do* that!' she said.

'What?' Kate looked baffled.

'That sulky thing you do when you're in a mood.'

'I'm not in a mood!'

'Yes, you are. I'm not getting at you! I'm just making the point that I've been there too. It's not a good place to be and I've not spoken about it since to anyone, except you. If Martin was pulled in for police questioning, especially for such a serious matter, it would hardly be his finest hour, would it? He's a professional with a reputation to protect – same as us.'

'I'm not accusing him of anything.'

'Aren't you?'

'No!' Kate said. 'I'm not!'

'Carmichael obviously thinks he's involved.'

They both fell silent: a simmering, resentful silence that dragged on and on. It seemed inconceivable that just last week they had been jumping on each other's bones. And now they were bitching again – a customary state of affairs in recent months – a complete head-batter as far as Kate was concerned. She'd rather be single-crewed facing an angry crowd on night shift than fight with the woman she loved this much.

Even if Stamp was an innocent caught in the crossfire, she was convinced that there was a rabbit off somewhere and the stench was coming directly from HMP Northumberland. She had a job to do and she would damn well do it.

'Does Martin know Kent well?' she asked.

'No, yes, I don't know.' Jo hesitated. 'He may have mentioned something about them working together in the past. I can't remember if he did or not.'

Bullshit!

Jo caught the look of a sceptic. 'OK, so he mentioned it . . . but only in passing. Happy now? I just don't believe he's involved, if that's what you're suggesting.'

That much had been obvious from the moment Carmichael mentioned the psychiatrist. Kate cleared her throat. She hated putting Jo in such an awkward situation, the police on one side and her friend, Martin, on the other. But she was well placed to provide inside information on people who might be hiding something that could help the investigation.

'I'm not one of your snouts, Kate.' Jo crossed her arms, glaring at her from across the desk. 'And I'd hate to think the reason you wanted me back on the team is to keep obs on Martin. If that is the case, then please say so. In fact, don't bother. I'll pass on this one, if it's all the same to you.'

'Quit, you mean? After what you walked in on this morning? Jo, you can't! If Sophie Kent turns out to be my unidentified victim, then it stands to reason Rachel could well be the third. If she isn't already dead, she's in great danger. Emily's your friend too. Doesn't she count?'

Jo didn't dignify that with an answer.

'For God's sake!' Kate said. 'I'm not trying to score points here, I'm asking for your help. The men pulled in after Sophie went missing all worked together at Coleby Prison in Yorkshire – only a few clicks from Kent's home, and not much further from the home of our other victim, Maxine O'Neil. There was a mass exodus when the prison closed down in 2002 and staff were dispersed around the country, but four of the men interviewed in connection with Sophie's disappearance washed up at HMP Northumberland.'

'I'm not saying Martin is directly involved in any wrongdoing. He was quickly ruled out of the Sophie Kent enquiry: as I understand it, he had an alibi, and the witnesses to back it up. Even so, he has knowledge of what happened ten years ago. I need to talk to him about Kent and two other prison officers.'

'I thought Lisa said there were four.'

'One has since died.'

'Who are the others?'

'Edward Harrison, an SO—'

'He's a PO now and public enemy number one. A nasty piece of work.'

'In what way?'

'In every way. Ask Emily, she hates him. The man's a complete pig. Who was the one who died and what happened to him?'

Kate knew where Jo was heading. 'Hung himself. His name was Ronald Cohen. He was a main grade officer. But you're right: dead or alive, he needs ruling out. There was no suicide note.' Kate glanced at the list she'd prepared for the briefing. 'What's Ashley Walker like? He's last on my list.'

'OK . . . but not very intuitive.' Jo began to blush.

'He tried it on with you?'

''Fraid so.'

Kate raised an eyebrow. 'He has good taste then.'

'Are you reviewing the original evidence?' Jo asked. 'In Sophie's case, I mean.'

Nice sidestep.

'After months of intense activity, the investigation went cold. Detectives were moved on to other cases and the enquiry wound down, although it was still very much alive.

I've got Hank liaising with the receiver on that job, feeding information to my lot up here.'

'Surely Kent, Harrison and Walker weren't the only ex-Coleby officers transferred up here. There must be others at the prison.'

'It should be easy to check.'

'Why are you so certain it's Sophie you found?'

'She fits the profile: her age, the timing of the abduction, the fact that she had no broken bones, had never been treated by a dentist, according to her father. Neither had our victim. Of course that could all be coincidental, but I'm fairly certain it's her. Don't ask me where the pearls fit in. If Sophie is the first victim, Maxine O'Neil the second and Rachel the third, then Cohen can be ruled out. He's been dead a while.'

'Five-year gaps figure somewhere,' Jo said. 'It sounds like you're on to something. Didn't they take a DNA sample for Sophie?'

'No match found.'

'Maybe someone made a mistake?'

Daniels shrugged. 'Human error is one possibility. The results could simply have been assigned to the wrong case file. Or it could have been deliberate: the evidence tampered with. My next step is to identify which it is.'

72

Emily closed the photograph album. She'd spent much of the evening in tears, leafing through happy memories, grieving for her dead husband and missing child, festering over her spat with Harrison and the rest of her team.

A sharp knock at the door made her jump.

She froze.

She hadn't heard a car drive up. It was a thirty-minute walk to the nearest village and her only neighbour had gone abroad.

Rachel?

Putting the album down, she rushed into the hallway and was immediately deflated when she yanked open the door. Stamp was on the step, a take-away in one hand, a bottle of wine in the other – a sheepish look on his face.

'Thought you might like some company?' he said.

Emily wanted nothing of the kind but moved back to let him in, a plan forming in her head. *Maybe he could still save the day.* Taking the food from him, she put it in the oven, opened the wine and poured them both a large drink. She joined him in the living room, sat down on the sofa and lit a cigarette. He didn't initiate conversation, just stood by the fireside as she raged about her day, her nightmare situation, lack of support from the police, from colleagues, from him too. From the prison chaplain, a man she described as 'even more deluded than Walter Fearon'.

'Can you believe that idiot?' She stabbed her cigarette out in the ashtray, exhaling smoke through her nostrils as she glanced up at him. 'If God exists, I'd like to know where he is right now. What terrible thing did I do to deserve what he's dished out lately?'

Her thoughts were all over the place: Robert, Rachel, Fearon – whose imminent release from prison she was determined to prevent, no matter what the probation officer said. Theoretically, Emily agreed with her. It would've been far better if the evil shit had been let out on parole with the threat of instant recall hanging over his head should he put a foot wrong. But it was too late for that now. Besides, would it really make any difference to an offender like him? Emily didn't believe so. South Yorkshire Probation Service couldn't keep him under surveillance 24/7.

He'd be up to his old tricks in no time.

Pausing for breath, she took a slug of wine, almost choking on the stuff before carrying on with her tirade. 'It's not good enough, Martin! There would be a public outcry if it got out that we release prisoners early, not because they deserve it, but because we're scared witless that they'll disappear into the ether if we don't.'

'Statistically speaking—'

She glared at him. 'Don't you dare quote statistics at me!'

'I was going to say that the sex offenders' register—'

'Is a joke!' Emily snapped. 'Prevents re-offending, my arse!'

'No system for tracking recidivists is perfect.'

'You can say that again! Sex offenders should serve indeterminate sentences with release dependent on professional risk assessment – end of story!'

'What do you think I'm doing here?' Stamp moved away from the fire and sat down. 'It's under review, the raison d'être for my research project.'

Emily knew that much was true. 'But you know as well as I do it'll take years to implement. Meanwhile, more children go missing and parents like me go through a living hell until they're found.'

She stopped ranting as the aroma of food reached them. She hadn't eaten all day and needed to if she was going to avoid collapsing in a heap in sheer exhaustion. She suspected Stamp hadn't either. Getting up, she set two places at the table, then went into the kitchen and spooned a small portion of food for her, a generous one for him and left the rest to keep warm in the oven.

Arriving back in the room, she put the food on the table, apologizing for yelling at him. 'Thanks for this, Martin. I must sound so bloody ungrateful.'

They ate in silence, lost in their own thoughts. His probably on their relationship, hers very firmly on her current situation and what she had in mind to do about it. A few mouthfuls in, she pushed her plate away. She couldn't face food with her stomach in knots. Then it all got too much for her and she began to weep.

Stamp put down his knife and fork. He leaned across the table, placing a hand on her forearm, his eyes misting up too. 'It's killing me seeing you like this, Em. Please let me take care of you.'

'I don't need taking care of,' Emily sobbed. 'I just need my daughter back.'

'I know. And I'll do anything I can to help you.'

'Will you?'

'Of course.'

Emily seized her opportunity.

She wanted him to bend some rules.

73

Detective Sergeant Robson had the floor. He was well into his stride, leaning against a desk at the front of the briefing room, feet crossed at the ankles, summarizing the investigation into Sophie Kent's disappearance. On the face of it, East Yorkshire force had done a good job. For months, they had worked the case intensively, pouring huge resources, both human and financial, into finding the girl. Thousands of actions had been raised and logged on to the HOLMES computer system, the intelligence collected, checked and rechecked several times.

'Eventually the leads dried up,' Robson said. 'Lisa spoke to the SIO.'

Kate's eyes found Carmichael. 'What you got for me, Lisa?'

'Kent was questioned at length. He married young. Pregnant girlfriend. Shotgun wedding forced upon the couple by her father, who died within the year. When Sophie was quite young, her mother became terminally ill. She left the family, quote "didn't want to be tied down by a kid she never wanted" unquote. As far as she was concerned, her life was over before it began.'

'Nice,' Maxwell said.

For once Carmichael agreed with him. 'She'd never make mum of the year—'

'Unless she was protecting the girl,' Jo suggested. 'I mean, making it easy for her. Can't be pleasant watching your mum fade away and die when you're eight years old.'

It was fair comment, Carmichael and Maxwell concurred.

'Anyway,' Carmichael said. 'That was the first place they looked, in case Sophie had run off to be with her mum. When investigators found Mrs Kent she was living in a hospice in Staithes, too ill to look after herself, let alone take care of a kid.'

As her young DC carried on talking, Kate glanced to her left. Jo was listening intently and scribbling on a pad. Grateful she'd remained on the case, Kate looked over her shoulder at what was written there, some of it underlined.

Three girls: 10, 15 & 20.
Five year gap.
All missing: February.
DNA switch: mistaken or deliberate?
Unwanted child?
Bill Kent: single parent.

It was nice to know they were thinking along the same lines.

Fairly certain in her own mind that the body in the morgue was Sophie Kent, Kate didn't intend sharing her suspicions with anyone outside of Jo and her immediate team. Not until she had hard evidence to back up her claim. Besides, she didn't want to upset her friend, Emily McCann. The poor woman had convinced herself that Fearon was behind her daughter's disappearance. To be perfectly honest, it suited the DCI to let her believe it for a little while longer, even though *she* suspected it wasn't.

Carmichael was still talking . . .

'Stamp was eliminated fairly quickly by the woman he was with.'

Jo's expression said: I-told-you-so. 'What about Officer Cohen?'

'Locked down in the prison when the girl went missing with umpteen witnesses.' Carmichael checked her own notes. 'Walker and Kent were both off duty, but therein lies the problem: it would appear that they spent most of the day together but gave conflicting statements when questioned. Timings were out by an hour or so. The SIO didn't have a lot of time for either man.'

'And Harrison?'

'Playing golf. His tee-off time confirms that. He was seen at the clubhouse afterwards by several fellow members of the Beverley and East Riding Golf Club.'

'Who was he playing with?' Kate asked.

Carmichael made a face.

Robson whistled. 'So Billy-No-Mates-Harrison hits a ball into the trees, disappears to look for it, goes walkabout for three hours, grabs the girl, then rejoins the course on the fifteenth so everyone sees him walking down the fairway for a pint the steward has already pulled. Very suspicious.'

'Exactly!' Carmichael said. 'My money's on the golfer . . . or Walker, who also happens to be the girl's godfather.'

'Emily never mentioned *that* to me,' Kate said.

'Maybe she didn't know,' Carmichael countered. 'Appar-

ently, he was more gutted than Kent when Sophie disappeared. Walker called her *his little princess.*'

Jo sat up straight, on high alert.

Kate could almost see the cogs turning. But before she had
a chance to open her mouth, the penny dropped. Bamburgh
was a fairytale castle far from home. Fit for a little princess.

Her mobile bleeped twice.

It was a text from Hank that she opened right away:

URGENT INTEL FROM AILSA. STAMP'S ALIBI UNSOUND.
CORROBORATING WITNESS – HOOKER FROM HULL –
GAVE SIMILAR ALIBI FOR SOMEONE ELSE IN EXCHANGE
FOR CASH. SHE WENT DOWN FOR P THE C OF J. NEEDS
LOOKING INTO. END OF MESSAGE.

Daniels looked at the others. Perverting the course of
justice, eh?

There were still four in the mix.

74

Leaving the front door wide open, Emily ran. Stamp was a few yards ahead, charging towards his BMW, his grey coat flapping in the wind, his arm outstretched, thumb poised over his key fob to open the car doors.

The lights of the car flashed twice.

Stamp got in, threw his coat on the back seat and slammed the door. He turned the engine over, but before he could drive away Emily jumped in the other side, breathless from tearing out of the house after him. She didn't speak immediately, just stared out of the front windscreen, trying to work out what to say to him.

They had argued when she broached the subject of Walter Fearon. She needed her friend's help to keep the inmate locked up beyond his release date, a transfer under the terms of the Mental Health Act the best way to achieve that now. Probably the only way – Emily couldn't do it alone. But he refused to assist, flying off on one before she'd had a proper chance to state her case.

Turning her body to face him, she asked him to come back inside.

He looked at her coldly. 'You are unbelievable, you know that?'

'It's a signature on a bit of paper, that's all!' She put her hand on his. 'Please, Martin. You said you'd do anything to help me.'

'You're asking too much, Emily. He's not mentally ill—'

'Oh no?'

'Not according to the law, he isn't.'

'Hey, we're the good guys, remember?' Emily didn't want another row but she wasn't backing down without a fight. She took a long, deep breath to calm the situation and talk some sense into him. If she argued, he'd ask her to get out and drive away. 'The law should be on our side, Martin. I'm asking you to section him, not kill him. Can't you see? It's the only avenue left open to me so close to his release. If there was any other way—'

'You can't seriously expect me to come up with a diagnosis for a medical condition he doesn't have!' Stamp shook his head. 'I won't do it. Don't ask me again. I won't stitch him up.'

'Don't be so bloody obstinate!'

His eyes were filled with loathing.

'What?' Emily glared at him. 'You want me to apologize for trying to do the best for my child? Well, think again. Her safety is the one thing on my mind right now. I don't give a damn about my job or yours. I just want to end this nightmare. Help me, Martin. You're my only hope.'

'Just listen to yourself!'

'No, you listen!' Emily slammed her clenched fist on the dash. 'Who cares if one more *fucking* prisoner is locked up longer than he should be? Newsflash: Belmarsh is full of them—'

'That doesn't make it right, Emily.'

'OK, I'm sorry. I shouldn't have said that.' She wasn't sorry at all. She wanted to slap him for being so bloody PC. 'You know how dangerous Fearon is. You said yourself he was a lifer in the making. Rachel's life is on the line here. Please, Martin, don't make me beg. If not for me, then do it for her. You've known her since she was a baby. Whether she's accepted you or not, you're the closest thing she has to a father right now.'

Stamp rounded on her, his anger spilling over. He told her how disappointed he was in her. Accused her of emotional blackmail. Playing with his feelings in order to get what she wanted. As far as he was concerned, her idea was preposterous, out of the question, totally unethical.

Emily didn't care about any of that. She wanted Rachel home where she belonged, out of harm's way. She didn't give a shit what she had to do in order to make that happen. She'd kill to get her daughter back.

75

It was almost midnight when Kate Daniels arrived home. She was totally spent but couldn't bear the thought of another night at the B & B. She hadn't even shut her front door when the phone rang. She swore under her breath. Ignoring the one in the hallway, she walked into the kitchen, chucked her overnight bag on the bench and picked up without checking who was on the line.

It was a nice surprise to find that it was Jo.

Kate sat down, wishing they were in the same room, talking face to face, a glass of wine, some night music, a few hours of passion ahead of them. *If she could keep her eyes open that long.* A kettle whistled in the background, nailing Jo's location in her mind. She imagined her standing by the ancient cooker in her tiny seaside cottage surrounded by gadgets and cookery books that were not her own, sitting down on the sofa to drink her tea – *that* sofa – Nelson snoring in his basket next to the wood-burning stove.

There was something wrong with the picture.

Kate wondered if the photo of the two of them was out on display, a reminder of happier times, not hidden away like stolen goods. The image of it sitting on the shelf in the kitchen cupboard on top of tinned tomatoes was so strong she could almost hear the roar of the sea above Jo's voice.

She'd been talking for a full ten minutes, hardly stopping for breath as she recounted another frantic phone call from Emily McCann. A distraught one by the sounds of it brought on by a bloody awful row with Stamp.

'She actually asked him to section Fearon?' Kate said. 'Good girl!'

'I might have known how you'd react!' Jo sounded pissed. *Again.*

'Well, I agree with her, don't you?'

'No, you don't! It would be so wrong to condemn anyone to a mental institution no matter what Emily may think they've done. I told her—'

'Bet that went down well.'

'She became totally hysterical.' A heavy sigh from Jo.

'You OK?'

'I'm fine. I just hate seeing her so distressed. She'll see sense when she calms down. At least, I hope she will. Martin and I don't always see eye to eye but on this occasion I must say I agree with him. We both reminded her that Fearon is an untreatable psychopath, not mentally ill—'

'Same difference.'

'You're wrong,' Jo said emphatically.

'Well, if you want to split hairs. You think the general public give a damn about that? All they're interested in is keeping scum like him off the streets for as long as possible.'

'That's what *she* said.'

'And she's right. People deserve protection from the likes of him. A medical diagnosis doesn't change that.' Kate stood up and opened the fridge. It was almost empty, so she shut it and flipped open the breadbin. No joy there either. 'Put yourself in her shoes, Jo. She's desperate—'

'I know she is, but she's not thinking straight. Her plan is flawed. Even if Stamp was willing or stupid enough to involve himself in an illegal conspiracy, she knows as well as we do it takes two psychiatrists to section someone, not one.' Jo yawned. 'Look, I'm exhausted and you are too. I'm sorry for calling so late. I'm tired and grumpy and . . .' There was a pause. 'I miss you.'

Kate smiled. 'Miss you too.'

The phone went down.

76

It was before six and still dark as Kate drove through leafy Jesmond on her way to Alnwick, her overnight bag on the back seat replenished for a further stay at the B & B. It was a pain in the arse living away from home, but a necessary evil sometimes. However, the way things were going she had the distinct impression it wouldn't be for that much longer.

Sophie Kent was her unidentified victim.

She was sure of it – now all she had to do was prove it.

Turning on the radio for company, an American commentator informed her it was Presidents' Day – George Washington's Birthday – a federal holiday in the US. *Lucky for them.* She'd welcome some downtime to herself. A few days off; an opportunity to get on her bike and take herself off somewhere quiet for a bit. The Northern Lakes via Hartside Pass would be her destination of choice: a warm cabin, a good book, a bottle of single malt and some decent food.

Christ! She was starving.

Moving into the outside lane, she overtook a slow-moving farm tractor, then pulled back in. Driving to and from incident rooms was often her best thinking time. The next twenty minutes passed in a flash as she debated whether or not to put Emily in the picture and out of her misery. Problem was, she remained convinced of Fearon's involvement in Rachel's disappearance. She was hardly going to entertain the possibility that Stamp might be responsible – or Kent, Harrison or Walker for that matter.

On the face of it, Martin Stamp was a great guy and good friend to Emily. He was smitten with her, that much was obvious. But in his rush to cement their relationship he'd acted out of character according to Jo. Refusing to back off and give Emily space to grieve after Robert passed away. Stamp was an obsessive then. Had he abducted Rachel McCann and, in so doing, handed himself yet another opportunity to play the hero?

The cliché 'two's company' sprang to mind.

And what of Senior Officer Ash Walker? Another man who'd reached out to the merry widow in her hour of need? Or another fucked-up individual with an ulterior motive? Had this mild-mannered, charismatic officer been manipulating people all along, including Walter Fearon? Had he placed the photograph of Emily and Rachel in the inmate's cell? That could just as easily have been Kent, Stamp, or PO Harrison – the obvious villain amongst them? Jo was sure Harrison was switched wrong and Sergeant Jane Lowther had discovered all three of them had both means and opportunity.

Some cases had no suspects. In this one, Kate was spoiled for choice.

A sign loomed out of the darkness, caught in the Q5 headlights: Alnwick slip-road off to the left, Bamburgh just fifteen miles further north. The answer lay with those pearls and that village somehow, Kate was sure of it. But she'd not yet come up with a credible scenario to explain how. Carmichael had rechecked the incident log and found no suspicious incidents that threw any further light on that particular theory. Well, actually, that wasn't strictly true. Lisa had found one . . . she'd happened upon it on the Bamburgh Research Project's blog. It involved not one but two children. They had drowned at the Bowl Hole next to Bamburgh Castle. The information might have taken them further had it not happened as far back as the eighteenth century.

But what if . . . ?

Daniels had hit upon an idea.

Why the hell hadn't she thought of it before?

77

By the time Kate reached the MIR her team were hard at work. She felt guilty for having abandoned them, but it was quality not quantity that counted when it came down to a night's sleep. Last night she'd collapsed into a long hot bath and passed out in her own sumptuous bed in sheer exhaustion twenty minutes later. Or was it the phone call with Jo before she retired that produced a peaceful oblivion?

In her office, she made a strong brew to kick-start her day and then called Hank, asking him to do something important for her. He'd completed his enquiries down there and was packed and ready to check out of his hotel.

'OK, see you later then.'

'Hopefully with something of value,' he said.

Hank and PC Ailsa Richards looked pretty chipper, considering the week they'd put in and the drive north to rejoin Northumbria's Murder Investigation Team. It was just gone one when they arrived.

Kate smiled as Hank approached, receiving a cheeky wink in reply.

In the past week, they had spoken several times a day but she'd still missed having him around to brighten her day. He was more like a cuddly big brother than a work colleague.

They looked out for each other in ways that other detective partners never did. She'd hate to lose him permanently, something that would happen if his wife got her way.

On closer inspection, he looked worn out, a tinge of pink to the whites of his eyes, the bags beneath a little more pronounced.

That didn't surprise her.

Late nights and early mornings reviewing a decade-old murder case was bloody hard work. It was an added strain living out of a suitcase away from home. She could vouch for that. She'd slept soundly for five hours solid in her own bed last night. It didn't seem like much, but she felt all the better for it.

'Any luck?' she asked.

'You bet,' he patted his briefcase and hauled it on to the desk to open it.

The report he handed over was no more than a few scribbles on an A4 sheet, handwritten by him – in a hurry, by the looks of it. She speed-read the document, her detective brain working overtime. It was a list of dates and times mainly, beginning with the initial missing persons report from Bill Kent.

She spotted the discrepancy as soon as she laid eyes on it – a ten-day lapse between the alarm being raised and DNA samples being obtained.

Bingo!

'An action to collect it wasn't acted upon,' Hank said. 'Can you believe that?'

Kate looked at the sheet of paper in her hand. He'd scribbled a simple explanation at the bottom – *one DC thought another had taken possession and vice-versa. Time enough for evidence tampering?*

Just as she'd suspected.

She raised her head. 'Now we're getting somewhere.'

Ailsa Richards grimaced. 'There were some red faces our end, boss.'

'I can well imagine.' Kate looked at Hank. 'Where did the samples come from?'

'Toothbrush and hairbrush. When the mistake was realized, the SIO sent someone with a bit of nous to do the job. The attending DS didn't flag up his visit, just called on spec, taking Sophie's toothbrush from its holder in the bathroom, the hairbrush from her dressing table where her old man said she kept it.'

'He didn't let Kent fetch the items for him?'

Hank was shaking his head. 'He says not.'

'Yeah, well, I still don't believe it.'

Ailsa grinned at Hank. 'Sorry, boss. Private joke.'

Daniels didn't question it. She was too busy taking in the interesting dynamic between Lisa Carmichael and the team's temporary recruit. Lisa looked pissed, an understandable reaction given that Hank was *her* supervision. He seemed really taken with his young mentee, was praising her efforts in Yorkshire, telling them all what an exceptional officer Ailsa was, giving the wannabe detective a verbal pat on the back for all the hard work she'd put in.

Daniels hid her amusement. She was about to make matters worse by giving Ailsa something important to do, stuff that would normally fall within Carmichael's remit. She had other plans for Lisa. But first she had an action to take care of.

'I want samples from Kent right away,' she said. 'Robbo, can you fix that up?'

DS Robson nodded but didn't move.

'Now would be good.' She waited for him to get to his feet. 'By the way,' she said as he reached the door. 'If he's at work, be discreet. But don't come back empty-handed. Even if he's just come off nights, wake him up. We can't afford to wait. If it is his daughter in the freezer, Rachel McCann's in big trouble.'

By the seven o'clock briefing, Kate was beginning to feel confident of a positive outcome in the case. A pristine uniform caught her eye as Sergeant Jane Lowther entered the incident room – the last one through the door. She was another officer destined for the CID, someone the SIO had a lot of time for.

'Any news of Rachel, Jane?' she asked.

'None you'll want to hear. She hasn't used her mobile phone once since she went missing or withdrawn any money from her bank account. It's not looking good.'

A sinking feeling in Kate's stomach made her lose her thread. Emily McCann had already been through so much. The sudden, undeserved misfortune of losing her husband was bad enough. If she lost her daughter too, her life was as good as over. Kate looked around her. Ailsa Richards was sitting with DC Andy Brown. They seemed to have hit it off during the course of the day and he'd taken it upon himself to show her the ropes and familiarize her with the room. Now that really would put Carmichael's nose out of joint. Ailsa already looked like she belonged there.

She'd fit right in with the rest of the team.

'You HOLMES trained, Ailsa?' she asked.

The young PC answered with a nod.

Another pout from Carmichael.

Ha! MIT's Golden Girl was sulking.

Kate bit her lip to stop herself laughing out loud. A little competition wasn't necessarily a bad thing in a murder incident room. In fact, it might work to her advantage. It would keep them both on their toes. 'Ailsa, take your lead from Hank. As soon as we have a body ID, your lot will reopen their room. I want you to check their system and feed anything you're not happy with to Hank as soon as you notice it. Lisa, I think we may also have missed something.'

'Boss?'

'I don't mean you personally. I'm not sure where those pearls fit in, but Bamburgh village is definitely the key. I want you to recheck with the back record team. Widen the original action to include *all* incidents that happened on or in the vicinity of the castle and beach, not just suspicious ones.' Giving Lisa a little smile of encouragement, she added: 'I'm only interested in this century.'

Lisa grinned. 'Yes, boss.'

As the team dispersed, Kate scanned the murder wall, asking herself a question: was she finally closing in on the killer she was seeking? The answer she came up with was yes. But then Robson rang in. Kent had gone walkabout and was nowhere to be found.

78

The prison was locked down tight. All inmates secured in their cells. Lights dimmed. Emily was standing with her back to the door as he moved towards her, crossing the threshold in silence. Unaware of his presence, she was somewhere else entirely, far beyond the perimeter of the floodlit prison grounds. She never heard his gentle tap on the door.

'Em?'

Turning round, she found Ash Walker standing there.

'Sorry,' he said. 'I did knock. Any news?'

Emily shook her head. She was getting desperate.

'How did it go with Martin?'

'It didn't.'

Walker looked puzzled. 'He refused?'

''Fraid so.'

'So what happens now?'

Emily gave a little shrug. It was as if she was at one end of a tug-o-war, the might of the Home Office at the other, a titanic struggle going on between them. She'd called and called, trying to get through to someone in authority, only to be fobbed off with the promise of a call back that never came.

'I've written to the Home Office and telephoned several times, but no one is returning my calls. I don't suppose they will – and I've no place left to go, Ash.' She choked on her words, close to tears again. 'Every morning when I wake up, for a split second I feel normal. Then I remember and the nightmare begins again. It's a curious thing, the mind. It is so used to life being a certain way it sometimes takes a brief moment to catch up with itself. It was the same after Robert died. There were occasions I set the table for three without even noticing, upsetting Rachel in the process.' Emily bit her lip, looking past him to the cell-block corridor beyond. 'If anything happens to her and that bastard is involved, I'll hunt him down, I swear. No matter how long it takes.'

'Short of ripping your clothes off and accusing him of sexual assault, I can't see what more you can do to keep him in.'

'Don't think it hasn't crossed my mind,' she scoffed.

'So what's stopping you?'

Emily just looked at him.

'I won't tell if you don't,' he said.

She shook her head. 'I couldn't do it.'

Ash met her gaze head on. 'He plays dirty, why shouldn't you?'

'I'm a better person than he is, Ash. Women who make false allegations are despicable in my view. It's taken years for genuine rape victims to be heard. I couldn't betray them. I just couldn't.'

'Even for Rachel?'

'Especially for Rachel. If I did, he'd make damn sure she was never found. I'd be signing her death warrant. That's assuming she's not already . . .' She looked away, her words trailing off, her emotions bubbling to the surface again.

Walker sighed. 'He made threats to kill in your presence, didn't he?'

'Yes, he did. But you think anyone will believe that now? The Governor, Harrison, the police – they all think I'm nuts.'

'I'm sure that's not true.'

'Isn't it?'

Walker tipped his head on one side, his eyes full of sympathy. 'They all know what it is you're going through. Come on, Emily. You need to get out of here. Let me buy you a drink.'

He helped her on with her coat. But as she bent to pick up her briefcase, she lost her composure in spectacular fashion. Walker put his arms around her and held her while she wept. As the sobs subsided, he kissed her ever so gently on the forehead. Then, without warning, her need for physical comfort overwhelmed her. Spontaneously she kissed him back.

Just how they managed to make it to her place, Emily didn't quite know. Her emotional need was so intense it obliterated everything else. Next thing she knew, she was lying post-coital in bed, staring at the ceiling in the small hours, a tear running slowly down her cheek. Walker lay on his side, stroking her hair. Then he fucked her again when she asked him to take her pain away for just a little longer. Afterwards, her body finally gave in. She fell into a deep and dream-filled sleep in the crook of his arm.

79

It was too early in the day to be pissed off, but Kate was – and it showed. Robson had the skills to handle a simple request. She'd ordered him to find Kent and take his DNA. He'd carried out the first task but blown the second and returned empty-handed.

'What do you mean, he won't give any samples?'

'He refused point-blank,' Robson said.

'On what grounds?'

'He said we already had Sophie's DNA.'

'Yes, we know that!' Kate yelled. Robson shifted his weight from one foot to another, looking like a troubled man. She wondered if he was dipping into his bank account again, gambling away money he didn't have. 'Didn't you explain that there might've been a problem at the lab?'

'Yes, although I wasn't very specific. I didn't want to tell him any lies.'

'Did I ask you to?'

'No, boss. But—'

'No buts, Robbo! I thought I made myself clear.'

'You did. But short of arresting him, what was I supposed to do? I told him there might have been a mix-up with forensics and he just said, "That's your problem."'

'Well, he got that right! It's a big problem now!' Kate gave him a severe look. 'OK, get him in here . . . No, cancel that. I'll speak to whoever dealt with him in 2001. The SIO, the FLO, *any-bloody-O.*' She pointed at him, a fierce look in her eye. '*Don't* disappear . . . you and I are going back just as soon as I've made the call.' She looked around her. 'Ailsa, you got a number for me?'

Ailsa nodded, avoiding eye contact with Robson.

'Get the FLO on the phone. I'll take it on line one.'

The call was put through within seconds. The DCI was calmer by then but still concerned that Robson wasn't up to speed and had taken the easy way out. Despite the time she'd given him to get his shit together, he'd come up short – probably because he didn't want a complaint against his name. Well, she had one. If she'd sent Hank it would've been job done. Hell, Lisa would've handled it better. It wasn't a popularity contest.

Identifying herself to the FLO, she explained her dilemma: Kent's refusal to cooperate, her theory that either a mistake had been made or else he'd switched the DNA to hide Sophie's identity in the event she was ever found.

'What's he like?' she asked. 'I mean *really* like.'

'He's an arse . . .' The comment was spoken in a pronounced Welsh accent, the officer's voice fading out as he turned his head away from the phone to yell at someone behind him, telling them to quieten down. The background noise ceased immediately. 'Sorry 'bout that, ma'am. It's like a zoo in here. I'm in the staff canteen. If you're asking did Kent kill his daughter, then no I don't think he did. That's the impression I got, anyway. He had no wife or partner at home so I spent more time with him than most. The man was in chunks.'

Kate tried to keep an open mind but she'd met parents who'd fallen apart before. She'd even sat next to one or two in front of the national press. She'd listened to their sob stories, heard their pathetic pleas for their kids to come home, knowing full well they weren't going to because they had killed the poor buggers. On the other hand, if Kent were innocent, he needed careful handling. If she put a foot wrong, she risked being branded as insensitive by everyone with a bony finger to point in her direction.

Thanking the FLO for his time, she hung up, grabbed her coat and went in search of Robson, still angry with him for cocking up the first visit. Kent could well be an innocent man, but Robson should have dealt with his refusal to give DNA, used gentle persuasion to get those samples, which is precisely what *she* was now planning to do. Up close and personal she'd be in prime position to make a judgement and, if necessary, a difficult call. If he wouldn't budge, she'd lock him up. She didn't have time to mess about.

80

The phone woke her suddenly. Reaching out from the covers, Emily grabbed it from her bedside table, almost dropping it in her rush to pick up. Speaking Rachel's name as she answered, she shuffled up the bed, taking in Walker's fit upper body as he woke too, reaching out for her hand, smiling at her through sleepy eyes.

It was Stamp's voice and not her daughter's that reached her ear.

'I've been thinking,' he said. 'I have an idea.'

Emily swung her legs over the edge of the bed, drawing the duvet around her, pushing the phone closer to her ear so Walker couldn't hear who was on the other end. Who was she kidding? It was the other way round, more like. Stamp would go ballistic if he knew she was with another man.

Walker sat up too, a question on his face. With a quick shake of the head, she let him know that it was not Rachel on the other end of the line.

'Can you hold on a second?' she said into the phone.

'Sure can.' All trace of their spat had gone from Stamp's voice.

Walker glanced at his watch, a horrified expression crossing his face as he realized the time. He tapped his wrist, his way of telling her he was very, very late for work. She nodded her understanding. To her relief, he got up immediately, pulled on his kit and gestured his departure. Her hand closed like a vice around the speaker as he whispered his apologies and made a quick exit, kissing her cheek on the way out of the bedroom, telling her he'd see her at work.

'Hello?' Emily said as the door closed. 'Martin, are you still there?'

'Certainly am – and on my way over.'

'No!' Emily didn't want him to see her now. She'd never hide her guilt. They had a future together potentially whereas she and Ash didn't. They had talked about it last night as they lay in the darkness. He understood that their night of sex wouldn't be repeated. He'd fulfilled a need and that was that. Stamp was still talking. She had to put him off. 'Can't it wait 'til I get to work?'

'You've changed your tune,' he said. 'You OK?'

'Yes, of course I am.' She lied. 'I'm just about to jump in the shower, that's all.'

'Nice image,' Stamp said, before he could stop himself.

'Later then?' Emily relaxed. 'My office, ten o'clock?'

Stamp smiled as he skirted a herd of cattle a farmer was shooing into a field on his left, one of which was refusing to obey his instructions. Taking the bend in the road, he applied the brake suddenly and let out a gut-wrenching bawl as he noticed Walker's battered VW in the lane outside Emily's home.

'Martin?' Her velvet voice again. 'Did you get that?'

Stamp felt so sick, he couldn't reply.

Level with the driveway now, he surveyed the scene. Emily had left her car out overnight, something she never did. It was parked at an angle to the front door as if she'd driven up in a hurry and couldn't wait to get inside. It didn't take a genius to work out what had gone on.

'Did you hear me, Martin?' Her voice again.

Stamp's emotions lurched between anger and betrayal. He didn't respond to the hands-free. Just then, the front door opened and Walker stepped outside, still tucking in his shirt as he ran to his car.

Inside the house, Emily flinched as the front door slammed and the phone went dead simultaneously. *Oh God, no!* Hanging up, she fled to the window. Opening the curtains, she looked out at the worst scene she could possibly have imagined, powerless to do anything about it. Walker waved at Stamp, got in his car and drove off. The psychiatrist glanced at her bedroom window, his arms resting on the steering wheel. She could see his devastation from where she was standing. He started his car and floored the accelerator. Seconds later he was gone.

As soon as Emily reached the prison, she went in search of him. Martin Stamp had been good to her since Robert died, so much so she felt she owed him an explanation. She found him on another wing, interviewing a young man who had agreed to take part in his research.

Taking a deep breath, she chanced her arm.

'Could you give us a minute?' she asked.

Greaves, the inmate being interviewed, got to his feet. He'd been detained at Her Majesty's pleasure for battering a 'friend' to death over a girl they were both keen on. He was a lovely lad: quiet, reserved, the absolute antithesis of the vicious thug his crime suggested he might be. His file contained glowing character references from his local priest, his family and friends, none of whom could shed any light on his loss of self-control, many having sworn under oath that they hadn't witnessed him losing his rag before. The sitting judge and jury thought differently.

Such a waste . . .

Of two lives, not one.

Emily stepped aside as he left the room, thanking him as he passed her by. When the door closed behind him, Stamp got to his feet. He was in a foul mood and immediately began stuffing his documents and laptop into his briefcase.

'Don't sulk, Martin. It doesn't suit you.'

'We've got nothing to say to one another, Em.'

'Since when? If you're referring—'

'Since I saw Walker sneaking out of your house at the crack of dawn. It brought new meaning to the words *a good screw*—'

'He wasn't sneaking . . .' Emily glanced out of the window, her attention drawn to Walter Fearon, who was tending the garden a little way off. 'Bloody marvellous,' she said under her breath.

'What?' Stamp looked up.

She used her eyes to point out Fearon. 'At your recommendation they take him off wing cleaners because he's a risk to me and put a bloody spade in his hand.' Emily shook her head. 'Does anyone round here have a clue about security?'

'You know what, Emily? In the last few weeks, I've seen a dark side to your personality I don't even recognize. You used to be so fair-minded, the champion of the underdog, the person who everyone could count on to do the right thing. You've changed – and not in a good way.'

Was it any wonder?

Emily didn't bite. In her position, she couldn't afford principles. Her daughter was in danger and the gloves were off. She wished he'd spare her the psychoanalysis and told him so.

'Are you telling me I'm on my own?' she asked.

'What do you think?'

'I think you're acting like a schoolboy. Jealousy didn't do Greaves any good, did it?' She regretted the words as soon as they had left her mouth. She wanted to take them back. She didn't want to fall out with him. She still needed his help. But from where she was standing it looked like she'd just blown her last chance. Should she leave him be? Let him calm down? There was no time for that. 'This morning you said you had an idea.'

'Yeah, a bad one.' He was walking towards her. 'Forget it.'

She blocked his exit. 'So you're not going to help me?'

He just glared at her. They were standing so close Emily could feel the heat – not to mention the hostility – coming off him. She was about to step aside when he spoke again. 'Know what the worst-case scenario is? Fearon gets out, does what he does best and like a boomerang comes right back, serving life!'

She slapped him hard.

On the gable end of C-wing, Fearon took a breather, sweat pouring down his face. He was part of gardening party being supervised by Kent, and was supposed to be working on the section of lawn closest to the corner of the building. He'd been given instructions to dig up the grass to make way for a new flower bed. Except the soil was rock solid and proving difficult to shift.

They were kidding, weren't they?

Fearon looked around him. He wasn't dreaming. There were no dinosaurs about, so this wasn't a scene from the Flintstones. It was slave labour, plain and simple. And it wasn't on. The blisters on his hands were weeping. The only upside was that it was so fucking cold, he couldn't feel pain.

Out of the corner of his eye, Stamp and Walker were approaching each other from opposite directions, some shitty looks passing between them. Their body language was choice. Fearon continued to observe the interesting dynamics. They were on a collision course, neither one giving way to the other. The SO's gait slowed as he neared the psychiatrist, the two men sizing up to one another like a couple of prize fighters at a weigh-in.

What was all that about?

'A word,' Walker said.

Ducking behind the wall so he could listen in, Fearon kept his head down. He pretended to work, knowing that if Kent saw him slacking he'd be hauled away for yet another bollocking. The dickhead was in one of his moods again. For a moment there was silence. Fearon assumed that Stamp and Walker had moved away but, seconds later, his ears pricked up as the psychiatrist said something intriguing . . .

'Come to gloat?' His tone was hard, abrasive.

'You tell me,' Walker replied. 'You're the shrink. Shame you can't recognize your own shortcomings.'

'What's that supposed to mean?' Stamp again.

'With Rachel missing, Emily needed some company,' Walker said. 'I obliged. I just happened to be there when you weren't. Right time, right place.'

'I bet you were.'

'Sex is a great healer, pal. You should try it sometime.' There was a short pause. Then Walker spoke some more. 'You don't see it, do you? Don't ask me why, but it's you she really wants. She told me so herself last night after . . . well, let's not get into that. I'm sure I don't need to draw you any pictures.'

No!

Meltdown.

Emily and Stamp?

Fearon's knuckles turned white as he tightened his grip on the garden fork. He smashed it into the ground with brute force, feeling the vibration travel up his arm, through the right side of his neck and into his head. This wasn't happening. It couldn't be. He threw down the fork. He'd had enough. But as Kent came charging towards him, he smiled, a vindictive plan forming in his mind.

81

The pretty village of Acklington wasn't far away, a short distance inland from the coast, less than a mile and a half from the prison where Kent worked. If you didn't know anyone who lived there, there would be no point ever stopping. Blink and you'd miss it – population less than five hundred.

When Kent opened the door, he looked neither happy nor surprised. Robson did the introductions and asked if they could step inside. Grunting his consent, the prison officer stood aside to let them in. Kate's driving glasses steamed up as she entered the house. Removing them, she slipped them into her jacket pocket, eyeing the shabby room.

An open window wouldn't go amiss. It was like a sauna in there.

An ironing board stood open in the centre of the room. Water bubbled out of the holes of the iron and on to the carpet beneath. A pile of uniform shirts had been dumped on the sofa waiting for attention. The flat-screen TV was tuned to a foreign football game. No photographs of Sophie on display, the DCI noticed.

Interesting.

'You know why I'm here?' Kate asked.

'Guess so,' he replied. 'But I haven't changed my mind. I'm not going to either.'

'I don't want to give you any more grief, Mr Kent. It would really help us if you'd cooperate.'

He didn't answer.

'OK, you leave me no choice. I'm sorry to have to tell you this, but I think we may have found Sophie, even though samples taken at the time she went missing tell us different. I need to clarify who my victim is once and for all. The only way to do that is to obtain samples from you. I take it Sophie is your biological child?'

'As far as I'm aware! Although, knowing my late wife, that can't be guaranteed.'

An evasive answer or an honest one?

'You do see our problem?' Kate said.

Hard eyes fixed on her.

Shifting the ironing board out of his way, Kent sat down, dropping his head into his hands. The DCI waited. She couldn't tell if he was going to admit switching his daughter's samples, leap up and lamp her one, or just crumble. He did none of those things, although he was visibly upset.

Kate asked herself if his grief was genuine. Or had he replayed this moment a million times over in the past decade to the point that he was able to treat them to an Oscar-winning performance? If so, he was playing a blinder.

She waited for him to look up. 'Will you give consent?'

'No . . . I won't.'

Pressing her lips together, she fought the urge to tell him not to be such a dick. *Time to up the ante.*

'After what I've told you, there are three reasons why you'd refuse to give a sample of DNA. One: you don't think we've done our jobs properly and you're angry. If that is the case, I can only apologize, sir. I'd be livid too, in your position.'

He didn't admit or deny it was so.

'Two: you're scared. You don't want to know who we found because if it is Sophie you have to face the fact that she's never coming home.' Kate spoke slowly, choosing her words carefully. 'Fear is also entirely logical. We're not robots, Mr Kent. Believe me when I tell you we feel the pain too, especially where children are involved.'

She paused.

He was nervous, waiting for her to verbalize the third reason. She wasn't going to make it too easy for him. She wanted him to sweat. She wanted those samples and would do anything to get them. Right now, the only way open to her was to apply a little pressure.

Robson looked at the floor. He knew what was coming.

As so he bloody should. He was a murder detective, a good one too until he fell from grace at work and at home. *His own doing.* Well, he'd had his last chance. More than one, if the truth were known. Kate wouldn't stand for a lightweight on her team. It was time they had a little chat. If he couldn't cut it, it was bye-bye, Robbo.

She eyeballed Kent. He was never going to love her but he'd respect her if she were straight with him. Even the worst scumbags responded to that. And this was no time to lose her bottle. 'I can see you've already worked out the third reason,' she said. 'That's right, isn't it?'

He didn't speak.

'OK, let me spell it out for you. You don't want to give your

DNA because you know full well who is in that Bamburgh grave – because you put her there.'

Still nothing.

'Have it your own way then.'

'You people make me sick!' Kent stood up suddenly, his eyes full of contempt.

Kate braced herself for an attack, verbal or physical, but it never came. The warrant card in her pocket suddenly felt heavier than it had ever done before. If this man was innocent – a homicide victim's father – then what she'd just accused him of was unforgivable. That didn't make her feel good. But she had a job to do. And she had to do it no matter whom she upset. Her first responsibility was to her victim.

'I didn't murder my daughter.' Kent didn't raise his voice as he made his feelings known. 'And for the record, I do think the police are a bunch of incompetent arseholes. I'll give you the samples. What's the point of refusing? You're going to arrest me otherwise, isn't that right?'

Daniels didn't reply.

82

Emily logged on to her computer, opened up her inbox and saw the message immediately. For a long while she sat there staring at the screen, her eyes fixed to the subject line: INMATE: X40965 WALTER FEARON. She hesitated, her right forefinger hovering above the mouse. The next few seconds could shape her future in ways she didn't care to imagine right now. This was a chance, her *only* chance of keeping Fearon behind bars a while longer.

All was lost if the answer was no.

Taking a deep breath in, she left clicked on the message, skim-read the text, then read it again. It was quite a long and considered reply, but only the first four words registered: *The Home Secretary regrets . . .*

A noise made her look up.

The door opened and Jo walked in.

Emily tried to act normal but fell woefully short of that.

Jo walked round the desk and got down on her honkers putting them on the same level. 'What's up, Em? Can I help?'

Emily couldn't speak.

'Martin told me you'd fallen out. Is that it?'

Emily shook her head, pointing at her computer screen.

Jo read the email, the light in her eyes dying as they moved over the text. She gave Emily a hug and a little sympathy. Her quest to keep Fearon in prison had failed miserably, her attempt to involve the Home Office a wasted effort. They both knew that.

'Did Martin tell you why we had a fight?' Emily asked.

Jo nodded. 'And that's your own business. You have nothing to reproach yourself for and you certainly don't owe him, or anyone, an explanation. He'll come round in time. He's angry now, but he'll see sense when he gets his head round it. Martin won't stay mad for long. He's got a big heart . . . almost as big as his ego.'

Emily managed a smile, appreciating Jo's attempt at cheerfulness.

Taking a compact mirror and a tissue from her desk drawer, she wiped her eyes. They were all red and puffy. In her race to follow Stamp to work she'd showered quickly and left the house devoid of any make-up, her damp hair scruffed back and clipped in an untidy mess at the nape of her neck.

'Martin is the least of my problems,' she said.

'What d'you mean?'

'Fearon gets out tomorrow.' Emily lowered the mirror. She was welling up again. 'I went to see him just now, tried to talk to him. He laughed at me. He's a serial sex offender whose walls are covered in pornography and he laughed at me! Who makes the damn rules, Jo? Them or us? I spoke to Harrison about it and he laughed at me too. As good as.'

'Let me guess: happy inmates keeps the lid on the prison, right?'

The answer was in the question.

'How the hell do they expect us to reduce offending behaviour if they allow the cons to drool over filth like that?'

Emily said. 'It's a bloody nonsense! I'm going to speak to the Governor about it later.'

'Don't waste your energy. You don't need another crusade right now—'

'Crusade? Is that what you think I'm on? For Christ's sake, Jo! What's wrong with you? Why won't anyone listen to me?'

Jo apologized.

Emily just glared at her, an invisible barrier between them. Clearly, Jo had something to add but was searching for the right words. Whatever it was, Emily had the distinct impression she wasn't going to like it.

'Have you heard from Kate?' Jo asked.

'No, why?'

'No reason.'

'Then why ask? Have you heard something?'

'No—'

'You're lying, I can tell.'

'You need to talk to her, Em. Tell her how you're feeling.'

'Yeah, right! Like she has time to listen. At least Lowther goes through the motions occasionally.' Emily stopped talking as a dreadful thought set her heart pounding. Panic set in and her mouth went dry. 'You're trying to tell me she found Rachel—'

'No, I'm not!' Jo pulled up a chair and sat down. 'Emily, you need to calm down and get some rest. I think you should go home and make an appointment with your doctor.'

'I don't need a doctor. I *need* Rach!' Emily was angry now and it showed. 'You didn't just come to hold my hand, did you? You came because Kate paid Kent a visit, demanding his

DNA. Well I can tell you now she's on a hiding to nothing. Did you know I was the one put the idea into her head?'

Jo nodded.

'I tried to take it back, to explain to her that it was all a mistake, but she ran with it anyway. Now it's all over the prison. She's wrong, Jo. It's Fearon, not Kent, needs watching.'

'No, Emily! You're the one who's wrong. It's illogical to think he's behind Rachel's disappearance. You know Kate almost as well as I do. You couldn't set her on a course of action she didn't want to take if you tried. If she's looking at Kent, there'll be a good reason for it.'

Emily just looked at her.

What on earth did that mean?

83

'You've got to talk to her.' Jo had her eyes fixed on Kate. 'She's in a terrible state and it won't take much to push her over the edge.' They were walking along the shoreline as the sun went down, the sea crashing on to the beach, Nelson racing ahead, his paws sending out plumes of sand every time he launched himself forward in pursuit of his ball.

Kate wasn't listening.

Her head was full of possibilities: Kent's DNA, miners, pearls, fairytale castles. What did it all mean and how did it fit together? When push came to shove, they were all just lines of enquiry that could lead her to a dead end. But only a brave SIO would drop one of them and put it in for referral.

Easier to pick one up.

'Kate? Are you listening?'

'Uhm . . . yeah,' Kate lied.

She'd spent all afternoon reading statements relating to Sophie Kent's disappearance. Something niggling at the back of her mind refused to bubble to the surface. The more she thought about it, the further away it seemed. Several names were now written on the murder wall at Alnwick Police Station: John Edward Thompson, Martin Stamp, Ash Walker, Ted Harrison and of course, the girl's father.

'It doesn't sound like you are.' Jo launched Nelson's ball in the direction of the car park, ensuring the dog didn't return to the water. 'Fearon gets out tomorrow and Emily is beside herself. Don't you think it's time you put her out of her misery?'

Kate looked at Jo. 'You didn't tell her anything?'

Jo stopped walking.

Seeing the hurt look on her face, Kate apologized.

Combing a hand through her hair, she studied Jo closely, wishing they were on a beach, equally beautiful, but far away: thirty degrees warmer, bikinis and flip-flops on, a sun-lounger and parasol, a good book, a sumptuous hotel bedroom just a step away – a night of unadulterated pleasure ahead of them.

In your dreams.

'By the way,' Jo said, as they set off again. 'Emily knows you visited Kent. Acklington is a tiny village. You were seen. Any news on his DNA?'

Kate shook her head. 'It's a priority job. Should have a result later. If our victim ID is confirmed as Sophie Kent, I'll 'fess up to Emily, I promise. She deserves to know the truth.'

'Yes, she does.' Jo paused, her expression grim. 'It won't stop her freaking out about Fearon though, will it? It'll give her something even more scary to contemplate. He may not be old enough to have killed Sophie Kent and deposit her body in Northumberland, but if he's working in tandem with an older sex-offender . . .'

Her sentence trailed off leaving an uncomfortable silence between them. They both knew that if Rachel had been targeted by Sophie and Maxine's killer, pound to a penny she was already dead. But they would deal with that when, *if,* victim ID was confirmed. There was no point either of them dwelling on it now.

They had reached the car park.

Jo opened the tailgate of her Land Rover Discovery. Removing a bright blue towel with doggie paw motif, she called Nelson to heel, slung one leg over him and began rubbing him down. Kate opened the door of her own vehicle, telling Jo she'd call her later when the DNA result was in.

Releasing the dog, Jo stood up to bid her farewell. But before Kate had time to climb in, Nelson shook himself violently, sending a spray of sand and salt water into the interior of her pride and joy.

Half-grimacing, half-smiling, Jo seized Nelson and brought him to heel so Kate could brush the debris off her seat. As she emerged from the car, her expression changed from minor irritation to revelation in a flash.

'What?' Jo said.

Kate looked at the ground beneath their feet. Then, hurriedly, she kissed Jo and the dog. Without another word, she got in the car, started up the engine and drove away, sending plumes of sand high into the air.

84

As Jo got smaller in her rear-view mirror, Kate spoke a name into her hands-free device. Pulling out into traffic, she floored the accelerator. The phone rang out unanswered. She was about to cancel and call someone else when Hank Gormley finally picked up.

'Hank, Sophie Kent's file is on my desk. Grab it and summon the squad for an emergency meeting.'

'You got something?'

'I bloody hope so.'

'You going to share it with me?'

The countryside rushed by as she explained what had been bothering her while walking on the beach with Jo, something finally registering as they said goodbye. It was a first: receiving vital intelligence from a dog. Hank laughed. But before he had a chance to respond to the information, her phone gave an audible alert of a call waiting. She put him on hold while she answered.

It was Matt West from the science lab.

'Hold on, Matt.' Switching calls again, Kate said, 'I'm hanging up, Hank. I've got Matt on the line. Can you check out the stuff I mentioned? Mine's strong and black, if you're offering. I'm only five minutes away.'

*

Both the coffee and the Murder Investigation Team were waiting when she arrived. There was an air of excitement in the incident room: arguing, banter, general chit-chat as detectives gathered round. An unscheduled meeting usually meant good news.

A complete hush descended as she took the floor, Sophie Kent's missing-person file in her hand. 'Ladies and gents, we have an ID,' she said. 'DNA match. No dispute. Sophie Kent *was* the first victim.'

Taking an A4 photograph from the file, she gave it to Carmichael to pass on. Naming a victim was guaranteed to provide a new impetus to the case. It was a breakthrough, yes. A cause for celebration, but a solemn occasion too. That much was evident from the team's reaction as the image travelled clockwise round the room. Even the most sensitive officers found it difficult to relate to a pile of bones. Kate was glad they were no longer dealing with that. The victim had now taken on a personality. She was real. Vibrant. Pretty, as the photograph showed: a ten-year-old tomboy with deep blue eyes and a cheeky grin. She had a name. Later, her image would be pinned to the murder wall as a reminder to them all.

Time to move on . . .

'When Sophie went missing, a number of suspects were interviewed at length, some of whom now live on our patch. You all know who they are.' Kate took a sip of coffee and set her cup down. 'Let's just concentrate on Kent for now. At the time, his clothing was retained and a forensic search of his car was carried out. This is where it gets interesting.'

The team were all ears.

'I was trawling through statements earlier today,' Daniels continued, 'and came across a forensic reference that later struck a chord with me. A few grains of sand were lifted from the handbrake casing of Kent's vehicle. Now we know for definite that she was buried in sand, that physical evidence takes on a new significance. Hank, did you check the continuity of the evidence?'

Gormley nodded. 'The constituency of the sand was never examined.'

'Because?'

'He explained it away. Told investigators he'd recently visited his terminally ill wife at a hospice near Staithes and took a walk along the beach afterwards. I believe this was corroborated at the time – the visit, I mean, not the walk.'

'Yeah, well, I'm not convinced.'

It was rare that two vital pieces of information came along at once. Daniels couldn't believe her luck. She could see the excitement on the faces of her team. She homed in on Carmichael.

'Raise an action, Lisa. I want the evidence box collected from Yorkshire. I want that toothbrush and hairbrush. I also want the sand sample taken to Matt West, under blue light if necessary. I need to know if he can establish whether or not the sand found in Kent's car came from Staithes. That means we need comparison samples collected from both Staithes and from Abbey Hunt, who brought plenty with her when she excavated the victims from our crime scene at Bamburgh. I want it done straight away. Let's see if we can nail this once and for all. Can I have a volunteer?'

Every hand in the room went up.

85

Fearon looked around his empty cell as keys jangled outside. His escort unlocked the door and, with a scowl that could kill a horse at five hundred metres, told him to move out. As he stepped over the threshold for the very last time, Fearon glanced up and down the corridor both ways. *No Kent?* Surely the dumb bastard wouldn't miss a final opportunity to lamp him one before he made his break for freedom?

He was marched down the corridor like a guardsman on parade. Jeers of 'Nonce!' rang out as he passed other cell doors. Fuck them, he thought. From here on in, he could watch TV, eat, sleep and crap when he wanted, even wear his own kit. The cons yelling at him were staying put. They had done their utmost to break him – gobbed in his food, stolen from him, taken a pop every chance they got – but he'd survived. He'd been fending off arseholes like them for years. He was free and clear. End of. Some of those he was leaving behind would live in this shit-hole the rest of their lives.

Giving them the finger, Fearon never looked back.

The journey to the discharge office took no time at all. It had seemed a much longer walk coming the other way. There were others waiting for release. Fearon was told to wait, then given the civilian clothes he'd worn on the day he arrived.

They were a little tighter now on account of the bodybuilding he'd been doing, courtesy of Her Maj.

Nice of her to take care of his physique that way.

A yellow line was taped on the floor to stop inmates crowding the no-neck sitting behind the counter. Sensing Fearon's gaze, the officer looked up, gave him the once-over. The screw was built like a nightclub bouncer: short cropped hair, impressive tats and bulging neck muscles beneath a pockmarked face not even his mother could love.

Consulting the list in front of him, he called out a name and prison number.

'Two-four-six-seven-zero Johnson, step forward.'

A puny kid Fearon didn't know shuffled across the line. The screw did the business and then handed him over to another escort for transfer to the main gate and release into the big wide world beyond. As he waited his turn, Fearon's eyes skimmed an official-looking notice on the wall, promising to care and protect inmates.

His snigger drew a look of suspicion from No-neck.

Finally, his name was called.

The screw beckoned him forwards, counted out the cash Fearon had had in his pocket the day he arrived, along with what he'd earned inside, a dead mobile phone, a crumpled pack of stale cigarettes but no lighter. The bastard had obviously confiscated that. Fearon was handed a travel warrant and discharge sheet with clear instructions what to do when he reached his destination.

Erm, he didn't think so. No, sir! He was going to be far too busy for that.

'The warrant will get you to Sheffield and is valid for today only, is that clear?'

'Crystal.' Fearon signed for his personal effects.

The screw handed him a half-sheet of paper. 'These are your reporting instructions. Now get lost.' Fearon turned away. As he made for the door, the officer had one last dig: 'See you soon, loser.'

Fearon grinned. 'Not if I see you first.'

Once outside the main gate, he felt many pairs of eyes on his back. Slinging his prison-issue bag over his shoulder, he gingerly made his way past a police traffic car. The driver gave him hard eyes as he walked by and then returned his focus to the main gate. Fearon relaxed. The pigs weren't after him. Not this time. Gate arrests were common. The police liked nothing better than to wait for a release date to pick someone up for outstanding offences. Today must be his lucky day. No one could spoil it. Not the Five-O, Kent or Harrison, certainly not that slag, Emily McCann. He just couldn't wait to get reacquainted with her.

Taking a final look behind him, he pulled up sharp.

'Well, well,' he chuckled.

Life was good.

This day was just getting better and better. He knew an arrest when he saw one. Kent was being helped into the police car at the main gate. Fearon waved at the cunt as the car sped by.

86

Kate Daniels sat tapping her fingers on the surface of her desk. Even though she was expecting Matt West to be put through to her office, she jumped when the phone rang out. There was no time for small talk. It was too late for Sophie Kent and Maxine O'Neil, but assuming Rachel McCann was still alive, Kate might just save her if she moved fast.

'Tell me what I need to know, Matt.'

Closing her eyes, she listened intently to the answer he gave.

'Sample A is not consistent with the original statement given by Kent. It doesn't match sample B: sand from Staithes. But it does match sample C: sand from your crime scene at Bamburgh. Although both locations are on the east coast, their properties are very different.'

Kate opened her eyes.

Matt's verbal report was clear. There was no hesitation, no ambiguity. These were hard facts – something she could work with – expert witness testimony that would hold up in a court of law. Unequivocal forensic evidence linking Kent's car to the Northumberland coast around the time his daughter went missing.

The words 'provable lies' sprang to mind.

It was a Eureka moment, a godsend to an SIO struggling

with a complex case spanning a decade or more. It put Kent bang smack in the frame for his daughter's murder. Thanking Matt, she put down the phone as a traffic car pulled into the car park outside her window, Kent's gaunt face peering out from within.

The interview strategy was simple. Drip-feed the information and let the suspect trip himself up. When she put it to the guv'nor, he agreed. She didn't hang around. Within fifteen minutes, Kent was seated in front of her and Gormley, with Naylor and Jo Soulsby watching via a video link next door.

Gormley introduced everyone and cautioned the suspect for the benefit of the tape, asking him once more if he wanted a solicitor present. He told them no, he'd done nothing wrong.

'Mr Kent,' Daniels began, 'I won't beat about the bush. When your daughter went missing ten years ago some sand was recovered from the handbrake casing of your car.'

'Was it? I don't recall that.'

'Then let me remind you. When asked about it, you told detectives that it must've come from a visit to Staithes. Remember now?'

'No, yes . . . vaguely. I was in a state of shock back then. With Sophie missing, I didn't know what I was doing or saying half the time.'

'Do you have any further explanation as to how it got there?'

'No idea. If that's what I said, then that's what I meant. It's the only explanation, unless it came off someone else.'

The DCI wanted more. 'Such as?'

'I dunno, people who'd been in my car.'

'Anyone in particular? I need names, Mr Kent.'

'Why?' When Daniels didn't answer, Kent moistened his lips and reeled some off: Stamp, Harrison, Walker and two other men – one of whom she already knew to be deceased.

'Clever!' In the adjoining room, Superintendent Naylor's eyes remained firmly fixed on the screen as he watched the interview progress. 'And a tad convenient.'

'How's she doing?' Jo asked.

'She's wondering if that was a deliberate ploy to queer her pitch.'

In the interview room, the DCI spoke again. 'You seem very sure about that.'

'We were on the same darts team,' Kent said with confidence. 'We all took turns to drive. Ask them, if you don't believe me.'

'I shall.' Kate glanced at the notes she'd made prior to the interview. It was important to hit him with the right questions. 'There were two items, a hairbrush and a toothbrush, recovered from your home. Items you allege belonged to Sophie.' She showed him the exhibits and asked him for confirmation, allowing him a little time. 'Mr Kent? Do they belong to your daughter?'

Kent shifted in his seat. 'I don't lie to the police. The CID collected them from her bedroom. Of course they're hers. Looks like them, anyway.'

'*Looks like them* isn't good enough,' Daniels said. 'Are they identical in every way? Very similar? Did she have stuff like this? Tell me what you meant by that.'

'She did have items like that, yes. That's all I can say. I'm not big on little girls' personal possessions. Are you?'

The DCI sat back and rolled her eyes at her DS, his cue to join in.

Linking his hands, Hank placed both elbows on the table. 'You're big on little girls though, aren't you, Mr Kent? You'll be telling us next that the darts team had access to your house as well as your car.' His expression was sceptical. 'I bet each one of the people you mentioned had been there at one time or another. Am I right?'

''Fraid so,' Kent said. 'I'm a friendly kinda guy.'

There was a short pause.

Daniels picked up the questioning: 'Do you like it here in Northumberland, Mr Kent?'

This seemed to throw him. 'Why is that important?'

'I'm just making conversation, trying to understand why you chose to settle in this part of the world.' He didn't answer. 'I like it here too. Out of interest, before you were transferred to HMP Northumberland, had you ever been to Bamburgh?'

'She's good.' Naylor winked at Jo. 'But I'm better.'

Jo grinned, enjoying his banter.

Kent didn't reply. He looked nervous.

'I'll ask you again,' Daniels said. 'Had you ever been to Bamburgh before you came to work here? It's a simple enough question.'

'No,' Kent said.

'On holiday perhaps?'

He shook his head.

'Never?'

'No!' He was angry now. 'Christ's sake, woman! I never wanted to come here in the first place. I didn't have a choice. I came to live in this region because of a job change.'

'Yes, I know all about that,' she said.

Naylor glanced sideways. 'Wait for it! She's going for the jugular. He's dead meat.'

Daniels held the suspect's gaze. A film of sweat had appeared on his brow. For the first time since the interview started he looked scared. It was as if he had only just realized the trouble he was in. Well, he'd blown his opportunity for legal counsel and she wasn't stopping now.

Time to give him a nudge.

'I'd love to believe what you say, really I would. But your evidence can be disproved. The sand recovered from your vehicle has now been forensically examined. It doesn't come from Staithes. In fact, experts tell me it's a physical impossibility. Geology is obviously not your subject . . .' She paused – but there was no reaction. Her suspect just sighed and looked away. So she pushed a little harder. 'Do have any idea where the sand came from, Mr Kent? No? OK, then I'll tell you. It came from Bamburgh beach.'

Kent's head shot up. 'You're having a laugh! I'd never set foot in this county until I came to live here, well after Sophie disappeared!' He glared at her. 'I don't recall how the sand got there. The police said there was sand. I just assumed it must've come from Staithes. Either you're trying to fit me up here, or someone very close to me is.'

In the viewing room, Jo huffed. 'Five minutes ago he couldn't remember any sand at all!'

Naylor didn't answer, just stared at the monitor in front of them. Kent was back-pedalling fast, telling the DCI he had no bloody idea how sand particles had found their way into his car, that his head had been in a mess at the time. He acknowledged that these were damning discrepancies in the statement he'd given, ones that now made him look guilty when he was anything but.

Daniels again. 'Are you guilty?'

'No.'

'I think you are. You knew fine well where the sand came from. You said Staithes to save your arse, but you knew all along it was Bamburgh. That's why you didn't want to give me a DNA sample, isn't it, Mr Kent?'

He said nothing.

Naylor looked up as Daniels entered the room, drinking water from a bottle. The interview had gone well. But she wasn't celebrating and the Super knew why. She had evidence enough to charge him. He'd lied about the sand. Probably planted dodgy DNA samples to throw police off the scent should his daughter's body ever turn up. As far as motive was concerned, he was the single parent of a girl neither he nor his late wife wanted in the first place. He'd had plenty of opportunity to kill her. He had a car, so he had the means to dispose of her body. But . . .

'He could have done it,' Daniels said weakly, palming her brow. 'But I'm not convinced. Her eyes flitted over the other three: Naylor, Gormley and Jo – in that order. 'Go on then. Hands up who thinks he did it.'

No one moved.

'Shit! That's what I thought. Did you see his face when I said the sand was from Bamburgh? He was incredulous. That's why I held off asking him where Rachel was. If he didn't kill his daughter, he hasn't got her. More worryingly, and he said it himself, if he didn't do it then someone very close to him did. Don't ask me why, but I think he's on the level.'

87

Live music meant the pub was always packed to the rafters. Not that Stamp was paying attention to the pretty folk singer in the corner captivating her audience with a melancholy tune. His focus was on prison officer Ash Walker, who was standing on the other side of the room enjoying a pint with one of the dog handlers from the prison.

Stamp was pissed, in both senses of the word.

He'd been in the pub since shortly before seven, getting more and more agitated as the evening wore on. He'd eaten nothing all day. The alcohol he'd consumed had gone straight to his head. He was over-emotional as well as angry. The last time he'd been this drunk was the day Emily married Robert McCann.

What a fool he was.

The presence of his coat draped over the seat next to him was intended to dissuade others from sitting down to pass the time of day. Grabbing his wallet from his inside pocket, he got up and pushed through the crowd to the bar where he ordered another Famous Grouse.

'Straight, no ice,' he said. 'Make it a double this time.'

The barman hesitated. 'You sure you haven't had enough, Doc?'

'Just pour, will you? What are you anyway, the alcohol police? Who the hell's counting, apart from you?'

'You've been putting a few away, that's all.'

He had too. He'd started on Tyneside Blonde with whisky chasers and then dropped the beer in favour of the shorts. This was probably his eighth this session and they were numbing his sensibilities nicely.

'Something wrong, Martin?' the barman asked.

'You could say that. You going to sell me that drink or do I have to go elsewhere?'

'I shouldn't . . .' He turned away and lifted a glass to the optic. 'Two measures, yeah?'

'That's what I said.'

The music stopped and the crowd showed their appreciation. Stamp looked over his shoulder. Some people were leaving. But Walker and his mate were sitting at a table near the door. Whatever was amusing them, it was sure to include Emily McCann, he thought. Served her right. She deserved no sympathy. She wouldn't get any either when he caught up with her.

He'd had it with her.

Having paid for his drink, he went back to his seat. As he did so, a burst of laughter reached him, the coarse, boisterous variety he assumed was the two men having a laugh at his expense.

Or Emily's.

Across the room, Ash Walker caught his intense gaze. He got up and wandered over in Stamp's direction, pint in hand. 'Buy you a drink before closing?' he said. 'No hard feelings.'

Stamp told him to shove his feelings up his arse.

Seeing Walker get the brush-off, his mate finished his beer, pulled on his coat and joined them. He nudged Walker. 'I'm off home before the wife comes looking for me.' Then to Stamp, 'I'm going your way, pal. Wanna lift?'

Stamp gave him a hard stare. 'If I do, I'll call a taxi.'

88

Emily struggled beneath his weight even though it was useless. The more she fought, the more she realized she couldn't get away. He had her pinned to the chair, her arms clamped in the vice-like grip of his fingers, his ugly, chewed nails digging into the skin on her wrists. Through filthy, smeared lenses, his eyes looked evil. She could smell strong alcohol on his breath as he laughed in her face, a sound so chilling it cut right through her.

Anyone looking on would know she was dreaming from the rapid movements going on beneath her eyelids, her incoherent mumblings, the way her body twitched and writhed under the blanket wrapped around her.

The telephone rang, shocking her to consciousness.

Disorientated, it took her a moment to realize she'd fallen asleep in a fireside chair. Groggily, she reached out and grabbed the handset. It was ten past eleven according to the living-room clock. Having just woken, her voice was deep, almost rasping as she answered with her name, only to be met with an icy silence at the other end.

The line was open but no one spoke.

Fearon?

'Hello . . .' Emily shivered. 'This is Emily McCann. Who's there?'

She tried to remember if she'd locked the door before falling asleep. Whether she had or hadn't, in their present state, the locks wouldn't stop anyone determined to get in. Reg Hendry was home from hospital but was still in no condition to fit new ones.

Why hadn't she let Ash Walker do it when he offered?

Still no response from the phone.

Emily sat up straight, discarding the blanket, shoving her feet into her shoes. She listened intently, not knowing if she'd just imagined hearing her daughter's voice because the urge to hear it was so strong. Was she still dreaming?

No. There it was again – weak and trembling – but definitely real.

Rachel was alive!

89

The vehicle was a piece of shit – a three-door Suzuki Vitara – but it suited his needs perfectly. It had off-road capability and wasn't flash enough to draw the attention of nosey parkers even if parked in dense woodland. Passers-by wouldn't give it a second glance. If they did, it would be just another poacher or a shag-wagon being used by a couple of saddos trying to get their rocks off in a lonely spot.

And this one sure was lonely.

Tyres crunched on frozen ground as he pulled off the track, slowed and stopped, well out of sight of the main road. He was agitated but also excited, like a cheetah waiting for an unsuspecting gazelle to offer itself as bait. Lighting a cigarette, he smoked it in the car before reaching into his jacket pocket. Taking out his weapon, he headed off into the night.

Racing along a country road at breakneck speed, Emily checked her rear-view mirror. Headlights were fast approaching from behind. One set only. Applying her brake, she indicated left, slowing her vehicle to a crawl while keeping her revs steady, should the approaching car stop.

It didn't.

It overtook and sped off round the next bend.

Blowing out her cheeks, Emily punched Kate Daniels'

number into the keypad of her mobile. Engaging first gear, she pulled on to the road again. Steering one-handed, she floored the accelerator as the number rang out.

Kate picked up, answering with her name and rank.

She was still at work.

'Rachel's alive!' Emily said.

Covering the phone, the DCI yelled above the din of the incident room. The urgency in her voice made everyone turn their heads in her direction. There was a hushed air of expectation as she resumed the conversation.

'She's at home?'

'Not yet. She rang me five minutes ago. She escaped. I'm on my way to meet her now.'

'No, Emily, it's unsafe! You must wait for backup. It'll take us at least fifteen minutes to reach you . . .' Covering the speaker, Kate told Hank Gormley to grab their coats. The rest of her team had all stopped what they were doing, barring Carmichael who was busy on a call. Kate picked up a pen. 'Escaped from where exactly?'

The line went dead.

'Shit! Hank, come with me.'

There was no time for debate. Racing out of the MIR, Kate redialled Emily's number but she didn't pick up. They needed to find her fast. Problem was, they didn't have a clue where she was heading. If Rachel *was* alive she'd have vital information to share. Kate didn't believe in the Almighty but she prayed for the girl to be OK.

With Hank on her tail, she took the stairs two at a time,

until her progress was blocked by a group of officers coming the other way.

'Move it! She yelled.

They didn't need telling twice.

In the front office, she barked instructions. 'Put a call out on the radio. Rachel McCann has escaped her captor. Her mother, Emily is trying to find her. All officers are to keep obs out for her car: it's a Land Rover Defender, blue with a white roof, '72 model – I don't have a reg. I'm going to make my way over to her place, see if I can spot her.' She looked at Hank. 'Come on! When we get in the car, just keep ringing her number. The silly bitch has no idea who she's dealing with.'

90

Martin Stamp glared at the barman as he covered the last of the beer pumps with a tea towel and dimmed the lights, notice of his intention to close up. He had no truck with the guy. He was OK as pub landlords go, a family man who lived on the premises, a village publican who tried his best to accommodate everyone – especially him tonight.

Saying goodnight he staggered off, pulling his car keys from his pocket, dropping them in the process. The ground came up to meet him as he bent to pick them up, his arm refusing to obey his brain. Or was it his eyes?

There were two sets of keys on the floor, not one.

He swayed as a size ten boot closed over them.

'Do yourself a favour . . .' the barman retrieved the keys and held them up between forefinger and thumb. 'Take a walk and leave these with me. I'll make sure the car is secure. I know your place. I'll drive over and collect you first thing in the morning.'

Emily reached the junction. She checked road signs. It had been ages since she'd been here. Rachel had mentioned the dirt road of a woodland park where her father used to ride his trial bike. It wasn't far. But which way was it? Right or left?

Right, definitely right, towards the village.

Or was it left?

Making a decision, she turned left. But after just a few hundred metres she realized her mistake. It was right. Definitely right. She should've known.

Calm down.

You can do this.

Emily swung the car round and raced back the other way, conscious that the phone call from her daughter might well have been a set-up, an elaborate trap to lure her away from the safety of her home. Rachel had been sobbing so hard when she called, she could hardly speak.

Was someone with her, forcing her to make the call?

Horrendous scenarios scrolled through Emily's head. Fearon was out now. The sick bastard was a killer in waiting. If he had her daughter, there was no telling what he would have done to her. What he might be doing this moment. Emily didn't consider the danger to herself. Rachel's safety was her only concern.

Would he trade – her for Rachel? Unlikely. Fearon hadn't an ounce of compassion in his body. But maybe she could find a way to help her daughter escape, even if it meant sacrificing her own life.

Spotting the turn-off, her eyes searched the eerie darkness as her headlights snaked along the road. She parked up. Apart from the ticking of the engine, all was still. Cautiously, she opened the door and stepped out into the night, calling her daughter's name.

The sound of the flick knife was unmistakable as the blade left its casing. There was no warning. Not much feeling either, just a punch to the back of the ribcage, then warmth as blood seeped into clothing. The second blow was worse. It sent a spray of red mist from the neck. Another blow. Now the blood gushed out with an audible spatter as it hit the surrounding vegetation.

Staggering . . .

Falling . . .

Knees buckling . . .

Hitting the ground head first on frozen soil. It was useless trying to crawl. It just made the blood pump harder.

It was cold, so very cold.

Breathe . . . breathe . . .

Rolling over was excruciatingly painful.

Face up now. A beautiful night. Clouds moving swiftly across the moon like mist. Tranquillity. Treetops. The hoot of an owl. Then silence. There were worse places to die than alone in this beauty spot. Except that wasn't strictly true. *He* was here – like the Angel of Death hovering a few feet above – fist clenched around the handle of the blade. Then like an image on the cinema screen, everything visible faded to black.

The hairs on Sam Bradshaw's neck stood up as his Border terrier suddenly bared its teeth and began to bark. Trying to get Spike to heel was useless at the best of times. The stubborn little bugger was going crackers in the undergrowth. Sam shone his torch to the left, listening for the sound of movement. Apart from a deep growl from the dog, all was quite. But Sam could smell nicotine on the air and he was desperate to get out of there.

'Spike! Heel!'

Sam sighed, his eyes scanning the woods.

He'd been walking here for years but tonight would be the last time. He was well spooked and was never coming back. Gingerly, he left the path to retrieve the dog. But as he lowered the beam, the ground began to turn red. Balking at the sight of blood, Sam called the dog again but still it wouldn't come. He was in sight now, pawing at wet leaves beneath the overhanging branches of a tree.

Sam bent down, managed to get a lead on the terrier and pull him away.

The body was almost covered with branches. All that was visible was the left hand, palm up, a brief glimpse of what looked like denim. The figure groaned. Sam ran.

91

There was a loud bang as the double doors of Accident & Emergency burst open. Someone yelled at Kate Daniels, telling her she couldn't use that entrance. It was for medical personnel only. Ignoring them, she took the lift to the mortuary viewing room. When she got there, the body was already on the slab and pathologist Tim Stanton was standing over it.

Guilt wrapped itself around her.

Stanton had been about to go home after carrying out a lengthy autopsy on an unconnected sudden death when this unfortunate and as yet unidentified assault victim passed away, handing her another murder case and him a headache to boot. There was little point in his going home, he told her, only to get hauled straight back by his favourite Senior Investigating Officer.

Kate appreciated that: she needed answers that only he could provide.

He held up five fingers, a sombre expression on his face.

She spoke via the intercom system. 'Any ID?' she asked.

'No, nothing . . .' he said. 'Which isn't a lot of help to you, is it? Dreadful business. Even his mother wouldn't recognize him.'

Her phone rang: it was Carmichael.

'I know who he is,' she said.

Emily could feel her bottom lip quivering. Quickly drying her eyes, she turned round. The doctor reminded her of her father: kind eyes behind steel-rimmed specs, cropped hair, almost white, tie a little askew. He looked jaded, like many of the doctors and nurses she'd seen walking the corridors during the hours she'd sat waiting, a watchful WPC close by – sent by Kate Daniels to guard the room and make sure no one entered who didn't belong there.

'Is she OK?' Emily asked.

The doctor nodded. 'Severely traumatized but in fairly good shape, considering. It appears she was out of it for much of the time, sedated by the man who took her.'

'Was she . . .?' Emily couldn't bring herself to use the words sexually abused. 'I didn't ask, I just couldn't bring myself.'

'I understand,' he said. 'And the answer is no. She appears to have been treated well, fed and watered. The damage is more psychological than physical, I suspect. She's resting now. You should too. It can't have been easy for you either.'

Emily's emotions came flooding out.

It was the best possible news . . .

Rachel was OK.

She was OK!

The sound of footsteps made Emily turn round. Kate was standing behind them, a grim expression on her face. She shook hands with the doctor, thanking him for taking care of Rachel. Then she sat down next to Emily and put her arm around her. Emily broke down then, the stress finally getting to her.

The doctor moved off down the corridor.

'She's alive, Em.' Kate hugged her friend.

'Thanks for coming,' Emily said.

Kate glanced away briefly. More guilt. She wasn't here because of Rachel and didn't quite know where to begin. So she just came right out with it. 'I have something to tell you, Emily. Martin Stamp is dead. I'm so, so sorry.'

'What?' Emily was stunned. She couldn't take it in. She wanted to know how. Was it a terrible accident? Was he driving? A heart attack? 'Oh God! This can't be happening again.'

She continued to throw questions out in quick succession, hardly stopping for breath.

Kate recognized the trauma in her voice. The same shortness of breath she'd witnessed so many times when families of victims were given shocking news. She'd heard it when she'd delivered the death message to the O'Neils. And again, just a few moments ago when she'd done the same to Stamp's only living relative, a younger sister, herself a doctor. The woman's world had collapsed when a Cumbrian police officer knocked on her door; refusing to believe that her brother was dead, she had demanded to speak to the senior officer dealing with the case. After a brief telephone conversation with Kate, the woman was now on her way east to identify her brother's body – what was left of it.

There was no denial from Emily: just blame and self-loathing.

'He's dead because of me,' she said.

'That's not the case,' Kate reassured her.

'Isn't it?' Combing both hands through unkempt hair, Emily clamped her lips together to stop herself from blubbing again. Accepting a tissue, she wiped her tears away and then pressed Kate for more information. 'You can't believe this a random killing? You can't!'

'I'm not sure what it is,' Kate said.

But that wasn't strictly true. She already knew who was responsible for Martin's death. Walter Fearon hadn't showed in Sheffield following his release, neither had he used his rail warrant. He'd left the institution with a prison bag containing a change of clothes and a few personal possessions. Crime scene investigators had found evidence that he'd washed himself in a stream close to where Stamp was discovered fatally wounded. Fearon had changed clothes, attempting to bury his bloodstained jeans and jacket. He'd legged it in a hurry, leaving the bag behind, when disturbed by a man out walking his dog. Stamp would've died in situ had it not been for the terrier. No doubt about it. His body might have lain undiscovered for months.

Now there was a manhunt going on and Kate was hoping that Fearon's luck had finally run out.

92

Emily told Kate that Martin had made her believe that life was worth living after Robert died and she'd pushed him away. They had fought over Fearon and she wouldn't listen when he tried to put things right between them. Rachel was all she could think of.

'That's as it should be,' Kate tried to reassure her.

Emily hugged herself. She wasn't convinced.

Kate cleared her throat. 'If it's any consolation, he wouldn't have felt a thing. According to the pathologist, he was extremely intoxicated—'

'And whose fault was that?' Emily paused for reflection. 'He died here, in this hospital, didn't he?'

He had. On the floor below, while the woman he loved sat within spitting distance, crying over a drama totally unconnected to his death.

'Kate?'

'Sorry?' Kate was miles away.

'I'm not daft,' Emily said. 'Martin must've been alive when they found him or they wouldn't have brought him here. He'd have gone straight to the morgue.'

'You're right, he was still breathing. But he was close to death, Emily. The body shuts down to protect itself in situations like these. Believe me when I tell you he didn't suffer. It would've been very quick.'

She didn't elaborate. Couldn't. Photographs had been sent to her iPad by crime scene investigators. It had been a frenzied attack: no fewer than seven stab wounds to the chest, one in each eye, the face slashed so badly that flaps of skin hung down where his cheeks once were. In her considered opinion, it had been a deliberate attempt to destroy his handsome features. According to Stanton, his jacket resembled Shredded Wheat by the time the last blow was struck. The injuries were some of the worst either of them had come across.

Fearon must've been covered in blood.

'It should have been me,' Emily cried again.

'Martin wouldn't have wanted that. He loved you, Em. We could all see it.' Kate changed the subject to Rachel. 'I expect they'll keep her in for observation.'

Emily gave a nod. 'I didn't think she had it in her, but she's come out fighting.'

'You should rest. You look exhausted.'

'I want to be with her when she wakes up.' Emily swivelled round to face the DCI. 'On the way here, she described an older man she'd been seeing – this Vic character Jane Lowther was on about. Fearon must have been pulling the strings, though. He must have! Is he still on the loose?'

'We're checking all known associates. If we haven't already picked him up by then, come lunchtime every force in the country will be looking for him.' Taking hold of Emily's hand, Kate chose her words carefully. Her friend was in a bad way but might hold vital information she was desperate for. 'It's important I find Rachel's abductor at the earliest opportunity, Em. Did her description of him mean anything to you?'

Emily shook her head.

'Are you certain?' Kate pressed her.

'Yes! Kate, listen to me. What about Fearon? He's been in and out of institutions since he was a small boy. He's street-wise. He knows every trick in the book and every low-life within a hundred miles. You've got to find him before he kills again.'

'We'll get him . . . eventually.'

'And when you do?'

'All I can do is build a case. The rest is up to the courts.'

Glancing at her watch surreptitiously, Kate realized that Jo would be there soon. Just as well. The SIO had so much to do and she didn't have time to sit and hold Emily's hand, much as she might like to.

'You don't understand, do you?' Emily didn't wait for an answer. 'It's a power thing with Fearon. It's me he really wants.'

'I don't believe he had anything to do with Rachel's dis-appearance, Em.'

Emily urged her to reconsider.

Kate listened carefully. What if Emily was right and she was wrong? Maybe Fearon *was* complicit in Rachel's abduc-tion somehow. Sex offenders often stuck together. 'Working in tandem' was the phrase Jo had used. It wasn't impossible that he'd masterminded Rachel's abduction from the comfort of his cell, but in order to do so he would have had to join forces with whoever killed Sophie and Maxine. And that was a stretch. Could it be that he was in cahoots with the older man, Vic? Whatever the story, the abandoned prison bag would put him away for the rest of his life.

93

Daniels looked around her. Hospitals had given her the creeps since her mother died in one. She'd walked the corridors in the small hours for weeks, praying she'd get better, experiencing the deathly hush when it was too late for the drunks, too early for the accidents to pour into A & E.

The smell of the place brought back unbearable memories.

A bell rang, signalling the arrival of the lift. As the doors opened, she expected to hear footsteps on the highly polished floor. But when no one emerged, she swung round to face the doors, her eyes scanning the gloomy corridor. Suddenly on high alert, she listened. But all she heard was the lift doors close again.

Fearon?

According to Jo, he was an untreatable psychopath who had it in for Emily. But surely he wouldn't risk coming here? Would he? As the hairs rose on the back of Kate's neck, she ventured a quick glance at Emily. The woman was oblivious to her concerns, so deep in thought that the lift probably hadn't even registered.

But still . . .

Telling Emily she'd get them both something warm to drink, Kate left her side to investigate. As she walked away, she caught the attention of the WPC guarding the door to

Rachel's room. Pointing at her own eye, the DCI sent a clear message to show vigilance.

There may still be a threat to the girl and/or her mother.

In the end, she found nothing untoward.

By the time she returned to the bench where she'd left Emily, Jo was comforting her. Kate handed them each a coffee she'd bought at the machine and sat down for a moment, extending a few last words of comfort. Then she stood up again, kissed them both and left for the station, telling Jo she hoped to see her later – her way of asking her to visit the MIR when she was done.

It was twenty past six when Kate reached the office. By seven the entire Murder Investigation Team had arrived. By the time they took their seats in the incident room, most had already heard what had gone on during the night. Kate gave the official version. Martin Stamp's death was shocking but, as murders go, it was cut and dried. It didn't require their input.

'Fearon is someone else's problem,' she said. 'Whoever abducted Rachel McCann was considerably older than she was. I'll be calling in on her later. She was sleeping when I left, but Jo will talk to her as soon as she wakes, try to get a better description of this Vic character. We know it can't have been Stamp because she knew him personally. For the time being, Kent stays in custody.'

'You think it was him, boss?' Maxwell asked.

Daniels pointed to the list on the murder wall. 'Or Walker, or Harrison, or John Edward Thompson . . . the TIE action still hasn't ruled him out.'

*

Jo arrived in the incident room two hours later. Kate could tell straight away she had some vital news. Rachel had described being kept in a windowless lock-up and she was keen to take them there.

'She knows where it is?' Carmichael was excited.

'She does indeed. The garage was empty apart from an old motorcycle and—'

'How did she get out?' Gormley asked, apologizing for the interruption.

Jo gave a half-smile. 'She's her father's daughter, Hank. She knew something the offender presumably didn't. Under the motorcycle saddle there was a set of tools. She took the lock off the door with them.'

'Outstanding!' Kate said, a biker herself.

'How the hell did she manage that if she was heavily sedated?' Brown asked.

'I guess the drugs had worn off by then.'

'While we had Kent in custody, I bet.' The comment had come from Carmichael.

Kate agreed. Her protégée had just taken the words right out of her mouth. 'Hands up anyone who doesn't think Rachel was the third intended victim?'

Not one detective raised a hand.

Jo was about to say something more when Kate asked another question of her team. 'OK, anyone here think that Walter Fearon was involved in Rachel's abduction?'

Still no takers.

'For what it's worth,' said Gormley, 'I think we're dealing with two separate incidents. Whatever is going on in Fearon's head, it's to do with his obsession with Emily McCann, not

Rachel. I think he killed Stamp because he was jealous of the friendship he had with Emily, something he may have picked up on at the prison. I could see it a mile off that day we bumped into them at the beach.'

'Yep, I could too,' Daniels said. 'Fearon might be vicious but that doesn't mean he's not intuitive. In which case Emily and Rachel need a safe house right away. They can't go home, that's for sure.'

'My house in Jesmond is standing empty,' Jo said. 'If it's acceptable to you and the guv'nor, Emily can use it until Fearon is no longer a threat . . . until you pick him up, I mean. She and Rachel have stayed over with me on occasions. They'd be happier there than at an unfamiliar place.'

'I don't know.' Kate yawned, then apologized to everyone. It was hot in the room and she was fading fast. 'It's your home.'

'It makes sense.' Jo threw a set of keys at her.

Kate caught them. They were *her* old keys. She recognized them from the little silver house on the end of the key ring. The sight made her sad. Too tired to argue the toss with Jo, she acquiesced. 'OK, I'll have a word with Ron. If he clears it, that's a done deal. Thanks, Jo. One more job I won't have to worry about.'

'There was something else in that lock-up.' Jo's tone was serious. 'Apart from the bike, I mean.'

Oh God! 'Why do I get the feeling I'm not going to like this?'

'On the contrary, you're going to love it.'

All eyes were on Jo.

'The scene Rachel described was completely bizarre. At

first, I thought she'd experienced some kind of drug-induced hallucination. She told me there was a table and two chairs set for a party in the centre of the room: balloons, paper cups, beautifully wrapped presents, a set of clothes . . .'

'I'm not loving it yet. What made you think it was something more than a hallucination?'

'She mentioned a set of pearls . . .'

94

The lock-up was exactly as Rachel had described it: a damp, claustrophobic space with a party scene at its centre. A paper cloth with a pink ballerina motif was draped over the table, on top of which were matching cups and plates, curly straws. Glitter sprinkled over the lot twinkled under a bare light bulb as it flickered uncertainly directly overhead, heightening the creepy image.

Staring at the table, Rachel was upset as it dawned on her how very lucky she was to have survived her ordeal. Kate gave her a hug and stroked her hair, nodded towards the door behind her, a heavy hint for DC Lisa Carmichael to take her home.

'This is beyond weird,' Hank said. 'There are some sick bastards around.'

Kate didn't answer. She was too busy thinking, her eyes fixed on the string of plastic pearls. They were not covered in glitter. Her impression was that they had been placed on the tabletop afterwards, the crowning glory, a finishing touch to the gross scene. Whoever the perpetrator was, it was clear that they were ready to kill again and would have done so had Rachel not escaped in the nick of time.

'Get SOCO in here!' she said. 'Or CSIs or whatever they call themselves these days.'

Hank went outside and gave instructions for the crime scene investigators to move in. The photographer immediately got to work, lighting the place up with a series of camera flashes to document what they had found for later use in court. Kate Daniels could almost see the distressed faces of the jury as they examined this lot.

When Hank returned to her side, she was mulling over the trio of prison officers still in the frame.

'I was just thinking,' she said. 'If Kent was off duty when Rachel went missing, then so too were Walker and Harrison. They were all on the same shift pattern according to their duty roster.'

'Good point,' Gormley said. 'Rachel's Vic could've been any one of them.'

'Yeah, but which one?'

Gormley shrugged. 'They're about the same age, vaguely similar in appearance. At her own admission, Rachel was legless when she met him, on subsequent occasions too, and heavily sedated after the abduction. I guess older men look much the same to an unhappy binge drinker. Short of showing her their family albums, we're screwed in terms of identification. She seems to have blanked out his face completely.'

'Understandable,' Kate said. 'She was seeking a father figure and found a monster. Jo is fairly sure the memory will return to her, given time.'

'Assuming the bastard we're after isn't someone else entirely,' Hank countered.

'Nah, Andy checked with the Home Office. Only six officers were transferred up here when HMP Coleby closed:

Kent, Walker and Harrison, plus Officer Cohen – who we know was deceased by the time Rachel went missing – and two others who couldn't cut it up here and were shipped out to establishments in the south. I had Andy chase them up. One was out of the country. The other works at Wandsworth now and he was on a training course. Half the prison service can verify that. It has to be one of those three.' She paused. 'Kent's in no position to refute the evidence we put to him. I had another go at him this morning, but he still won't cough.'

'Doesn't mean he's not guilty.'

'True.' Kate sighed. 'Do we know who owns this place?'

'Not yet. Robbo's checking it out.'

'Whoever killed Sophie took Rachel, agreed?'

Gormley nodded.

'Then the way I see it is this: Kent can't prove he didn't kill his daughter but if he agrees to my proposal, he can rule himself in or out of Rachel's abduction. If she fails to ID him, he walks.'

'You going to run an ID parade?'

'Not necessary if he agrees to let her take a look at him.'

Hank raised an eyebrow. 'You think he will?'

Another flash from the camera.

'Only if he's not guilty,' the DCI said.

95

'It's not him.' Rachel's head went down.

Daniels felt guilty. It wasn't the outcome either of them had hoped for. When she'd asked Rachel McCann to face a suspect *she* thought might have been Vic, the girl had gathered her courage and jumped at the chance. But the man she was looking at now was not the man who had abducted her. She was standing so close to Kent, she could almost touch him through the glass. There was no hesitation in her answer, no doubt either. Why should there be? She knew Vic personally. They had got drunk together. He'd courted her almost. They had never been intimate, but she knew him well.

'Is that it then?' she said.

'I'm sorry, Rachel.' Kate swept her arm towards the door. 'Come on, I'll walk you to reception.' She led the disappointed twenty-year-old out of the viewing room and along the corridor. Hank was coming the other way, a question in his eyes. The DCI shook her head – almost imperceptibly – letting him know that Kent was in the clear.

'Will you organize a lift for Rachel?' she asked him.

'I'm fine,' Rachel said. 'I can get the bus.'

'No, you won't. Your mother would kill me!' Kate insisted. 'You were in hospital overnight and it's a long way back to Jesmond.'

'Oh, we're not staying at Jo's place now,' Rachel said.

'Since when?' Kate was outraged.

Hank hovered close by. He had that look. The one that meant he knew something the DCI didn't. That wasn't a good place to be. Particularly in the middle of a level one murder case when your boss hasn't been to bed and things aren't exactly going to plan.

Rachel looked puzzled. She'd picked up on the unspoken aggro between them. 'Is there something wrong?' she asked.

'Course not,' Kate lied. 'I was under the impression you were staying there for a few days until we get things sorted out, that's all. I'm always the last to hear of a change of plan, aren't I, Hank?'

Rachel looked at her accusingly.

Kate lowered her gaze to hide the fact that she was withholding information. Rachel didn't understand what was going on. Why should she? She hadn't yet been told about the death of Martin Stamp and therefore had no clue about Fearon or the threat he posed to her and her mother. All the professionals, including the doctor who'd treated her, agreed it was best not to add to her anxiety by telling her there was a second, equally scary, psychopath on the loose.

'So why are you acting like my mum does when she doesn't want to worry me?' Rachel asked. She wasn't fooled by the attempt to fob her off. 'I'm a grown-up now, Kate. You guys don't have to protect me, you know.'

'It's not that, Rach . . .' Gormley flicked his eyes towards his boss. 'Kate's a grumpy bugger when she's been up all night. She's pissed with me for cocking something up. I can't tell you what it is, but it's nowt for you to worry about. Happens to us all from time to time.' He grinned. 'What's the worst that can happen? She'll either forgive me or sack me.'

It was a complete fabrication, but Rachel appeared to swallow it. Kate moved quickly on, asking her to wait in reception while they found someone to take her home. Then she and Hank walked back through the double doors to the corridor beyond. As soon as they were out of sight, she rounded on him.

'Mind telling me what the hell is going on?'

'Fearon was spotted by a social worker in Sheffield earlier. The woman called the police and the idiots rang Emily—'

'Before ringing us?'

'Wanker probably wanted to play the hero.' Gormley made his best mindboggling face. 'Emily rang Jo saying she no longer required her place. Jo rang me when she couldn't get hold of you. That's how come you were the last to find out.'

Kate was appalled. 'Well . . . did they get him or not?'

Gormley shook his head. 'He was gone by the time the local plods arrived.'

'Jesus! So they don't even know if it *was* him. What if it's a false report, Hank? What then? I saw Stamp's body when that bastard had finished with it. It wasn't pretty, I can tell you. A vengeful attack is one thing, but that was rage, pure and simple. There's no telling what he'll do if he gets hold of Emily. I want the name of the numpty who told her she was safe to go home on my desk in ten.'

Gormley lifted his hands like she was holding a gun.

'Don't yell at me. It's hardly my fault.'

'Who the hell else would I yell at?'

Kate was pacing now, visibly tired and angry with it. False sightings of offenders had taken many an SIO's eye off the ball and put lives at risk, occasionally with disastrous consequences. It was unwise to take one woman's word that Fearon was no longer in the area, no longer a serious threat to Emily McCann. Kate pulled up abruptly, took a deep breath in and then let out a big sigh, trying to calm herself down.

'Contact the social worker concerned. Check out just how well she knows him. We can't afford to drop our guard.'

'You want me to fix up a panic alarm at Emily's place?'

'Oh, that'll work. The Stint is fifteen miles from the nearest nick. It'll take for ever to get there in an emergency.' Kate shut her eyes and then opened them again, letting out an almighty sigh. 'I'm sorry, I didn't mean to have a go at you. And yes, I want an alarm – in fact I insist on it, even if it is utterly useless. If Emily argues, you can tell her I won't take no for an answer. Now go!'

'Can't you talk to her? Explain you're not happy—'

'You think she'll listen?'

'She might.'

'No, she won't. You know how stubborn she is. She certainly won't be pushed around. She just wants to go home and get her life and her kid back to normal. And who can blame her? She won't play the victim either, not for him, or anyone. It was all I could do to persuade her to go to a safehouse in the first place!'

The door behind them creaked open.

Rachel looked worried and vulnerable as she stepped into the corridor asking them not to be mad at her mum, telling them she was the one who'd wanted to go home. She'd been listening at the door and completely misread the situation. Her eyes were filling up. She was scared to death.

'You think Vic is coming back for me, don't you?'

'No, honey.' Kate pulled her close, rolling her eyes at Gormley. *Vic was only half the threat.* 'We'll find him, Rachel. You have my word.'

96

Kate slammed her hand on her desk.

'What do you want me to do?' Hank asked.

'The only thing we can do. Bail Kent out for further enquiries.'

'You sure?'

She nodded. It wasn't a brave decision. She firmly believed that whoever had taken Rachel had killed the others, so Kent was off the hook. Besides, she had to sleep. She just had to. She'd been working for thirty hours solid. Her concentration was dropping like a stone and it would only get worse the longer she went without rest. Asking Hank to take over, she set off for the B & B. Rachel was safe now. The other victims were long dead and another few hours would make no difference to the case.

As she drove, the macabre image of a little girl's tea party in that filthy lock-up kept going round and round in her head. It brought to mind her father's dead twin, the aunt she never knew. Mary's death had affected him greatly. Still did, decades later. These two unconnected events and Rachel's alertness in leading them to a crime scene had given her a glimpse into a killer's past.

She called Jo.

'You were right about an act of devotion,' she said.

'You found the lock-up?'

'Yep, and I'm betting the person we're after lost a daughter or sister at an early age. He's marking an anniversary of some sort, as crazy as that sounds. A birthday in all probability. It means Lisa can now concentrate her efforts on the back record checks and search specifically for an incident involving a young child. I just wanted to thank you and let you know where we're at.' Her voice broke. When they were together, she often used to debrief with Jo on difficult cases and had always felt better for it. It wasn't so easy now they were living apart. 'Actually, I just wanted to hear your voice.'

'Get some rest,' Jo said. 'You sound shattered.'

Kate wiped a stressy tear from her cheek.

Words failed her and she hung up the phone.

At the B & B, she fell into bed but couldn't settle. After only three hours' sleep, she showered and made her way back to the station, arriving shortly before four p.m. Ron Naylor was there when she arrived, her sounding board should she require one, he told her.

A hastily arranged briefing focused on Kent's release on bail. There was universal agreement within the squad that he was an innocent victim rather than a perpetrator of murder. With no time to indulge that thought, Kate turned her attention to the two men still in the frame. She had reason to suspect Harrison and Walker and sufficient cause to make an arrest.

They were brought to the station under protest an hour later, Gormley and Carmichael interviewing Harrison, the DCI and Brown having a crack at Walker. But after two hours of intense questioning, neither pair were any further forward. Both suspects refused a request to take part in an ID parade, denying any involvement in Rachel's abduction, the disappearance of Sophie Kent or the murder of Maxine O'Neil.

'Well, that was predictable,' Kate said as she left the interview suite.

'Bail them out.' Naylor was resigned. 'There's no hard evidence to hold them.'

'Apart from the fact we know one of the arseholes is responsible,' Hank scoffed. 'Harrison was a dick throughout the interview. I could happily have punched his lights out.'

Kate was only half-listening to his tirade. In her mind's eye she was picturing Walker in the interview room, his uniform on. It set her wondering what shift he was working, a plan forming in her head.

There was an alternative to a straight ID parade.

She looked at Maxwell. 'Were they both at work when you picked them up?'

He nodded.

'Any idea if they've gone back?'

'They did. I dropped them off myself. Thought it was the least I could do, given that their vehicles were at the prison. Walker was quiet in the car but Harrison . . . well, let's just say he didn't shut up the whole way. He kept bleating on about an official complaint. Said the Governor was going to hang you out to dry.'

Kate shrugged. Like she gave a shit. She was used to being complained about.

'I got the impression he started at two, if that's any help, boss,' Maxwell said. 'So finishing at ten would be my best guess. Walker is probably the same. You want me to get on to prison admin and check it out?'

'No, someone might tip them off. Call Jo and ask her to do it surreptitiously on my behalf. Do it right away. But tell her it's strictly hush-hush.' She looked at Robson, who was sitting beside the window, a flurry of snow falling gently behind him. 'Robbo, assuming Neil comes back with the right answer, I want you to speak to division and organize a street identification at the prison at ten o'clock. If they argue about the lack of notice, just refer them to me. Tell them I'll let them know when and where to collect the witness. I'll sweet-talk Rachel. I'm sure she'll agree to go through with another ID.'

Gormley and Naylor exchanged a grin.

'If Mohammed won't come to the mountain . . .' Hank said. He didn't bother with the rest.

97

The Area Command Inspector's tone of voice was evidence enough that it hadn't gone well. Two hours before the planned street ID it had begun to snow steadily and by ten o'clock he was dubious of a good outcome. Emily and Rachel met him in the prison car park, travelling under their own steam in Robert's Land Rover. It was a smart move. The Traffic car reported all sorts of problems getting there. Regulations prevented Daniels from taking part, fairness demanding that she stay away. No chance to influence the witness, no fear of being accused of that. Fair enough, she thought, time to back off and let uniform sort it.

Parking in a bay near the prison gatehouse, the man in charge looked out of his window as the Land Rover Defender pulled up alongside. The doors opened almost immediately, two females emerging, transferring to his car as instructed, brushing snow from their clothing as they slammed the doors.

As they waited for the shift change, the officer turned to face them, having a word with Emily, then telling Rachel exactly how it would go down when staff walked out of the gatehouse. That included the reason why she was there, even though it probably sounded like he was stating the obvious.

Experience had shown that in circumstances like these it was advisable to be prescriptive.

There was no room for error. He didn't want the witness doing or saying anything inappropriate, anything that might render the evidence inadmissible.

He smiled at the girl, an attempt at reassurance. 'Rachel, you're here to see if you can identify the man who abducted and held you captive in a garage in Northumberland. You must appreciate that you may not see the person responsible. However, if you do, you must indicate to me – in the clearest way possible – that you have seen someone you recognize. Do you understand?'

'Yes, perfectly.'

'I can't prompt you in any way. For example, I couldn't ask is he the man in the red jumper or anything like that. *You* must describe and point him out to *me*: That's him, he's wearing a red jacket, a blue jumper, a yellow scarf or carrying a suitcase or whatever. Agreed?'

Rachel gave a little nod.

But as the minutes ticked by, the weather worsened. It was a complete white-out by the time the finishing shift trooped out. As they filed past the Traffic car en route to their own vehicles, they all looked the same dressed in uniform parka jackets with hoods pulled tight around their faces. The whole thing was a bloody disaster, an outcome the Inspector conveyed to Kate Daniels at the earliest opportunity.

'This is Alpha One, ma'am. No joy here, I'm afraid. We weren't able to make a street ident. By the time the shift cleared the gate they all looked like Nanook of the North. It was impossible for Rachel to tell one from another.'

Kate punched her steering wheel in frustration.

'OK, return to base,' she said. 'And thanks for the assist.'

'Don't thank me yet. I was clocked by security in the car park. They kicked up a fuss when I arrived, gave me a bit of earache for not clearing it with them first. Think you're in for the high jump for not giving them any notice, ma'am.'

'That's received, Alpha One. I'm shaking in my boots. Actually, I'm on my way there now to eat humble pie. Apologies if you got it in the neck.'

Parked just a short distance away, Kate had already received a summons from the Governor. He was screaming for answers, wanting to know why she'd locked up three of his bods, thrown them out again and then positioned a Traffic car on his doorstep without a word in his shell-like. She was about to tell him to butt out. It was prison service property, that was true, but she was on police business, investigating a very serious matter. He'd just have to put up with her doing her job.

Well, almost.

Naylor wanted her to wear kid gloves and calm troubled waters. She hoped the Governor wouldn't turn out to be a prat or she'd find that extremely difficult in her present mood. With very little rest in the last few days, she was exhausted and ready to call it a day. 'Can you ask Rachel and her mother to hang on for me, Alpha One? I'll rendezvous with them in the car park in five.'

'No problem,' came the reply. 'Sorry we weren't able to help this time.'

'Don't worry about it. You did your best.'

Half a mile from the prison, Kate passed the Traffic car going the other way. He flashed his lights in lieu of a wave. She did likewise and drove on, arriving a few moments later. Emily and Rachel were sitting in the Defender in the staff car park. Pulling up alongside, Kate wound her window down and offered a few words of apology for another aborted attempt at identification. Then she made her way into the jail to keep her appointment.

The Governor was furious. He had every right to be. It wasn't every day that a member of staff was locked up by the Murder Investigation Team, let alone three. But he was an OK bloke and – without giving too much away – she managed to placate him. Her investigation had been an arduous one, an intense couple of weeks, but she reassured him that it was as good as over with just a few loose ends left to tie up. That was stretching the truth a bit, but he accepted it with good grace, even offered to walk her from the admin block to the main gate.

No hard feelings.

They fell in step, chatting about the recent spate of bad weather as they walked. But as they neared the gatehouse, Kate stopped listening to the man by her side, or rather his voice faded out of her consciousness as she noticed something odd through the chain-link perimeter fence . . . Emily's Land Rover was only just pulling away. More worryingly, there was someone following . . . a suspicious second vehicle . . . skirting the car park . . . no lights on. Kate did a double take – just to be sure her eyes weren't deceiving her – then she started running.

Charging into the gatehouse in a panic, she banged loudly on the inner security window. The duty officer jumped to attention, abandoning his newspaper when he saw the Governor racing into the building behind her.

'Rewind the CCTV!' Kate yelled, pressing her ID to the glass. 'Now, man! DO IT!'

Taking his cue from the Governor's nod, the officer did as she asked.

Three pairs of eyes scanned the image as it rewound at speed until Kate told him pause it, then run it on at normal speed.

'Freeze it there!' she said.

Pressing the pause button again, the officer stopped the tape, leaving the image of the unlit car on screen. Without being asked to do so, he zoomed in on the car. One person only inside.

Instinctively, Kate knew who it was.

'Let me out of here, quick!' She moved towards the exit. 'Call for backup and keep hold of that tape.'

It seemed to take for ever for the inner and outer doors to open and close. Then she took off, sprinting to her Q5. She started the ignition and sped off like a woman possessed.

The narrow country lane was winding and unlit, the Q5's wipers struggling to cope with the bleaching snow. Each load that was wiped away was quickly replaced by more big white flakes that settled on the windscreen, obscuring her vision. Peering through it as best she could, she did a double-take, closing on a sight up ahead that was confusing: white lights rotating in the darkness.

'Shit!' Panic set in.

As she depressed the brake, slowing the Q5, her phone rang.

'I know who did it,' Carmichael said.

98

As soon as she got home, Emily told Rachel to set the fire while she went into the kitchen to make some tea and toast for supper. Twenty metres short of her driveway, moving headlights changed direction and stopped. The lights were cut. A car door slammed shut and a figure moved swiftly towards The Stint on foot.

Daniels hardly had time to digest what Carmichael had told her before the image up ahead became clear. The lights she'd seen were the headlights of a car, flipped on its roof and spinning in the road like a breakdancer. Applying the brakes sent her bag and other items shooting forward into the foot-well. The Q5's backend slewed across the road and she had to compensate by steering into the skid before finally bringing the car to a halt.

Putting her hazard warning lights on, she got out, the phone still in her hand as the spinning vehicle came to a graceful stop. It wasn't Emily's car, or the suspicious vehicle that followed her from the prison car park – the same vehicle she suspected of colliding with this car and causing it to crash.

Steam was billowing from the engine of the upturned car

and there was a strong smell of petrol in the air. The driver was trapped inside.

Kate swore under her breath.

'Boss?' Carmichael was yelling down the phone. 'Boss? You OK?'

'Lisa, I've come across an RTA. Get on to Control. I need immediate assistance.' Giving her exact location, Kate took a mini-Maglite from the door pocket of the Q5 and scanned the scene. The crashed vehicle's front windscreen was out – a side window too – but there were no passengers as far as she could tell. 'I have one casualty, but there may be more. Ambulance and fire service personnel required.'

'Leave it with me,' Carmichael said. 'I'll sort it.'

'Lisa, Emily is in danger. A suspicious vehicle tailed her from the prison. I was following when I came across this lot. The prison should've called for backup already, but tell Control they'll need to find another route through Felton. The stricken car is sideways on. The B6345 west of Acklington is completely blocked.'

Fearon tried the front door. It was locked. Silently, he moved round the rear and saw Emily through the window. She'd nicked her finger on a bread knife and was searching in a cupboard for something to put on it, leaving the knife unattended on the bench.

Stealthily, he moved away.

When Emily heard the window break, she froze.

Rachel!

Her eyes darted to the knife block. She grabbed the largest knife there and bolted from the room, reaching the living-room door just as it slammed in her face. She tried the handle but it wouldn't budge.

In the living room, Fearon kept his shoulder to the door. Grabbing Rachel by the hair, he pulled her head to one side so it was almost parallel with her shoulders. He stared deep into her eyes, sniffing her perfume, the same one her mother wore. The girl was too terrified to struggle, her whole body rigid, eyes fixed on the cold steel blade in his hand.

'Walter, please listen to me,' Emily called through the door. 'Let my daughter go. Take me instead. That's what you want, isn't it? That's what you've always wanted. Mr Stamp told me so.'

Emily wished Martin were here now. She was calm, despite the sound of Rachel's hysteria from the other side of the door. Careful not to make a sound, she searched the drawer of a small side table. Finding the key she was looking for, she moved to the cupboard under the stairs and opened the gun cabinet Robert had fitted against the far wall. Removing the shotgun with trembling hands, she fumbled in her first attempt to load the ammunition. Cursing under her breath, she tried again, determined to do whatever was necessary to protect her only child.

99

Kate Daniels didn't hear the officer in the control room. Her phone was in her hand, but her arm was by her side as she stared at a pair of lifeless eyes. The young woman was hanging upside down from her seat belt. She looked about twenty years old; not a pretty girl by any stretch of the imagination, but she had beautiful hair, the colour of bronze, styled asymmetrically as if she'd made a real effort tonight. To the left of her lolling head, on the interior of the car's roof, a gift lay on its side. It was wrapped and lovingly tied with a bow, suggesting the girl had been on her way to a party.

Her last, poor kid.

'. . . 7824: please respond. Are you able to offer medical assistance?'

Blinking snow from her lashes, Kate swallowed down her grief for the girl. It felt surreal, standing there in the middle of nowhere in the glare of the Q5's headlights, staring at a stranger, the snow falling silently all around her, a voice from the control room cutting through the deathly hush.

When she lifted the phone to her ear, her voice was flat. 'Come again, Control.'

'Are you able to offer assistance? Control over.'

'Negative. It's a fatal . . . the casualty's neck is broken.'

'Stay with the vehicle, 7824.'

'That's a negative . . .' Drawing her eyes away from the dead girl, Kate's thoughts returned to Emily. She lifted her torch, scanning the scene. Even with the Q5's capability, with dense bushes on either side of the narrow road, there was no vehicular way through and it would take longer to find another route. 'I'm making my way to the priority job at The Stint, Control.'

'Yes, we're aware of that. Officers have been dispatched.'

'7824, my battery is low. Please use the force radio from now on, over.'

Leaping over the steaming chassis, Kate sprinted up the road, arms like pistons, willing herself to cover the ground to Emily's home less than a mile away. As she ran, all she could hear was the sound of her own heavy breathing. Slipping on the icy surface, she strained to see over hedgerows as the road twisted and turned.

And there it was up ahead . . .

A tiny light in the darkness.

Exhausted and panting for breath, she ran on. As she neared the property, she could see that the kitchen light was on inside the house but, as she rounded the final bend, a dark shadow appeared behind a curtain of snow. She stopped running and approached with caution, trying to get some breath into her lungs. A 52 plate, dark-coloured Renault Clio was parked just short of the gateway. Lights off. Driver's door wide open.

Shining her torch inside, she leaned in. The car had been hotwired and a hypodermic needle lay on the passenger seat, a tourniquet strap next to it.

Fearon would be pumped up and capable of anything.

Kate turned to face The Stint. The tiny cottage was backlit in the moonlight, a Christmas-card image covered in fresh snow, exactly as it had been on the day Emily and Robert moved in. That was party night too, an open-house celebration for a wonderful couple beginning a new life together.

A gunshot pierced the night air, stopping her dead in her tracks as she walked toward the house. The sound sent a shiver up her spine. She spoke quietly on the radio: '7824 to Control, shots fired at The Stint. Where the fuck is my backup?'

Kate knew she had a decision to make. There were two women in the house and one drugged-up male, presumably armed with a shooter. Another gunshot sent her heart banging in her chest. There was no time to waste.

Swallowing down her fear, and despite advice from the control room to the contrary, she decided not to wait for her colleagues to arrive. Not that anyone would've blamed her. She was unarmed, at an obvious disadvantage, but she was also a police officer with a duty to preserve life.

Emily and Rachel were still inside. She couldn't leave them to the mercy of Fearon.

She crept into the house. The hallway light was off, the bulb crunching under her feet as she entered. She listened. Total silence. To the left of her, Robert's gun cabinet was empty and there was a faint smell of cordite in the air, the internal door blasted open. In her mind's eye, she could almost see the weapon in Fearon's hand, poised to blow her head off the minute she entered the living room.

Through a crack in the door, she saw blood.

One cream-coloured wall was covered in it.

The torch caught a flash of denim, about forty-five degrees to her right on the floor.

Male, not female.

She blew out her cheeks, relief bringing tears to her eyes.

Fearon was lying on his back, a gunshot wound to the right side of his chest, a bloody knife in his hand. He wasn't moving. His eyes were shut but she was taking no chances. Kicking away the knife, she kneeled down beside him and felt for a pulse.

Still breathing.

She felt sick as she stood up straight, her imagination working overtime. For a moment she just stood there, trying to restore her breathing to normal. She didn't want to turn round for fear of what faced her on the other side of that room. But the sound of a faint whimper sent her spinning in that direction.

Emily's pathetic figure was slumped against the wall, bloodied and still, Robert's shotgun by her side. Rachel was curled up in a foetal position beside her mother, her face pale with shock, unable to take her eyes from the psychopath that was Walter Fearon.

100

Flashing lights turned the snow blue as it continued to fall in eerie silence. The Stint was now a crime scene. A WPC had been posted outside the front door, instructed to keep out unwanted visitors. Emergency vehicles were parked haphazardly on the road and on the driveway, transportation for the range of professional personnel who had swarmed to the scene when alerted by Control: crime scene investigators, photographers, paramedics and, of course, Kate Daniels' own team of murder detectives.

Fortunately, no forensic pathologist had been summoned.

Not yet, anyway . . .

Kate took a deep breath.

Not long after she'd entered the cottage, armed support had burst through the door, training their guns on everything that moved. For anyone who hadn't seen them in action and didn't know how professional they were, it was one of the most frightening experiences imaginable. Rachel had gone into shock and they had quickly been stood down.

Kate was standing in the front porch, holding on to her, an arm securing a red blanket the ambulance crew had placed round her shoulders. The girl couldn't stop shivering. Was it any wonder? Fearon's attempt to kill her mother had been the last in a series of horrendous incidents most people wouldn't encounter in a lifetime. Martin Stamp had been right about him all along.

And so had Emily, up to a point . . .

On her first day back at work she'd made a prediction that he would kill his next victim. Little did she know that Stamp would be the person he'd vent his rage upon; or that an attempt on her own life would follow the vicious killing of her lifelong friend. Though she had received a single stab wound to her left side, the injury was, thankfully, not life threatening. She'd been treated quickly at the scene by paramedics and was now being taken by stretcher and deposited in an ambulance, a sight that made Rachel weep all over again.

Leading her to the same ambulance, Kate shut the door and watched it drive off into the wintery night. When she turned round, Hank was leaving the house, a pair of wellington boots and a police-issue waterproof over his suit. As he got closer, she moved her fingers slowly across her throat, a question in her eyes.

He shook his head.

Fearon was still breathing.

101

A further trawl of the incident log for Bamburgh had led Carmichael to a sad revelation. Ash Walker had been fifteen when his parents brought him to the Northumberland village to spend time with his grandparents in a rented holiday cottage. The old couple had gone off to walk their dog, leaving him in charge of his five-year-old sister. The pair of them had been playing on the rocks when she was swept out to sea by a freak wave. She drowned.

The wall of silence the Murder Investigation Team had expected failed to materialize – far from it. Walker had been keen to share details of his macabre acts of devotion, and the traumatic death that had started it all. He described, as if it had happened only yesterday, the sight of rescuers pulling his sister's dripping corpse from the water. Helpless and alone, he had followed as they carried her up the beach and laid her on the dunes to commence the frantic effort to revive her.

In his head, Bamburgh Castle had become a living memorial to her, the motive for the killings not far from one put forward by Jo Soulsby early in the enquiry.

Ten years ago, on what would have been her tenth birthday, he'd killed his *little princess*, Sophie Kent, laying her to rest in the very same spot where his sister had lost her fight for life. He'd got the idea of dressing her in adult clothes when he overheard one paedophile admit to another that he'd killed and buried a young girl in a woodland grave in Yorkshire years before.

He was laughing as he told Kate Daniels, 'The nonce who did it was a Geordie, as it happens.'

Instead of reporting the matter to his superiors he'd copied the MO in the belief that the same paedophile would be blamed if Sophie's body were ever discovered. To prevent the remains being identified, he'd slipped into her bedroom while visiting her grief-stricken father and substituted another kid's hairbrush and toothbrush for Sophie's. The traces of Bamburgh sand that had implicated her father had been a mistake; Walker hadn't realized that grains of incriminating evidence from his shoes had been transferred to Kent's car during a darts night out – his only error in the whole affair.

Five years on, he'd killed Maxine O'Neil, a fifteen-year-old who looked exactly as he imagined his sister would have, had she lived. He'd seen the talented dancer's picture in the local press performing in a Christmas concert at school. He'd watched her for a few weeks planning to make a move. Then, one day, out of the blue, he spotted her waiting at a bus stop, a sign that she was the right one. Stopping his car, he offered her a lift. When she refused, he got out, rendered her unconscious with a single blow and bundled her into the boot. When she came to and refused to celebrate the prearranged birthday tea he'd lovingly organized, he killed her.

'Some kids,' he said, 'are never grateful.'

Walker had thought of everything. He'd carefully selected

remote locations where there were no neighbours to report strange sounds or comings and goings. He'd chosen the presents, the gift-wrapping and paper plates following the theme his sister had loved – princesses and ballerinas – perfect for her special day. The dresses he'd picked out for his victims were almost the same as the one his sister was wearing the day she died. Not quite, but nearly: red polka dots, matching ribbons for their hair, short white socks and his mother's white shoes with a strap across the front. And pearls like the ones belonging to his grandmother that his sister loved to play with.

The guy was sick.

In interview, Walker confirmed Kate Daniels' supposition that Rachel McCann had been his intended victim number three. His sister would have been twenty within a few days and Rachel was the right age for him to carry on his monument to murder, had she not managed to escape.

However, he denied any involvement in DCI Gordon Munro's case. The murder investigation that had frustrated the North Yorkshire SIO seemed doomed to remain unsolved . . .

Until Kate began replaying Walker's statement in her mind. His account of the 'Geordie nonce' who'd bragged about killing a young girl and dumping her in a woodland grave conjured up an image of John Edward Thompson sitting in the interview room, trying not to draw attention to himself. He'd been questioned by officers investigating the Yorkshire murder, but claimed he was abroad at the time. It turned out he'd served time in HMP Coleby, on the wing where Walker had been employed. Further actions led them to his former cellmate, who soon began to sing. As a result,

Thompson was arrested. He was currently awaiting trial for the North Yorks murder. So at least one ex-SIO would be able to enjoy his superannuation without a niggling unsolved case to keep him awake at night.

Chris Ridley, the historian who'd helped Kate track down a set of pearls for comparison, received a commendation from the Chief Constable for services rendered to the Murder Investigation Team, even though the police only managed to trace one other set and it was never a full-blown line of enquiry.

Emily McCann made a complete recovery from the stab wound to her side. When Fearon had shoved Rachel aside and charged at her like a bull, probably planning to shred her face as he had done her friend and colleague, Martin Stamp, Emily hadn't hesitated to pull the trigger of Robert's gun. The CPS accepted that she'd acted in self-defence and no charges would follow. As for Fearon, he too had recovered from his injuries and could now look forward to spending the rest of his sad life in prison.

When the Bamburgh enquiry ended, Ailsa Richards didn't want to go home. She put in for a permanent transfer to Northumbria with aspirations of one day rejoining the Murder Investigation Team. Lisa Carmichael had offered her lodgings and they were now the best of mates. Kate Daniels couldn't promise her a job, but she would see what she could do.

Though the case was closed, Kate still had one more thing to do before she could lay it to rest. With a heavy heart she drove to Acklington village to make her peace with Bill Kent and apologize for the trauma she'd put him through. He'd hear nothing of it. He was grateful that his ten-year ordeal had finally come to an end. Sophie now had a proper resting place – maybe not quite as pretty at Bamburgh beach, but somewhere he could go and talk to her.

The sound of Robert's bike was distinctive as Rachel dropped the machine into the corner – knee down – using the force of gravity to maintain stability. Then confidently sped off along a winding road through stunning countryside, heading for home. She rode well, Kate shadowing her; their trip over Hartside the first of many in the years to come. It was a favourite destination of Kate's, the one she turned to whenever she sought solitude after a harrowing case. The summit had far-reaching views on a good day. It was a place she only ever visited alone, with one exception: Jo Soulsby. Now she was happy to share it with Rachel, and hoped she would grow to love it too.

Hank, Jo and Emily turned to greet them as they arrived at The Stint. Since the trauma of that February, Rachel had moved out and returned to her studies. Today, she'd gone home. Surrounded by friends, she was ready to celebrate her father's life, draw a line under the past and start over . . .

The five of them wandered down the garden to the riverbank, a casket already in place. Emily looked a little reticent as her daughter neared the water's edge and emptied out her father's ashes into the water and watched them float away.

She looked round. 'No more tears, Mum.'

'No more tears,' Emily repeated.

As mother and daughter walked off arm in arm to begin a new life, Jo made her excuses and left. Kate watched her go, her face pained with regret. During the Bamburgh enquiry, they had come close to rekindling their relationship, only to be pulled apart by circumstances. Since then, Jo had accepted Naylor's invitation to return to work for Northumbria's Murder Investigation Team, but she'd given Kate the brush-off. Their relationship was destined to be platonic from now on.

'Get a grip!' Hank said. 'Could be worse.'

'Oh yeah?' Kate levelled her eyes at him. 'What would you know?'

Digging a hand in his pocket, he pulled out a plain white postcard and handed it to her. It was postmarked the Nether-lands and addressed to her in Fiona Fielding's flamboyant hand. Kate swore under her breath. She'd been so busy, she'd forgotten to text the artist her home address.

'Aren't you going to read it?' he asked.

Kate grinned. 'I know what it says, Hank.'

'Ahem . . .' He made a crazy face. 'I think you'll find this one's a little different, boss. I thought I'd better rescue it from your in-tray and deliver it personally before the team got their hands on it and posted it on Facebook or Twitter. It's a bit more interesting than the usual stuff on there.'

'Er, what have I told you about reading my mail?'

Kate turned the card over. Instead of her usual four words – *Are You Hungry Yet?* – Fiona had planted a bright red lipstick kiss on one half of the card. On the other, she'd written four new words: *Two Lips From Amsterdam.*

Kate laughed out loud. 'Come on,' she said. 'It's my shout.'

Acknowledgements

The idea for this book was mine but many people have contributed along the way – all of them deserve a loud round of applause. First and foremost, my brilliant agent at AM Heath, Oli Munson; my Pan Macmillan editor, the one and only Wayne Brookes; my wise and wonderful copy editor, Anne O'Brien; and last but not least, my publicist, Philippa McEwan, who looks after me so well.

Thanks must also go to the unsung heroes, especially editorial assistant Louise Buckley, who will be married before this book hits the shops – congratulations, Louise! Also to everyone in the art department for producing the cover, the sales and marketing team who work extremely hard on my behalf, and the booksellers and readers who have supported me since day one.

Were it not for my very own 'close protection team' I would not be a writer. So thanks to my family for putting up with my other self, the one who slopes off for days on end to play with words: Paul, Chris, Kate, Caroline, Max, Frances and Mo – you are all simply amazing.

extracts reading groups
competitions books new
discounts extracts
extracts discounts events
competitions books reading groups
new extracts
events books
new books
extracts reading groups
new this reading groups
interviews
events extracts events
discounts new
new books events interviews new books extracts
events new events
discounts extracts discounts

www.panmacmillan.com

extracts events reading groups books
competitions books extracts new